HOME GAME

Paul Quarrington

1983
Doubleday Canada Limited, Toronto, Canada
Doubleday & Company, Inc., Garden City, New York

Also by Paul Quarrington
THE SERVICE

Many people (read most) know more about baseball than I do. These people helped very much in that regard: Solomon Schepps, Robert Irwin and Nick Pashley Indeed, they are so knowledgeable that any questions regarding the game should be taken up with them.

I would also like to mention these fine people: Karen Gold, who read the manuscript and suggested certain changes (all but one of which I made. Sorry, Karen), they improved the book immensely; Janet Turnbull, for all her support; Dean Cooke, like-wise; Thad McIlroy, Boy-wonder, who not only gave me encour-agement and advice, but also bought me several hundred dollars worth of beer; Kim Fedderson and Anne McCourt, who have great taste in literature and always say they like my stuff; and my good buddies Marty and Jill Worthy who gave me all sorts of things, not the least of which was food.

This book is for my father.

ISBN 0-385-18422-0
Library of Congress Catalogue Card Number 82-45602

Copyright © 1983 Paul Quarrington
All Rights Reserved
Printed and Bound in Canada by John Deyell Company
FIRST EDITION

Designed by Irene Carefoot
Jacket Design by Matthew Berger
Jacket Illustration by Jon McKee
Cover Concept by Gar Reeves-Stevens

Typeset in Century Schoolbook Roman by AES Company

Canadian Cataloguing in Publication Data

  Quarrington, Paul.
     Home game

  ISBN 0-385-18422-0

  I. Title.

  PS8583.U27H65   C813'.54   C83-098043-1
  PR9199.3.Q37H65

HOME GAME

The land is mostly water.

Although Michigan is officially listed as the twenty-third largest state, if one were to include all of the water, eleven thousand inland lakes and twice as many rivers, it would rank in the top ten. It touches four out of the five Great Lakes, every one except Lake Ontario. (I, sitting here in Toronto, am looking out my window at that one—it is grey, rough, and if not dead, at least dying.)

First, of course, were the Indians—they gave it its name, "Michigan" = "large lake". Which of the lakes the Chippewa meant we don't know. Personally, I think it must have been an Indian inside joke. "Here is large lake." "Which large lake?" "Who cares?"

Then came the Irishmen, and the Finns. They saw the water, decided it would make for wonderful irrigation, and became farmers. This was a mistake. The land was indeed good land, but good in a different way, filthy rich in minerals. It choked the life out of the crops, and the men resigned themselves to a hard life, a struggle just to maintain poverty.

Then came the blacks—but that was all right, for no fool could demand "What right have you to be here?" when he himself had no right, rhyme, or reason.

All this would change, of course. The minerals would come up out of the ground, and huge cities like Detroit would blossom, or whatever it is that cities like Detroit do.

But not now. Listen: In 1957 they finished building the "Big Mac", the five-mile bridge that spans the Straits of Mackinac. Before that the Upper Peninsula, cold and hard to tame, was almost a world of its own. To get there you either had to know exactly what you were doing, or else you had to have absolutely no idea, in which case you got there by accident. Most people got there by accident.

On October 14, 1938, Mr. Roosevelt, getting a little edgy, went on the radio and stressed the need for a reexamination of national defence requirements. Above the Straits of Mackinac it went largely unheard, the transmission skipping among the rivers carefree and wild.

The last time most of the people there had listened to the radio was about a week back, when the New York Yankees beat the Chicago Cubs four games to none, thereby winning the World Series.

Emotions tend to distort the voice and make it difficult to understand.

—*Canadian Protection Services' Guide for Radio Communication.*

Pa said, "S'pose he's tellin' the truth—that fella?"
The preacher answered, "He's tellin' the truth, awright. The truth for him. He wasn't makin' nothing up."
"How about us?" Tom demanded. "Is that the truth for us?"
"I don' know," said Casy.
"I don' know," said Pa.

John Steinbeck,
The Grapes of Wrath

BOOK ONE

Chapter 1

THIS STORY WAS told to me by my grandfather who claims to have heard firsthand accounts of all events and was present at some of the more important ones. To say he inspired it would be a lie. In fact, he threatened me with bodily injury if I did not write it down.

Nathanael (Crybaby) Isbister wondered if anyone could see him.

The countryside was filled with the fog that falls with the sun. The skies were lined with heavy clouds, and no moon shone.

Isbister had found a spot where the blacktop took a sharp bend to the left, calculating that he would be caught in the glare of approaching headlights. But then he noticed that the road didn't straighten until some fifty feet beyond him and he thought, my God, what if they're surprised by the sight of me standing here, they could go right off the road. A little old wizened lady from Detroit with a wart on her nose could have a cardiac arrest and drive into the trees. He backed off a bit then, until he was standing in a spot which he calculated would just be missed by approaching headlights. He realized that if he stood there, no one could see him. So he took his sign, a sheet of cardboard with the word "ANYWHERE" written with charcoal in big block letters, and stuck it out with his long arms, letting it fall within the projected beam of approaching headlights. It occurred to him that nothing would be so frightening as a pair of disembodied hands holding a sheet of cardboard that read "ANYWHERE", so he withdrew it and stood still.

And wondered if anyone could see him.

He had found the cardboard and the charcoal in a clearing in the neighbouring forest. There several drifting hobos had formed a lopsided circle around a dying fire. They were passing among themselves a bottle of lord-knows-what.

3

Isbister probably would have stayed with them, but for the look of recognition that had clouded one hobo's face when Nathanael spoke his name.

"Isbister!?" screamed the man who owned the face, choking on the lord-knows-what and bringing it back up from halfway down his throat. "Are you Goldenlegs Crybaby Isbister?"

"All I said was I'm called Isbister."

"I know what you *said*, but what I'm asking is . . ." The hobo raised himself to his feet. It took about thirty seconds. "Are you also known by the cognomens of Goldenlegs and/or Crybaby?"

Isbister rocked himself on the balls of his feet, shrugged, and grunted, "Yeah."

"Tell us about Ernest Rosewood!" This was from another of the men, who seemed to have been passed the realization along with the bottle of lord-knows-what.

"Well—" Isbister brought up his right forefinger and drove it into the palm of his left hand. He began to move it back and forth across the skin, making short and circular motions with it. "He was a great fighter."

"Say it again! Say it again!" A third hobo was up on his feet and thrashing drunkenly with his arms. "Tell us about how he demolished Herbert Forster!"

Isbister's moving forefinger stopped momentarily and then continued across his palm. He spoke quietly and with effort. "That fight should never have been held."

"Bullshit! Forster was a good man!"

"Are you kidding? Are you crazy?" Isbister's throat tightened up and he spent several seconds clearing it. "He was fifteen pounds lighter"—his forefinger kept moving all the while—"and almost a head shorter."

"So what? Fulton Grange was two heads shorter and twenty pounds lighter than Lance Pitman, but nobody ever said boo 'bout that, on account of Grange won!"

"You know what happened? You know what happened?" demanded Isbister. "The doctors . . ." He cleared his throat again. "The doctors said there's some connection in the brain, in what they call the *medulla*, that connects the senses to the brain and ties it all together, and Rosewood knocked it all to pieces in Forster's brain, just knocked Forster's head so hard this connection snapped loose, and Forster can't see now, and can't hear now, and. . ." Isbister's finger was moving frantically and he realized with horror that his eyes had brimmed with tears that were about to spill.

"An accident," said one of the hobos in protest.

"AN ACCIDENT??!" The tears spilled over. "That happened two minutes after Rosewood made a cut above Forster's eye that you could have put a suitcase in . . . but they never stopped the fight . . ."

"There he goes! There he goes!" came the voices with delight. "There goes *Crybaby* Isbister!"

"I AM NOT CRYING!" shrieked Isbister. "You see, when I get excited, I hyperventilate. I breathe too fast. And that activates the tearing reflex. That's how . . ." He stopped to rest because it was difficult to talk through the sobs. "That's how actors pretend they're crying, you know, they hyperventilate . . ."

"Imagine that—meeting Crybaby Isbister, and him crying and everything."

"I'm not crying!" Isbister looked around frantically, saw the cardboard and the piece of charcoal, grabbed them and darted from their lopsided circle.

Nathanael Isbister was six foot two and very well built. His nose had been broken repeatedly in his youth and now, at thirty-eight, lacked any definition. His ears were slightly cauliflowered, and his eyes were darkly deepset, driven into his face. His hair, once golden, was an odd collection of colour and curls. His appearance was formidable and threatening. This was why people loved to call him "Crybaby" Isbister.

The "Goldenlegs" was from a long, long time ago.

A truck pulled over to the side of the road. Isbister picked up his tiny travelling bag, ran awkwardly to the cab, and jumped up and into it.

" 'Anywhere?' " demanded the driver when Nathanael was half-way in. "I thought I knew every town around here, but I never heard of 'Anywhere.' Where 'bouts is it?"

Isbister nodded before him. "That way."

"Past Burton's Harbor?" The driver was a tall, blond-haired man with a baseball cap placed backwards on his head. He pulled at the stick shift and the truck roared out on to the blacktop.

"That's right."

"Well, that's a shame, because I can't take you through Burton's Harbor, on account of us being not allowed to carry passengers."

"Oh."

"But if you want, I can let you out at the town limits, and then I'll stop at a cafe on the other side, and you can scoot on through and meet me, if you want."

"We'll see." Isbister tried to smile at the man beside him. The driver grinned back heartily and worked the gears. Nathanael noticed that the truck driver's teeth were extremely small and yellowed. The man had a boyish face, but the lines around the eyes were heavy and slack.

"I been driving for forty-two hours straight," announced the driver. "Only stopped for a couple of whizzes and food. But not to sleep."

Crybaby Isbister realized that he was supposed to be impressed by the fact that the man had forgone sleep for almost two days, so he whistled through his teeth and asked, "How in hell do you guys do it?"

"Every guy got his own way. What works for one guy don't do dick on a stick for another. You know what I do?"

"What?"

"I ask myself riddles."

"Yeah?"

"Yeah. Like this—what has five legs, two heads, and lives in the bottom of a valley?"

"What?"

"Huh?"

"What's the answer?"

"Oh—I don't know. I gotta think about it for a little while."

"You don't know the answer?"

" 'Course not. It wouldn't be any good if I knew the answer. What good would that be? This way I got something to think about."

Isbister sighed. "How do you know there *is* an answer?"

"Way I figure, buddy, there's gotta be. You gotta figure that in this great big world somewhere there has *got* to be something that has five legs, two heads, and lives in the bottom of a valley."

Isbister nodded and watched the moonrise.

There was a silence then that the driver filled with whistling. Isbister spent the silence trying to determine what the tune was. It seemed to vacillate between "Auld Lang Syne" and "Camptown Ladies".

Then the driver asked, almost shyly, "Know any riddles?"

"Yeah." Isbister drew himself forward on his seat. "I know a riddle. It goes, what walks on four legs in the morning, two legs in the afternoon, and three legs in the evening?"

The driver grinned, sensing it was a good one. He plucked the backwards cap from his head and ran his hand through the thinning blond hair. "What walks on—what is it?"

"Four legs in the morning, two legs in the afternoon, and three legs in the evening."

"Four legs, then two legs, then three legs," muttered the driver. "Morning, afternoon, evening." He replaced the baseball cap, forwards this time, tugging it down hard so that he had to tilt his head back to see the road. "What walks on them legs?" he asked himself quietly. "Jesus."

"Wrong," whispered Isbister softly, so the other man couldn't hear.

"WHAT THE HELL WALKS ON THEM LEGS?!" shouted the driver, delighted with the riddle. He turned to Isbister. "You know the answer?"

"Yeah—you're not giving up are you?"

"Don't be radickallus!" boomed the driver. "I'm gonna get it soon . . ."

In fact, he didn't get it for almost half an hour. Isbister appreciated the opportunity to be alone with his thoughts, although at the time he would have been hard put to say what they were. He was drifting off to sleep when the man beside him shouted, "A doggy!!"

"Huh?" Isbister started. "Did you hit a dog?"

"Nope. That's the answer to your riddle, ain't it, a doggy?"

Isbister yawned and asked, "How do you figure?"

"I figure it this way, chum. In the morning a dog walks on four legs, 'cause that's how many legs he's got. That's the easy part. But in the afternoon it's *two* legs . . . know how come? Because in the afternoon he gets hungry, right? So he starts begging for food! Right? But in the evening, he's on three legs, 'cause he's gotta take a pee!" The driver laughed. "It was hard, but I got it, didn't I?"

"You got it." Isbister settled back and closed his eyes.

Nathanael Isbister was born at 12:15 A.M., January 1, 1900, in New York City. His father, John Isbister, had raced down to the

Times office and arrived there panting. "My son . . ." he gasped, falling across the desk of a bespectacled editor, "My son was just born! He's the CHILD OF THE CENTURY!!!"

Without saying a word the editor directed John Isbister to join a long line of men, all of whom claimed to have sired the child of the century.

Nathanael was, in fact, the fifty-seventh child to be born in the new century, and that was in New York City alone.

As we all know, the child of the century was Tekel Ambrose, who was born in Burton's Harbor on January 1, 1900, at 12:00:05.

Chapter 2

NATHANAEL GOT DOWN from the cab just outside Burton's Harbor's town limits. He smiled at the driver. In return, the man flicked the brim of his baseball cap, stuck his thumb in the air, winked, and said, "Doggy." Crybaby smiled again and walked away.

He stood in a belt that lay nakedly between country and city. The trees and hills had died behind him; there were miles before the first houses, the small tarpaper shacks of Niggertown, began to pop up crookedly.

Isbister sighed; and looked around vacantly; and wondered how he had ended up where he was.

The night had cleared—the sky was a rich and full one. The moon and stars were bright and biting. Isbister kept his head up in the air and walked, not down the road that lay ahead, but into a useless, vacant, and sterile field.

He met a cow. Some kind of renegade, he supposed, a skinny old bossy that stood in the middle of nowhere and chewed cud that must have taken her all day to accumulate. He addressed her. "Evening, Gertrude."

The cow tilted her head inquisitively.

"What," asked Isbister slyly, "has five legs, two heads, and lives in the bottom of a valley?"

The cow appeared to consider it. Her chewing took on a ruminating quality, like an old man eating biscuits over a checkerboard.

"Mind you," added Isbister, "I don't know the answer."

Suddenly the cow flicked her head backwards over her right shoulder and lowed a low moo.

"No," answered Nathanael, "doesn't even sound close to me."

The cow began another moo, jerking her head in the same manner. Isbister crossed his arms and shook his head emphatically. The moo became as loud as a foghorn.

"All right, all right!" Crybaby pointed in the direction of the head-flick. "That way?"

9

The cow resumed a peaceful munching and Nathanael trudged off.

Nathanael Crybaby Isbister had a very peculiar way of walking as a result of a horrible accident. From what I understand, his knees and ankles couldn't work right. His legs would rise inordinately high and swing around in short semi-circles. His feet splayed off in opposite directions and landed flatly. I don't really have it exact in my mind—my grandfather has tried to show me on numerous occasions, but his arthritic twigs aren't up to it.

Speaking of my grandfather, at this point he makes his first formal entrance in the story.

Three or four miles from the city of Burton's Harbor is a town called Alexandria, which is a pretty grand name for a collection of three hundred inhabitants, three buildings, and maybe forty-five houses. This is where my grandfather was. He had just recently found himself a new profession, that of musical ethnologist. How it occurred to him, I will never know. What my grandfather did was stand on various street corners with an elaborate-looking machine in front of him that had knobs and flanges and great spools of tape. He would wait, well dressed and bespectacled, until an old lady hobbled by. Then he would step timidly forward, removing his fedora, and proffering a pale hand.

"Pardon me, ma'am."

(The ancient ones would wrinkle their faces at the sight of yet another drummer.)

"I'm from Roundrock University, Department of Ethnomusicology and Culture, E-T-C."

(Then their wrinkles would fade.)

"I was wondering, ma'am"—my grandfather would pretend to be powerfully embarrassed by the proceedings—"if you have lived in this region all of your life?"

"Why . . . yes. Yes, I have." It always seemed to be a revelation to the woman herself.

"Then, ma'am, I was wondering if you could cast your mind back to when you were a little girl . . ."

And their eyes would mist.

"Do you remember, as a child, singing songs?"

The ladies would nod, think momentarily, then nod again.

"Well, ma'am, I am compiling a volume of native American folk

music with the aid of my newly developed portable voice recording machine here.'' He would pat the contraption affectionately.
''If you would be so kind as to sing a song into this microphone, it
would prove vastly beneficial to my studies.''

Sometimes this coaxing was all that was needed; other times
he'd have to work on it a few more minutes before the ladies
would sing:

> *Camptown ladies, sing this song, doo-dah, doo-dah!*
> *Camptown racetrack four miles long, all the doo-dah day!*

My grandfather, in the throes of academic ecstasy, would leap
to the machine and start adjusting dials and tuners.

> *Gotta run all night, gotta run all day . . .*

It was the only song they ever sang. Before the end of the first
chorus they would be stomping out the beat on the sidewalk and
clapping with their gnarled hands.

> *I bet my money on a bob-tailed mare,*
> *Somebody bet on the bay!!*

''Thank you!'' my grandfather would shout. ''That was beautiful! Simply beautiful!''

Old ladies can blush pinky-red as a sunset. They clasp their hands
and turn coyly from side to side and look every bit as cute as a
seven-year-old.

''That one *surely* must go into the songbook. Will you give me
your name, dear lady?''

They would protest. ''Oh, goodness gracious, everybody knows
that old song!''

''Aha! You may think so! But never before have I heard anyone
resolve from the diatonic right back into the diatonic! That is precisely the sort of regional difference that I am devoted to finding.''

''Oh?''

''Oh, truly. Your name, dear lady?''

When the name came, it was always all three, first, middle and
last, and sometimes a ''widow of so-and-so, daughter of so-and-so''
and sometimes a *''Miss''* that was so heavy it might qualify as an
immoral proposition directed at my grandfather—charming old
bastard he was, even when he was younger. ''Delighted!'' he
would squeal.

Then, after a few minutes of small talk, the songstress would inquire if it would be possible to purchase a copy of the songbook.

"It will travel mostly in scholastic circles," my grandfather would say regretfully. Then he would get an idea. "But, I say! If you were to give me your address, I would send you a copy."

After the address had been given (along with a standing invitation to tea), the ladies would ask, "And how much is the book?"

"Oh, my dear madame, for you it will be free of charge."

"I couldn't!"

"You couldn't? Very well, then. A nominal charge to cover printing costs and mailing, perhaps?"

"Of course."

"Shall we say . . . $4.97?"

"Oh!"

"Too much, my dear?"

"Not at all, not at all . . ."

Anyway, my grandfather was happily working his way through the elderly female populace of Alexandria when some mechanical genius noticed that the newly developed portable voice recording machine was not plugged in. There wasn't even a cord. He and some other men tore it apart to find a complex system of elastic bands designed to give the spools an illusion of movement.

The men then gave chase to my grandfather.

Nathanael Crybaby Isbister wandered his lonely way across the useless field, peering up occasionally at the sky. Suddenly a little man ran by, so quickly that Nathanael wasn't sure he hadn't imagined him. Then, quick upon the little man's heels, came an angry mob, red-faced men with pieces of wood and one or two shotguns.

Nathanael Crybaby Isbister watched them rush by, listened to their muffled grunts and threats, and quickly his eyes welled with tears. He cursed something aloud—probably the taint of excited hyperventilation.

Now, you can either buy this or not, no skin off my teeth. I only write what my grandfather tells me. It has to do with that cow, Gertrude.

She was no ordinary cow.

To begin with, her name wasn't Gertrude at all, but rather "Beatrice the Bovine Beauty". In her youth she had been a star of vaudeville. Beatrice could dance, moo a tune, do subtraction and addition, and even read the minds of the audience. It's true if you want it to be. Say a spinster should stand up. (Beatrice's back would be turned of course, and she was blindfolded.) Beatrice's assistant would call out, "Is this lady married?" Silence from Beatrice the Bovine Beauty. "Is she single?" Beatrice would mooooo, and anyone could tell there was no doubt in her mind.

Then, one day, in a field beside some theatre, she met a bull. She was never to know his name. To say that he had his way with her would be a gross understatement. Beatrice was in an orgiastic state for almost twelve hours. When morning came, the bull cleared the fence with a lazy vault and slowly strutted away. She never saw him again.

Her spirit broken, she gave up showbiz and moved into the vacant, useless, and sterile field. There was just enough grass for a cow that was too heartsick to have an appetite. It was lonely, which suited Beatrice fine—there was no one to see her in her misery. And there were no bulls, false-hearted creatures that they are.

Now, the reason I'm telling you all this is that, in the direction that Beatrice had flicked her head, there was indeed a valley! And that's not all.

You readers can pick and choose what to believe at this point.

Nathanael Crybaby Isbister came upon the valley and chuckled with appreciation for Gertrude (Beatrice). And because the valley was Anywhere, he began to descend into it.

Suddenly there were trees again, trees that held out the starlight, and Nathanael found himself in almost pitch-blackness. He held out his arms and described wide arcs with them, like a minesweeping device. The grade began to steepen and Isbister was forced to quicken his pace. The faster he got, the more he winced from the pain in his bad legs. He was almost running when the ground gave away completely. He fell for a split-second, landed on his keester, and found the moonlight upon him once more.

The answer to the truck driver's riddle is: this particular dog. The one that was looking (twice), anxious and concerned, at Isbister's face.

The dog, otherwise an ordinary mongrel, had two heads joined together at almost right angles high on the neck. Two tongues drooped from two mouths, and four eyes focused from the edges to make up for the fact that neither of the heads could look directly at Isbister. And between his forelegs hung a shorter, misshapen fifth leg.

Isbister screamed, doubted his sanity, got up to run, turned back to double-check his eyes, and whispered, "Oh, my God," all in the space of a breath.

One of the dog's heads tilted in the questioning way animals have; the other head, finding itself suddenly lower, pushed up until both were level again.

Nathanael decided that the thing to do would be to turn and continue quickly on his way. Which he did. Unfortunately, he had not walked ten steps when he realized with terror that the creature was trotting merrily along beside him.

Crybaby refused to look at it. He muttered through the side of his mouth, "Get away. Scat. Shoo. I don't like you. Neither of you."

The dog barked, just once, although there was a doubleness to it, a kind of simultaneous echo.

Isbister stole a glimpse of the thing. The fifth leg was taking ineffectual swipes at the air in a futile attempt to assist locomotion. Crybaby's head snapped forward again. "Skidaddle. Vamoose."

Suddenly the dog's image was no longer blurred on the rim of Isbister's vision. Crybaby relaxed momentarily. But then the creature was in front of him, leaping about playfully, and it had a stick. One of the mouths gripped its end while the other snapped at the air, the angle putting the stick about an inch away from its bite.

The two-headed, five-legged dog dropped the stick in front of Isbister's feet.

"Oh, my God," he thought, "it wants to play fetch."

Crybaby's mind raced towards an idea—throw the stick into the thick brush and then hightail it out of there. Nathanael reached down and plucked it up; one of the dog's heads took a puppy's nip at his hand. He raised the stick and hurled it far into the greenery. And then he ran. Because he had bad legs, the effort of running made him wince and breathe in short, pained gasps. Anyone seeing him, though, would remark that he was running extraordinarily quickly.

But not quickly enough. In some seconds the creature was before him again. The other head was holding the stick—it deposited it in front of Nathanael. Isbister picked it up and tried the strategy again, running as fast as he possibly could.

The creature kept returning.

Twenty minutes later, Crybaby held the stick high above his head. The dog, excited and panting, took twisting leaps into the air in a spirited attempt to get it back. Every so often it would bark with the strange double echo.

Isbister said, "Okay, okay—I'm gonna see which of you guys is smarter, Fido or Rover." Fido was the right head, Rover the left. Rover was slightly bigger, and Fido's eyes were askew. "Now, most dogs fall for this, but we're gonna see whether two heads are really better than one. Got it?"

The dog yelped and flew into the air. Isbister batted it down joyfully. "Okay, Fido! Okay, Rover! Here we go!!" Nathanael brought the stick back as if he intended to hurl it with every ounce of his strength. The dog crouched down and both sets of eyes peered warily. Then Isbister threw his arm forward mightily, emitting an Olympic "Aaaaaooooffffff!!!" The dog flew off in that direction.

Rover had just barely noticed Nathanael drop the stick behind his back in the split-second before it was thrown. The resultant double-headed confusion caused the dog to spin around quickly and drop to the ground.

Isbister laughed loudly. "Both you guys fell for it! Ha, ha! Two heads aren't better than one! You're both stupid!"

The dog got up, its tail between its legs, and crept shamefully toward the stick. Both Fido and Rover took short, reproachful glances at Isbister. He stopped laughing.

"Okay, okay, guys, I'm sorry. It was a dirty trick."

The dog emitted a sharp, double-edged yap.

Isbister picked up the stick and threw it high, pointing at it help-fully. The dog's spirit came back in a second and he bounded after it. They played a straightforward game of fetch for a few more minutes.

The voice came from behind Isbister just as he felt something hard and metallic pressed against his lower spine.

It sounded like a nine-year-old with bronchitis holding his nose. "Okay, you ugly, conniving dog-napper. Get those arms up high! You're in a whole gobba trouble."

Nathanael raised his arms hesitantly. "Dog-napper?"

"Yeah, you smelly, lop-eared bastard. Dog-napper is what I said, and dog-napper is what I meaned."

"Look, kid, I didn't nap your dog."

There was a sharp pain in Isbister's ankle and the voice said, "Watch who you're calling a kid, you mangy snake-in-the-grass. I'm old enough to be your daddy, 'cept I bet your mother was so ugly I couldn't get close enough."

Meanwhile the two-headed, five-legged dog and hunkered down close by, and was watching the proceedings happily.

"Hey, listen," said Nathanael, "let me turn around, eh? I'm not armed."

"You got a stick," said the little voice. "Drop the stick."

Nathanael did so. "Now can I turn around?"

"I got a gat, so don't try nothing or you'll find yourself in conversation with St. What's-his-name."

"Okay."

"Peter."

"Huh?"

"That's what St. What's-his-name's name is. Okay. Take one step forward and then turn around real slow—and keep your hands up high till I say you can let them down, or I'll blow your guts all over the ground."

Jesus, thought Nathanael Crybaby Isbister.

So he spun around slowly, not an easy thing to do with his awkward legs. And when he had turned 180 degrees, he saw nothing. He looked down.

Now, my grandfather has, in an old seafarer's trunk, a broadside advertising Major Mite from when he toured the United States in 1891. At that time he was about thirty-five, but still youthful and extremely handsome. The picture, reproduced from a photograph, shows him with wavy blond hair, parted down the middle and fashioned into elaborate curlicues over his forehead. His upper lip is adorned with a handlebar moustache. He has clear eyes, a strong nose and chin, and his smile is long and rakish, full of life.

He is dressed in an ornate military uniform, but the form and size of his muscles show through instantly. He is turning his head slightly to the left, obviously offering forward what he considers his most photogenic angle.

Major Mite appears to be the epitome of male looks and physique. The broadside points out in great big letters that he is twenty-two inches tall.

Of course, that was a lie. He was, in fact, four full inches over two feet. And in the forty-odd years since the picture was taken he had grown a bit. When Nathanael Isbister laid eyes upon him, Major Mite was grizzled, wrinkled, and knocking on three feet.

With both hands he held a revolver, a huge old-fashioned Colt, that he obviously found a little hard to keep in the air. His arms shook under the strain.

The only thing remaining true to the broadside was the Major's eyes. They glared at Isbister, burning and sparkling with inner force.

The dog sprang happily over to Major Mite. They were about the same size. "Hello, Janus," said the tiny man. "I knew I'd find you."

"I call him Fido and Rover," announced Nathanael quietly.

"Well, maroon, he don't got but the one name, and it's *Janus.* Moses and Murray, you'd think if you were gonna steal a dog you'd at least have the courtesy to find out its right name!"

"I didn't steal him," said Crybaby. "I found him. I was just playing with him."

"A likely story, mule-face," muttered the Major. "In case you ain't noticed, you big galoot, there is something, shall we say, *unusual* about Janus. Namely, he got twice the normal allotment of heads, and a extra leg, although he don't need it! Now, do you think dogs like that just wander around ever'where?"

"I wondered about that."

"Oh, you did, now, did you? You, Curly, are full of fabrications! Why, if I didn't have this gun in my hands, I'd thrash the truth out of you! I'd tear you apart limb from limb! I'd . . ."

"Why would I steal the dog?" interrupted Nathanael patiently.

The dog, meanwhile, was turning both of its heads from one speaker to the other, as if it understood totally what was being said.

"Why!?!" shrieked the little man. "On account of he's the biggest draw since Beatrice the Bovine Beauty! Leastwise, as far as animals is concerned. He's worth his weight in gold!"

"Oh, yeah? Well, I happen to know that despite its two heads it's just as stupid as any other dog."

The dog, as if reminded of its embarrassing fiasco, snarled through both mouths.

"That's all the proof I need!" shouted Major Mite. "Janus just positively fingered you as his abductatator! If you hadda been playing with him he would have liked you!"

"Aw, he's just mad because I played a tr—" Isbister considered the words that were coming out of his mouth, and stopped them.

"What you say?"

"He's mad because I played a trick on him!" shouted Nathanael.

"Trick? What kind of trick?"

Isbister shrugged. "I pretended to throw the stick, but I really just dropped it behind my back."

The midget took a step nearer Nathanael and studied his face. "Ooooh," he said quietly, "you are *nasty.*"

Chapter 3

BUT WHAT OF my grandfather? Well, what that sly old dog did was this: he headed into the thick of the forest and climbed a tree. There he threw off his spectacles and respectable jacket, mussed his hair, and rolled up his shirt-sleeves. Then, as the mob roared underneath, he dropped among them and joined in their menacing mutter. "Let's get that guy!" he said. "Lord knows we got enough trouble without the likes of him running around!" The men around him grumbled out agreement. Before long my grandfather was directing them, leading them. "Hey, you! Make sure he ain't in that haystack over there! He's a tricky sonnabitch!" "Hey, Baldy, check out that drain-pipe!" The men responded like automatons.

My grandfather led them throughout the county until well into the morning. He was tireless in the pursuit of the outlaw. And he was ruthless in what he said they should do with the outlaw once they caught him—"Hang him by the bollickers and let vultures pick at his eyes!"

With the dawn came a kind of excited fatigue. The men went to a bar—it wasn't supposed to be open, but one of the posse's members was the owner. There my grandfather told stories. "When I first started in the Law Enforcement field . . ." Law Enforcement!? Can you believe it? "It wasn't like today. No siree, when I started there wasn't none of this paperwork and ass-callousing and head-scratching. It was 'Bang! Bang!' ", and my grandfather let off two mighty shots with his forefingers, blowing off the imaginary smoke and staring with a mixture of hardness and compassion at his imaginary victim.

When the men asked him what he was doing in their town he winked and pointed to a mouth screwed up tight. They bought him beer and wine and whisky, and when he finally passed out they carried him gingerly upstairs and laid him down to sleep.

Major Mite, with a wave of the Colt 45, told Isbister to "Move!" The weight of the raised gun almost caused the midget to topple over backwards.

"Where," asked Nathanael, "are we going?"

"We are going back to the ten-in-one, on account of I don't know what to do with you, so we have to ask the Doc. But if I had my way, I'd tear ya from limb to limb!"

Janus suddenly felt contrite about his betrayal of Nathanael, and went over to lick at his hand.

"Go away," said Nathanael. "Look at the trouble you two got me into—just because you can't take a little joke."

Janus began to whine quietly.

"Oh, knock it off," demanded Isbister. "Thanks to you guys, I may be torn from limb to limb."

"And don't think I couldn't do it, neither!" shrieked the high-pitched voice from behind. "I know what you're thinking, Buster! You're thinking I'm a little on the short side! Right? Well, lemme tell you something and you better listen good—little man beat a big man every time if the little man's in the right and keeps on coming!"

And thus was Nathanael transported out of the valley.

From behind came grunts from Major Mite as he tried to level the mammoth pistol into Isbister's back.

Other than that, they walked in silence.

My grandfather and I are in a quandary, i.e., how to fill up this interim. As I just said, Nathanael and the Major walked in silence. My grandfather was passed out drunk. Beatrice the Bovine Beauty wasn't up to much, just chewing cud. (But *not* wallowing in self-pity, mind you, not Beatrice.)

My experience as a writer (two published novels, mixed reviews, modest sales) tells me that what I should do is pry open Nathanael's mind. I should reveal his thoughts, as he was no doubt considering his past right that very instant. But my grandfather says no—and for emphasis he slams his cane on my tabletop.

"Why not, you old feeble fool?"

My grandfather's eyes and veins bulge and he says, "Beeecause—" through a clenched tooth. Then he relaxes with a sigh. "Leave the poor man alone," he says—then, afraid of the sudden gravity in his voice, he sings a crackling chorus of "Camptown Ladies".

What I will do is relate a tale from Major Mite's past.

When the Major was fifteen years old, Mulcher took him to Europe, where he caused quite a sensation. Mulcher is, of course, Morris M-for-Magnus Mulcher. You've all heard of him. If you haven't, pretend you have. He was the most famous impresario and showman of his time, and he started off by managing Major Mite.

When Mulcher first met the Major, the latter was ten years old and a perfect specimen of a boy in every way, except that he was only a little over a foot tall.

The Major's real name was Donald Pfaff.

His father was an iceman who was convinced that Donald's diminutive stature was a result of approaching sterility. His first child had been normal, if not slightly taller than average. Then came Donald, only a quarter as big as someone you would call a runt. The third child, reasoned Mr. Pfaff, will be no child at all, and my tool will lie wilted and useless until the day I die.

If Mrs. Pfaff had been the only woman in his life it wouldn't have mattered much. But there was Norma, a local whore who boasted the biggest set of breasts the county had ever seen. (Compared to the world record holder, of course, Norma was modest.)

And so Mr. Pfaff hated the sight of Donald, and did everything in his power to make the child's life miserable. While his older brother played baseball (a new game, so new it wasn't even called baseball, but rather rounders, and was different from the game we know in many ways), Donald would have to help his father with the ice route.

As they stood at the customer's back door, Mr. Pfaff would make jokes about Donald:

"When Dr. Brandston delivered the boy, he looked at him, then went right back to the missus and poked around inside some more. He said, 'If they're gonna come this size, you probably got two or three more at least.' "

Mr. Pfaff never laughed at his little jokes; he just made them and took disdainful looks at the child. They weren't anywhere near the truth—at birth Donald had weighed ten pounds and was a difficult delivery.

The housewives never laughed at his jokes either. They said, "But Mr. Pfaff, he's so cute. Come here, Donny . . ."

And while Mr. Pfaff said, "He ain't cute. You say good things come in small packages, I say so does poison. You think he's so damn cute, you can have him." Donald climbed up on the ladies' laps where he was fondled and clucked over. He like to wedge his tiny head deep within their bosoms.

Morris M-for-Magnus Mulcher was meanwhile pursuing, in the same town, a career as an alcoholic. It so happened that one night he found himself in the same tavern as Mr. Pfaff, who was no slouch himself when it came to drinking. Mr. Pfaff had been saddled with the care of Donald while his wife was at some kind of church meeting.

His father said, "The only good thing 'bout being his size is you could crawl right into a broad's pinko." This is the way Mr. Pfaff talked in barrooms. "Yes siree—right up and into it, and you could lie around in there just as easy as can be. Why, you could even smoke a ceegar in there!"

The men around Mr. Pfaff laughed and one said, "Yuh, it'd be nice, okay. They say that when a man's born he comes out of a little hole—then he spends the rest of his goddam life trying to get back in!"

And the men laughed again, all except for Morris M-for-Magnus Mulcher. He was a solitary drunk and always chose the table furthest in the corner. There he'd dream of transatlantic balloon flights and ladies who could smoke cigarettes with their lowermost orifices.

I'll bet nobody else in the world dreamt like Morris M-for-Magnus Mulcher. His dreams went:

Just numbers.

If you were to walk up to M.M. Mulcher and ask what 12% of $6,867 was, he'd mutter the answer as if it was how he took his coffee.

He just had a head for figures. And that's all—numbers, dollar signs, and percentages were all his brain would hold.

Of course, I'm simplifying things. Morris M-for-Magnus Mulcher was as human as any one of us. He had compassion, for example— he had once been very kind to an old apple lady. He explained very carefully to her how to run the most profitable street corner apple stand—how to buy in quantity, commission urchins to sell door-to-door for 26 percent total sales, how to set up a bookkeeping system for credits and debits, all of that.

And Morris M-for-Magnus had lusted after women in some vague way. The only avenue of release he knew about was prostitutes. He could understand them. Whenever he gave one ten dollars he wondered what percentage she received. And whenever her eyes twinkled and shone at the money, he felt the warmth in his breast that is brotherhood.

So, in his way, M.M. was just like you or me. He was kind, good, and lonely. It wasn't his fault that all he knew and understood were numbers, dollar signs, and percentages.

Now, for example, all this loud talk of "pinkos" was foreign to Morris M-for-Magnus Mulcher. He sipped at his whisky and tonic and thought:

It was not a good thought, so he frowned. Any thought or dream that did not terminate in at least three figures was of no use to him.

Suddenly there was a little creature standing on his table. A tiny doll dressed in rags. But it *moved!* M.M. Mulcher was astonished. The boy was only a foot high, but perfect. An angel's face, coy and innocent. The boy looked at M.M. and said, "Quick—lemme have a sip of your drink."

Morris M-for-Magnus Mulcher stared at the tiny boy standing on his table. It was like lightning:

and his mind started ticking over zeros a mile a minute.

He held his glass up to the tiny boy's mouth. Donald guzzled at it, smacked his lips, and drew a sleeve across his mouth. "It's cheap stuff," he said. In those days his voice was so high it could barely be heard.

"I will buy you some better brand," M.M. Mulcher said quietly.

"Naw, my old man'll hit me. That's the old fart there, drinking with his buddies and making stupid jokes about me."

"Which man is your father?" asked Morris M-for-Magnus.

"The peckerhead over there with the beer gut and the moustache."

"Is your father poor?"

"My old man?" Donald shrugged. "I guess so. Isn't everybody?"

"How would you like to be a showman?"

"Huh?" Little Donald Pfaff was confused by this man. He asked slowly, "Whaddaya mean, 'showman?' "

"What I mean is this. I will hire people to teach you how to sing and how to dance. Then we will rent halls. Only halls with a capacity of 500 or more. We will sell tickets at two dollars a head. Our intake will be $1,000 per show. We subtract the cost of renting the hall and advertising, approximately $200. This leaves $800. Of which you will receive ten percent. That is $80. You will earn $80 per diem."

"Hey, Mac," squeaked little Donald, "ya don't gotta teach me how to sing. Listen at this:" Then the boy went into the highest-pitched and most exuberant rendition of "Molly Malone" that the world has ever heard. The barroom dog whimpered mournfully and hid. Donald accompanied himself with various hand gestures—when the lyrics involved anything female, he would mime acts of self-abuse and wink at Morris M-for-Magnus. The word "cockles" was illustrated by Donald's clutching at his own microscopic genitals.

Halfway through, M.M. Mulcher reached forward and clamped his hand around the tiny boy's head. The song continued, muffled through the skin, for several seconds before it stopped. Then the miniature limbs began to flail madly, fighting for release. Mulcher let go.

Donald Pfaff was beet red and furious. "What kinda thing is that to do, Mac?! How'd you like to get your head stuffed down a crapper, huh?"

Morris M-for-Magnus Mulcher smiled slightly and said, "Why sing for free when you could become rich doing it?"

To calm himself, Donald bent over the whisky and tonic on the table as if it were a drinking fountain, tilted it towards him and guzzled. Finished, he said, "You got a point there, Mac. 'Cept for my old man wouldn't let me. He needs me to help on the ice route."

"I will talk to him," announced M.M., and he left to do just that. Donald watched the ensuing transaction—it involved about forty-five seconds of haggling and a ten dollar bill. Then Morris M-M-for-Magnus Mulcher returned to the table and said, "Let us go."

"Ten bucks, eh?" asked Donald.

M.M. Mulcher nodded.

"Jesus . . ." muttered the tiny boy, and he swallowed back something in his throat. "Ten lousy bucks."

"You will soon be rich." said Mulcher.

Donald shook his head once and brightened like a light. "Yeah! I'm gonna be a *showman!*"

Donald jumped down from the table and took a last look at his father. Mr. Pfaff had rejoined the general conversation and seemed to have no intention of saying farewell to his son. So Donald looked away.

"Let's go, Mac!" he hollered up to Morris M-for-Magnus Mulcher.

They walked from the barroom, little Donald galloping to keep pace with his newfound guardian.

True to his word (and much to Donald's disgust) Mulcher hired teachers. Donald had a singing teacher, a dancing teacher, a dramatics teacher, and, worst of all, a diction teacher. This man was to teach little Donald how to speak properly. Which was next to impossible. He was also supposed to educate Donald in the art of lively repartee.

"I say," the teacher would begin, "you are an exceedingly small fellow." Then he would raise his eyebrows in expectation of the witty retort.

"And you eat the crust offa a bear's ass," was typical of little Donald Pfaff.

After several months of training (torture to the boy) they were successful. Donald would say (with exaggerated openings and closings of his mouth), "I may well be small, my good sir, but nigh-ther are you an ex-ceed-ing-ly big fel-low for say-ing so." If the teacher asked, "What is the weather like down there?", Donald would enunciate, "It is ver-y cool and re-fresh-ing, thank you, for all of the hot air pass-es well a-bove my head."

As far as all the other things went—the singing, dancing, etc.— Donald was a natural. In a few months he could put on a show that would have been good even had he been regulation height.

Morris M-for-Magnus Mulcher knew that something was still missing. It was the diction-and-lively-repartee teacher who had the inspiration. "It is all very well, his singing and dancing and razor-sharp witticisms, but after all, he is just a dwarf named Donald Pfaff. However, if he were something other! Not the aristocracy, of course, that would be too presumptuous. But *military!*"

And Major Mite was born.

From his first show, at the age of eleven, Major Mite was a success. The audience went wild at the sight of the miniature boy dressed in army regalia.

The Major would strut onstage and launch into a rapid tap dance atop a special platform. He would sing patriotic songs which, although hard to hear, left not a dry eye in the house. For the second half, Major Mite would answer questions from the audience.

"Major, how tall are you?"

"Well, sir, I do reach the ground. I dare say that is tall e-nough."

Ladies would usually ask, "Have you found a little girlfriend?"

The Major found it hard to resist telling the audience how he'd lost his virginity before he ever even knew he had it, but he always said something like, "I have met man-y girls, but they u-shu-a-ly put me in-to a per-am-bu-la-tor with the rest of their dolls."

"How tall would you like to be?" someone would shout.

"Sir, I am not dis-sat-is-fied with my stat-ure. But, I must confess, it *would* be plea-sant to take a bath with-out the use of a life pre-serv-er."

"Don't you find it hard to climb stairs?"

"Let me an-swer you in this man-ner, my good wo-man: when I reach the top of the stair-case, I e-rect a flag and claim it in the name of the U-nite-ed States of A-mer-i-ca."

"Where do you get your clothes?"

"I get them from my clos-et."

"But where do you *buy* them?"

"I buy them from the rack—at the toy store."

At any rate, both Major Mite and Mulcher became rich—M.M. much more than the Major, of course. Morris M-for-Magnus began to be known as a great showman, and he even began to think like one. He decided that it would make for a great show if the Major was teamed up with a giant, so he contracted Angus McCallister from Cape Breton Island.

McCallister, at seven feet, two inches, was the tallest *man* that has ever lived. I emphasize "man" because Angus was not technically a giant. Giants are produced by a malfunctioning pituitary gland, and sometimes are close to nine feet tall. They are sickly and prone to disease, particularly, for some strange reason, in their feet. They almost always die young.

Angus, on the other hand, was ridiculously healthy. His chest measured a full seventy inches (still the world record), and his arms were as thick as trees. He was beefy and burly in the style of Cape Breton, with a long red beard and flaming grey eyes.

In other words, Angus was as big as a healthy, normal body can get, and he quite deserved his billing of "The Strongest Man Alive". You got paid fifty dollars if you could fight him for more than a

minute—no man ever collected the purse. He could pick up anything smaller than a house. Legend has him pulling out oak trees
by the roots, and who am I to mess around with legend?

Angus McCallister and Major Mite formed a duo the likes of
which have never been seen before or since. Standing together, the
Major was about an inch shy of the top of the Cape Bretoner's
boots. The Major could perform a soft-shoe in the hollow of
Angus's palm. And Morris M-for-Magnus became richer.

So, when the Major was fifteen, M.M. decided it was time to
broaden their horizons. Thus he, the Major, and McCallister boarded
a steamship and tooted away for Europe.

(Angus picked up the Major (who, incidentally, was about eighteen inches tall now) and held him to look over the railing at the
fading U.S. of A.

"Donny," he whispered, Angus being the only one who addressed
the Major that way, "I've heared tales o' the whores overseas that'll
rip yer pants. An' no' very dear are they, neither, or so I'm told.
No' only that, but in Europe ye'll be famous. They love wee people. Did ye ken that King Henry the Eighth was wee?"

(If you people out there want to talk like someone from Cape
Breton, read the above passage aloud, moving only your bottom
jaw.)

"Bullshit!" giggled the Major.

"No, no!" Angus laughed. "Sure an' he was wee! No more'n
two foot. An' le' me see—well, o'course, Napoleon was wee.
Ever'one kens that."

"Ya big ape! He was short, but he weren't short like me!"

"He was!" Angus pretended to be deeply insulted by this lack
of faith. "An' his whole army was wee, too, for he wanted none
bigger than he! Ye donna ken it for ye've no' been ta school."

"Neither have you!"

"That's true, too. I guess I've read it in a book."

"You don't know how to read, you enormous galoof!" cried
the Major, and he batted Angus ineffectually on the cheek.

"Ah! Ye're right there, Donny. I donna. Then where did I ken
about Napoleon from? Where? I know! I dinna read it, an' I dinna
hear it—I made it up!")

Angus and Major Mite were fast friends despite the difference in
age—Angus was almost thirty, but he had a certain childish quality
and was forever teasing the Major. After shows the two would go
look for trouble together.

They had a favourite trick they like to pull. Angus always wore a pair of overalls that were extremely baggy—there was ample room inside for the tiny Major. So in he would climb and out they would go.

McCallister would go to a whorehouse and, being flush with money these days, rent the best-looking girl on the premises. In her room, Angus would look away coyly and mutter, "I'm no' like other men . . ."

The girl would say, "I should think you ain't."

Angus would shake his head with woe. "Ye donna understan'. It's me peter."

"Your hah?"

"Me peter. It's no' like them o' other men."

"Big, hah?" the girl would ask with a curious mixture of fear and delight.

"Ah no—it's no' that. It's no' so big, really. It's jest that . . . ah, hell, I'll show ye." And Angus would go to work on his fly-buttons. The girl would watch, spellbound.

Then Major Mite would poke his head out of Angus's pants with a broad grin and a "Hi!"

I've got my grandfather going now. Whenever he's reminded of that stunt he starts laughing. He's one of those people who laughs sucking in. It lasts about three seconds before he commences coughing.

Now—Nathanael and Major Mite are nearing their destination. My grandfather is groaning on the edge of sleep, devastatingly hung over. So it's time I got to that story I was going to tell about Major Mite.

Well, the Major and McCallister and Mulcher weren't an overnight success in Europe but, once started, their fame grew like a vine. All manner of people, the wealthy and the royal, invited the young Major to balls and receptions.

Major Mite was incredible—he had found a talent for mimicry and at these gatherings he would impersonate people like Wellington, Nelson, and Napoleon.

Napoleon was the best. With his hair greased and combed forward, the Major bore Bonaparte an uncanny resemblance. Then, hand in waistcoat, he would strut back and forth, his brow furrowed and eyes dark and brooding, full of strategic genius.

The Major delighted his way around Europe, and at night he and Angus would go out drinking and whoring. Mulcher was exquisitely happy—all that his work entailed was keeping the stories of the Major's and McCallister's nocturnal romps out of the papers.

One day they received an invitation for the big one—a performance for Queen Victoria.

It was held in one of the largest rooms in the Palace; there Angus and the Major went through their stuff, and although the Queen never allowed a smile to crack her face, she announced at the conclusion, "Delightful."

McCallister and the Major were personally introduced to her as she sat upon a huge and ornate throne amid purple velvet and jewels. Angus knelt before her in supplication and the Queen said, "Big." The Major did likewise and she said, "Tiny. Very." Then the pair withdrew.

It was customary when leaving the Queen's imperial presence to back out, even though the door was two hundred feet away across an unbroken stretch of marble. This was no problem for Angus, whose long legs carried him backwards as fast as another man might run. For the Major, however, it was more difficult. In order to keep up with Angus, the tiny boy would take two or three steps backwards, and then twirl around and charge madly for a second or two. Then, with another twirl, he would resume his regal backward strut.

The Queen's court was delighted by this breach of protocol, particularly one of the Royal Dogs. The mutt ran for the little Major and began to yelp and bark, circling menacingly. It was not a very big dog, but the Major was terrified—it was, after all, bigger than he was. So the Major tried to scare him away with a series of whispered threats. He even abandoned his techniques of lively repartee. But the dog kept barking and snapping.

Finally Major Mite flew frontwards toward the door in a panic. The dog pounced, and the two grappled about on the floor until Angus plucked the boy out of the fray.

Safe in his friend's arms, the Major spoke these now famous words to Queen Victoria: "Your Highness, I believe it is time to feed the dogs."

That is the way legend has it, at least. I have it on good authority that what the Major actually said was, "Hey, lady!! Why don't you feed that goddam mutt?!?"

Legend has a way of trimming rough edges.

Chapter 4

IN THE MIDDLE of a field stood a huge tent. Sometime ago the canvas had probably been a blinding bright red, but time had faded it to a pale pink. Here and there rents and tears had been repaired with thick stitches, like those on Frankenstein's monster's neck. Behind the huge tent were two smaller ones—lopsided staircases of four steps each led to their openings.

Crybaby and his tiny abductor walked toward the tents—pale spotlights lit the scene, making it milky and dreamlike in the night.

Describing a semicircle around half of the big top was a series of large wallboard posters, each with a light of its own. There were eleven of them in all, and Crybaby was forced to walk past them by Major Mite.

These were the pictures that leapt into Nathanael's eyes:

i

Large gold letters spelled out "STELLA—800 LBS. OF WOMAN". Beneath them was a round cloud in a pink, polka-dotted dress. The artist had almost given this cloud a face of beautiful simplicity —large, childlike eyes and full, feminine lips. But then, between these, he had attached a hideous sow's snout.

Every limb and appendage, right down to the little toe, was balloon-like. The artist had taken especial care with her breasts, making sure that each gigantic globe was distinct.

ii

The second poster was the artist's conception of Major Mite himself. He had chopped off about forty years of age and, by placing the Major beside a yardstick, almost a full foot of height—the Major barely cleared the two-foot mark.

In the picture Major Mite was decked out spectacularly in military fashion: medals and pistols, swords and braiding, all made larger so that the Major could look even smaller, buried beneath their weight.

The artist gave Major Mite enormous locks of blond hair and put a twinkle into the blue eyes. Beneath the painting he had spelled out, "THE SHORTEST MAN ALIVE."

iii

As would seem logical, next to this was announced "THE TALLEST MAN ALIVE", and up soared a fellow whose name, apparently, was Davey Goliath. Where the Major had been pictured with a yardstick, Davey stood beside a tree, dwarfing it by twice again. He was shown to be a fine figure of a man (a little lanky, of course) with an impishly boyish face—freckles and tousled red hair.

In the picture he was laughing.

"Who are all these?" asked Isbister of the Major.

The tiny man pointed over his shoulder (although Nathanael couldn't see) and said, "Second from the left is me." Although this is old news to you and me, it was something of a surprise to Crybaby.

"So you're Major Mite, eh?" he said. "The picture doesn't look like you."

"Agh!" snapped the little man from behind. "It ain't supposed to, nimrod. Keep moving!"

iv

"ZAP—THE WILD MAN FROM BORNEO " was one of the artist's most ambitious works. First of all he had painted a scene of dense foliage, a jungle full of exotic fruit trees and multi-coloured cockatoos. Then, in the middle of it all, wearing an expression of savageness you could never imagine, stood the wild man, Zap.

From head to toe he was covered in hair, dark and matted like fur. His teeth were long and pointed, as was his head. His crown came together above his eyes like a pin. In his hands he held a hunk of raw meat, and the artist had drawn two or three trickles of blood dripping from the wild man's mouth.

v

"MADAME TANYA", according to her picture, was some gorgeous woman! The artist had dressed her in the last of Salome's
veils, thin and transparent so that you could see right through. The
body inside was enough to make you groan. Firm breasts and big
hips.

Her face, what you could see of it, was delicious in every sense—
large, almond eyes, a ruby red mouth formed into a child's pout.
The only thing the artist had added that did not conform to Every-
man's ideal of womanhood was a beard. A large, curly one that
hung down to her breasts. It was bushy and full, and any member
of the House of Jonah would have been proud to be its owner.

That is what this story is about, sort of.

"I'll bet it's fake," said Nathanael over his shoulder to the Major,
hooking a thumb towards Tanya.

Major Mite did not respond.

"What the . . .?"

vi

"THE HISSLOP SISTERS" were every bit as gorgeous as Madame
Tanya; in fact, all three women were almost identical, except that
the Hisslops didn't have beards.

The painting showed them in skimpy underthings—brassieres
and panties—and somewhere near the midriff the two were joined
together. And in case anyone should miss the point, the artist had
spelled out in big, block letters, "SIAMESE TWINS".

vii

"THE ALLIGATOR MAN" was just that, with a slash across the
middle—he had the body of an alligator and the head of a man.
The picture showed him crawling around on the ground in typical
reptile fashion. But from his neck rose a handsome human head
that had a handsome human face.

Nathanael Crybaby Isbister said, "I don't buy that one."

The Major said (very quickly, it seemed to Isbister), "While bearing the child still within her, THE ALLIGATOR MAN's mother witnessed, on safari in deepest Africa, the death of her own husband at the hands of a crocodile's jaws. Prenatal impression produced the hideous monstrosity that you now see before you."

"I don't see him before me."

"Shaddup."

viii

"JANUS, THE TWO-HEADED FIVE-LEGGED WONDERDOG" we've met already. Having done so, we realize that the artist may not be as good as we once thought. For one thing, the fifth leg in the painting reached to the ground and seemed every bit as sturdy as the other four. For another, the two heads were completely separate and free of each other, whereas we know that in reality they shot off awkwardly and were no little nuisance to the animal. And as if all that wasn't bad enough, the artist had made Janus a pureblooded collie. He probably had a tiny bit of collie blood in him, but then again he probably had a tiny bit of every breed's blood somewhere inside.

Nathanael even said to him, "Is that supposed to be you guys?"

The dog glanced up at the painting and yapped. Isbister thought it did so proudly.

"I wish you two would quit pretending you can understand everything I say," demanded Crybaby—to which the dog made no reply.

ix

"THE RUBBER BOY" made for a strange picture—he was quite a nice-looking young man, but every limb and feature was stretched. It was as if you saw the boy in all the funhouse mirrors all at once. In the picture the boy was reaching through a window that was twenty feet from him.

Nathanael saw the picture and said to Major Mite, "I'm double-jointed."

The Major said "Shaddup," so Isbister started on Fido and Rover (Janus).

"I really am," he said. "I can bend my finger right back to my hand."

Crybaby, just to reassure himself, grabbed his left forefinger and pulled it backward until it lay flat against the back of his hand. Then he released it and said, "Ouch."

x

This was perhaps the strangest picture of all. Imagine, if you can, a hippopotamus, standing erect and crammed into a tuxedo. When you've done that, the writing "THE HIPPOPOTAMUS BOY" becomes redundant.

xi

A black picture, covered with shrouds of night.

Somewhere within the shadows lurked the face of a man, but it was obscured and hard to make out.

The poster was clearly the work of another artist.

The writing, an ornate script done in gold leaf, said "DOCTOR SINISTER."

They rounded the other side of the big top. The only light came from the moon, and it was hard to make out the figures. They stood in a small group, gesticulating wildly and talking all at once. Isbister could discern three voices: a regular man's baritone, a high-pitched squeaky tenor, and an arrhythmic series of guttural grunts.

As they moved closer, Nathanael could make out the words.

"For crissakes, Doctor!" boomed the baritone. "Why bother?"

There was a loud grunt here and a sound like a cat whose tail has been stepped on.

"He'll get it soon," came the tenor. "It's simply a matter of patience and perserverance."

A match flame burned the darkness and was transformed into a floating, glowing coal. Someone had lit a cigar.

"Now here, Zapper," squeaked the high voice. "Smoke this."

The lighted end moved in the air—it shone redder as someone sucked in. Then came a scream as from an outraged orangutan, and the ember shot into the air, flying past Isbister's left ear.

"What goes on?" whispered Crybaby.

"Aaagh!" came a scream from behind him. "What bastard fired a ceegar at me?"

The squeaky voice piped in the blackness. "Major? Have you returned?"

"I have returned, but I expected a more cordial welcome than to get ceegars thrown at me!"

"It was but little Zap," returned the tenor.

"You tryin' to get that maroon to do the Wrigley routine again?"

"He's going to get it soon!"

The baritone came in. "He's not going to get it soon! He's an idiot."

"He'll hear you!" squeaked the tenor.

Here came a complicated series of grunts.

"Did you find Janus?" asked the tenor.

"I found him and the egg-sucker what stole him to boot!"

"I didn't steal him," said Isbister quietly. "I was just playing with him."

"Lies!" shouted Major Mite.

"We shall go to my caravan to discuss it," announced the tenor.

With another "Move!" from the Major, they walked.

The moonlight silhouetted the three men from behind. One was fairly big, muscular, and walked with a determined strut. His hands were thrust deeply into his pockets. Next to him was a short, frail figure who stumbled occasionally and once toppled all the way to the ground. He was up in a second.

The third figure was tiny and hunched over. His arms dangled at his side, his knuckles almost brushing the ground. Sometimes he would spin around like a dervish, but it was quick, much too quick for Isbister to make out anything of his face.

They walked to a trailer, an old one that used to be attached to a horse. But the horse was long dead, and the wooden wheels were buried deep into the ground. They walked up some lopsided steps and entered.

It was a tiny caravan to begin with, being the home of a solitary man, and a small solitary man at that. The five men and one dog would have been cramped for space had it been empty, which it was not*. Isbister was pointed to a minute rocking chair in the trailer's least crowded corner. He went to it and wedged his posterior in snugly.

---

*Among other things, this caravan contained: 984 books (most of them on the floor), 28 books in manuscript form, a writing table a foot deep in papers, a pipe organ, a wooden flute, a concertina, a banjo-ukulele, a chessboard, an easel, 43 bottles of liquor (half of them half-empty), 17 paintings, 23 etchings, most of a bicycle, 4 chairs, a hammock, a lamp with a base that was a naked lady, a ship in a bottle, a wind-up Victrola, a wireless (that didn't work), and a large box that was full to the brim with love letters.

The four other men stood around him.

You know more or less what Major Mite looked like.

Next to him stood a man only a little more than a foot taller, who said (in a high-pitched squeaky tenor) "I assume you've met the Major." This man had a long, droopy moustache that covered his mouth. Nathanael wondered, idly, whether this was why his words came out so quietly. He was an old man, wrinkled and wizened—bald on top, long and shaggy about the ears. His nose was long and thin and twitched back and forth like a rabbit's. He said, "This is the Alligator Man."

The tallest one said, "Hi," in a regular baritone. He had a rugged face—hard lines and pockmarks. What there was about him that was like an alligator was not to be seen.

The little man with the moustache said, "And this is our little Zap," and put his arm around the same in a fatherly manner.

Zap, if he stood upright, would probably have been just under five feet, but he was hunched over to about half of that. I've thought hard about how to describe him, and this is the best I could come up with: he looked like Jerry Lewis, covered in hair, doing an impersonation of Lon Chaney as the Hunchback of Notre Dame. He had a twisted nose and ill-matched eyes, one big and the other both smaller and lower on his face. He was dressed in a scanty fur covering, *à la* Tarzan. His skull was shaped oddly, rising to a tiny point near the back. He was what is known as a "pinhead," or, more scientifically, a microcephalic—both terms mean about the same thing.

When introduced Zap grunted and stuck his finger into his right nostril. He then made what seemed to Nathanael to be a very hideous face.

"I," said the little man with the moustache, "am Doctor Sinister." He grinned and showed that he was missing one of his front teeth.

Isbister allowed himself a silent chuckle.

"Now," said Dr. Sinister, beginning to pace back and forth in the little caravan, "you have been accused of stealing our dog, Janus. This, needless to say, is a heinous profligacy. What have you to say in your own defence?"

"I . . ." began Nathanael.

"I'm sorry, I'm sorry!" interrupted the little Doctor. "I neglected to ask you your appellation. Will you please excuse me?"

"Sure—it's, uh, Isbister."

Dr. Sinister's eyebrows rose high on to his forehead. Then he said, "Very well, Mr. Isbister, you may continue."

"There's really nothing to tell you," said Nathanael. "See, I was just walking along, and I came upon a slope that went down into a valley. I started down it, but it was steeper than I thought and I lost my balance. I have bad legs. When I hit bottom, Fido and Rover were there looking at me."

" 'Fido and Rover'?" asked Dr. Sinister.

Major Mite explained irritably. "That's what Curly calls Janus."

"I see," said the little man. And then to Isbister, "Pray proceed."

"Well, I tried to lose the thing, but I couldn't. I ended up playing fetch with them. Then he" (meaning Major Mite) "came along, threatened me and brought me here at gunpoint. That's all."

"That story wouldn't hold water at the bottom of the ocean!" shouted Major Mite.

"Major!" snapped Dr. Sinister. Zap grunted in a similar tone. Then the Doctor proceeded. "There *are* certain things that warrant further explanation. For example, Mr. Isbister, *why* did you begin a descent into that valley?"

"I wanted to."

"Yes, I imagine you did. Now, could you try to respond to the query without engaging in tautology?"

"Personal reasons, then," said Nathanael.

"Your reticence does little to persuade of your innocence," said Dr. Sinister.

"Why is it important?" demanded Isbister. "Can't I go where I choose?"

"Yes, I suppose you can. All I'm asking is that you expand your story somewhat. It is, as it stands, rather controvertible."

Nathanael Isbister stood up. "Look, if you want to press charges, do it at a police station. I'm leaving."

The Alligator Man was the only one of a stature comparable to Nathanael. He stepped forward, took his hand from his pocket, and put it on Isbister's chest. "Sit down, Mac," he said quietly.

Nathanael stared in horror at the hand on his chest. It was covered with green scales.

Nathanael sat down in the tiny rocking chair once more, and the Alligator Man quickly replaced his hand in his pocket.

After a moment's silence, the tiny Doctor asked quietly, "Are you *Nathanael* Isbister?"

"Why do you ask?" returned Isbister sullenly.

"Because if you are Nathanael Isbister I might be more inclined to believe your tale."

"Crybaby Isbister?" asked Major Mite. "I thought he was dead."

A tiny smile had come to the Alligator Man's face. "Nathanael Isbister? Yeah . . . yeah, that's him! I saw him play once . . ."

"I fail to see why my story should be any more believable just because I happen to be . . ."

A remarkable change had come over Major Mite. The midget was grinning broadly. "Ain't this something'?" he marvelled. "Nathanael Crybaby Isbister, sitting right here."

"I'm not him," stated Nathanael. "I'm not him, and I'll tell you what else, I stole the dog."

The Alligator Man said, "I saw you play once. You're him, okay."

"So I'm him!" shouted Isbister. "But I stole the dog!"

Dr. Sinister stared hard at him. "Why did you steal the dog?"

"Why? Because he's the biggest draw since Beatrice the Bovine Beauty. Leastwise as far as animals is concerned."

"I told him that," said Major Mite. "He didn't know Janus from a hole in the ground. Called him Fido and Rover."

At this point Zap moved forward to look at Isbister. He brought his furry face to within inches of Nathanael's. Zap's mouth hung crookedly and stupidly open, and his uneven eyes were crossed. After studying Nathanael he stepped back and grunted loudly.

Janus added to this a short, double-edged bark.

The other three men said, almost in unison, "Nathanael Crybaby Isbister."

Confronted with his identity and unable to get away from it, Nathanael felt the tears begin to spill from his eyes.

Except for this sobbing there was silence in the tiny caravan.

Dr. Sinister said quietly, "I suppose that proves it."

"Now!" I shout at my grandfather, waking him from his slumber on the couch. He gets up with a start. "Whatwhatwhat?" he demands, his old eyes bleary.

"Now's the time to expound upon Isbister's past," I tell him.

My grandfather climbs to his feet awkwardly, mocking under his breath my use of the word "expound." He crosses over and stares at the paper in the typewriter. "Naw, not now," he says.

"Look, I can't just keep writing about how he's always crying, and why everyone has heard of him without explaining . . ."

"Listen, sonny, you don't know shit about writing books. That's why the first two were bombs."

"They were not!" I protest.

"They stunk," my grandfather responds. He reaches over my shoulder and pulls the paper from the machine, racing his eyes over it. "Okay," he decides. "Now it's time for the Hisslop girls."

"Okay. Right after I explain . . ."

My grandfather plucks up his cane, an old thick shillelagh, and for a few minutes he pursues me around the table, swinging blindly. Finally he connects with the back of my head, and I go down. When I come to there is a new piece of paper in the typewriter. Across the top it says:

INtroDucINg thE HisLoP SiSers

I sigh.

Violet and Daisy Hisslop were, at the time, in a diner in Burton's Harbor. They were sharing a grilled cheese sandwich and drinking coffee.

Violet and Daisy were joined at the hip; the bones there were fused together. Had they been born nowadays, the doctors would have little trouble separating them, but coming as they did from the past and from a poor family, they remained linked together. If someone had offered them the operation they would have refused. Each thought, dimly and never voiced, that she drew life from the other. Daisy felt that if she were separated from Violet she would surely die. Violet felt the same way. Of course, their greatest fear was that the other would die first.

This fear manifested itself at night, in bed, when there was a frantic race between the two sisters to go to sleep. Neither could stand it if the other drifted off first. So both had become inveterate pill-takers and drinkers. Each bedtime was a mad dash toward stupor. They would stuff themselves with drugs and gin, and by the time they lay down sleep would come over them in less than a minute.

They had found one other way to avoid this terror, and that was to people their bed, preferably with a young man. That way, if one should go to sleep, the other could avoid "death" by fervent and arduous love-making with the bedmate.

This had its drawbacks, especially for the bedmate. If Daisy should nod off, Violet would go to it with the young man. This would wake up Daisy, and while the sated Violet drifted away,

Daisy would engage the young man. Which would wake up Violet. You see how this worked out. Daisy and Violet would spend half the night asleep, half the night making love. The poor bedmate, however, was denied the sweetness of slumber.

Now it was no problem for the Hisslop girls to find young men, despite the oddness of their connection. They were extremely attractive women. They had auburn hair, bright blue eyes, and pale, pearly complexions, almost white. Their figures were firm and rounded. Young men were invariably won over by their beauty and great charm. And the Hisslop sisters had been through quite a number of them.

That's why they were having trouble deciding about the young man sitting over in the diner's corner, eating a piece of apple pie.

"I'm positive," announced Violet. "It was about four weeks ago."

"No, I don't think so," said Daisy. "I think I would remember *him*."

The Hisslop sisters shared a mischievous giggle.

The problem at hand was a serious one. If they hadn't slept with the man, then they could well have found one for that night. If they had, however, slept with him, they would have to search for another. Although they had little trouble getting young men, it was, because of the situation outlined above, impossible to get the same man on more than one occasion.

Violet was adamant. "A month ago. He was the one who liked to . . ." She completed the sentence by whispering into her sister's ear. Daisy cupped her hands over her mouth and her eyebrows shot up on to her forehead.

"But," asked Daisy, "wasn't that man much shorter?"

"No, no, it was him!"

The young man, being heavily involved with his apple pie, had not looked up.

Violet announced, "I'm going to ask him."

Daisy said, "Oh, don't! I'd be too embarrassed."

For all their sexual activity, the Hisslop girls were very shy, especially Daisy. Violet was a little more forthright and usually had her way.

"I'm going to ask him," she said again—and although Daisy was positively mortified, they climbed down from their perches and crossed over to where the young man sat.

"Excuse me," said Violet.

Daisy giggled.

The young man looked up.

Violet continued, "You probably don't remember us . . ."

My grandfather woke up in his hotel room. From below him came the sounds of many men in a bar. He descended the staircase into their midst.

And was greeted with hearty applause. Most of the people there were the same men he had led in the posse.

He accepted their ovation gracefully, bowing from the waist. "Good evening, law-abiding citizens of this fair community!" They drew him up to the bar and began to ply him with drink. The owner-bartender, an extremely fat man with a little beard, engaged him in conversation.

"I suppose," said the fat man, "that you've come to investigate the gambling problem over in Burton's Harbor."

"How did you find out?" snapped my grandfather.

"Just put two and two together," smiled the fat man, pleased that he'd figured it out. "They got a gambling problem there, you're an expert in law enforcement, so, you're going to investigate the gambling problem."

"If you tell anybody," my grandfather whispered, "I'll have your licence revoked so fast it'll make your head spin."

"You can count on me, sir!" said the fat man. "I won't breathe it to a soul."

"Okay," nodded my grandfather. He glanced around to make sure no one was listening, then he leaned closer to the bartender. "In your opinion, how bad is the gambling problem in Burton's Harbor?"

"Well, sir, here in Alexandria we say that they got three types of people over there. They got the religious guys, they got the freaks, and they got the gamblers. And that's all they got."

"They told me all that in the briefing," said my grandfather irritably. "I was hoping you could give me some more *inside* info."

"What you want to know?" asked the fat man helpfully.

"That's more like it. What I want to know is, you ever hear any names of places? Places that they gamble in?"

The fat bartender shook his head.

"Don't forget, pal, one nod from me and your place goes out of business!!"

"I think maybe I heard *one* name from someplace . . ." the fat man said. "I don't know if anything really goes on there. I ain't never been there."

"Let's have it."

"Place called the Fulton Arms Hotel."

"Over in Burton's Harbor?"

The fat man, being rather caught up in the crime-fighting aspect of the conversation, answered, "Affirmative."

"If anything comes of that lead, I'm going to make sure you get a special commendation."

"Thank *you*, sir!" The bartender gave my grandfather a double whisky, on the house.

I knew it, I knew it! I knew my grandfather was senile! I've just been glancing over the pages, and I see that night and day have gotten completely mixed up. This last section is about sixteen hours ahead of the rest of the story! And now, to make matters worse, I've been instructed to introduce a whole new set of characters. This is getting to be too much. There's only one thing to do.

Start a new chapter.

Chapter 5

BROTHERS TEKEL, MENE, and Peres sat at the head of the table.

Tekel, the oldest, lowered his head in prayer. All around him, around the huge table, the men did likewise.

Brother Tekel was a frightening-looking man. His hair was witch-black and spilled to his shoulders. His beard, immaculately cared-for, hung down nearly to his waist. He was clad in black robes. Eyes, small and dark, burned from deep within his face. He was tall and gaunt, with a large hooked nose and a tiny slit mouth. His cheeks were so hollow they formed pools of shadow on either side of his face.

His brothers, Mene and Peres, looked much the same—but for some reason less frightening.

Tekel's face suggested fires in the night, clouds across the moon.

His voice in prayer had an edge like a razor blade.

When he finished all the men at the table said, "Amen," and began to eat in silence. They made their meal from grains, vegetables and fruit. Elsewhere in the huge house the women and children were making a meal of grains, vegetables and fruit—they also were eating it in silence.

All the men were "Brothers"—they referred to each other that way—but Tekel, Mene and Peres were fraternal brothers as well. At the meal's completion, Tekel rose, as was custom, to address the "Brothers".

They listened with total concentration, absentmindedly picking bits of food out of their long, immaculately cared-for beards.

And Tekel spoke, his voice as soft as a whisper:

" 'Having therefore these promises, dearly beloved, let us cleanse ourselves from all filthiness of the flesh and spirit, perfecting holiness in the fear of God.'

"Perfecting holiness," Tekel repeated, "In the FEAR of GOD by cleansing all filthiness—of the spirit, and of the *flesh!*"

The Brethren nodded. The point had been made.

"When Father Jonah did found us here, he did write, 'The Holy House of Witness must be and grow as a dignified addition to the Community.' Above all else—if nothing else—we must command respect. We must show the townspeople how to cleanse themselves, and in order to do this, we must have respect."

Then Tekel Ambrose launched into one of the tangential and biblical asides that he was known for. He said:

" 'And the Lord spake unto Moses, saying, Command the children of Israel that they put out of the camp every leper, and everyone that hath an issue, and whosoever is defiled by the dead:

" 'Both male and female shall ye put out, without the camp shall ye put them; that they defile not their camps, in the midst whereof I dwell.' "

The Brothers (even though they were unsure what Tekel was going on about) nodded slowly.

"When Father Jonah did found us here, he was not able to foresee the cancerous intrusion of a people as lacking in dignity as the House is glorified in it. I do make reference, of course, to one Doctor Sinister (hear his very name!) and the troupe of misshapen outcasts!"

Here Brother Tekel's voice rose, as it did whenever he spoke of one Doctor Sinister and the troupe of misshapen outcasts. And then, almost shouting:

" 'All the days wherein the plague shall be in him he shall be defiled; he is *unclean!*

" 'He shall dwell alone!' "

Tekel fell silent, savouring the effect. He was like a dark magician who had just produced a rabbit from a hat: a fat, black, imbecilic rabbit with foot-long fangs.

Quietly, now:

"I have heard, Brethren, that our Holy Family has been made reference to by name—*by name!*—at that loathsome establishment. This cannot be tolerated. It will not be.

"When our Holy Family is mentioned by name, the townspeople . . . laugh. If allowed to go unchecked, ere long the townspeople will laugh at us on the streets! They will point and jeer, as if it were *we* the defiled, *we* the unclean!

"Thusly, I recommend we enter said establishment—I know it to be outlawed, but what choice have we?—and challenge them to a *game.*"

Here Brother Tekel Ambrose smiled grimly. The "game" mentioned was, of course, baseball. Brother Tekel Ambrose was arguably the best baseball player in the world.

"I suggest we challenge them accordingly," he continued. "The winner of the game shall remain in Burton's Harbor. The loser shall depart."

Although the three brothers had discussed this before, Mene now came up with an objection. It was his role to vocalize any objections that the other Brothers might have.

"Why should the misshapen outcasts agree to play?" he asked. Around the table some of the bearded men nodded.

"They shall agree to play," said Brother Tekel knowingly. "We will handicap ourselves to an extent that they feel they may win. We will offer them any monies got by public admission." Tekel nodded. "They shall play."

Now I know that the above makes for pretty strange reading. When my grandfather first told me about the House of Jonah I made several rude noises and suggested that he be committed. For once in his life he remained cool, calm, and collected. All he said was, "Look 'em up in a encyclopiddiya."

> House of Jonah, The: Also known as the Witnesses of Jonah; an off-shoot of the Hutterites. Founded 1896, by Edmond Raillery (Father Jonah). Original community, Burton's Harbor, Michigan.
>
> The beliefs of the House of Jonah prohibit the eating of meat and any commerce not based upon a bartering system. The men do not shave; all sport long, immaculately cared-for beards.
>
> At their founding the Brethren of the House of Jonah numbered 112. In 1970 there were approximately 10,000 members scattered across the United States and Canada.
>
> In the years between 1930 and 1940 the House of Jonah achieved considerable fame for their baseball team. Although never admitted into a registered league they played many exhibition games. Their most outstanding member, Tekel Ambrose (1900 -   ), was arguably the best baseball player that ever lived.

There you have it. And now, pretending that I'm still copying out what it says about the House of Jonah, I flip the pages into the letter "I". "H" and "I" are in the same volume, you see; my grandfather, although he's watching carefully, suspects nothing.

There, in "I", I find:

> Isbister, Nathanael (1900 - ?) Arguably the best baseball player that ever lived. His professional career went from the years 1923-25, and his

batting average was .412. Much of his fame was based upon his prowess as an outfielder and base-stealer. He was called "Goldenlegs" Isbister. In 1925 he sustained an injury to his legs that rendered him useless as a sportsman. He turned then to sports reportage and radio broadcasting. His emotional outbursts earned him the nickname "Crybaby."

In 1938 he disappeared and was not heard from again.

Isbister, Nathanael (1900 - ?) lowered his face into his hands and wept. Dr. Sinister motioned to the others in the caravan. Major Mite and the Alligator Man left with nods, leading Zap by both hands. Janus lingered behind, settling down into a corner.

Then Dr. Sinister began to talk quite merrily, as if unaware that he was in the same room as a huge, weeping man.

"I expect," said the little Doctor, drawing over another chair, "that you're quite surprised to find us here like this. Not that I can blame you. Aggregations of this sort are supposed to be rather mercurial, that is to say, motile, moving from town to town, yes? And, as you perceive, we seem to be stuck here. The truth of the matter is that we are indeed stuck here, immobile and stagnant, a carnival of cataleptics, totally incapable of recrudescension. I'm afraid that I could not move this trailer even if Floyd were alive, which he is not. Floyd, the equine extraordinaire, is no longer with us, a direct result of his being dead. But enough of these caballine reminiscences."

The Doctor leaned back and pulled a huge cigar from somewhere within his coat. He lit it and continued.

"You see, Mr. Isbister, we were at one time nomadic. Indeed! No more than a fortnight in any one town. Strike the tent! Rein the horses! Hee-ha!" Dr. Sinister succumbed to giggling that threatened to hurl him from his perch. "But upon arriving in this town, or environs, no sooner had we set up when great rainclouds filled the sky from end to end, whereupon we became the unhappy recipients of subitaneous precipitation the likes of which have not been seen since biblical days, I am sure. It was, in a word, nasty. The ground became a scoriac quagmire and down we sank. When the ground was once more rigescent we were ensnared. Ah, well . . .

"I, although ever the optimist, felt that we had had it, but for some unaccountable reason, some sociological factor that I have yet to fathom, the people of this community have a sedulous appetite for human oddities. Every day brings a near-capacity crowd.

Thusly, we have survived and almost prospered for what I estimate to be the better part of two years, stuck, quite literally, in this one place. Very," said the little man, "feracious."

Nathanael Isbister, his eyes drying, looked at the fellow.

Dr. Sinister stretched forward an empty hand as if to touch Nathanael's face. Isbister pulled back quickly and suspiciously.

A cigar appeared in Dr. Sinister's hand, already lit and smoking.

"Do you indulge?" asked the Doctor—his own cigar was stuck in his tiny mouth.

Isbister chuckled lightly and accepted it. "A magician, eh?"

Dr. Sinister looked, for a moment, sad. "Yes, I'm afraid."

"Huh?"

"When you say 'magician' you mean 'prestidigitator,' 'a master of sleight-of-hand'. That, alas, is all that I am. I regret to say that to my ears 'magician' is something of a cacemphaton. Observe: have another cigar." The Doctor raised the empty hand and a lit cigar materialized between his fingers. "Nothing to it," said Dr. Sinister, tossing the stogie into an ashtray. "Utterly ludibrious. A matter of mechanics."

"I still don't see . . ." began Isbister.

"The truth of the matter is that I have but one wish in life. No, wait, I tell a lie—I have, in fact, two. One is to produce the perfect entertainment. This is within my grasp. The other, howsomever, is unattainable. It is insuperable, the proverbial squaring of the circle, but it is my wish nonetheless. I wish that I could raise my hand . . ." He did so. "And that the cigar would be there . . ." It was, in a twinkling. "And that I would have no idea how it came to be there. Dr. Sinister shook his head. "In this particular instance, I know only too well."

"Yeah? How?"

"Oh, well, I'm not going to say. It's not at all important."

"But, you don't *really* think? . . ."

"Yes! Yes, I do indeed," said Dr. Sinister emphatically. "I've every confidence and troth. One day I'll simply . . ." He stretched forward his hand and yet another cigar appeared.

Isbister looked at him eagerly.

Dr. Sinister shook his head. "Afraid not," he muttered.

Nathanael chuckled to himself. "How can the cigar appear if you keep putting one there?"

"Now *that* is an excellent query, my friend. I'm afraid I'm . . . afraid."

"Afraid."

"Rather. 'Terrified' is not putting too keen an edge on it."

"That the cigar wouldn't be there."

Dr. Sinister nodded. "That nothing would be there." Then he sparked up. "Enough of this talk! In my heart of hearts I know full well that one day . . ."

The little Doctor reached forward his empty hand and snapped the bony fingers.

Isbister was surprised, for nothing materialized.

Nathanael looked quickly to search the Doctor's face—there were seven lit cigars crammed into the tiny mouth.

Isbister laughed uproariously while Dr. Sinister removed the cigars one by one. His words became more and more intelligible as he did so—"IwahwabwabgowasnityeIquite enjoythaonem self—yes, it was rather good, wasn't it?"

Nathanael asked, "I suppose you know how they got there?"

"Yes, I do, as a matter of fact. But in this instance I don't mind as much, for it had such a remarkable effect on the audience."

Both men laughed loudly. Nathanael had a big, hearty guffaw that came as easily as his tears. The Doctor giggled, squirming around in his seat as though he were being tickled by some invisible being.

Isbister finished first and looked at the little man. Dr. Sinister's face folded up with laughing-lines and laughing-crinkles so easily that Nathanael imagined he had spent the greater part of his life doing it.

When the Doctor finished there were tears running over his wrinkles. It took him a while to recover. He finally sat back, exhausted from his merriment. "How lovely," mused the man, "is a cachinnation."

"Why," asked Nathanael, "do they call you Dr. Sinister?"

"I'm not truly a doctor," confessed the little magician. "That is, not a medical doctor. Actually, I'm no sort of doctor whatsoever. It is just that when I came to head this aggregation (better put, when the aggregation came to me to be headed), the members were so struck with my erudition (which I personally consider sciolistic) that they appendaged to my cognomen various labels of learnedness: Doctor, Professor, et cetera." The little man dwelt on something. "I've no idea why I said 'et cetera', Mr. Isbister. 'Twas an unfortunate morology. 'Doctor' and 'Professor' were the only ones. At any rate, it was 'Doctor' that remained, being, as it were, slightly easier to elocute."

"But why," persisted Nathanael with a grin on his face, "do they call you Doctor *Sinister?*"

"*I* thought of that! Don't you think it idoneous?" The little Doctor fashioned his face into what was supposed to be something sinister. He squinted, and wrinkled his nose.

It made Isbister burst out laughing.

"Uh-huh," said the tiny man. "Well, then, I call myself Dr. Sinister because I am more or less left-handed."

" 'Sinister' means 'left-handed'?" muttered Nathanael. It was half question, half dim recollection.

"In an archaic sense. It comes from shields, you know, such as knight-errants were wont to lug about. The left side was called 'sinister' and the right, 'dexter'. Now here is something that is remarkable in an unremarkable way. My Christian name is Poindexter, i.e., 'right-pointing'. My name has both left and right in it: Poindexter Sinister. Do you find that remarkable in an unorgulously remarkable way?"

"Nope," answered Isbister candidly. "Seeing as you tacked on the Sinister part yourself."

"This is true," agreed the little man. "I did that so long ago I've come to view it as my inherited name."

"Which was what?" asked Nathanael.

"Frip." It sounded like a little hiccup.

"Frip?"

"Frip. Poindexter Wilhelm Frip. Isn't 'Frip' ghastly?"

"What kind of name is it?"

"Other than ghastly, I can't say for certain. I have studied nomenclature on a purely amateur basis, and the best I can offer is that it is some offshoot of the french 'frepe' which means, I hesitate to appendage, 'rag'. There is also an old English word, 'frippery', which alludes to ornamentation, supercilious finery, so on and so forth. The way I speak is an excellent example of 'frippery', filled as it is with words I have culled from various dictionaries, am uncertain as to the meanings of, and employ with insulsity."

"Why do you talk that way, then?" asked Nathanael.

"I'm afraid it is a prerequisite for my vocation. People do not wish to pay to see a dwarf. They will, on the other hand, expend their money freely in order to see a 'homuncule'."

"I see," said Isbister.

"Do you?" asked Dr. Sinister. "I'm so glad."

"Major Mite is a—what is it?—homuncule?"

"I should say so!" exclaimed Dr. Sinister. "Of course, today he is obtenelinated. Two feet, ten inches. He shot up—a giant amongst homuncules is our Major. When he was young, though. . ." A smile came to the Doctor's face. "Just over a foot and as talented as could be wished."

"When I was a kid," recalled Isbister, "my mom used to tell me to clean myself up, and she'd say this poem: 'You must always comb your hair, for Major Mite might be hiding there.' "

" 'And make sure your ears are good and clean, for Major Mite is bad and mean,' " responded Dr. Sinister with a chuckle. "He's the stuff of legends."

"You know, he's crazy," said Nathanael.

"Hardly crazy, Mr. Isbister! He is lent to impetuousity, I will grant you that, and a tad vociferous."

"Threatening people with a gun, I call that crazy."

"Well, Mr. Isbister, I am afraid you are not one hundred percent sympathetic with the intricacies of our existence. There are ten people here—ten human oddities. 'Freaks' if you will. We are despised in town—pointed and stared at, made the butt of objurgation. When we venture outside this encampment we do so with a modicum of trepidation. In Major Mite's case this manifests itself in a firearm. I rather doubt that it was loaded."

"You're not a freak," remarked Nathanael.

"I suppose not."

There was a silence here, until Isbister asked, "What's the matter with the Alligator Man's hand?"

"What is amiss with his hand is amiss with the rest of his body, save, mercifully, his visage. A skin condition, basically. The epidermis is scaly and exudes a distinct green tincture."

"So you call him the Alligator Man?"

"Usually I call him Ally, as we all do. Professionally, of course, he is the Alligator Man."

Nathanael Isbister snorted.

"What would you have me call him?" asked Dr. Sinister. "The Man With the Hideous Skin Condition?"

Isbister shrugged and changed subject slightly. "Major Mite handed me some line about his mother having seen his father . . .' "

"That would be the rhesis used in the show. 'While bearing the child still within her, THE ALLIGATOR MAN'S mother witnessed, on safari in deepest Africa, the death of her own husband at the hands of a crocodile's jaws. Prenatal impression produced the monstrosity that you now see before you."

"Any truth to that?"

Dr. Sinister seemed hard put for an answer. He stared ahead for a long while, moving his tiny chin back and forth, warming up to speech. He said, "Mr. Isbister, we have a redundant caravan, being as one of our members, the elastic Rubber Boy, has left us ultroneously following a heated debate concerning funding and remittance and the lack of the same. Would you care to spend the night in it?"

Nathanael thought initially to decline. Ordinarily the offer of shelter would have been accepted straightaway, but this time he had misgivings. Of the four men he'd met, one was a midget psychopath, another, although charming, seemed not to be operating with maximum sanity, another was covered with green scales, and the last was hairy head to foot, extremely ugly, deformed, incapable of speech or thought, and likely to attempt to devour anything in sight.

But Nathanael was tired and miles from Anywhere. (How in hell, he wondered, did I wind up here? An accident.) He felt friendly toward Dr. Sinister, and (though he would never have admitted it) he had taken a liking to the grotesque beast Janus, or, as he still persisted in calling it mentally, Fido and Rover. So he nodded and said, "Thank you. I ain't had a bed in a long while."

Dr. Sinister led him to a caravan that was also half-buried in the ground.

Janus, four eyes looking dreamy, followed behind.

Chapter 6

I AM NOW going to attempt to reestablish the simultaneity of this narrative, which my doddering old grandfather screwed up. Therefore, we see the morning sun rise—the day will be a good one, cloudless and warm. The air will have a cool nip to it, though, and more leaves will redden. Still more will tumble to the ground. A wind, sharp and purposeful, will push across the earth. (My grandfather, having read this passage over my shoulder, is now doing a silly burlesque of a ballet dancer, prancing about the room.)

The sun is in the sky—it is 10:00 A.M., the following day.

Now, here is what our characters are up to. (Those we have met so far.)

Daisy and Violet start up in their bed. Beside them is the young man from the diner, who, it turned out, hadn't known them after all.

Daisy asks, "What time is it?" and Violet, squinting to see the clock on the table across the caravan, says, "Ten. We have to get ready."

The man beside them snores loudly, having managed to go to sleep only some twenty minutes ago. The girls look at him and giggle.

Daisy pulls up the sheets to cover her nakedness and tells Violet, "Wake him up."

"You wake him up—you're next to him." Violet leaves her breasts bared, and lies back sleepily. Daisy is pulled down with her.

"I don't want to," says Daisy.

"Oh, all right!" snaps her sister. Violet reaches across and hits the man lightly on the head a few times. Daisy clutches her sheet higher, looking away. Finally he wakes up with sputtering noises— "Wha-, wha-, wha." When the man opens his eyes, Violet modestly raises her sheet too, and tells the man, "You have to leave now."

"How long did I sleep for?" he asks.

"For a long time," peeps Daisy from behind her sheet.

"Hours and hours," assures Violet.

The man shakes his head and gets out of bed. Both girls follow his naked body with their eyes, giggling occasionally.

When he is gone, they rise, wash, and dress, an operation that requires great cooperation and coordination.

Violet says, "He had a tiny willy, didn't he?"

Daisy is shocked, goes beet red, slaps her sister on the naked belly, and says, "Oh, Violet!"

"But he did, didn't he?"

Daisy lowers her eyes and nods. In a few minutes they will be dressed for the show. They wear a single skirt, which will be doffed to show miscreants that they truly are joined together. Underneath it they wear G-strings; that is, a single string with two sequined flaps attached to it. Because of their union at the hip, standard underwear is out of the question. Their upper parts are covered with multicoloured brassieres. Most of their time they spend on their faces. Although they are beautiful, it takes a long while to remove the traces of excessive drinking, pill-taking, and sleeplessness.

In the caravan beside theirs, the Alligator Man is peering through his window, watching the Hisslop Sisters. He is in love with them (although he prefers Daisy just a tiny bit more), and he spies on them every morning. As they dress, the Hisslop girls will often toy playfully with each other's bodies, caressing naked breasts and bottoms.

The Alligator Man knows they would never give him a chance, so he has never approached them. He just stays by the window and watches them dressing. When he sees a young man in their caravan, it makes his stomach double up painfully, and he hits the walls of his room. He curses his scaly green skin for making him so ugly and then abuses himself mercilessly, angrily. When all is over, he pulls on the little swimming trunks that are his costume and walks toward the big tent.

Major Mite has been up for hours.

He has cleaned his caravan and polished all his fake medals and swords. He has spit-polished his tiny leather boots. He has made certain that his trousers have a sharp (if short) crease to the leg. Dressing in his costume, his uniform, takes him almost two full hours, making sure that everything is letter-perfect. His hat is three fingers' width above his brow, his sword falls at a slight backward angle of twenty degrees, his gold braiding descends to just below his breast, his fake medals are evenly spaced and go across according to chronology and down according to importance. He has cleaned his gun, blowing dust from the empty barrels. He has shaved, brushed his teeth, and plastered his thinning hair flat on to his head.

He always finishes dressing with fifteen or twenty minutes left before the show. He spends that time pacing his caravan. His steps are short but uniform. At either end he clicks his heels.

While he does this, he thinks about Angus, his friend.

Zap sits in a corner, crouched down and hugging his knees. All alone and in the darkness, his hairy face goes through a rapid series of expressions for no reason at all. By turns it looks happy, then outraged, then sad, then questioning, then happy, then confused . . . always coming back to questioning . . .

His tiny eyes dart about the room's empty corners.

He is naked now; in a few minutes, Dr. Sinister will come to dress him up in his Tarzan outfit. Zap knows how to put it on himself—he has been taught to but he can't be relied upon. During the phase when Zap was allowed to dress himself for the show he showed up naked on more than one occasion, brandishing a member that was enormous considering his size. He shook this member menacingly at the audience, and Dr. Sinister was forced to give one or two refunds. Another time he came dressed in one of Dr. Sinister's old tuxedos, complete with bowtie and cumberbund. How he managed to get into it was a mystery—most thought that it was one of the other people playing a joke.

Suddenly Zap emits a long, anguished yowl. It fills the tiny caravan. When it dies away, a smile comes to his tiny, ugly face. Then he looks questioning once more, and his eyes dart about the room.

Doctor Sinister knows that he should go dress Zap, but he still has much unfinished business to attend to. The first is to transcribe into his diary a passage from a novel he's been reading. It is, "While I would not call her wart a beauty mark, neither would I turn her out of bed on its account." The passage amuses the little Doctor a great deal, and he spends a few minutes repeating it aloud and chuckling. Underneath it, in his diary, he has put "*Simone*!!"

Next, Dr. Sinister opens his mammoth dictionary, covers his eyes and stabs down with a finger. It lands upon:

> Pestilential, conveying or causing or of the nature of pestilence, foul-smelling.

"Pestilential," he says to himself. He thinks of how he could use the word in his function as master of ceremonies. This is his way of expanding his fripperish vocabulary. He repeats "pestilential" once expanding his fripperish vocabulary. He repeats "pestilential" once more and then leaps to the pump organ.

Standing on the machine is a yellowed page of manuscript paper, blank except for these four chords:

The Doctor plays them and adds a variety of fifth ones. This one appeals to him most:

A stark chord, the sound of an iron fence on a winter's morning. He dips his pen and writes it down.

From there he flies to another of the caravan's corners, where a painting easel stands. The work upon it is covered with an oily rag which he snatches away to reveal a young girl of perhaps seventeen, naked, one foot in a steaming bath. Dr. Sinister smiles at the work until something strikes him. Then he scowls.

"Must fix those titties," he mumbles.

For a minute or two he mixes colours, nine or ten of them, until he has a pinkish glob on his palette. From this glob he picks up a tiny drop with his brush and gingerly applies it to the girl's left nipple. Dr. Sinister leaps backward and looks at his creation. He seems satisfied.

In his desk drawer is a thick sheaf of papers, dog-eared and smudged, which constitutes a novel the Doctor is writing, tentatively entitled *The Sorcerer*. Snatching up the last few pages he reads quickly throug them, mouthing the words beneath his thick walrus moustache. Then, with a flourish, he adds the next sentence. It is " 'All right,' he said. 'If that's the way it must be.' "

Then he is done except for one thing—he stands in the centre of the caravan and raises a hand. In a twinkling an apple appears.

"Nope. Miniscule," he whispers. He shakes his head and leaves the caravan, munching peacefully.

Nathanael Isbister is awake, too, and has been for quite a while. Along with his other ailments (bad legs, excited hyperventilation), he is also cursed with insomnia. It takes him hours to fall asleep and then he is awake what seems only minutes later.

He has spent this time playing with the two-headed Janus, wrestling about on the floor of the caravan.

At one point one of his legs buckles underneath him, and Nathanael cries out painfully, tumbling to the floor. Janus looks at him (twice), concerned. "Damn legs," explains Nathanael. He raises a hand and strikes hard at the offending appendage. It makes him wince horribly. "Goddam legs," he says—and after resting a moment, resumes play with the grotesque creature.

Soon Dr. Sinister will rap lightly on the caravan's door and ask whether or not Mr. Isbister wishes to attend the exhibition of extraordinary eccentricities. Mr. Isbister, having nothing else to do, will accept.

Mene, Peres, and Tekel Ambrose are making their way to the outskirts of town where they will find the freak-filled tent. They walk in single file (Tekel in the lead) and keep their bearded heads lowered to the ground. Young children rush to taunt them, but the brothers do not give them the pleasure of so much as a flicker of response.

They dress in long, black robes and their feet are bare. They trample over pebbles, stones, and shards from Coke bottles, never altering their rhythmic pace.

His thin lips moving quickly, Tekel prays. His dark eyes are screwed up tightly as he leads the way.

My grandfather has been spirited to Burton's Harbor and booked into the Fulton Arms Hotel. He is gazing out the window at the town, a dirty collection of warehouses and factories. Rivers and lakes sparkle around the curve of the earth.

Behind him on the bed is a slightly obese woman whom my grandfather has lured to his room under the pretense of being J.R.R. Janson, famous writer of western prose. The girl has a thing about cowboys, although she has never seen one in all her life.

My grandfather told her to never mind the fact that he was dressed like all the other goldurned eastern dudes. He just did that, he explained, because in his regular duds he had to waste too much time beating up slickers who had nuthin better to do than make fun of the way a man dresses. 'Sides, he went on, way a man dresses don't amount to piss in the sea. It's the way a man thinks is important. They way he feels. The way, he repeated (fastening on to one of the woman's breasts), he feels.

Now the girl is fast asleep and, I should add, blissfully happy after having made love to J.R.R. Janson, famous writer of western prose.

As my grandfather looks out the window, three men pass by on the street before him. Three men dressed in black robes, walking in a ridiculously uniform single file. All three sport black beards that tumble on to their chests.

My grandfather, a particularly avid baseball fan, recognizes Tekel Ambrose, who is, in his opinion, a better all-round player than Babe Ruth. Maybe even better than Nate Isbister was before an accident deprived him of his miraculous legs.

My grandfather wonders, idly, what Tekel Ambrose is up to, but has on his mind a more pressing problem—that is, what to do about the gambling problem in Burton's Harbor. He has no interest in stopping it, mind, but he does want to figure a way of getting his finger into that plump pie.

Little does he suspect (bright as he may be) that the answer is walking underneath him on the street in a ridiculously uniform single file.

Of the other characters (the ones we may term "minor", although it seems to me this is something of a mistake):

The truck driver is snoring loudly, taking one of the many naps he takes while driving a load from point a to point b.

The hobos encountered on page three are sound asleep, zonkered on lord-knows-what.

Beatrice the Bovine Beauty is chewing cud and *not* wallowing in self-pity.

Morris M-for-Magnus Mulcher is dead.

Major Mite's father, Mr. Pfaff, is also dead.

Angus McCallister, on a farm in Cape Breton, has been working his fields for hours, pulling behind him a plow.

And myself, whom you may or may not consider a character without the slightest fear of hurting my feelings, I am far from being born. My grandmother, my grandfather's wife, has a seed inside her that in a few months will produce a man-child, who in time will place a seed in a lovely lady, which will produce yours truly.

My grandmother is not to see my grandfather ever again (a fate which does not displease her); my father is never to know his father (a trauma which will leave him remarkably unaffected psychologically); and I am not to know my grandfather until my life has been spent some twenty-odd years. At this time he will show up at my doorstep, crinkled like a leaf in autumn, barely able to support himself on his thick wooden cane. He will stare at me with his light, unfocused eyes and address me thus: "I hope you got a pile of paper and a new typewriter ribbon, boy." Pushing me angrily aside, he will make for the sofa that will become his bed and base of operations. When I ask him, "Who the hell are you?", he will become maudlin, affecting tears. "Don't you recognize me, son? I'm your dear old grandpappy." After producing various certificates and papers, he will convince me that he is indeed that relation to me, but I will remain unimpressed. He will then begin to relate to me the tale of a game of baseball, a game that becomes the fulcrum in a great many lives. Hearing him out will take hours and hours, after which I will bluntly demand, "So what?" He will tell me that

I am his collaborator and that the two of us are to set it down, novel-style. I will balk, claiming an inability to cease work on a tale of sordid sex between sordid people in sordid places. I will produce the papers in question. My grandfather, in an exemplary action, will whip out a cigarette lighter and burn them to ashes.

Chapter 7

"SHOW-TIME, LADIES and gentlemen!"

This was Doctor Sinister's chant. He stood atop a soap-crate in front of the big-top and intoned, "Showtime, ladies and gentlemen! Showtime!"

Before him the people pressed forward eagerly. Nathanael saw that they were for the most part poor. The men were dressed in the green coveralls of factories and farms. The women were squat and shabby, their unkempt hair hidden under scarves. Children stood by their parents' legs, dirty and strangely silent; they had wide eyes as they stared at Doctor Sinister.

The little Doctor motioned towards a boy that stood close to him. "Come hither, my lentiginous lad," he said, "I'm more than a trifle concerned with your hygienic habits! Do you assuetudinally clean your aural orifices, by which I refer to your ears?" The boy backed away, confused and hesitant; as he did, Doctor Sinister reached out and seemingly removed from one of said orifices a pink sponge-ball.

Now, this did not evoke the wave of delight and enthusiasm you might expect. While Nathanael was amused by the trick (he brought his huge hands together a couple of times, then realized that no one else was clapping), the other townspeople stared forward glumly. Even the smallest children were unaffected, shifting their feet impatiently. Doctor Sinister threw the ball up and away. No one but Isbister noticed that when it reached its zenith, the ball disappeared.

From where he stood beside the soap-box, Nathanael twisted his head around to search the little Doctor's face. Dr. Sinister shook his head and mouthed the words, "I know."

Then he addressed the audience again. "My dear friends, if you would be so gracious as to queue up here in front of me, we could transact business on the following basis. In exchange for fifty cents, I will give you a tiny rectangular piece of paper embossed with the lone word 'ADMIT'. Although superficially and upon first hearing this may sound somewhat one-sided, allow me to inform you what that tiny piece of paper will enable you to do!" Here the Doctor's voice became rhythmic, slamming into the word "you" over and over again. "*YOU* can see the legendary Major Mite, the smallest man that ever lived! *YOU* can see the absolutely phenomenal young Davey Goliath, whose feet stride the terra firma but whose head reaches to the outer stratosphere! *YOU* can see Zap, fearsome savage from pestilential Borneo, link between the simian and homo sapiens! *YOU* can see Madame Tanya, the lovely lady of the hirsute visage! *YOU* can see the Hisslop sisters, fated to live their lives out side by side, connected by a fusing of blood, bone, and flesh! *YOU* can see the Alligator Man, the hideous prodigy of prenatal impression!!"

(On the outskirts of the small crowd were three bearded and robed men. Nathanael Isbister noted them and thought briefly that he recognized the tallest. Their presence was strange and incongruous, but before Isbister could dwell on it there came another "You.")

"*YOU* can see the curious canine Janus the Wonderdog who has not one but *two* heads and not four but *five* legs! *YOU* can see the Rubber Boy—er, no, you can't! But *YOU* can see the Hippopotamus Boy, in all likelihood the most unsightly human being upon the face of this planet! *YOU* can see myself, Doctor Sinister, swami and mystic magician! All for fifty cents! Fifty small cents! Half a buck! Four infinitesimal bits! Five-oh pennies! Fifty cents!"

The people had their money ready. They had had their money ready since before Doctor Sinister had started his harangue. They moved forward and bought their tickets (Doctor Sinister producing change from thin air, not that anyone noticed), then they walked silently into the big tent. The last three to do so were the bearded men. The tallest one gave Dr. Sinister one dollar and fifty cents, and the two had the following exchange:

Dr. Sinister said, "Nice to have you boys come to a show."

The tallest bearded man said, "We have not come for your show. We have in no wise come to be entertained, and that is what the word 'show' would imply."

Dr. Sinister said, "Indeed? Why have you come then?"

The tallest bearded man said, "For reasons which will remain our private knowledge for the meanwhile."

The three men walked in a ridiculously uniform single file into the big tent.

Isbister told Dr. Sinister, "I don't have fifty cents."

"Yes, you do, my friend! It's right here on your head."

Isbister felt the little man's hand rifle through his curls. When it came back there were two quarters in it. Isbister smiled, then asked, "Who were those guys?"

"I'm a tad surprised you did not recognize them. They are members of a religious organization that is known as the House of Jonah."

"Goddam Tekel Ambrose!" shouted Nathanael Isbister. "I knew I'd seen him before. We played them once, you know. Exhibition game, somewhere down south, I think. Goddam, is he ever good. I remember, he hit one right out—" It struck Nathanael that he was talking about baseball with enthusiasm, so he shut up abruptly.

Doctor Sinister smiled and said quietly, "Let's go inside." They did.

The first thing that caught your eye inside the big top was a small iron cage that contained Zap. He cowered in one of its corners as the people pointed and jeered at him. Every so often he would leap at the bars, enraged, snarling with his pointed teeth. The people would rear back *en masse.*

Doctor Sinister leaped to the stage. "Ladies and gentlemen, ladies and gentlemen!! Please do not taunt the Wild Man from pestilential Borneo!" he shouted. "We certainly do not want a re-eventuation of last year's unfortunate occurrence!"

This stilled the crowd, although not one of them had any idea just what this occurrence was.

Zap stuck out his tongue at the people and, in the brand-new silence, let loose a loud fart.

"Ladies and gentlemen," continued Doctor Sinister. "The jungles and furzy gorses of pestilential Borneo are peopled by creatures exactly similar to this particular specimen. We call him Zap. Not quite animal, not quite human, straddling a fine line 'twixt the two. As you perceive, he is hairy head to foot. His skeletal structure is less human than simian, that is, ape-like."

Nathanael, watching Zap, saw the tiny thing stand up at this point and lean against the bars of his cage like a man might lean on a mantelpiece at a cocktail party. Then Zap leapt up and grabbed the overhead bars, commencing to swing back and forth.

"His skull," continued Dr. Sinister, "rises to a patently perceivable point. By all scientific measurements and extrapolations, his brain could be no larger than a small apple!"

Zap dropped from the bars and collapsed on the floor of his cage, covering his ugly and hairy face.

(Near the stage were two young boys. One turned to the other and said, "Wanna see how stupit he is? Lookit this." The boy took a dime out of his pocket and flicked it through the bars of Zap's cage; it landed near his face. Zap sat up on his haunches and picked up the dime. He turned it over and over beneath his bigger eye, examining it. Then he flicked it back at the boys. The boys laughed, although the youngster who initially threw the dime laughed a little less, being as the dime accidentally caught him in the eye on the return flick.)

"Howsomever," continued the doctor, "Let me assure you that Zap is to some degree humanoid. If some one among you would like to riddle him a simple arithmetical problem—?"

"Four take away three!" someone shouted.

Zap fell backwards on to his butt and, raising his hands, brought up two fingers from each. These four he held three inches away from his eyes and stared hard at for several long moments. Then one by one they fell away, until three were gone. Only the middle finger of his right hand remained erect. With this he motioned fervently at the audience.

"He is absolutely correct!" shouted Doctor Sinister. "The answer is the solitary 'one'."

"Four plus seven!" shouted someone else, and around him people chuckled.

Zap began to raise fingers laboriously, biting at his tongue. After almost two minutes he had all ten up. He stared at these and then screamed. He howled and leapt at the bars, reaching through with a hairy arm and trying blindly to grab someone from the audience. The people laughed loudly at his frustration.

Nathanael brought up a forefinger and drove it into his palm; he started making short circular motions with it across the skin.

Zap fell forward on to his stomach and cradled his tiny head in his hands. His eyes moved calmly through the audience, looking from face to face. They settled on Isbister, and the two stared at each other. For a split-second Nathanael thought he detected in the Wildman's eyes a flicker of intelligence. But then Zap grunted loudly and emitted another fart.

"Next, ladies and gentlemen," said Dr. Sinister, walking away from Zap's cage, "something I'm sure will warrant intense feneration, that is, the legendary Major Mite, the shortest man alive!"

Here there was a smattering of applause, and murmurings among the audience—"I dint know there really was a Major Mite . . .", "I thought he was just in fairy stories . . ."

Out strutted the Major, the tiny man dressed in military finery. His dignified gait carried him quickly to the centre of the stage where he clicked his heels and bowed deeply.

Meanwhile Dr. Sinister had flown to the back of the stage where there stood an enormous pump organ. Leaping on to the bench, he drew out three chords in a wheezy fanfare. Then Major Mite began to sing:

> *Oh, I am the Major,*
> *The minute Major Mite.*
> *No bigger than a baby,*
> *Just two feet in height.*
> *I've been the whole world over,*
> *And many things did see;*
> *But the smallest thing, the tiniest thing,*
> *Was indubitably me!*

The Major's voice, though high-pitched, was craggy and worn. It wandered on- and off-key haphazardly.

When he finished singing the words, Major Mite launched into a soft-shoe with his tiny feet. The dance was well executed, but by the time he was through he was breathing heavily, and was red in the face and sweating. He jumped up on to a high stool and sat there catching his breath while Dr. Sinister tried to lead the audience in applause. Other than Nathanael, however, he was unsuccessful. The rest of the people stared forward, waiting for something.

"At this point," said the Doctor, "Major Mite would be pleased to deinturbidate any obfuscation . . ." The little man shook his head violently and said, "He would be pleased to answer any questions that you good people might have."

There was a long silence. The people obviously had no questions. Nathanael impulsively called out, "Major!" The little man broke into a grin and turned his head toward the direction of the voice. "Yes, my good sir?" he articulated. Nathanael realized he hadn't thought of a question. After a few seconds he asked, "Where did you learn to sing and dance?"

"My teach-er, sir, was the re-nowned show-man and en-tre-pre-neur Mor-ris M-for-Mag-nus Mul-cher."

Of course, Nathanael knew that. For years the names of Mulcher and Mite (and McCallister) were inseparable.

Nathanael thought that by asking a question he could get the others started, but that wasn't so. They still just stared straight ahead, waiting for something. So Nathanael called out, "What is the biggest drawback for a little guy like you?"

Major Mite dwelt on the question, pulling at his chin. Finally he enunciated, "I sup-pose, sir, the big-gest draw-back would be that while the ep-i-gram con-cern-ing the plent-i-tude of fish in the sea is app-lic-a-ble to your-selves, it is cer-tain-ly not so for me."

(By which the Major alludes to Alvira Ford, who being both tiny and rather beautiful, was the only girl the Major ever loved in his life. This opens up a whole other story, and quite a good romantic one at that. You see, when Major Mite's unprecedented success came, it brought with it the usual number of copies and pretenders—all but one have faded into obscurity. The exception is, of course, Commander Gnat, who was a match for the Major in every way. He was as small, he was as handsome, he was as talented. Morris M-for-Magnus Mulcher took on Commander Gnat as a client, and the two tiny men battled each other for fame and popularity. Then, one spring day, Mrs. Ford brought to Mulcher her daughter, then seventeen. Alvira was, as I've said, rather beautiful. She had a wide mischievous grin and bright blue eyes. Her hair was a collection of golden ringlets and curls. And, although there is inevitably a certain amount of deformity with any little person, she had a pretty good body.

(For both the Major and the Commander it was love at first sight and proposal at first speech. Alvira could not decide between the two. Thus began the most famous rivalry the carnival world has known. The would-be lovers did war on every conceivable front. Murder attempts were perpetrated by both sides. They filled Alvira's ears with lies about the other, they made her promises they could never keep. Alvira kept vacillating between the two, sometimes seeming to favour the Major, sometimes the Commander.

(Morris M-for-Magnus capitalized on it, of course, promoting the feud, even making reference to it on the billings. For him it was big bucks. This is the way he thought of it:

and who could argue?

(Finally, though, Alvira settled on one of them. It was the Major. They were married and lived together for a blissful two years, at the end of which Alvira vanished. With Commander Gnat. Alvira was gone for three years, at the end of which she reappeared. Upon Alvira's swearing to remain ever faithful to the Major, the two had a reconciliation. However, this was only to last a year, at the end of which Alvira again ran away with Commander Gnat. Some months later, she returned. Then she ran off again. It goes on and on . . .

(Look at it this way. The Major, Commander, and Alvira were as famous then as movie stars are today. Well, you know what movie stars are like, getting married and divorced, fooling around with each other's wives and husbands, etc., etc. What we have here is the same sort of thing, except that for certain reasons we are restricted to a field of three participants.

(Hold on, here—a voice has risen from the audience, and it is not Nathanael's . . .)

"Hey!" a man called out, encouraged by Isbister. "How's come you're so small?"

The Major turned his head in the direction of the voice. "For the same reason, my good man," he articulated, "that you eat the crust offa a bear's ass."

The response got the most applause of the afternoon.

Dr. Sinister strode to the front of the stage where he addressed the audience. "I should like to present the batrachian wonder of the world—turn away, ye of fragile constitution—the famous Alligator Man!"

From behind a curtain he came. His appearance made the audience gasp, and Nathanael's forefinger (making circular motions against his palm) began to move at a furious pace. The whole of the Alligator Man's body, up to his neck, was shiny, scaly, and very green. If you look closely at the back of your hand, you'll see that it is intricately lined and segmented. All of the Alligator Man's skin was like that, only the segments were many times larger, and the lines easy to see from a distance. And they shone with a very green glow.

Dr. Sinister said, "While bearing the child still within her, the Alligator Man's mother witnessed, on safari in deepest pestilential Africa, the death of her own husband at the hands of a crocodile's jaws. Prenatal impression produced the hideous monstrosity that you now see before you."

The Alligator Man's face was extremely grim. His was the kind of face you see in barrooms, handsome and hardened, brooding over a glass of beer. It was a tanned brown and didn't seem to belong on top of the green body.

He stood there and was stared at for about three minutes. Then he turned around and walked back to disappear behind the curtains.

"Ladies and gentlemen," said Dr. Sinister, "I'm sure you all are cognizant of the biblical tale of David and Goliath. With us is a young man whose genealogical lineage has been authentically linked to the Brobdingnagian of that epical story. Would you please make welcome the tallest living human being, Davey Goliath!"

Nathanael remembered the poster from outside, with the picture of the man dwarfing trees, the young man with the broad smile and gleaming eyes. It was decidedly not a picture of the man who walked on to the stage.

For one thing, he hardly *walked*, he hobbled. He supported himself with two gigantic canes and took tiny, tiny steps. His feet were twisted so that it was the outer sides that made contact with the ground.

The other main difference was in the face. There was no broad smile, only a pained slit with no colour in the lips. There were no gleaming eyes, only a pair of spectacles almost an inch thick—the lenses were yellowed and obscured whatever lay behind them.

But that he was the tallest man in the world was not to be argued. He seemed to be over ten feet tall.

Davey Goliath worked his way slowly to the centre of the stage and stood there. The massive canes trembled to support him.

"Mr. Goliath is twenty-one years of age," chimed Dr. Sinister, "and is eight feet eleven and one half inches tall! He tips the scales at 439 pounds!"

8'11½" is quite hard to imagine. Just think: whatever room you're in (unless you live in a palace or something) would be too small for Davey. Look up at the ceiling and imagine a young man hunched over to avoid bumping his head on it. His great weight had nothing to do with excess fat—in fact, scaled down you would think him slender and frail. His shoes were almost two feet long, his fingers as long as other people's shoes—all these outmost appendages were awkward and seemed crippled. His brain simply couldn't get messages to them quickly enough, if at all, and they couldn't get messages back. If you were to burn Davey's hand, he wouldn't know. The message "Ouch" would get lost on its way to the brain. Or, if you put a log in front of him, he would trip over

it. The eyes would see it, and the brain would urgently start trans-
mitting, "Step over it! Step over it!", but the feet would never
know. The body was just too great a kingdom for the little monarch,
the mind.

As if the mind didn't have enough problems of its own.

Dr. Sinister told the audience that he was willing to forego af-
frontry should his veracity be reproached. Then he told them that
he wouldn't even mind if they thought he was lying about how tall
Davey was. Any man or men from the audience could come up
and measure him. Dr. Sinister indicated a stepladder that could be
used.

Two men, obviously carpenters, jumped up. When Dr. Sinister
offered them a tape-measure one of the men waved him away rudely,
producing another from his overalls pocket. The two men went to
work.

A curious transformation came over Davey's face. Whereas before his expression had been simply a grimace, concentrated on
the effort of holding himself up, it now spread, first with appre-
hension, then with fear, and finally out-and-out panic.

One of the men climbed to the top perch of the stepladder and
touched the measure to the giant's temple. Davey began to sweat,
his lips trembling.

Dr. Sinister crossed to him and patted him on the wrist, which
was as close as he could possibly get to Davey's shoulder.

"Is it the hunter?" the giant whispered, or so it seemed to Isbister.

"No, no, son," returned the little doctor quietly. "It's just two
gentlemen from the audience."

The other carpenter placed the bottom of the tape to the floor
and shouted, "Yep! Eight foot eleven and one half inches!" With
that it was over, and the giant Davey Goliath hobbled off stage
about twice as fast as he had hobbled on.

The tears were welling in Nathanael's eyes—it was a matter of
sympathetic excitation producing the reflex hyperventilation.

Dr. Sinister, then, without a word of introduction or commentary, proceeded to do some magic tricks. Almost all of them gave
the illusion of something being pulled from thin air, which was
surely the Doctor's main talent, that and vanishing them back into
thin air again. Balls, scarves, rabbits, birds, cigars, books, flowers,
fish, eggs, and salamis came from, and went to, nowhere. Dr. Sinister stood there all the while shaking his head slowly. Toward the
end of the display he seemed to lose control—from one hand he
would bounce a rubber ball, his other would be brandishing a

knife, and no sooner would he return these to nothingness than two more objects would appear. Then things started coming from his mouth at the same time, yards and yards of ribbon, two or three eggs. Various furry creatures ran away from him, birds flew, it seemed, from his ears. When the Doctor was through, Nathanael tried to lead the audience in spirited applause; they patted their hands together quietly, politely. Isbister heard one small child say, "It's up his sleeves."

Dr. Sinister took grand bows, his long white hair bouncing about madly. Pulling himself up abruptly, he said, "You will make me erubescent with your kind applause. I wish to thank you for allowing me to demonstrate the goetic art of Merlin, sorcerer extraordinaire, with whom I had the goluptious pleasure of apprenticing under while I was still a sprout of some fourteen years. And now," he continued, "a phenomenon ne'er before seen in the canine world, to wit, Janus, who, as his mythical name implies for your inference, has not one but *two* heads, and also who, which you could not infer from any implication from his mythical name, has not four but *five* legs! JANUS!"

Out trotted the wonderdog to centre stage, where he hunkered down, two long tongues drooping, and watched the audience closely.

"Note," demanded Dr. Sinister, "that both heads have total motor facility!"

Janus blinked both sets of eyes and opened both mouths.

"Both heads share common vocal apparati!" said Dr. Sinister.

Janus barked his strange double bark—Nathanael had a strong impulse to scream out, "Stop pretending you understand everything!"

To demonstrate the motor abilities of the short fifth leg Dr. Sinister bent over and offered his hand in the familiar "shake-a-paw" manner. Janus took several short swipes at it with the misshapen leg and finally planted it in the Doctor's palm. "Pleased to meet you, Janus," said Dr. Sinister, pumping the tiny paw energetically. "Yawp!" returned the wonderdog.

"Next," announced Dr. Sinister, "the rarest of sibling relationships, first personified by Chang and Eng born in 1811 in Siam, whenceforth we derive the appellation 'Siamese Twins', the lovely Hisslop Sisters, Daisy and Violet!"

The girls walked onstage and shared a graceful curtsy within their single dress. Nathanael was immediately struck by their beauty and thought, like everyone else in the place, that they were simply identical twins. Someone in the crowd vocalized the notion: "It's a fake!"

"Let all modesty be thrown asunder then!" boomed Dr. Sinister, and the girls undid the skirt and let it fall to the ground. Despite the hundreds of times they had done this, it still made them blush a light pink.

The shedding of clothes showed that high on the hip there was a mottled flesh-like scar tissue that joined the two girls firmly together. "Miscreants behold!" shouted the little Doctor and, after a moment or two, raised the skirt for the girls. Daisy hastened to fasten it.

Then Dr. Sinister produced two saxophones (not from thin air, mind you, but from a stand near the back of the stage) and introduced the song "Lilies in Summer", written by himself. Then he jumped to the pump organ and began to play the accompaniment.

The Hisslop Sisters blew on their instruments frantically, embellishing the tune with fast riffs and arpeggios. They played in a style much like New Orleans jazz, throwing in sevenths and flattened thirds. To much of the crowd it sounded atonal, weird. Nathanael, after a while, found himself strangely drawn into it.

Both girls closed their eyes tightly while playing and kept time with their whole bodies. When they finished they looked out sheepishly, embarrassed, at the audience—their look was one of "I'm sorry, I don't know what came over me." After a little bow to acknowledge the applause (nonexistent except for the sound of Isbister's huge hands being brought together), they turned and fled the stage quickly.

Dr. Sinister said, "We should now like to introduce to you Robert Merrill, otherwise benamed 'The Hippopotamus Boy' which, cruel through it may be, is an unavoidable and idoneous cognomen. Be you thankful." This last phrase was caught only by Crybaby and a few others who stood close to the stage, being as Dr. Sinister almost whispered it. With it, the curtains flew apart at the back and the Hippopotamus Boy was visible.

The audience sucked in its breath as one. Robert Merrill was surely the ugliest man that ever lived. His head looked as if someone had fused several cauliflowers on to it. There was one growing from the back of his head, one from his forehead, and one from his lower jaw. Bone shot from his upper jaw through his mouth, turning his lips backward, making his mouth a useless, drooling opening. The whole bottom half of his face shot out grotesquely (hence "The Hippopotamus Boy"); his nose was simply a little lump of skin, hardly noticeable. His eyes were buried deep into the cauliflower skin and seemed dark and unseeing. He appeared to have no ears, and the hair on his huge scalp was thin and sprang out in insane patches.

The effect of Robert Merrill upon Crybaby was devastating. In a second Isbister was bawling unabashedly.

Robert Merrill craned his head awkwardly to the sound of the sobbing and gazed upon Nathanael. From his mouth came a long groan, broken here and there. He was, in fact, speaking, although no one, not even Dr. Sinister, could understand him.

Elsewhere in the audience a woman fainted with a short, breathy scream. Slowly the Hippopotamus Boy turned his head in her direction. The groan that was his speech became louder, more insistent.

The children began to jeer at him; the men murmured sullenly. The Hippopotamus Boy turned and walked behind the curtains. It took some moments for the people to settle down. Nathanael's eyes didn't dry, even after he could no longer see the boy.

Dr. Sinister's voice was bright and cheerful. "From the snow-laden hills of pestilential Russia comes to us Madame Tanya, who adds to the unquestionable endowments of femininity the remarkable asset of hirsutity. Make welcome the Bearded Lady, Madame Tanya!"

Madame Tanya was hardly the bombshell portrayed outside. She did, however, possess the endowments of femininity the Doctor mentioned. She was dressed very modestly, but her breasts were obviously large and pendulous. Her hips were full, her buttocks rounded. The face, however, was not such an open-and-shut case. Even without the beard it had an ambiguous look to it—a large, jutting jaw, a pronounced forehead and nose. Her dark hair was ruthlessly bobbed close to her scalp. The beard, however, was a gem: long, full and curly, reaching down to the heavy bustline. It was a very dark brown.

It occurred to everyone that this could easily be a fake. It was either a woman with a beard stuck on, or a man with padding beneath the blouse and long skirt. To this end, Dr. Sinister announced that following this portion of the show there were two additional tents that could be visited for the meagre and paltry sum of one quarter of a dollar, two small bits, twenty-five pennies, two-five cents.

(These are the little tents Nathanael had noticed the night before, called in the trade "blow-offs".)

In one, continued Dr. Sinister, Madame Tanya would submit herself to any examination that would satisfy the skepticism of the examiner.

In the other the people could view Stella, the fattest woman in the world, the ultimate in obesity, the pinnacle of portliness.

But first, said Dr. Sinister, let us prevail upon Madame Tanya to tell us how she keeps her whiskers in such mollitious condition.

Madame Tanya had obviously learned this by rote, and gave no attempt to infuse it with any emotion. Her speaking voice was a husky mid-range.

"You should never," she began, "use too hot a curling iron on the beard. This makes it brittle and destroys the fine sheen. This secret was taught to me by members of the House of Jonah."

The audience chuckled at this reference to their resident religious fanatics.

With that came a voice that rose like a crow in the night. *"How dare you!?!"*

Chapter 8

THE VOICE ELECTRIFIED the place. The townspeople reared back, gasping, children clutching madly to trouser legs. Major Mite jumped on to the stage shouting, "What the hell?!" Zap threw himself against the bars of his tiny cage. Isbister drove his forefinger into the palm of his hand.

Dr. Sinister alone remained perfectly calm and at ease, his tiny rabbit's face screwed up quizzically.

With a furious flurry of black, Tekel Ambrose ascended to the stage. He raised his arms and demanded silence. He got it. It was a heavy silence, as if the very air had become fat. Tekel let it sit there for a full minute as he turned his dark eyes upon every person in the place. Then a single finger arose to point, accusingly, at them all.

"How dare you laugh?" It was almost a whisper. "How dare you laugh when the name of our sacred aggregation is mentioned upon this sullied platform?" And then, to the people on the stage, "How dare you mention our name?"

Dr. Sinister asked, "Is that a rhetorical question, or would you care for a response?"

"There can be no response," stated Tekel Ambrose. "I am aware that not every man deems our way of life worthwhile. I am aware that there are those who can argue convincingly against it from a theological standpoint. I am aware that we are considered mad. I was not, however, aware that a man could not live by his beliefs without the fear of public ridicule!"

"Oh," said Dr. Sinister, "it was hardly public ridicule . . ."

"What would you call it, sir?" shouted Tekel. "I call it public ridicule, to be mentioned in this place. Townspeople! Have you thought cogently of where you are? Not only a place of entertainment, but entertainment of the basest sort! These . . ." Tekel cast about for a word, "*people* are not to be looked at and wondered over. They are to be cared for, they are to be pitied. This man . . ."

73

he said, pointing at Poindexter Frip (a.k.a. Dr. Sinister), "makes his living by allowing you to see nature's abominations! Townspeople, what need have you to see her abominations when you are all so blind to her wonders?"

This bit of rhetoric was lost on the audience; they weren't paying any attention to Tekel's words, although they were too frightened by his dark, angry looks either to leave or heckle.

Major Mite sauntered up bully-like, pulling up his trousers. He stood in front of Tekel and did his best to look menacing, staring into the waist of the black robes. "Hey, Mac—in case you ain't noticed, we got a show goin' on here. Why don't you mind your own beeswax?" Then he added sneeringly, "Why don't ya go play baseball?"

Tekel Ambrose nodded and addressed Dr. Sinister. "I think our two aggregations are at odds with each other. Each would be much happier if the other left. Why do we not play baseball? Why do we not play baseball, and the winner shall stay, the loser be banished?"

The little doctor ruminated momentarily and then said, "One reason for refusing this miratory challenge would be that you people, having a semi-professional baseball team, would win, being as we do not have a semi-professional baseball team, nor, truth be told, so much as a baseball."

Tekel Ambrose said, "I do not propose that you play our whole team. Just the three of us—Mene, Peres, and myself."

Without knowing exactly why, Crybaby Isbister pulled himself on to the stage. This was hard to do with his awkward legs. He crossed over to Dr. Sinister and said, "They're the three best."

Tekel said, "I will play with one hand tied behind my back."

Dr. Sinister pulled on his chin.

"We shall play a public game, and any monies had by admission shall be yours. Our games ofttimes net up to a thousand dollars," Tekel added.

Dr. Sinister asked, "Do you have horses?"

If the question confused Tekel Ambrose he didn't show it. "Yes."

"If we lose, can we borrow them to transport our housings?"

"Yes," stated Tekel. Then he turned to Isbister and said, "You realize that only actual members of this man's so-called troupe may participate."

It startled Nathanael—there had not been a flicker of recognition on Tekel Ambrose's face when Isbister had climbed on to the stage.

"Well," said Dr. Sinister, "I think we shall play baseball, then."

"Shall we set the match at three weeks from this day?"

"Three weeks. Fine."

"The place?"

"There is a useless, sterile field that lies nearby," said Dr. Sinister. "We could make the pitch there."

"It shall be done. We have no further business here." With a furious flurry of black, Tekel Ambrose descended from the stage. He and his brothers strode from the tent.

The townspeople left after them, some to see the fattest woman in the world, some to check Madame Tanya. Left in the tent, upon the stage, were the rest of the freaks (with the curious exception of Major Mite), Nathanael Isbister, and Dr. Sinister.

"A remarkable godsend!" said the little man. "A true magnality! Not only shall we have our caravans uprooted, freeing us for the noctivagation that our vocation requires, it appears that we shall set out on our odyssey with a thousand bucks!"

The other members nodded.

"I had thought to ask them for assistance at any rate," continued Dr. Sinister. "A true magnality, a remarkable godsend! Mr. Isbister, you chose a particularly propitious and pinguedinous day to spend with us!"

"Yeah, those House of Jonah guys are real good ballplayers," said Crybaby. "You don't stand a chance."

"Good! We shouldn't want to win. Just think—travel! New towns, new faces! Which town was it you girls wanted to return to?"

The Hisslop sisters twisted with embarrassment. "Peoria," they said in unison. There was a young man there with remarkable stamina.

"And David shall see his parents in Washington." The young giant struggled to put a smile on to his pained face. "Ally can see his home in Florida." The Alligator Man grunted, but contentedly. "Zapper and I shall again see the historic sights! And Major Mite, he shall visit Cape Breton and be reunited—where is our Major Mite?"

"I'm standing right here, wanting to upchuck," came the squeaky high-pitched voice. The Major was standing in the tent's opening, his tiny frame lit up by the daylight.

"Feeling somewhat out of sorts, Major?" asked Dr. Sinister. "A touch queachy?"

"I feel sicker than I ever did before." The midget strutted to the stage and jumped up. He looked at the people assembled there and, true to his word, it seemed as if he might throw up at any moment.

After a long silence he said, "You wanna know what I just did? I just run after that guy, and I said, 'Okay, Mac, we'll play ball. But we don't want none of your goddam charity.' I said, 'You show up with nine players, and as for tyin' your hand behind your back, stick it up your rosey-red for all I give a care, but when it comes time to play, you better have both of 'em unencumbered, 'cause you're gonna need 'em!' That's what I said."

Crybaby smiled. Dr. Sinister said, "Whatever made you do that?"

Major Mite shouted, "On account of I don't happen to be acquainted with the practice of doin' something with the expressed purpose of losing at it!"

The midget began to strut up and down like a caged lion.

"But, Major," said the Doctor, "you yourself have often spoken querimoniously of this town, how tired you were growing of Burton's Harbor."

"That ain't got nothing to do with nothing! All I know is, if a guy says play ball, you play ball! You don't lie down and lose like that."

The remark left a stunned silence, until Dr. Sinister said, "But how can we possibly—"

"Aw, for God's sake, just think about it. Now, Ally, he's a regular guy, nice and big. He could play all right."

The Alligator Man said, "I played ball lots when I was a kid. I could probably do all right." He was pleased with the Major's confidence in him.

"Violet and Daisy is nice healthy girls," continued the Major. "You're okay, Doc. Tanya's all right. I'm okay."

"But what of the rest of us?"

"We all got uses. Now, Davey there, he could pick a pop fly right out of the air like it was nothing. And Bobby—" The Major looked at the Hippopotamus Boy and asked, "You figure you could play, Bobby?"

The boy nodded his huge, misshapen head ponderously and groaned what was meant to be a "Yes".

The Major said, "Sure you could. And Zap . . . well, maybe he couldn't do much . . ."

This elicited from the Wild Man a long scream and several thrashes from his hairy hands.

"But we got two secret weapons," said Major Mite. "One is, I go up to Cape Breton and get Angus. He's the biggest, strongest man in the whole, entire world. He could bash those balls to hell and back! He could—"

Dr. Sinister shook his head sadly. "He's old, Major."

"I can say 'Nuts' to your 'old' crapola, Doc! He's the strongest man that ever lived."

"He may possibly be," said the Doctor resignedly. "What might our second secret weapon be?"

"Well, he's standing right here watching. Only the great Nate Goldenlegs Isbister!"

Crybaby said quickly, "Ambrose said only members could play—"

The Major said, "You can bend your finger to touch the back of your hand, right?"

Janus barked, which the Major took for affirmation. "Then you're a Rubber Man if ever I seen one."

"Now, listen—" said Nathanael, "even if I wanted to play, which I don't, I got bad legs."

"You batted .426 in 1924!" shouted Major Mite. "You led the league in home runs *and* stolen bases! You could throw to home plate from centre field! You don't need your legs!"

"What good is it throwing to home if I can't run to catch the goddam ball?" asked Crybaby.

"Well, hell, your legs ain't cut off! They're still attached to your body! You ain't crippled!" shrieked Major Mite. "Besides, you could coach us. You're the only one knows anything about baseball, besides me."

"I got places to go . . ." murmured Nathanael.

"I say we play to win!" shouted the midget Major Mite. "Now who's with me?"

The Alligator Man said, "Me, Major." The Hisslop sisters (who were eyeing the famous Nate Isbister) said, "We are," (Violet) and, "Please help us, Mr. Isbister" (Daisy). Zap grunted, Janus barked, and Robert Merrill groaned—all unquestionable support for the enthusiastic Major. Davey Goliath said, "Let's play to win."

Dr. Sinister said, "Well, that's a majority. Play to win it is. Will you help us, Mr. Isbister?"

Nathanael Crybaby Isbister looked at the faces. They ranged from beautiful to hideous, and all were looking at him. Finally he said, "I'll coach you. I won't play, but I'll coach you."

There was enthusiastic applause.

BOOK TWO

Chapter 1

ONE THING THAT is rather worrisome is the matter of Tekel Ambrose's hatred for Dr. Sinister. It shocked the little Doctor as much as anybody, for the encounter you just read about is the first conversation those two men ever had. Dr. Sinister bore Tekel no malice; indeed, contrary to Ambrose's complaint, the Doctor regarded the dark bearded man with great respect.

Tekel Ambrose's life was a hard one. The House of Jonah had no truck with such things as electricity or machinery. Their farming was done with the crudest implements and beasts of burden. They rose at sunrise and worked silently throughout the day, making use of every minute of sunlight. Only when it was pitch dark would they go back to their huge house; there they would have the day's one meal—grains, vegetables, and fruit. Tekel Ambrose had never eaten meat, nor had he ever been tempted to.

Tekel Ambrose was unmarried, and had never in his life been with a woman. I am not sure whether he was ever tempted in this regard. He certainly never gave any signs of it. If there was any joy in Tekel's life, it was baseball. But this, too, is doubtful, for his face was always black and gloomy, even out on the diamond. When he smashed the baseball to hell and out of the park, his only reaction was a flash in his eyes like lightning at midnight.

(Now, about baseball. It was Tekel's father, Jemehiah Ambrose, who originally came up with the idea. It was founded on necessity— the House of Jonah was starving. A cruel winter had robbed them of most of their food, and since their religion ruled out commerce except on a barter system, the store owners of Burton's Harbor didn't want much to do with them. They wanted money, of which the House of Jonah had none. Jemehiah scoured through the writings of Father Jonah, Edmond Raillery, hoping to find some answer.

(It was not promising. Edmond Raillery was against everything. All the things which you and I might consider joyful, like booze and sex and big cigars and thick steaks and funny jokes and movies and songs and literature, all of that was out. "True joy," wrote Edmond Raillery, "is to be found only in Labour, in the striving toward a single goal. It is far better to concentrate upon hitting a ball to a straight and true course than to indulge in any activity that is purely sensational." It struck Jemehiah that Father Jonah was referring to baseball. Everything fell into place. The House could play baseball. It wouldn't be offering entertainment, because for the House of Jonah it would be Labour. It was work. If people paid money to watch them do it, that was their business. And, because they got the money in that way, it was, in a sense, barter. Then they could barter with the monies got by this bartering. It was pretty convoluted thinking that Jemehiah went through to come up with the idea, but the trickiest part, the biggest snag, he glossed over like nothing. Implicit in this scheme was the idea that the House of Jonah come up with not just a baseball team, but one of the finest around, so that people would want to pay to see them. This, to the mind of Jemehiah Ambrose, was no big problem.

(Indeed, it was accomplished within a year. With the same determination with which they worked the fields, the men of the House of Jonah worked on baseball. It was simply a matter of concentrating upon the straight and true course of a hide-covered ball. The men were in the finest physical condition to begin with, so things like running and swinging bats meant nothing.

(In a few years, they had become almost too good. The local teams wanted nothing more to do with them, being sick and tired of sound trouncings, e.g., 53-2 against the Granville Giants. The major leagues offered to draft the whole team and set them up in the American League, but they had to refuse. They couldn't be paid for playing baseball, although it was all right to play baseball and have people pay them for it. So they came up with the idea of handicapping themselves. Sometimes only three or four of the Brothers would show up to do battle with the opposition. They would tie hands behind their backs, bind their feet together—once or twice they pitched blindfolded. Although all of this sounds like playful antics, it was done in complete seriousness. The players stood on the field, perfectly sombre and long-bearded, and beat the pants off everybody. They played the major league teams in exhibition games and invariably won. They toured the country and brought back to Burton's Harbor tons of money that could be bartered with.

(Mene, Peres, and Tekel were young teenagers when all this started; they were to emerge as the team's strongest assets, particularly, of course, Tekel.

(Now, all this about "arguably best player", etc. You are probably saying to yourself, "I've never heard of either Tekel Ambrose or Nathanael Isbister." Good point. Surely the best player award must go to someone we've all heard of, like Ruth, Gehrig, Heilmann, or Cobb. But you must remember the way an authority's mind works. He doesn't want to talk of someone that every Joe Blow knows about, because that makes it seem like he's doing a half-ass job. So the historians and trivialists of baseball dug deep into the past and came up with these two names: T. Ambrose and N. Isbister.

(Both have lifetime batting averages over four hundred. Both could hit the ball right out of the park. Tekel Ambrose's other talents lay mostly in his arms. He could pitch a no-hitter just as easy as I can spit. He could throw the ball with an inhuman accuracy to any point on the field. In this respect, historians and trivialists tell us, he surpassed Nathanael Isbister. *But*, and my grandfather doesn't mind me telling you this being as it's what he calls "public information", what Isbister had over Ambrose was legs. Wonderful, miraculous legs. That man stole more bases in two seasons than any man in the game's history. He stole home more often than any other man in history. And out in centre field, no hit escaped him, no matter how far or fast he had to go to get it.

(The reasons you haven't heard of either man are (a) Isbister's professional career was only two and a half years long, too short to make sure that he wasn't some fluke, just a lucky kid who kept getting the breaks, and (b) Ambrose is disqualified by some minds on the grounds that he played for a non-league team and that a great many of his games were not documented in the official fashion. Reports about the great Tekel were passed mostly from mouth to mouth.

(Now, where was I? I fear my mind is getting as doddering as my grandfather's, who, reminded of baseball, has switched on my tiny TV set to watch a game. He doesn't like it much these days—too many damn teams, he says, and not one with a hero. In the old days, they had heroes. Oh well. I've remembered now—I was talking about Tekel, and this was a lengthy parenthetical aside. Therefore . . .)

Why did Ambrose hate Dr. Sinister and his troupe of misshapen outcasts so much? Well, one reason is that Tekel Ambrose, as a Brother of the House of Jonah, was against entertainment of any sort. He disliked Mrs. Loopenville, who ran the local repertory theatre. He disliked Mr. Druck, who ran the local movie house. He fervently disliked Mr. Jimpson, who ran the local burlesque, where they had naked ladies. But he didn't hate them. He only hated Dr. Sinister.

Another reason might be that Dr. Sinister made money out of other people's misfortunes. Ambrose used that argument in the last section after all. But it doesn't really hold water, because (as even Tekel must have suspected) Dr. Sinister divided whatever money he got with all the members. He even set aside an equal share for Zap, the Wild Man from Borneo, keeping it in a safety deposit box in his trailer. Not only that, but Dr. Sinister was not without talent himself. He was a magician, he played the organ, he delivered the running commentary—in short, he worked ridiculously hard for a mere pittance. He was nowhere near as well off as Tekel, who hoarded his barterable money because he had nothing to spend it on. Besides, the other members of the troupe were there of their own free will—Dr. Sinister had no chains around their ankles, he had no contracts signed in blood. They were free to come and go as they pleased.

In my humble opinion, from what my grandfather has told me, I suspect the real reason is something like this:

Every now and then, weather permitting, all the carnival members would go on a picnic, out into the fields. And one day they went into a field where Tekel was working, worshipping his god Labour. The scene Tekel saw was something like this:

Beneath an apple tree, Daisy and Violet Hisslop asked Davey Goliath if he could pick them some of the nice apples from high up on the branches. Davey, grinning for once, hobbled over and stretched his arm up high, right to the top, and plucked the two biggest, reddest apples. He gave them to the two sisters. Violet said, "Now you sit down, Davey, and we'll kiss you on the cheek," and Daisy said, "Ally! Davey wants to sit down." The Alligator Man, who had been rough-housing with Zap and Janus, came over reluctantly. "Again? Tell him to make up his mind," he snapped at Violet and Daisy. The Alligator Man went behind Davey and took his elbows, and Davey lowered himself with his assistance. When Davey Goliath was sitting on the ground, Violet and Daisy both bussed him on the cheek, turning him a pale pink. Then Daisy said, "And Ally gets a kiss too, for helping us with Davey!" The Alligator Man turned away sullenly, saying "Skip it," and went back to his rough-housing. Zap leapt up on to his back and covered Ally's eyes with his hairy hands. They stumbled around in tandem, Janus circling around them, yapping with his strange double bark.

Major Mite, Robert Merrill, and Dr. Sinister sat nearby on a blanket. Major Mite was concentrating on an anthill in front of him, watching the activity of the insects. Occasionally he would say, "Look at them bastards move!" Robert Merrill, wearing a neck-brace that Dr. Sinister had fashioned for him, worked upon a piece of paper with a quill and ink. The Doctor was nose-deep in a thick, leather-bound book.

Robert Merrill, the Hippopotamus Boy, handed a sheet of paper to Dr. Sinister, who read aloud:

The ants scurry, scurry,
Always in a flurry,
Ever in a hurry,
They never stop to rest!
I wonder, do they know,
That with just a single blow,
Their home could be razed low,
That it would be their death?

Dr. Sinister added, "Full of facund, Bobby. Very well done." But Major Mite was troubled. "How can you raise something low?"

The Doctor answered, "Not r-a-i-s-e, Major, r-a-z-e."

"Don't make no difference to me, Doc, I can't spell," said the Major. "All I want to know is, how can you raise something low?"

"Raze, r-a-z-e, is homophonous, to wit, to destroy something totally, that is, wipe it out." Dr. Sinister returned to his book, which was a thick novel.

"I still don't get it," muttered Major Mite. Robert Merrill took the paper back from the Doctor, struck out the word "razed" and wrote over top of it "laid". His handwriting was ornate and flowery. He gave the paper back to the Doctor, who re-read the entire poem with the substituted word. It pleased the Major.

"Now I get it," he said. "It's funny, ain't it, them little boogers running around without a nevermind about yesterday, today, or tomorrow. Funny."

Dr. Sinister nodded, without looking up from his novel.

On another blanket sat Stella, the only member we haven't met so far. She sat like a small mountain, the fat spilling on to the ground as if the sun were melting her. It was impossible to distinguish the parts of her body that stuck out of her white, tent-like dress, they were so blown-up and distorted. Near the top of the pile sat her face—a tiny nose, a full mouth, and two sparkling sea blue eyes. She was laughing at something Tanya had said to her.

Tanya lay stretched out in the sun. She had stripped down to her underthings, and it was obvious that the large breasts did belong to her, as did the full bottom. The face, however, squinting against the sun and darkly bearded, seemed extremely masculine.

So this sight greeted Tekel Ambrose:

A small, hairy man with pointed head and teeth . . . a dog with two heads and five legs . . . a man nine feet tall . . . two girls joined together . . . a hideously ugly boy . . . a man with green skin . . . a dwarf . . . a fat lady . . . a woman with a beard lying almost naked in the middle of the day . . . and, sitting in the middle of it all, a small man peacefully reading a novel.

It was then that Tekel Ambrose began to hate that small man.

Because: Tekel Ambrose thought of himself as a good man. But, if he was, it was only because he had never done anything bad. His regimented lifestyle didn't allow choices between good and evil, noble and ignoble actions. Tekel realized instinctively that this was the first test he had ever been put to. He realized that what the Bible would have him do, what Jesus would have done, would be to love these people. To embrace them with all their deformities and ugliness. But, searching for the first time within his soul, Tekel Ambrose came up with fear, revulsion, and disgust. Accepting simply that he had failed, he had only one wish—to be rid of them all. And in particular, the little man with the shaggy walrus moustache who sat in the centre of the freaks and calmly read a novel.

Having agreed to coach Dr. Sinister's team, Nathanael Isbister immediately regretted it; however, he had a strong sense of honor and would never go back on his word, no matter how impulsively given. He had agreed because he was basically a soft touch. Throughout his life he had found it impossible to say no to any request made of him.

The members of the troupe pressed Isbister to begin his coaching immediately. He said, "All right! We'll start in half an hour. First of all go and put on some clothes that you don't mind getting dirty. And I mean *filthy!*"

They agreed and ran out eagerly. Isbister, Dr. Sinister, and Zap remained behind. "Aren't you gonna get changed, Doctor?" asked Crybaby.

The little Doctor looked down at his ancient, threadbare tuxedo. "The possible inturbidation of this suit is a matter I view with insouciance," he said. "I've many more."

"Suit yourself," said Nathanael.

"We must go inform Stella of this transpiration," said Dr. Sinister. The little hairy Zap reached a hand through the bars of his cage and flipped the latch free. Pushing the door open, he sprang out and up in one motion, landing in Dr. Sinister's arms. "My, my, my," the Doctor muttered, "aren't you eager and avid, leaping from your latibule like that."

"Stella's the fat lady?" asked Nathanael.

"Oh, yes, very fat. A lovely person. Come along."

Dr. Sinister took Zap's hand, and the three men left the big top. They crossed over to one of the smaller tents. As they ascended the four rickety stairs, a young man with a stone face and a shiny black leather jacket ran down past them. Dr. Sinister turned to watch the young man storm away into the surrounding fields.

"That boy," he told Isbister, "is always in attendance. Never at the show proper, mind, only to view our Stella." He shook his head, slightly bewildered.

Upon entering the little tent, the first thing that Nathanael noticed was a strong smell. It was mostly cheap perfume, but underlying it was the pungent odour of manure.

Then he noticed the mountainous woman sitting in the enormous throne-like chair. He ran his eyes slowly over the rolls and curls of her body, the flabby crevices and gigantic curves. Finally his eyes settled on the face. The fat lady's mouth broke into the sweetest of smiles, and she said a quiet, "Hello."

Zap broke away from the Doctor and clambered up on top of the fat lady, snuggling away until he was comfortable. "Hello, Zapper," Stella said, and, raising an arm (the fat drooping a foot down from the bone of her forearm), she began to pet the hairy man's pointed head.

"Stella!" said Dr. Sinister excitedly. "The most innugacious thing!" Whereupon he related the tale of Tekel Ambrose's challenge, their acceptance, Major Mite's demand, and their subsequent decision to play to win.

"I say 'bravo' for the Major," stated Stella. "I'm almost ashamed of you, Pointy."

"I was inhebetated by the prospect of departure. Mind you, they shall still be victorious in this laquearian contest."

"What a pessimist!" said Stella, and Zap grunted (or so it seemed to Isbister) angrily.

"But they are a first-rate baseball team!" argued Dr. Sinister. "I confess total ignorance of that game. However, there is one thing that could conceivably potentiate a victory. This, Stella, is Nathanael Isbister."

"I was wondering when you were going to introduce me. Pleased to meet you, Nathanael." She proffered a hand that compared to the rest of her was only plump. Nathanael accepted and shook it lightly.

"Are you familiar with baseball?" Stella asked.

"Stella!" chirped Dr. Sinister. "Nathanael Isbister was perhaps the finest combatant the diamond has ever witnessed! Not to mention his long and immensely popular career in sports reportage."

"Oh! I'm sorry, Nathanael, but I've never heard of you. Can you forgive me?"

"Absolutely," smiled Isbister.

"He is going to coach us," explained the Doctor. "Indeed, his tutelage will begin within the quarter-hour."

"Well, bring round the barrow when you're ready," said the fat lady, and then she turned to study Nathanael's face more closely. "How did you happen to be here when all this took place?"

"Oh, I was just wandering around, and I ran into Fido and Ro— er, Janus."

"And the Major, convinced that Mr. Isbister had stolen said wonderdog, abducted him hither at gun-point!" Dr. Sinister giggled loudly and Stella laughed—hers was a light, easy laugh, like birds upon clouds.

"Yeah," chuckled Crybaby. "And then the Doc here said I could spend the night, so I did, and I went to see the show, and Ambrose showed up, and—well, ma'am, I guess I just got caught up in it."

"A lucky thing for us," noted Stella. "Are you on vacation, Nathanael?"

For the first time since entering the little tent Nathanael became uneasy. He shuffled his feet and said, "No, ma'am. I . . . quit radio and newspaper work."

"Why?"

"Oh, you know, the grind just kind of got to me. You know how it is." Isbister waved his answer away, furthering the impression that it wasn't the truth. Stella noticed his uneasiness and changed the subject. "What did you think of the show?"

"It was real interesting. I've never been to a . . ."

"A freak show?" suggested Stella.

"Yeah. Never been to one before."

"Oh." Stella smiled and stroked the little Zap, who was at this point snoring loudly in her folds. "What was the crowd like, Poindexter?"

"Hardly pandemic," said the little man. "And a trifle pusillanimous, given to pococurantism."

"I had quite a few in here," said Stella. "Over twenty-five people, I think."

Isbister suddenly noticed that Stella's chair was hooked up by various cables and chains and, in fact, dangled about an inch off the ground. Following the link-ups, he arrived finally at a graduated metal shaft with an arrow trembling high up on it. He realized that Stella was sitting on a huge scale. Edging even closer, he saw that the metal needle indicated a point just above "615".

Stella saw him looking and added, "You realize that some of that is this chair. Not much, I'll agree, but some of it."

Nathanael smiled and could think of nothing to say.

"Stella," said the Doctor, "is very likely the fattest woman in the world."

"Oh?" muttered Isbister stupidly.

"Quite a claim to fame, eh?" asked Stella—then she chuckled lightly. They all three laughed, and Zap stirred happily in his slumber.

"Well," said the doctor, "it's almost time. I shall go fetch the wheelbarrow."

These references to wheelbarrows are due to the fact that Stella's enormous weight made for a problem. She couldn't move very easily—for all practical purposes, she couldn't move at all. (So, for example, the strong smell that Isbister had noticed was due to her throne being, in fact, a commode. The perfume was an attempt to hide the odour.) There was, directly behind where she sat, an opening in the tent. Dr. Sinister would wheel the barrow up behind it (it was one he'd designed himself, a high one with a side that folded down) and all Stella would have to do was roll over backwards, into the pillows of the barrow, and she could be transported.

This was what they did, then, when Dr. Sinister announced time for practice. Nathanael offered to push the thing. He wheeled her behind the Doctor, and they talked as they went.

"This is very kind of you, Nathanael."

"Don't mention it," said Crybaby. "I used to push my mom around, you know, when I was a kid. She was crippled."

"I don't think I'll be able to do anything," said Stella, "except offer moral support."

"That's something I could do with, anyway," answered Nathanael.

Up ahead, Dr. Sinister was talking to Zap as they walked hand in hand. "I think you shall easily learn this game," the Doctor said. "Although I am at best a sciolist, there is not much to it." Zap grunted loudly and picked diligently at his nose. The Doctor continued. "A spherical object, to wit, the ball, is batted about and caught. Very eximious."

The other members stood around in the middle of the field, having changed to old clothes. The Alligator Man was pleased that he'd been able to watch the Hisslop sisters dressing twice already that day. The girls had been excited, and more playful with their lovely naked bodies than usual; their four nipples had been pert and richly pink. They had pulled on an old skirt and sweatshirts.

Nathanael set down the wheelbarrow and walked toward the assembled players. As he arrived, a baseball came towards him, a quick, hard throw. Isbister snapped out his hand to catch it—his palm stung sharply. Looking, he saw that the ball had come from the Alligator Man, who said, "Found it in my trailer. Got a bat, too." Ally held it up.

" 'Kay, forget the bat for now." Nathanael held up the ball and turned slowly, showing it to everybody. Then he dropped it to the ground, so that it rolled a few feet away from his feet. He did nothing, just stood there—as did everybody else. This situation lasted for a long moment until Isbister said:

"Okay, now that's the first thing we've got to learn. What you guys should have done was jump for that ball. Each and every one of you. You gotta learn to go after a loose ball just like you breathe. Without thinking about it." Nathanael picked up the ball again. After a moment, he let it drop to the ground.

The midget Major Mite came scrambling to get it before the others had taken a step.

"And that's how you gotta go for it, too!" said Isbister. "Just like the Major did." He repeated the dropping of the ball.

This time, the Major, Dr. Sinister, the Hisslop sisters, and the Alligator Man pounced into the vicinity of the ball all at the same time. A moment later, an excited Zap jumped into their midst, and a moment after that, Davey Goliath pitched forth from where he stood and fell face first to the ground. One of the Hisslop sisters shouted, "Davey! You'll hurt yourself!" With a rapid series of double-edged barks, Janus was there too. Robert Merrill, his head in the neck-brace, came to the pile next—because of the weight and awkwardness of his head, he walked fairly slowly and with care.

Stella, unable to move from her wheelbarrow, shouted encouragement to them all. Beside her, Madame Tanya stood still as a statue and looked on with disdain.

From within the brace of people, Major Mite shouted, "I got it! I got it!" Daisy Hisslop shrieked, "Ally! That's *not* the ball!" Zap's grunts came loudly, interspersed with loud howls. Major Mite was persistent—"I got the booger, now everyone get up offa me!" Janus barked, and Robert Merrill groaned unintelligibly. Davey Goliath, lying on the ground, slowly reached forward with a long hand and began to poke it around blindly, groping for the ball.

Isbister had to chuckle at the voices coming from the writhing human pile. Dr. Sinister was saying, very quietly and calmly, "Excuse me, I believe I have retrieved it. I believe I have." Daisy and Violet shrieked and giggled, the Alligator Man cursed with determination. Major Mite's shouting was nonstop, "All right, get up offa me, I got it! So help me, I'm gonna brain somebody, lay off it, Al! Daisy and Violet, I'm giving you fair warning, and I don't care if you are girls, I'm gonna . . . Yow! What bastard bit me? Janus, your days are numbered!"

Stella said, to the bearded woman beside her, "Go on, Tanya! It looks like fun."

Tanya said a very simple, "No."

After a few minutes, things settled down, with all the members sitting on the ground exhausted.

"All right!" said Crybaby happily. "Now, who's got the ball?"

Everyone came up empty-handed, until Zap reached up and removed it from his mouth. Then they all laughed for a good, long moment.

"Well," said Nathanael Isbister, "I don't know how much talent we got on this team—but we sure got some spirit!"

Our friends didn't know it, but they had another ace up their collective sleeve.

My grandfather slipped through his own shirt-sleeves two cuff-links embossed with fake rubies. He pushed a rhinestone pin through his tie. He washed and slicked down his hair. Then, with an arrogant swagger, he descended into the tavern of the Fulton Arms.

He ordered a double whisky and, to pay for it, peeled a twenty dollar bill from a huge, thick roll (mostly newspaper, of course). He puffed on a Cuban cigar (stolen almost two years ago—he'd been keeping it in a jar with pieces of apple, awaiting just such an occasion). And then, using a mystical method he himself had originated, he began emanating thoughts of richness and untold wealth.

It worked. Three or four men came and sat down near him. "New around here?" asked a gruff voice.

My grandfather ignored them; with a snap of his gnarled fingers he shouted, "Garçon! Another double whisky—and not that house pigslop, either. The very best!"

"New around here," came the voice again, this time making a statement.

"Are you speaking to me?" demanded my grandfather rudely, without looking at the man.

"Yeah," the guy answered sullenly. "Excuse me."

"What is it you wished to know?" snapped the weasel.

"Just wondered if you were new around here, that's all," muttered the man.

"I am merely passing through. Were it not for a foul-up with my traveling schedule"—he pronounced it "shed-ule"—"I would be nowhere near this godforsaken hole-in-the-ground."

Another of the men asked, "Where you headed?"

"Not that it is any of your business, sir, but I am going to Chicago, for the annual meeting of the shareholders." He said this curtly, as if he hoped it would bring the conversation to an end. Naturally, he hoped no such thing.

"Shareholder in some company, eh?"

"No, sir. I am the president-owner of a company, attached to which are some twelve hundred shareholders."

"What kind of company?"

"Ladies' undergarments."

"No kidding?"

"Of course not. I do not kid. Another whisky, boy—and *move* it!"

"What's your name?"

"I am J.M.M."—my grandfather squinted craftily—"Brassiere."

Yesterday I thought of something to compare what happened to my grandfather with. It was something culminative, like a storm (first grey clouds peeked above the horizon, etc.). But today it won't come to me, which proves a hitherto unknown medical fact, i.e., that senility is contagious.

What happened then (*sans* the comparison, even though it was a dilly) is that these men asked my grandfather if he'd like to engage in a little game to while away his stay in Burton's Harbor. My grandfather suggested cribbage, vetoed by the others on the grounds that they had no board. One of their ranks suggested poker. My grandfather's eyes popped open. His mouth fell apart moronically. And he said, "Isn't that—*illegal?*"

"Not for money!" they shouted in unison. Just a friendly game between gentlemen. (Ha, ha, ha. I wish you could see the old "gentleman" now, sleeping in his stained underwear on my sofa.) My grandfather agreed reluctantly, and they retired to one of the rooms upstairs.

Now this was a game filled with many hustlings. They let my grandfather win for a while; for a while, my grandfather let them let him win, and then he started losing, so they thought, Jesus, even when we let him win, he loses. Someone suggested a little "spice". Shall we spice up the game a little, say, a penny a point? Who carries pennies?! demanded my grandfather, feigning anger at his losses. I only have bills! Like a spoiled and ill-tempered child, my grandfather dumped his money on the table, and the playing began in earnest, along with the drinking.

(My grandfather had, and still has, an almost mystical concept of alcohol. He feels that if he gets drunk enough, it puts him in contact with the gods, the deities of drunkenness, and no harm can befall him. He practises this especially when playing cards.)

The hustles vanished in straight order. They played hi-lo Chicago, wild card follows the deuces, high spade in the hole, and you gotta declare. After a while, my grandfather had accumulated a huge pile of money—he was smiling blissfully, and felt a warm contact with all the forces that be. No harm could come to him, he was abandoned to, and at one with, the cosmos.

He was drunk as a coot.

Then he began to lose. His pile of money dwindled slowly, like a pile of snow under a hot sun—slowly, but surely and steadily. He began to whimper. He poured more alcohol down his gullet in an attempt to reestablish contact; alas, it was too late. Still his money disappeared.

Indeed, my grandfather was losing with such determination that the men he was playing with soon became bored with him. They began to speak conversationally, above my grandfather's drunken moans. Stuff like:

"I hear there's trouble over at Arnie's factory."

"Yeah?"

"Yeah."

"Trouble?"

"Yeah. You lose, Mr. Brassiere."

When my grandfather had but a lonely five-spot sitting in front of him, one of the men said, "You hear the news? House of Jonah gonna play the freaks."

"What in hell for?"

"Well, seems that Tekel Ambrose challenged them to a game, and the loser has to leave town. Don't have to guess who that's gonna be. It's five to stay in, Mr. Brassiere."

"You mean the freaks said okay? Since when can they play baseball?"

"The way I heard it, the freaks are just in it for the money. They get the whole gate. They're probably itching to leave town anyway."

"I suppose so. Well, that's one game we won't get any action on."

"Shit, yes. It's gonna be a bloodbath. Professional calibre baseball team playing a bunch of freaks. No one would believe it. You lose, Mr. Brassiere."

My grandfather, at this point, had reached his zenith of intoxication. Or his nadir, depending on how you look at it. All his money was gone. The above conversation had been soaked up by his sponge-like brain, but how deeply it had penetrated is impossible to judge. He leaned back and with all his being sought some other-worldly contact. Whether or not he achieved it is likewise impossible to judge. All we know for sure is historical fact. My grandfather closed his eyes and said these words: "Gentlemen. I am willing to bet on the freaks." Then he and his chair toppled to the ground.

$$\bigcirc$$

Major Mite, meanwhile, early the following morning, dressed himself in a sedate grey suit, complete with bowtie and miniature fedora, packed a tiny travelling case and walked away from the trailers without a word of farewell.

$$\bigcirc$$

Doctor Sinister heard him leaving but said nothing. The Doctor was up and about in his own overcrowded caravan, busily composing a letter. Finished, it looked like this:

Dear Mr. Ambrose,

Although it makes me a tad erubescent, I confess a marginal knowledge (banausic!) of baseball. However, even a scant memoration of the rules expergefacts the realization that said rules must perforce be modified. Par exemple, (a lusory one, admittedly) we cannot don appropriate uniforms; having attended at the exhibition, you are aware of the prodigious sibling bonding that produces this metagrobolization. Thusly, I would ask to change said rules, hoping that you will be assentaneous to these revisions—if not, we shall negotiate. The other matter at hand is that of umpireship. Proleptically assuming that any man I suggest will be viewed with platic suspicion, I have the matter in your capable hands. I know you to be an honest man.

Yours,

Poindexter Sinister.

And although I risk ruining the continuity of the narrative, I will now show you the reply which arrived about a week later.

Dear Dr. Sinister,

Of the first two bits of business: by all means, adjust the rulings in any manner you see fit. Of the second: there is a man perfectly suited to the role of umpire. Mr. Doubleday's own grandson, Dustin, came to Our House yesterday to make my acquaintance. He agreed to officiate. I was sure you would have no objection. He strikes me as being a man of the highest moral integrity. I remain,

T. Ambrose

Chapter 2

BEFORE YOU CAN even begin to understand young Davey Goliath (who didn't show up for practice the next morning and was nowhere to be found) you must know a story.

It begins long ago, in Ireland. There, in 1761, was born James Byrne. Young James was a giant. When he went to London at the age of twenty one, the billing placed him at eight foot four, "and in full proportion accordingly". Of Mr. Byrne, we know very little. He is said to have been of a gentle disposition (like our own Davey) and none too bright.

Now enters the other character of our little melodrama, one Dr. John Hunter. Dr. John Hunter was at the time the most famous surgeon in all of England, the founder of the science of comparative anatomy. There was nothing about this natural world that did not fascinate Dr. Hunter, and no ends he would stop at to satisfy that fascination. He wondered how a deer's antlers grew, for example. So he selected fifty deer that exhibited different stages of antler development and slaughtered them. He spent hours happily taking apart their heads. He wondered about the effects of poison on the nervous system. To this end he poisoned thousands of animals: dogs, cats, horses, rabbits, cows—in short, anything he could get his hands on. The number of insects Dr. Hunter wondered about and dissected out of wonderment must number into the millions. Myself, I wonder about Dr. Hunter.

When Dr. Hunter saw the advertisement for young James Byrne, it sparked his curiosity. He went to see him and decided that science could learn much from a study of that enormous skeleton. After the show, he ran backstage and asked the giant point-blank if he could have his body when he died. He offered to pay a lot of money for that privilege. James was aghast. He said a terrified No!, turned and fled.

But the seed was planted and the nightmares began. Young James started seeing Dr. Hunter everywhere—lurking behind buildings, peeking out of windows, following him down the dark cobblestone streets. And always, always, Dr. Hunter had with him a huge cauldron full of boiling water, which he stirred like a witch from Macbeth. "To clean the bones!" he would call to James. "We need to have your bones clean!"

How much of this was the young giant's fantasy and how much actually took place is a matter of opinion. And it matters nary a whit as far as James Byrne was concerned. All he knew was, everywhere he went that damned Dr. Hunter was there waiting, stirring his monstrous kettle. "To clean the bones! We need to have the bones clean!"

This drove James to drink, as one can easily imagine. Myself, I need nothing so dramatic as seeing a man with a giant kettle to boil me. At any rate, after one long day in the pub, young James walked outside, tripped (as giants are prone to do), bashed his head on the road, and contracted pneumonia. He was only twenty-one.

As he lay on his deathbed, the image of Dr. Hunter became even more clear and terrifying. James and his few sympathetic friends devised a plan. His body would be placed in a huge box, weighted down with metal, and unceremoniously deposited at the bottom of the Irish Sea. Dr. Hunter could never get him there. So, thinking that he had outwitted the surgeon and escaped the giant kettle, young James Byrne died happily.

Friends, it grieves me to tell you that it did not work. The undertaker who had been conscripted to prepare the body was actually in Hunter's pay. Some say it was Hunter himself in disguise. It matters not—at some point on the long trek to the sea, Byrne's friends stopped to wet their whistle, and the crate containing the giant's remains was spirited away. And James Byrne went into the kettle, so that his bones would come out clean.

If you go to the Royal College of Surgeons in London, you can see James Byrne's skeleton.

Now, this story (which I'll wager was never heard by any of you) is well known among (you'd never have guessed) other giants. And its effect upon them has been the same as with Byrne. Terror. Total terror. Patrick Cotter (7'11") arranged to be buried twelve feet deep in rock. The opening was first layered with iron bars and then bricked up. Other giants have invented Hunter-proof coffins— two-foot thick iron slabs with a myriad of padlocks.

So it was with Davey. Despite Dr. Hunter's having been dead for almost a hundred and fifty years, Davey still saw the man with his giant kettle, grinning at him. Remember when Davey was being measured by the men from the audience, he seemed to say, "Is it the hunter?"; we know now he was in fact saying, "Is it *Hunter?*"

Some days were worse than others for poor Davey. On the morning of the second baseball practice, he had gone out early to the field, his aim being to limber up a bit. But arriving there, he saw steam pouring up from behind some bushes, and heard a craggy voice intoning, "Clean, clean, we need them clean! Clean as a whistle, with a pearly sheen!" The bushes parted, and Dr. Hunter's face emerged with a foot-long Sardonicus smile and a wrinkled, winking eye.

Davey Goliath turned and fled with his canes. He fell into his trailer and locked the door several times. He had three bolts, four padlocks, and seven chains. Then he lay down on the bed and wept.

Nathanael Isbister noticed immediately that Davey wasn't there, for he had wanted to measure the giant's hand. He, Dr. Sinister, and the Alligator Man had planned a trek into Burton's Harbor in order to get equipment, and Crybaby had realized that the giant's glove would have to be custom-made.

He asked Stella, whom he had wheeled to the practice, where the boy might be. She told him the Dr. Hunter story.

"Jesus," muttered Crybaby. "Oh well, I guess we'll just have to do the best we can." He plucked a little notebook out of his back pocket and took a pen from behind his ear. "Okay, Stella, let's take a look at your hand." Stella held it out, and Crybaby took it into his own. The two hands were as different as night and day. Isbister's was large with swollen knuckles. The skin had been worked to shiny callouses, covered with scabs and scratches. Stella's was ghostly white and underlined with light blue veins. As I've pointed out before, compared to the rest of her it was only plump. "My, it's tiny," said Nathanael, continuing to hold it. "We'll have to buy you a kid's glove." After a moment he let go the hand and wrote, "Stella—kid's glove" in the little pad. "Are you right-handed?" he asked her—she nodded, and Nathanael made an "R" beside her name.

Suddenly a hairy hand was thrust up in front of Isbister's nose. The nails were sharp and pointed. Crybaby jumped back, alarmed and frightened; then he heard the musical tinklings of Stella's laugh. "Zapper wants a glove too," she chuckled.

The furry little man looked up at Crybaby with a moronic grin and then shrieked loudly. Isbister turned away and walked up to the Hisslop sisters. "Ladies," he said.

The girls twisted coyly and said, "Good morning, Mr. Isbister," in unison.

"We're going into town to buy equipment," he told them. "I'll need to know how big your hands are, and if you're right- or left-handed." Violet, who was the right-sided sister, said that she was left-handed, while Daisy, on the left, was right-handed. They held up their hands for Crybaby's examination. After looking at them for a bit, Nathanael let his focus change until he was concentrating on the soft mounds of their breasts, which rose splendidly even in the baggy sweatshirts.

The Hisslop girls had long, graceful fingers—Nathanael decided they would take a man's small size, and wrote that down. He thanked them and turned to walk away—Violet's voice stopped him.

"Mr. Isbister!" He turned towards them. "We were wondering . . . did you ever meet Babe Ruth?"

He smiled. "Sure."

"Well—" began Violet (Daisy looked away, as if the conversation did not involve her), "we were wondering. You know those stories they tell—that he would stay up all night, drinking and . . . being with women?" Violet vocally added a sly underline to the word "being".

"Yeah?" asked Crybaby.

"We were wondering if they were true." Even though Daisy was looking away, she began to colour rapidly as her sister said these words.

"Yup," said Nathanael. "He played some of his best games after a night of drinking and being with women." Isbister returned the word "being" with the same sly underscoring.

"And no sleeping?" asked Violet.

"Sometimes he didn't sleep for days on end." Isbister watched as the Hisslop girls' eyes popped open with dreamy wonderment. Then he smiled again and walked over to Dr. Sinister.

"Morning, Doc," he said.

"Mr. Isbister!" The little man reached inside his tuxedo and pulled out the final draft of the letter which we have already seen. "I have spent the morning preparing this ecphrasis. I now present it to you, should you care to opine."

Nathanael read through it and handed it back. "Real good," he told the Doctor. "We can get a rule book in town."

"Capital," said the Doctor.

"Now . . ." Isbister raised his little notebook. "Are you right-handed or left-handed?"

"Aha!" beamed the little man. "Herein lies yet another entelechy of my name, i.e., Poindexter Sinister, which contains both right and left. View it as a parvanimity if you will, but that same duality is possessed by myself manually. To wit, I am to some extent *both* right- and left-handed, in a word, ambidextrous, although I favour my left hand if given freedom of choice." Dr. Sinister smiled beatifically.

"Well, well, well . . ." Isbister wrote that down (at least, as much of it as he could understand). "A switch-hitter. You know, Doc, I think you may be our pitcher too."

"I shall do my best to suppeditate that function."

Suddenly a hairy hand was thrust in front of Isbister's face again, accompanied this time by a vicious fart. Nathanael looked down at Zap's ugly and hairy face.

"Little Zap wants a glove!" exclaimed Dr. Sinister.

"Sure looks like it," said Nathanael. "But . . ."

"I know that you are wondering if his limited mental capacities warrant using him at all. He is definitely not umbratile. But I think it would be no great or ugglesome problem to impress upon our Zap that he should by his own ultroneousity attempt to retrieve a ball from the air or hit one with a bat."

"You think so?" asked Nathanael.

"I do, indeed."

Isbister wrote down, "The Doc—man's small; Zapper—medium . . ." Then he hesitated. "Is he right- or left-handed?"

The Doctor pulled on his chin. "I've never noticed. Remiss in my role as scriniary. Hmmm . . . he exhibited his right hand. Perhaps he's right-handed."

"Yeah, but see, if he's right-handed, his glove goes on his left hand."

"I see, I see!" mused the Doctor. "He raised his right hand, yes? Therefore, that must be the hand he wishes gloved."

"Well, okay . . ." Isbister wrote down an "L" beside Zap's name. The Wild Man from Borneo strutted away, scratching solemnly at his chest.

Isbister glanced over at Dr. Sinister. "You know the Hippopotamus Boy?"

"I know him as well as any man does."

"Well, is he okay?"

"I see what you are asking! Indeed, he is okay. Perfectly cogent. His inability to speak is purely mechanical and has to do with the bone projecting through his mouth. But that idiasm has nothing to do with his intellect. Converse with him, and his part in the dialogue will be written in a pad which he carries expressly for that purpose."

"Uh-ya." Isbister walked over to Robert Merrill. It was hard enough looking at the boy, with his huge misshapen head—but in addition, Robert gave off a stench that was quite hard to live with at close quarters.

The Hippopotamus Boy extended a notebook; the top sheet said, in an ornate and flowery handwriting:

> Good morning, Mr. Isbister! I am very pleased to make your acquaintance. Please feel free to call me either "Bobby" or "Robby". I think we can win this game with your excellent help. My hand appears to be of a normal size, and I favour my right. If there is anything I can do for you at any time, just ask.

Nathanael read the note, and smiled at the boy despite the monumental ugliness and horrible stench. "Thanks a lot, Bobby," he said, walking away. "I think maybe we can take this game, too."

Madame Tanya stood a few feet off; it struck Crybaby as he approached her that she looked a lot like Tommy Drivotch, a guy he'd played with in the minors. Except, of course, that Drivotch didn't have those large melon-shaped breasts attached to his chest.

"Good morning, ma'am," said Nate.

"Good morning, yourself," came the husky answer. "Don't call me ma'am." This last statement had nothing to do with her sexuality, it was merely a denouncement of politesse and social protocol. "Just call me Tanya."

"Okay, Tanya. We're going into town to buy gloves and such like that, so I need to know how big your hand is."

Madame Tanya raised a hand that was every bit as big as Nathanael's, equally calloused and well worked. Hers, though, had immaculately manicured nails that had been polished to a shiny pink.

Accordingly, Isbister wrote down "Tanya—man's large". "And are you right- or left-handed?"

The answer was "right". Crybaby marked that down.

Then he looked for the Major—who, as we know, slipped away in the wee hours of the morning. Crybaby spent a long time looking at the team members before he was absolutely certain that the midget wasn't among them. "Hey, Doc!" he bellowed.

Dr. Sinister was playing catch with Zap; or at least he was trying to. He would toss the ball lightly through the air at the little hairy man. Zap would let it bounce off whatever portion of the body it happened to hit. Then Dr. Sinister would say, "Now, throw it back, Zap! Come on, son, pick it up and throw it back! Participate, lad, participate!" Zap would stare at him and pick at his nose. Finally Dr. Sinister would retrieve the ball himself, and the whole process would begin anew.

Dr. Sinister turned his head to Nathanael. "Yes, my friend?"

In the middle of Crybaby's question ("Do you know where Major Mite is at?"), a quickly thrown baseball bounced off the top of Dr. Sinister's head. The little man reeled dizzily for a moment or two, then looked at Zap—the Wild Man from Borneo had fallen to the ground and was covering himself.

"You've got it!" said Dr. Sinister. He returned his attention to Crybaby. "The Major? You ask where he is at, and I fear I cannot morigerate, for the good gentleman is this moment in transit. Ask me his destination, though, and I will answer fleetly, Cape Breton."

"Cape Breton?"

"That very place! For it is there that dwells his lifelong companion and (in his opinion) saviour of the baseball team, Angus McCallister."

"He's gonna bring him back here?"

"Angus will no doubt come *motu proprio*."

"Hey, don't forget that Ambrose said only members of the troupe could play."

"Angus was with us for many years, and his contract, being as it was always nonexistent, has yet to be terminated."

"And this guy's big?"

"Big, yes," nodded the Doctor. "I search my fripperish vocabulary and cannot find a more apt word. Big. Suits Angus to a T, big does. Big."

"Good," nodded Crybaby.

"But old," muttered the Doctor. "Very old."

"Well," said Crybaby, "I guess I got all I need to know. Let's go go into town and get the stuff."

If Nathanael thought that going into town was merely a matter of climbing into the old pickup truck and driving away, he was sorely mistaken.

First of all the Hisslop sisters came up and gave Dr. Sinister a huge bag of laundry for the dry-cleaning. It was thrown into the truck. Tanya and Stella also had clothes to be laundered, although nowhere near as many as Daisy and Violet. Robert Merrill came up with a large stack of books from the public library, mostly poetry and historical romances. He then handed the Doctor a list of books he'd like taken out. Dr. Sinister scanned the list. "*The Light of Noon?* You've had that before, Robert." The Hippopotamus Boy moved his huge head laboriously and wrote on his little pad:

I liked it.

Dr. Sinister nodded.

Then the little Doctor began his own preparations. The troupe had a large caravan that served as a kitchen; Dr. Sinister went there first, armed with a little clipboard, and checked off various foodstuffs that were needed. He then went to his own caravan and spent several minutes inside, finally emerging with a tiny iron box, secured by a padlock. Apparently it was full of money.

The Alligator Man jumped up into the truck driver's seat, and Nathanael and Dr. Sinister got up into the cab beside him. Janus the wonderdog jumped into the back, nestling down among the library books and bags of laundry. Nathanael Isbister called to the remaining troupe members, who were standing around waiting to wave them off, "You guys keep on practising—just throw the ball around until you get used to its feel." They nodded and waved.

The Alligator Man rammed the starter until the engine sparked, then slammed his foot down heavily. The pickup truck raised a huge cloud of dust and roared away.

The Alligator Man was sullen on the way to town. He stared ahead determinedly and kept the truck moving at about seventy miles an hour. He took corners without slowing a bit. This distressed Nathanael (his foot constantly working an imaginary brake) but not the Doctor, who chattered happily above the rush of wind. "As I see it, we'd best proceed thus. We will stop at the sports equipment store—no, better to go to the laundry first—no, the library. Neither of you fine men have shown signs of nutation. I rethink, and conclude that you two had best drop me off, and go to the sports . . . Aha! But I have the money. Of course, I could always give it to you. This fremescence is not getting me anywhere. I shall silently ratiocinate . . ." (Which he does for three seconds.) "I have it!" Etc., etc.

Their first stop wound up being the sports store. Nathanael and the Alligator Man milled around, picking up bats and swinging them, putting on gloves and pounding their hams hard into the pockets. Nathanael would dump equipment that met with his approval on the counter, where the man behind it was tallying the figures. The Alligator Man, though, would ask Nathanael first, "Hey, Crybaby"—Nathanael cringed every time his nickname was used "what do you think of this bat?"

Finally all the equipment was piled up, except for the special items. Nathanael asked the man, "What's the smallest glove you got?" The man produced a tiny, tiny glove that was for tiny, tiny children. They took it.

Then they needed two big ones. "How big?" asked the store owner. While he looked on incredulously, Nathanael spanned almost two full feet with his hands.

"Jesus . . ." muttered the man. "I'll have to order them. No, wait a minute. Here . . ." The store owner disappeared down some stairs in the back, and returned a few moments later with two enormous gloves. "They sent me these for the display window," he explained. "I don't think they ever thought anyone would use them."

Just before they left, the store owner motioned to Nathanael. "You know how that guy kept calling you Crybaby?"

Isbister began to rock back and forth on the balls of his feet. "Yeah?"

"You Crybaby Isbister?"

Before Nathanael could say anything (he was about to deny it), the Alligator Man said, "Damn right he is."

"Son of a toad!" exclaimed the man. "Whatever happened to you?"

"He became a nun," answered Dr. Sinister, and the three men, each with a big box of equipment, walked out the door.

Driving away, the Alligator Man said, "What the hell's the matter with you, anyway? Anyone would be proud of being Crybaby Isbister, but you always say you ain't him, or you start bawling . . ."

Crybaby's fists balled up instinctively; he kept his silence.

The Alligator Man did not let up. "And what happened to your legs, anyhow? All anyone ever heard was that they got broke. Well, how did they get broke? And how come you gave up being on the radio, anyway? You must have been making pretty good money, eh? And how come you gave up writing for the newspapers, anyway? And how come you won't tell anybody that you're Nathanael fucking Crybaby Isbister?!"

Crybaby brought up a huge fist and began to swing it hard at the Alligator Man's face. Just before it hit, though, he pulled it back sharply—and began to cry. He buried his face in his hands, and they were soon dripping with tears.

He was comforted by Dr. Sinister, who told him, "I am just like you."

Through his sobs, Nathanael asked, "You are?"

"Indeed," said the little man. "I always deny being Crybaby Isbister."

They drove to the laundry, dumped the clothes, and went on to the library. That building sat in the town square, along with two hotels (The Fulton Arms, for one), city hall, and a liquor store. In the middle of it all was a large square of green grass, where old ladies wearing several sweaters sat on benches and tossed bread crumbs to pigeons.

"I shall go to the library," announced Dr. Sinister.

"I'm gonna go into the Arms for a while," muttered the Alligator Man. "How long you gonna be?"

Dr. Sinister did some mumbling computations. "Library. Patents . . . hmm . . ." and then said, "why don't you return in one hour?"

"Okay." The Alligator Man (his green hands thrust deeply into his pockets) jumped from the cab and marched into the tavern of The Fulton Arms.

Hearing a strange double-edged bark, Dr. Sinister said, "I note that the hitherto somnambulant wonderdog is again among the waking."

"I'll take him for a walk in that little park," said Nathanael—his eyes were just drying.

"If you wish," said the Doctor. They went to the back of the truck and unloaded the books and Janus.

Alone with Fido and Rover, walking him to the tiny park, Nathanael said, "That Alligator guy has sure got a chip on his shoulder."

"Yawp!"

"Stop that. I wonder what his problem is. He got a pickle up his ass or what?"

"Yawp!"

Nathanael laughed loudly. "I told you to stop that!" He took off after Janus, and they ran on to the grass. Nathanael's legs buckled under him painfully and he tumbled down, but before he had a chance to cry out, Janus pounced on top of him and they began to play-fight happily.

Around them, on the benches, old women with several sweaters on opened their eyes in horror at the spectacle of the man being attacked by a two-headed, five-legged dog.

My grandfather tells me, "Put in about me and that Alligator goomer in the barroom."

"Ancient asshole!" I scream. (I'm not usually like that, please understand, but these past couple of weeks with the old geezer have been pure torture.)

"Lez have a little respect for your elders, boy!" He brandishes his cane menacingly.

"Look, what can I say about you and him in the barroom?"

"See, I was in the barroom. Right? Just minding my own beeswax, trying to think my way out of a little problem I had, namely, this baseball business. So, I'm standing there at the bar, and all of a sudden this guy comes and stands beside me. And he just looks like anybody you might see in a barroom—little slapped-around kind of look, hard times, usual stuff. He says, 'Gimme a beer,' to the bartender, and the barkeep obliges him, naturally enough. But then this guy takes his hand out of his pocket to grab his beer—and damned if that hand ain't green!"

"So what did you think?"

"I thought, 'Lookee that—a green hand.' "

"And what else?"

"Nothing else. Just, 'Lookee that—a green hand.' "

"Ancient asshole," I mutter (not loud enough for him to hear).

He hobbles away, saying, "Lookee that—a green hand."

When Dr. Sinister came out of the library, his arms full of historical romances for Robert Merrill (and Abner Doubleday's official rule book for himself), he noticed a commotion in the little green park. Quickly dumping the books in the truck, he ran over.

The crowd was mostly young boys and old ladies. The women cried out things like, "It's the Devil's work!" while the children sang out, "It's a monster!" They threw small stones and pieces of wood.

In the middle of it all stood Nathanael and Janus. The dog barked and snapped defiantly with both sets of teeth. Isbister cried and bellowed, "It's just a dog! It's just a damn dog!"

Dr. Sinister sprang into the throng and held up his arms. "Ladies and gentlemen!" he called out in his most theatrical voice. There was an uneasy, chilled silence. "Ladies and gentlemen! Whether it be the work of Mephistopheles or nature's monstrosity is not for us to judge! We are merely spectators of existence! Howsomever, if you are impressed by the sight of Janus the Wonderdog, brought to you here on display, assuredly you would be impressed by the other prodigious eccentricities for which we are the vanguard! I am Dr. Sinister, manager of a troupe of truly wondrous people! Why, my good townspeople, if you were to visit our site (Highway 10 and Route 5), you could see the legendary Major Mite, the tiniest man breathing today! *You* could see David Goliath, descendant of the biblical Brobdingnagian! *You* could see the Hisslop sisters, beautiful naiads both, bound together forever by a fusing of flesh! *You* could see the Alligator Man, hideous and batrachian product of prenatal impression, empirical proof of that erstwhile theoretical scientific phenomenon! Why, *you* could see Tanya, the hirsute lady! The eldritch Hippopotamus Boy! *You* could see Zap, authentic and dasypygal denizen from pestilential Borneo! And Stella, the greatest example of gulosity, tipping the scales at eight hundred pounds! All of those wonders are yours to see, yes, it is true! Please extend this invitation to others of your acquaintance, and do not fail to accept it on your own behalf! Dr. Sinister's Troupe of Extraordinary Eccentricities is, for a short time, situated at Highway 10 and Route 5, admission a mere and pitiful fifty cents!" He began to drag Nathanael and Janus out of the circle. "Do not forget that name, ladies and gentlemen! Dr. Sinister's Troupe of Extraordinary Eccentricities! Thank you and good day!"

They put Janus into the cab of the truck and locked the doors. "Damn them," muttered Nathanael. Janus lay down on the torn seat, cradling both of its heads sadly. Crybaby looked around and noticed the liquor store. He took an involuntary step toward it and then swung around, back to the Doctor. "What do you have to do now?" he asked.

"I must (a) purchase some cigars for the Wrigley impersonation and (b) attend to on the behalf of Mr. Goliat (such being David's patronym) some business in the municipal building. Mayhap we should do (b) first, seeing as that edifice is right behind us." He jerked a thumb over his shoulder and they went in. Dr. Sinister walked down a hallway until he came to a door marked PATENTS OFFICE. He rapped lightly and walked in.

There was a tiny lady, quite old, with a pink pince-nez upon her nose. She sat behind a desk piled high with papers. When she saw Dr. Sinister, she allowed herself a small smile. "Hello, Poindexter," she said quietly, her voice as shy as mice.

"Hello, Amanda," said the little Doctor. "How are you?"

"Fine, thank you," she returned. "And yourself?"

"I am pretty bobbish, thank you, and all the better for your asking. This gentleman is Mr. Isbister."

"Pleased to meet you," said the old woman, and then she turned, very businesslike, to the papers in front of her. "Well, Poindexter, I believe there is only one new addition in Section 782, Subsection 7e, and I don't believe it is anything you and David would be interested in." She pulled out a sheaf of papers. "Here it is. The diagram is fairly explanatory."

Dr. Sinister accepted the papers and flipped through to the back. There he found several diagrams that depicted a coffin underneath the ground that was connected via a chain to a bell above the ground. Nathanael looked on with wonder. "What is it?" he asked.

"You see, it's a safeguard against being buried alive," answered the Doctor. "Should the buried party awaken with vitality and vitesse, he has but to pull the chain (which causes the bell to ring) and people will be alerted to his insalubrious predicament. But, as Amanda has noted, it is not the sort of thing we're interested in." He handed back the sheaf of papers to the woman. "Amanda, might I show Mr. Isbister No. 8738, Section 782, Subsection 7e?"

"Certainly," she answered. She went to a filing cabinet, rifled through for a bit, and extracted some papers. Dr. Sinister in turn handed them to Nathanael, who noticed immediately that the names at the top of the patent were "Poindexter Wilhelm Frip; David Gray Goliat".

Dr. Sinister pointed out a series of complicated drawings and measurements. There were various cross sections and close-ups of those cross sections.

"This is rather ingenious, if I do say so myself," said Dr. Sinister. "The sides of the coffin are some two feet thick, fashioned out of lead, and in this middle section here, you see—?" he pointed to a cross-section and Isbister nodded, "it will be electrified with the aid of a generator that is housed inside the coffin proper. Thus, it could not be cut open because the metal of the saw (in conjunction with the natural laws of physics) would cause an electrical shock of quite some little magnitude. In a word, zzzzaappp!!!" Dr. Sinister gave the papers back to the little lady. "David and I think it should suffice, although we're constantly checking to see if anything better should happen along. Ours is not foolproof, the elenchus being that the generator could break down, eradicating the electrical field. Goodbye, Amanda."

Dr. Sinister and Nathanael walked through the door. "Davey wants to be buried in that?" asked Crybaby.

"If that is the best that is available when his time comes."

"Why doesn't he get cremated?"

"Cineration is against his religious views. He is fervently religious, young David is."

"You know, Doc, Stella was telling me about that Dr. Hunter and everything."

"Yes, I know," said the little man.

"Well," continued Nathanael, "don't you think it's a little . . . whacky? I mean, maybe he's a little off in the head?"

Dr. Sinister shrugged his shoulders.

"I mean, maybe you should try to help him solve *that* problem instead. This Hunter guy's been dead for over a hundred years, for God's sake."

They were now walking slowly along the sidewalk, heading for a cigar store.

"Nathanael," said Dr. Sinister, "the human brain is an extremely complicated piece of machinery. The one we are discussing has been developing for over twenty years under rather unusual and remorative conditions. Myself, I lay no claims to understanding it. Years ago, a younger man, I might have done what you suggest, that is, I would have sat Davey down and explained cogently and rationally that Dr. Hunter was not to be feared, due to his being very dead. But now that I am older I am not so presumptuous as to think my rationality could battle the workings of that brain. Therefore, I offer him comfort.

"If a child is crying in the night, Nathanael, afraid of the darkness, you could say to him, 'Child, there is nothing in this darkness to fear. There are no bogeymen, ghouls, flibbertigibbets, or pigwidgeons.' But you would be missing a great point—to wit, that it was the darkness itself the child feared, and the darkness will always remain. And, dear Nathanael, it is a thing to be feared. Therefore, you hold the child, and that is all you can do.

"If David wants assistance in the construction of a Hunter-proof coffin, that is what he will get from Dr. Sinister. Besides which, there likely isn't time for anything but, in Davey's case. I am afraid that pituitary giants are not blessed with longevity; to be one is lethiferous. That is, young David's days are sorely numbered. Here is the cigar store—are you coming in?"

"I just remembered something I better do," said Nathanael. "Can you lend me five bucks?"

Dr. Sinister produced the money, saying, "Consider it an advance on your coaching remuneration."

Nathanael walked quickly to the liquor store and bought three big bottles of whisky.

Poindexter Wilhelm Frip was born in England a little over fifty years before this story took place. He was the fourth child of eleven, and poor children they were, too. Dr. Sinister's childhood reads like something straight out of Dickens. (It doesn't really, the way I write, but it *could*.) He was taken out of school at eleven and put to work in a factory that made boots and shoes. At fifteen, he joined the military by lying about his age and (trickier yet) his height. He fought until he was twenty.

Now, a careful reader will point out that someone around here is lying, either the good Doctor or myself, for Poindexter Sinister stated upon the public stage that he was apprenticed to one Merlin when he was fourteen. However, both of us are telling the truth.

Merlin (real name not available) was one of the young boy's co-workers at the shoe factory. He was, from all reports, a positively obscene old man. He sported a long, matted grey beard and had a wrinkled hole in his face where his left eye had been poked out. His ears were folded up as if someone had tried to put them into an envelope. His nose was red, bulbous, and constantly oozing white stuff. Merlin smelled as if he ate garbage (not out of the question), he burped and farted as if he alone inhabited the planet, and he had a nasty habit of picking his nose and ears, rolling the pickings into little balls, and flicking them skyward with his gnarled fingers.

It was Poindexter Frip, working beside Merlin at the factory, who first noticed that the balled-up pickings seemed to vanish when they reached their zenith in the air. At first he thought it was merely his imagination, so he spent the next few days watching carefully until he was absolutely sure. The pickings *were* disappearing. Then he spent a few more days trying to overcome his fear of the old man. Finally, he asked quietly, "How do you do that?"

The old man laughed grotesquely. "*Do* it?!" he bellowed. "I don't *do* it, boy! I don't do nuffin'. I don't do nuffin'." Merlin picked up a nearly finished shoe from in front of him. "I just ain't able to hold on to fings, that's all." The shoe vanished in a twinkling. "Can't hold on to nuffin'. Not jobs, not womens, not nuffin'. And then, as if all that ain't trouble enough, fings I can't 'old on to has a 'orrible habit of comin' back when I don't need 'em." The shoe appeared on top of his head. Merlin laughed his blood-chilling laugh. "See, boy? The shoe's on me *head!* It's on me bleedin' head! Not on me foot, where a shoe belongs, it's on me head!" Merlin laughed again, and Poindexter Frip, terrified by his first encounter with first-rate, top-notch lunacy, busied himself at his work.

Walking home, though, he found the old man behind him. "I can't hold on to nuffin'!" screamed Merlin, hobbling with a club foot that he kept bound in dirty-grey bandages. "Not jobs, not womens, not nuffin'. I'll stand ye to a draught, boy, aye, that I will do."

Any chance of declining ended immediately when Merlin grabbed the boy by the collar and pulled him into a pub. Although the lad struggled, it mattered not a bit. Merlin pulled him up to the bar and demanded two pints of bitter. The old man dug into a pocket and came up with two coins, which he handed to the publican. The publican turned away, and then back again. "Where's the money?" he demanded.

"I just gave it to ye!" shouted Merlin.

The publican studied his empty hands. "No you didn't."

"I'll not pay twice for the same mug!" shouted Merlin angrily. "If ye can't hold on to money with your fat, greasy fingers, that's your concern."

The publican was studying his empty hand. He had felt the coins being pressed into his palm, he was sure he could feel them in his fist, but when he opened it, nothing. Reluctantly, he turned away.

"Nobody can't hold on to nuffin'." said Merlin. "Drink away," he directed young Poindexter Frip. The boy raised his mug, huge in his tiny hands, and took a small sip. Initially, he wanted to spit out the strong, golden ale, but he forced himself to swallow. He felt the tiny bomb go off in his stomach, felt the heat spread around his body.

"That's a good lad," said Merlin. "That'll put hair on yer chest. You want hair on yer chest?"

The young boy nodded and shrugged that he supposed so.

"Why!?" shouted the old man. "You want to be a ape? You want to be covered with hair and look like a monkey?" The old man giggled under his breath. "All the young boys wants to be apes," he said quietly. "Take another sip, boy, so ye'll turn into a ape."

Poindexter Frip did so—it went down a bit easier this time.

"Boy," asked Merlin, "ye know how nobody can't hold on to nuffin'?"

The lad nodded.

"Ye reckon ye can hold on to sumpfin'?"

The lad nodded again, uncertainly.

"Well, 'ere, hold on to this watch." The old man passed him a gold-plated pocket watch. "Put it in yer pocket, quick, and hold on to it good."

The boy did so.

Merlin grabbed his drink and downed about half of it straight away. The beer trickled out the side of his mouth and rolled into his thick beard. He wiped away the drops with the back of his ragged sleeve. "Boy," he demanded loudly, "can ye read?"

Poindexter Frip nodded once more, taking a sip of his draught, a larger sip that went down almost smoothly.

"And how much do ye read?" asked Merlin. "A lot? Ye stay up nights to read?"

"I don't read that much," whispered the lad.

"Aye," nodded the old man. He brought his one eye closer. "Ye'll make a good ape, ye will. I can almost see the hairs poppin' out all over yer body. Still fink ye can hold on to sumpfin'?"

"Yes." The boy took another sip.

"Well, 'ere, you hold on to this billfold. Put it in yer pocket, quick, and hold on to it good."

Merlin took another large guzzle at his mug, leaving just a mouthful or two behind. Then he said, "Boy . . . where does dragons live?"

"They don't," whispered Poindexter Frip.

"Ah!" The old man stuck a twisted finger in the air and winked with his one eye. "I've long wondered about that!" he said. "I've long wondered where dragons live, but now I know that they don't. Still fink ye can hold on to sumpfin'?"

"Yes," muttered the lad.

"Well, 'ere's another watch ye can hold on to. Put it in yer pocket, quick, and hold on to it good." Merlin finished his drink quickly. "Now, aye-up, boy, down yer draught. I knows a place where they doesn't know me."

Poindexter Frip took a long series of small sips until his mug was empty. Then they left, just as a small commotion began among the men who were sitting near them.

Outside on the street, young Poindexter almost made an attempt to dash away from the old man, but he remembered the things he was holding and hesitated. Old Merlin saw his start. "If ye've got a mind to run away, boy, run away! It's a fing a ape's got to be good at, runnin' away—ye need yer practice."

"Your things," said Master Frip, and he began to dig into his pockets.

"Agh!" exploded the old man, and he produced both watches and the billfold from thin air. "Ye can't hold on to nuffin' neither! Nobody can't hold on to nuffin'."

The boy watched, open-eyed with wonder, as the objects returned to the nothingness they had come from.

"Now," shouted old Merlin, "I says I knows a place where they doesn't know me! Are ye comin'?"

"How do you do it?" asked Poindexter.

The old man turned away angrily and started hobbling off. "I told you, I don't do nuffin'. I just ain't able to hold on to fings."

The boy trotted after him.

"Nobody can't hold on to nuffin'. You shouldn't ask the same question twice, lad. Fink of a new one each time."

On the way, Merlin dashed into a pawnbroker's while the boy waited for him outside on the street. When the old man came out he had three pound notes in his gnarled fingers. From there they went into a pub called The Square and Compasses. Merlin sat the boy down in a corner and went to the bar for two mugs of draught. When he came back he said, "There's a young man behind the bar can hold on to his money. I doesn't begrudge 'em it if they can hold on to it." He chuckled mirthlessly.

They then proceeded to drink the night away, mostly in silence. Every so often, though, Merlin would speak to the boy. "Know why I works at the shoe factory, lad? Of course ye don't. I works there 'cause they makes me. The police does. If I quits or so much as misses a day, I'll be right back in Old Bailey. They fink it's gonna change fings. As if it could change anyfing. Ye know what's important, boy?"

The boy shook his head.

"Not bloody much, that's what." It was sentences like that one that plunged the two back into silence.

Meanwhile, young Poindexter was getting quite drunk, for the first time in his life. And as he looked around him, he felt a peace descend. It was as if a fat, six-foot pigeon had come down to nestle the boy in her bosom. Although all the faces he saw belonged to strangers (and most of them hardened and ugly), Poindexter felt a strong pull of brotherhood in his heart and wanted to touch them all.

And there was no face so ugly as that of his companion. When Merlin wasn't speaking, his mouth was curved into a cruel slashing frown. His one eye was dark and bloodshot and stared ahead as if sightless—where his other eye should have been was a red, wrinkled thing that looked for all the world like an asshole. When Merlin spoke, all of his features joined together in a kind of spastic dance, bouncing around mindlessly on the leather of his skin.

But even for Merlin, the boy felt affection.

"Ye like the drink, do ye?" snarled the old man, guzzling greedily at his own. "Well, there may be hope for ye yet. Boy," asked Merlin, "what would you call a lizzyard that were twelve foot long?"

"A lizard?"

"Aye, a lizzyard of twelve foot. What would ye call the beast?"

"I don't know," confessed the boy.

"It seems to me, boy, that ye might call it a dragon."

"I suppose so."

"Then ye've lied t' me!" the old man bellowed sorrowfully. "All the world asks, 'Merlin, why isn't ye a better man?' and yet they lie t' me each and every one! 'Cause ye said dragons didn't live nowhere, and yet they've got lizzyards of twelve foot and if that ain't a dragon, nuffin' is!"

"Where do they have these lizards?" asked Poindexter Frip.

"*Where?!*" shouted Merlin. "I'll not tell ye. It's in books, if ye care to know. Read books."

"Will you show me how to make things appear and disappear?" asked the lad hopefully.

The old man laughed loudly, so hard that it drove tears from his one eye and, oddly enough, even from the empty socket. And then he bent closer to the boy. "If ye tell me where the dragons is, I'll show ye how to make it *look* as if fings is comin' and goin'."

In the morning, Poindexter Frip woke up, sick and scared, with the first rays of the sun.

He was sick for reasons known too well to all of us. His head was foggy, his stomach screamed, his eyeballs ached, and death would have been a mercy.

He was scared because he didn't know where he was. He lay on the floor of a small room—a room that was more crowded than his caravan was to be some forty-odd years in the future. There were books and papers everywhere, all scattered about as if after a cyclone. There were globes and maps and empty bottles. There were clocks and magnifying glasses and telescopes and empty bottles. There were candles and inkwells and solar charts and empty bottles. In the middle of it all was a desk at which sat the old Merlin, working with a quill and ink. He was covered with black splotches.

There came to Poindexter Frip dim recollections from the night before. Of fleeing from some men who wanted to beat Merlin to a pulp (although he couldn't remember why); of staring at the moon; of trying to hit that same heavenly body with their urine; of singing songs that he had never known the words to (and singing them flawlessly, if his memory served); of Merlin's making things appear and disappear in a dazzling display outside in the night—apples, balls, candles, daggers, eggs, footwear (something for every letter of the alphabet if I cared to—the reason I don't is that it would not indicate that the thing most often produced was a beer bottle which the old man then made disappear in a fashion that even you or I could execute, although not so rapidly).

The Merlin that starred in these dim recollections was a different one. This one laughed a great deal, and danced with his club foot on the cobblestones, hurling out greetings at every animate and inanimate object, and was given to slapping Poindexter Frip on the back in a friendly, almost fatherly, fashion.

The one that stared at the waking boy was the old one again. He pointed at a lopsided bookcase and snarled, "We got a hour before the shoe factory, lad. Start findin' out where's the lizzyards." And then he returned to his own work.

Slowly and painfully, Poindexter Frip walked over and pulled down a massive leather-bound volume. The lizzyards were not there.

Poindexter Frip took up residence with the old man, both to spend more time in pursuit of the lizzyards and to ease the situation at his own home, which was sorely overcrowded.

It has been suggested that Merlin introduced the lad to such acts as buggery and fellatio; this may or may not be true. However, we know for certain that Merlin did take great pains to make young Frip carnally knowledgeable on the matter of the female of the species through a long succession of prostitutes that he brought up to his squalid quarters.

What business is it of ours, anyhow?

Some weeks later, the lad shouted with delight, dropped a book on the floor, and told Merlin that in some of the desert areas of the Americas there was a lizard called the Gila Monster, and that this creature had reputedly attained a length of twelve feet, tip of nose to tip of tail.

"And don't fink that's the only one, neever, boy! But it's enough."

Thus Poindexter Frip began his tutelage in the art of prestidigitation.

Merlin never admitted that he was employing sleight-of-hand when making things come and go. (He never denied it, either.) I feel that it was this reticence that made our Dr. Sinister such a firm believer in Magic (note that upper case!) and gave him the faith that one day he would just raise his hand and something would be there, just like that, and he wouldn't know how it had happened.

In the year that Poindexter Frip spent with Merlin, he learned much. He learned the art of magic (note that lower case), and he learned that there was far more to the world than the slummy London streets he was accustomed to. He made up his mind to see the rest of it, and accordingly joined the military.

So this stage of Poindexter Frip's upbringing is almost complete, except for one incident which I will now relate, thank you very much:

This particular evening began like many others—that is, with Merlin proclaiming, "I knows a place where they doesn't know me!" The two went out and began to wend their way toward it. (Incidentally, the boy Frip had become one of alcohol's biggest fans and was developing a capacity that was truly remarkable considering his diminutive stature.)

At any rate, en route to this place they passed an agitated throng of people. Investigating, they saw that the group (mostly young boys and old women) were busy pelting a man with small stones, and screaming, "It's a monster!" and "It's the Devil's work!"

The man (who had given up trying to bat away the rocks and simply stood there) was distinctly horrible-looking. His nose appeared to have been cut vertically down the centre, and the two halves pushed to either side of his face. His mouth was lipless and slanted, his eyes ill matched and asymmetrical. So the people pelted him.

Merlin dashed to the centre of the throng with a thunderous burst of the vilest obscenities. Still the rocks were thrown at the ugly man. Merlin snarled, grunted, and made horrible faces. One or two of the stones were thrown at him, but most still went at the ugly man. Finally Merlin withdrew his organ from his pants and shook it menacingly at the crowd. He was pelted with a barrage of rocks. Then he took flight, and the people pursued, throwing their stones at his back. For an old man with a club foot Merlin could move with surprising speed, but it still took him almost half an hour to lose all of the crowd.

Then, as the two sat exhausted in a pub, Poindexter Frip asked, "Why did you do that?"

Merlin's answer was shouted angrily. "Because it's *me* what deserves it, boy! *ME!*"

Chapter 3

IN 1908, JACK NORWORTH and Albert von Tilzer wrote a song that began, "Take me out to the ball game." The fact that this song has been popular for seventy years tells us something.

"It tells us," screams my grandfather, "that baseball is one hell of a game! It's man against the laws of nature, that's what it is. See, boy, once that ball gets wallopped, it's flying through the air like a bird. Just like a bird! It's nature holding it up there, just like a bird. Then it's the *man* gotta get it down. Get it?" (This is as eloquent as my grandfather waxes, I'm afraid.)

But the geezer has a point, one which Nathanael tried to impress upon his unlikely team. As he put it:

"Now, one thing you guys should never forget is that when we get out on that diamond, there's gonna be three forces in action. One is us, the other is Tekel and his bearded weirdos," (the troupe members chuckled loudly) "and the last one is Mother Nature herself. Now, she's not playing sides, she's just playing. She can be either our friend or our enemy, and what it depends on is how much we understand her. We got to be able to say, 'Okay, up at bat we got us a right-hander. He's standing like this here.' " Nathanael illustrated a typical pose. "Now, the pitcher's been pretty fast today, okay? All this stuff makes a difference. There's a strong wind headed from the north. So, you say to yourself, 'Mother Nature being what she is—reliable—I bet that ball's gonna come right over here.' Now, it ain't that easy, because the batter knows ol' Mother Nature too, and he's gonna try to trick her a bit. Right at the last moment he's gonna choke up on his bat, he's gonna spread his feet a little further apart, he's gonna turn to the right . . . he's gonna do *something*. But we're gonna keep our eyes open, and we're gonna think ol' Mother Nature, and we're gonna do okay! Okay?"

The players shouted "Okay!" in loud response, being very much taken with Nathanael Isbister's monumental enthusiasm. It is just

118

as well they little suspected that Crybaby's enthusiasm was merely a cover-up for an even more monumental depression.

"Okay," shouted Nathanael, "you all got your gloves on. Now, I'm gonna hit some out to you. Not only do I want you to think about catching them, I also want you to think about Mother Nature. Remember, from the time the ball touches the bat until the time it arrives in your glove, it's Mother Nature's game all the way. Now, go!"

As far as catching went, the team looked like this:

The Alligator Man was all right. He had an accurate innate sense, and started running toward the ball as soon as he heard the crack of the bat. His glove hand was sure and steady. Moreover, he played aggressively and was quickly bathed in a heated sweat.

Madame Tanya was also pretty good, although sluggish. Her movements seemed listless—but wherever the ball came down, Madame Tanya was there. If someone else was there to receive it, she would step back and let him. If she was there alone, she would snap at the ball, almost as if irritated, with a smooth arc. Then she would return the ball to Nathanael, throwing it "like a girl", that is, bringing it around, instead of over, her shoulder.

Dr. Sinister wasn't much good, simply because he couldn't run very quickly on his short, skinny, and aged legs. If a ball came close to him, however, he would pluck it from the air almost effortlessly.

The Hisslop sisters posed a problem. At first, they would both shield their eyes and quiver with fright, allowing the ball to land a foot or two behind the pair of them. Asked about it, it became clear that both sisters had expected the other to catch the ball. After that, the problem reversed—both sisters would try energetically to receive it, and their arms would get tangled and confused. The ball would again land a foot or two behind the pair of them.

Robert Merrill was, in a word, pitiful. His lack of mobility hindered him, but even so, he seemed remarkably uncoordinated. His gloved hand often waited feet away from where the ball would eventually fly.

As for Zap, the Wild Man from Borneo, it's hard to say. Sometimes, seeing his friends running for the ball, he would fly off behind them—and once or twice, by means of jumping on various backs and tripping up various legs, he managed to catch the ball. Most of the time he stood around idly, grunting and pulling various grotesque faces. His glove he switched from hand to hand, foot to foot, even covering the pin of his head with it.

Janus was by far the best of the bunch. He caught easily seventy percent of the balls hit by Nathanael. And the two heads were never in conflict either—it was if the two minds had worked out some complicated system of etiquette. One of the heads would pull away at the last second, and the other would get the ball.

Nathanael was wondering how he would tell them that they wouldn't be allowed to play.

So that's how we stand, thus far. Davey is still in his caravan, sleeping and dreaming a trouble dream. Major Mite is on a train.

If we look across the field they are practising on, we can discern a tiny silhouette. From this distance, it is obviously a four-legged creature, but we are too far away to say what particular kind.

Practice over, it is now late in the afternoon; Dr. Sinister excuses himself and announces that dinner will be ready in half an hour. The little Doctor takes Zap with him. The Hisslop sisters go to change—the Alligator Man leaves some seconds later, both eager and angered by the thought of seeing their naked bodies. Robert Merrill leaves to begin his new books. Stella and Tanya sit on the ground, savouring the last of the daylight, while Janus lies panting beside them. Nathanael Crybaby Isbister goes over and sits beside them.

Nothing is said for a long time, until Crybaby mutters, "You're pretty good, Tanya."

Madame Tanya shrugs manfully with her shoulders; the large melon-shaped breasts shake.

"But," continues Nathanael, "you didn't put much into it."

Tanya turns and looks dead into Crybaby's eyes. Her face is stone and untelling. "Why should I?" comes the mid-range husk.

"Well, if we're going to win this game, we've got to give it everything we've got," answers Nathanael.

"Two days ago," says Tanya, "if someone were to have asked me what I least wanted to do, I might have said play baseball."

"Oh yeah?" Nathanael wonders briefly why Stella isn't saying anything; she is merely listening patiently to the conversation.

"It seems to me that people should have better things to do than batting a little ball around and trying to catch it," says Tanya. She lies on her back and closes her eyes against the light.

It is Nathanael's turn to shrug, after which he is at a loss. After a few moments, Madame Tanya continues. "Maybe you were right,

Mr. Isbister, when you said that it was Mother Nature's game. But do you think that makes me think fondly of it? I'll tell you right now, I think Mother Nature is a bitch."

"Oh yeah?" responds Nathanael.

"Yeah," says Madame Tanya, as she pulls her fingers through her beard. The "yeah" has the "wanna-make-something-out-of-it?" tone that has caused so many fights through the years. Then Tanya sits up, her breasts rolling forward majestically. "Yeah," she repeats, and this time it is simply an affirmation, with no overtone or undercurrents. "I'll play," she tells Nathanael, "but please don't expect me to be enthusiastic about it. In fact, don't ever expect me to get enthusiastic about anything." She stands up and walks away toward her caravan. Following her with his eyes, Nathanael notes an alluring wiggle to her buttocks.

"Don't think badly of her, Nathanael," says Stella. Then she changes subject quickly, as she asks with a giggle, "Did you like my moral support at the practice today?"

Nathanael preoccupied, nods slowly. Then he asks, "Wanna go for a walk, Stella? I mean, I'll wheel you around, if you want."

"That would be nice, Nathanael. In fact, there is something I'd like to show you."

Crybaby fetches the wheelbarrow and pushes Stella up into it. His hard hands sink softly into her flesh and fat. Then she motions with her tiny hand in a certain direction, and Nathanael pushes off.

At dinner, Nathanael Isbister was silent. What Stella had showed him was a patch of dandelions—the weeds grew far away from anything, in a small cluster that measured only a few square feet. From a distance they looked normal, the bright yellow biting into the green and brown of the fields. But Stella had told Nathanael to look closely, and he had—to find that the dandelions were square. "Also," she told him, "they're twice as big as they should be." They were enormous, the heads of the weeds, and unmistakably rectangular, as square as they should have been round. Crybaby pulled one up to examine it.

"Ain't that something?" he muttered.

"I was the only one who knew about them," said Stella from her wheelbarrow. "I saw them while we were on a picnic, but I didn't show them to anybody, not even Poindexter. I thought it would be wonderful if they were left alone."

"Oh," said Nathanael. "Maybe I shouldn't have picked one."

Stella giggled. "Maybe you shouldn't have. Although sometimes there is a good reason for picking flowers."

Nathanael smiled and extended the weed in mock chivalry. "A flower, my good lady?"

Stella accepted it in the same spirit, turning her eyes away coyly and blushing a light pink. She held it gingerly between her plump fingers. "Now it's our secret, Nathanael," she told him. "Only we know where the square dandelions grow."

He nodded.

"And now," she said, "I guess we should be getting back for dinner. It should come as no surprise to you, Nate, that I am hungry."

Dinner, Isbister found, was all in all a pretty strange affair. The night's dish was spaghetti, which the Doctor had prepared in a huge cauldron on top of a black, pot-bellied stove. Robert Merrill did not partake of it, because his always-open mouth did not permit him to chew. He sat at the long table with a flask and a straw, the end of which he placed far into his orifice, to some point where presumably he could get some suction from it. He took very small pulls and worked hard at swallowing the stuff. Even so, a lot of it dribbled out and down his chest. The sight of the remarkably ugly boy eating in this remarkably ugly way did not seem to affect anybody (except Crybaby) in the little caravan that served as the dining place.

The Alligator Man hung his head low over his plate, shovelling the food in rapidly. Every so often he would turn his eyes up, mostly to the Hisslop sisters who sat across from him, and more than once in Nathanael Isbister's direction. It was a black look he was giving out—Isbister had a hard time ignoring it.

Daisy and Violet did pretty well, though, chatting amiably throughout the dinner. Daisy even told the Alligator Man, "Gee, Ally, I thought you played ball very well." For this compliment she received a very rapid black look, which bothered her not at all. Violet said, "I thought we all did very well, didn't you, Mr. Isbister?"

"Well," said Nathanael, still thinking of the square dandelions, "it could have been a lot worse."

"Davey's still not out of his caravan?" asked Daisy.

"I fear not," answered Dr. Sinister, who was busily hovering around the pot, dishing out the sauce and noodles. "I shall go see if I can't be demulcent after dinner."

Nathanael's appetite, which had been waning while watching Robert Merrill eat, now took a nosedive as Zap set upon his own meal. The little hairy man took up the spaghetti in his hands and spent a few moments trying to roll it into a ball. When he found that this was impossible, he simply stuck the mess into his face and began chomping and mulching and making all manner of revolting noises. In less than a minute he was through, his face covered with red tomato sauce. Dr. Sinister regarded him and tsk-tsked with his tongue. "Expect no invitations from the aristocracy, my boy," he said quietly.

Tanya and Stella were quiet throughout the meal, but for different reasons. Tanya was simply being sullen and untalkative. Stella's silence was due to the fact that she was far too busy eating to talk. Nathanael watched in disbelief as three, then four, then five plates of spaghetti disappeared into her.

"Ally," said Violet Hisslop, "are you going into town tonight?"

This was the question the Alligator Man hated most, for it meant that the girls were again in quest of a young man for their bed. He hated that question so much that he felt a violent need to get drunk, so he nodded simply.

"Will you take us with you?" asked Violet.

"Yeah, yeah, yeah," snapped the Alligator Man. "I'll take you in, but I ain't gonna wait around to take you back."

"We'll find our own way home," said Violet. Daisy looked up and said, "Thank you, Ally," She received no response.

"No hitchhiking, girls," said Dr. Sinister; having finished with the spaghetti, he was now dishing ice cream into little bowls.

Violet Hisslop looked at Nathanael. "Mr. Isbister, would you care to see the sights of Burton's Harbor?"

(The Alligator Man's head jerked up sharply to stare at Nathanael Isbister. Crybaby realized in a split-second what the chip on Ally's shoulder was, but needed no such unspoken threats.)

"No, thank you," he said. "I've seen just about as much of Burton's Harbor as I can take."

"If you care to," said Dr. Sinister, "you can assist me. I am once more to endeavour to teach our young Zap to perform a gay canard, namely, the Wrigley impersonation."

"Jesus Christ, don't you ever give up?" growled the Alligator Man.

"No," said Dr. Sinister.

Zap, having eaten the spaghetti with his hands, now undertook to get the ice cream into his mouth with the use of his knife and fork.

"You can visit me after, if you want," said Stella who was eagerly awaiting her first bowl of ice cream. "I don't have much to do in the evenings."

"All right," said Nathanael. He pushed his plate away to make room for dessert—there were three or four bites gone.

Janus was eating in the corner, where two bowls sat side by side. Both heads dug in wolfishly. Janus, too, was eating spaghetti.

Then dinner was over. Janus lay down promptly and went to sleep. The rest of the troupe members dispersed to pursue their singular activities.

Now, Dustin G. Wrigley, as even Nathanael Isbister knew (though he'd been out of touch with practically everything for a long, long time), was a famous politician of the day and had been in the limelight for over a quarter of a century. He was known to be honest, cards-on-the-table-wise. (Given the historical perspective I now have, I could dispute that, but what the hell.)

(Don't I use an awful lot of parentheses?)

Dustin G. Wrigley's one peculiar mannerism was the way he smoked his cigar. He held it between his second and third fingers, high up at the first knuckle joint. Therefore it was very easy to do an impersonation of him, and indeed, such impersonations were quite popular. All one had to do was hold a cigar in the prescribed manner and there could be no doubt who one was pretending to be.

This is why Dr. Sinister, in his never-ending pursuit of a more entertaining entertainment, had thought that for Zap to do this would be very titillating and tickling for the general public.

As can be gleaned by the Alligator Man's remarks both recently and in Book I, Chapter Four, Dr. Sinister had yet to be successful. It was easy enough to get Zap to hold the stogie correctly (all one had to do was place it between his hairy digits), but upon the first puff Zap would scream and hurl the cigar at some object distant or near.

Dr. Sinister and Nathanael walked out of the eating caravan, leaving Zap unattended for a moment. Then the little Doctor leaned over to Crybaby and whispered, "I have a new plan, and a subdolous one it is, too. Perhaps Zap's reluctance to smoke is based upon a formidolian incomprehension as regards how normal a social activity it is. True, he has seen me indulge. But he has seen me do a great many odd things, not all of which I have held up to him as exemplary. Therefore, Nathanael, when he comes upon us, he shall find us both smoking and enjoying it a great deal.''

Dr. Sinister waved his hands in the dusk, and two lit cigars materialized between his fingers. He handed one to Nathanael, who sat on the steps of a nearby caravan, and turned to fetch Zap.

"Hey, Doc," called Nathanael, turning the little man around. Crybaby gestured with his cigar. "You know where these smokes came from?"

Dr. Sinister nodded. "I know," he said quietly.

In a moment he came back, leading Zap by the hand. Zap's eyes darted about suspiciously, as though he knew something was afoot.

"Mr. Isbister and I are just enjoying a halituous refreshment," said Dr. Sinister. "Isn't it halituously refreshing, Mr. Isbister?"

Nathanael drew on his cigar deeply, exhaling with a pleasured sigh. "You bet, Doc," he said, "it sure is fine."

"For centuries," continued Dr. Sinister, "civilized man has sought sensual pleasure in tobacco."

"You bet," said Nathanael.

Zapper's eyes moved from one to the other slowly, narrowly.

"Yum yum," said Dr. Sinister.

"It sure is good," said Nathanael.

Suddenly Zap let loose with something that was half yowl, half grunt, and began pawing the air frantically.

"Oh, would you care for one, Zapper?" asked the Doctor. "Certainly, my boy, certainly." He produced one (from the pocket of his worn tuxedo), lit it, and put it into Zap's hands, Wrigley-fashion. "Puff," he told the hairy little man. "You will enjoy."

Zap crossed his eyes as he raised the stogie up, so that he could keep his eyes on it. He put it to his lips, pulled in, and then screamed.

If Nathanael hadn't jumped up, the cigar would have hit him right between the eyes.

"No, no, Zap, it's good!" said Dr. Sinister, winking at Nathanael. "It is merely what we term an 'acquired taste'. Isn't it delicious, Nathanael?"

"Yeah," grunted Isbister, staring hard at the pinhead.

By this means, in a minute or two Zap was grunting-yowling for another cigar. One was lit and handed to him. Nathanael, taking no chances, crept around until he was standing directly behind the little man as he took his first puff. However, if Nathanael hadn't jumped up, the cigar would have hit him right between the eyes.

They repeated this process seven or eight more times—and no matter where Nathanael moved to, it seemed as if he was always jumping out of the path of the burning cigar.

Dr. Sinister was plainly exasperated. "I've only one more plan for this luctation," he sighed. "If this fails, then the general public shall forever be denied the pleasure of a Wrigley impersonation as performed by a Wild Man from pestilential Borneo." He took out a cigar, lit it, and handed it to Zap. "Here, son," he muttered, defeated, "have a smoke."

Zap looked at the cigar for a long time, his furry brow furrowed. Nathanael ran for cover behind one of the caravans. He listened for the outraged howl . . . it didn't come. When he peeked out (expecting a smouldering projectile), he saw Zap lying on the ground in a relaxed fashion, puffing peacefully on the cigar.

"It worked!" he shouted. "It worked, Doc!"

Dr. Sinister, sitting on some caravan steps, was cradling his head in his hands and looked far from pleased.

"What's the matter, Doc?" asked Nathanael. "It worked, didn't it?"

"Yes," muttered the Doctor. "I was trepidatious, though, that this would happen. That particular cigar, Nathanael, is imported from Havana, and costs almost two dollars."

He sighed again; both men watched the Wild Man from Borneo puff happily on his cigar.

After that, Isbister went to the little tent that served as a showplace and home for Stella the Fat Lady. He found her, seated on her throne, thumbing through a huge pile of yellowed newspapers.

"Hoddo," he said, pushing aside the curtains that made the doorway.

"Hello, Nate!" she responded happily. "Boy, were you ever a good baseball player!"

Isbister shuffled with his feet despite himself, and once more indulged in the idiosyncratic mannerism of driving one finger into the palm of his hand. "You been reading about me, eh?"

"Yes, indeed. Look here . . . 'Goldenlegs Isbister once more stymied the opposition by his astounding field work. He batted a single, two doubles, and a homer for his team and kept Olson, the losing pitcher, at bay for fear of his ability to steal bases. This young man (only twenty-three) may well prove to be the sport's greatest player.' " She laid the paper on her lap and asked, "What's all this keeping the pitcher at bay business?"

The question relaxed Nathanael, mostly because it didn't have anything to do with what really happened to him. He sat down on the floor in front of the throne, beneath Stella's pudgy feet. "Well, in baseball you can steal bases. See, if a guy's on first base, he can kind of sneak to second base while the ball's in the air from the pitcher to the catcher. So the pitcher has to keep an eye open to make the play to first so the runner won't try anything. See, he can throw the guy out . . . catch him while he's off the base. What the paper means is that the pitcher was so worried about me stealing bases that he couldn't concentrate very well on pitching to the batters. Get it?"

"Nope," giggled Stella.

"Where'd you get all those papers anyhow?"

"I've kept them. For no special reason, I guess—I just find it impossible to throw anything away. They're from all over the county . . . this one's from Peoria, here's one from Boston . . ."

"That one you got there must be fifteen years old."

She looked at the date and nodded. "I was just starting out with the Doctor then. I've been with him longer than anyone."

"How old were you?"

"When I first started? I would have been eighteen, I guess."

"So how'd you get started in this business?"

"Well, there was no troupe of extraordinary eccentricities back then, there was just the Doctor. He travelled around the country in a little caravan, pulled by an old nag named Floyd. And he put on magic shows.

"I was a pretty lonely girl back then. I suppose I only weighed about three hundred pounds, but still, life wasn't much fun. I was working in an office as a secretary—everyone there thought I was some kind of monster. The other girls used to giggle every time I walked by. And as for boyfriends—well, forget it. So I spent a lot of time by myself, going to plays and movies and museums and art galleries and anything new that happened along. So I heard about the magic show, and I went to see it.

"Well, you've seen Pointy do his stuff. It's pretty amazing, isn't it? I was spellbound. And he looked such a nice man, too. He wasn't bald then, and hadn't so many wrinkles, but his eyes were the same. Those gentle, old eyes. So I kept going to see him again and again. Every night I'd be there—and sometimes I'd be all alone in the audience. Anyway, one might after the show he came up to me and said—I'll always remember—he said, 'I trust you do not keep coming in order to see me make a mistake.' He just made a nice little joke. So I laughed and said no, then he said, 'I'm glad, because Floyd and I are leaving this very night and having not made any mistakes thus far, I was very much afraid that we would leave our most frequent patron unsatisfied.' Well, Nate, when I heard he was leaving it almost broke my heart. It's hard to put into words. It's just that Dr. Sinister and his magic and his old horse Floyd and his tiny rickety caravan had so little to do with the world—with the world I was living in, the world where I was laughed at, where money and business were all anyone cared about, where . . . I mean, Pointy's world just had nothing to do with any of that. And it's not as if Pointy was trying to escape from the rest of the world. His world seemed *realer*, somehow. And even if it wasn't, at least I felt at home in it. I felt at home for the first time in my life. So I asked him if I could come along. Just like that— five minutes after I'd met him. And he said yes, without a moment's hesitation.

"Now, Nate, don't think it was Pointy's idea to exhibit me as the fat lady. I became his assistant in the magic act. But I kept gaining weight, and gaining weight, until finally it was almost impossible for me to move. Then I suggested I be the fat lady, and Pointy said all right.

"And then the other members came, one after another. The first two were the Major and Angus. You haven't met Angus yet, but he's a magnificent creature. When we first met them—it was in Atlanta—they were drunks. You see, their manager, Morris M-for-Magnus Mulcher, was the only one who could keep them under control, drinking-wise. When he died, they fell apart.

"So, one night they came to a show. Nate, it was the funniest thing I've ever seen. In reel these two drunks, covered with mud, their clothes torn and old, screaming and swearing and waving whisky bottles around—and one's the tiniest thing you've ever seen, just the size of a little boy, and the other is *monstrous!* Enormous! They started to heckle us, saying that I was fake, that I had to take off all my clothes to prove that I wasn't really four or five people. They said that the Doctor was doing his act with mirrors, and that they'd seen better shows in washrooms. As much as I love them both now, I'd have to say they were vile.

"And when they finally quieted down, Pointy said, 'Major Mite, Mr. McCallister, I am deeply honoured to make your acquaintances.' Nate, those two old drunks just broke into tears on the spot. They came and hugged Pointy, they kissed his forehead; they shook his hand so much I was afraid it would fall off. We put them to bed, we cleaned them up, I sewed them some new clothes—and they stayed with us.

"Next came little Zapper, from out of nowhere. One morning we found him sleeping on the ground outside of the caravans. He had a little note pinned to him that said, 'This boy is a total idiot, incapable of speech or thought. I felt that perhaps his gruesome appearance might make him useful in your show. He is yours, if you want him. The boy is called Zap.' It's still a mystery where he came from, but he seemed happy with us, so we didn't spend much time trying to find out.

"Janus was brought to us by a farmer. He said, 'Lookee this doggee. He's yours for three bucks.' Janus was just a pup. The farmer was scared stiff of the little thing, and would have given him to us, probably would have paid us to take him. The farmer said that the dog's name was Fido and Rover. So Pointy gave the man ten dollars, changed the name to Janus, and the dog's been here ever since."

Nathanael was about to interrupt, to note his preference for the former name, but Stella talked eagerly on . . .

"Bobby . . . Merrill, the Hippopotamus Boy . . . we found in a little train station—that is, the Doctor did. Pointy was going off somewhere (I can't remember why—it probably had something to do with one of his ex-wives), and at the train station there was a little commotion. Bobby had fallen asleep on one of the benches there. In those days, he used to wear a hooded cowl, like a monk, to hide his face. But the stationmaster had pulled down the hood while he was asleep, and he'd called the police. Bobby was sick—he had a fever and he hadn't eaten for weeks—so he was trying to fight. Pointy stopped the police and said he'd look after the boy—and that's what he's done ever since.

"Nate, if you only knew what Bobby has been through . . . and he was just fourteen when he came to us. He's never had a home; he's just been wandering around the country, only daring to come out at night, going through garbage to find something to eat . . ."

Stella was silent for a moment, but then, remembering the thread of her story, she continued on.

"The Hisslops came to us after that. They were quite famous, and working for one of the really big shows, but they were having trouble with their adopted parents. If you want to call them that, 'parents'. They were a couple of real heels, these two. They more or less bought Daisy and Violet from their family, put them into show business, and never gave them another thought. The woman was a drunkard—she'd spend her spare time beating them. The man was a drunkard, too—but he spent his spare time doing different things to them, if you get my meaning. So, when the girls turned twenty-one, they ran away. They'd run away before that, understand, but the police kept bringing them back. Now that they were of age, there wasn't a thing their 'parents' could do . . . and so they've been here ever since.

"Next came Madame Tanya and the Alligator Man. They'd been working the same carny, somewhere in Florida, but it folded, so they came to be with us.

"And then, just about a year ago, Mr. Goliat came with his son Davey. This is the first show Davey has been with—he'd wanted to be a lawyer, and he'd even gone to college. He was just able to squeak through a year or so—then he went and grew a couple more inches, and he had to quit. He couldn't hold the pencil in his hand anymore, and it took him too long to get from class to class. Not only that, but his eyes were getting weaker, and the Dr. Hunter dreams were getting worse. So there was only one thing left for him to do—come be with us.

"We had a Rubber Boy up until about a week ago—that's whose caravan you're staying in. But he was just a young man, and a little restless, so he left. And Angus left too, I'm not really sure why. He said he wanted to farm some land up in Cape Breton, where he was born. I'm not sure. The Major misses him pretty bad—they've been best friends ever since the Major was fifteen years old.

"So that's the history of Dr. Sinister's Exhibition of Extraordinary Eccentricities. Now it's your turn."

"My turn?"

"Yup," nodded Stella. "Please forgive my curiosity, but it's as fat as the rest of me. Can't you tell me something about yourself?"

"Not much to tell," grunted Isbister.

"Nate," said Stella, reaching for another newspaper, "these are full of stories about you, about how good you were, until we get to this one—" She held up a yellowed paper and pointed to a story on the front page. "You know what it says?"

Nathanael shrugged. "Not exactly."

She read from it. " '*Nate Isbister Hospitalized.* Goldenlegs Isbister, baseball's wonderboy, was brought into St. Mary's Hospital today suffering from injuries to his legs. The nature and cause of the injuries are not known, but doctors said it is highly unlikely that he will ever play again. They reported that Isbister sustained multiple fractures and lacerations. Isbister himself was either unwilling or unable to comment.' "

"Stella—" began Nathanael.

"And then, we have these papers." She grabbed for another. "Not with stories *about* Nate Isbister, but with stories *by* Nate Isbister." She pointed to various articles, all on the subject of sport, that bore Nathanael's name on top.

"Stella—" Nathanael began again.

She spoke in a quiet voice. "Nate, don't tell me anything if you don't want to, but—there's so much here. There must be so much in you."

"There isn't," he protested. "It's all there, in those papers."

She smiled gently. "All right, Nate. We'll talk about something else."

Isbister got to his feet. "Not tonight, Stel. I've had a long day. I think I'll turn in."

"Mad at me?"

"Hell, no, I ain't mad. I'm just tired." He walked to the doorway, then turned around to half face her again. "I ain't mad," he said, and then he was gone.

Isbister found Janus asleep in front of the door to his caravan. "Ho, there, Fido! Ho, there, Rover!" he called. The dog jumped up excitedly. "Come on in," said Crybaby. "I'll fix you a drink."

When the Hisslop sisters returned home (with a young man in tow) they saw that the light in Nathanael's caravan was still burning. Daisy and Violet were both quite drunk, but the sight sobered them for a moment. In the silence they heard a low moaning and soft sobs. "I wonder," asked Daisy, "if he's all right?"

Violet shrugged. "I guess so," she said.

"Maybe we should go see," suggested Daisy.

"He's a big man," said Violet, "he'll be okay." Violet took the young man's arm, and they pulled him toward the caravan.

Daisy asked, "Do we have any gin at home?"

"Haven't you had enough?" countered Violet testily.

Daisy's response was a simple, "No."

For all her truth and honesty, Stella has been misleading both Nathanael and us. She has implied that she began life plump and continued to pack it on from the word go. Perhaps she herself has come to believe this; perhaps she simply sees her first fourteen years of life as insignificant. The fact remains, however, that during these years it was only Stella's cheeks that were fattish, and pleasantly so. Her first woman's body (which came early, at age twelve) was as well proportioned as one could imagine (and I, stuck as I am in this place with the old geezer, can imagine some lulus!).

Stella Stinton was born in Albany, New York. Her father, Oscar, was a salesman, specializing in the recently developed storm window, which he sold door-to-door. Nowadays, in her more pensive moods, Stella would often speculate that the irony of her existence started here, right at the beginning—for on beastly days, days full of thunder and torrential rains, her father's business would boom. While other children's dads—carpenters and painters—would see the downpour and decide to stay at home, Oscar Stinton would clap his hands joyfully, grab his samples, and plunge outdoors. He would come back soaked to the bone but grinning broadly. And at dinner he could not stop talking—"They never think they need 'em until you show them that they do. 'Lookee that rain sperl the rugs,' I tell 'em. 'Jumpin jeepers,' they say. 'Gimme some o' them gizmos!' " Oscar would laugh loudly and eat with good appetite.

Oscar Stinton's wife was of German stock, a pleasant woman, but rather on the simple side. Her life revolved around food. The daylight hours were devoted solely to its preparation—sausages, cabbage rolls, wiener schnitzel, latkes, varenyky, potatoes in every conceivable permutation. If something good happened, it was cause for a feast of epic Roman proportion. If someone were feeling poorly, food was the only reasonable cure. And if things were rolling along normally, a good, hearty meal would ensure that they continued to do so.

So Mr. and Mrs. Stinton had rather insular worlds, separate and self-contained, yet dependent upon each other. The father's was concerned totally with storm windows—from this world came money, which was transported across to the mother's. This world produced food, which went back to the father's, where it would fuel the selling of storm windows. Back and forth across a six-foot universe. This intergalactic reciprocal trade agreement worked well, except that it was too small to include Stella's world. For it was a child's world, and infinitely large.

When Stella asked a question, her father would say, "How should I know? All I know is storm windows." Her mother would say, "How should I know? Eat, *Liebchen.*"

Then there was Janet.

Stella had been walking home from school one day when a commotion attracted her attention to a tiny hillock that lay in the middle of a field. On the top stood Janet—she had hiked up her schooldress so that her underwear was plainly visible, the better to free her legs, which she was using to dissuade pretenders to her reign of the small summit. These pretenders, all of them boys, could make no headway. Each attempted ascent was countered by a well-placed kick which sent the boy rolling down again, howling miserably. And while she awaited another, Janet would twirl around gleefully, laughing at the top of her voice. The boys were being beaten so badly that they had lost all interest in Janet's panties (which was what had drawn them there in the first place—she had been dancing) and had only one thought in mind—control of the hill. But even a coordinated mass assault from all sides was ineffective; Janet's feet, landing on faces and groins indiscriminately, proved too daunting.

As Stella neared the fray, the boys decided to call it off, and were backing away sullenly. One boy called out, "Anyways, we kin all see yer unnerwear!", and the others, hoping to add sting, pretended to laugh. Janet, regarding them with a small smile, reached down and pulled the panties to her knees, still holding the dress well above her waist. The boys turned and fled, much to Janet's delight. Then she noticed Stella. "What are you staring at?" she demanded. "Don't you have one?"

Immediately Stella sensed the challenge, the exhilaration that it offered. "Sure do," she returned. "Prettier than yours."

"Let's see it," said Janet, and Stella promptly and proudly displayed herself. Janet regarded her studiously and said, "Well, yours has more hair, but I don't think it's prettier."

"Maybe not," nodded Stella, and both girls pulled up their pants. Then they began to walk together, in no specific direction.

From that day forward they were fast friends. To Stella, Janet was almost the key to the mysteries of the universe. It was not that Janet knew things, because she didn't—but she knew where to look, and she was not afraid of barriers or closed doors.

And more than that, she was fun. One day, Stella told Janet about her father's business, the selling of storm windows. Stella did not comment on it one way or another, she merely stated, "My dad sells storm windows." There was volumes more she wished to say, but she had no words.

It didn't matter—the next day Janet showed up with a pair of wire-cutters. "Come on," she ordered, "let's go get some of them storm-windows." And they sneaked down the backyards, first breaking the glass, then ravaging the wire inside.

(Until, of course, Oscar Stinton mentioned at dinner [vegetable soup, roast lamb, mashed potatoes, carrots, peas, turnips, devil's food cake and ice cream], "Business sure is booming. Some punks been bustin' the windows, and the people says, 'Some punks been bustin' 'em, sell me some more.'")

As they grew into their bodies, Stella and Janet spent long hours comparing them. "We're both gonna have big tits," Janet would say. "But you got bigger hips." These conversations inevitably turned to the topic of sex, and the girls would wonder if it was as much fun as they suspected it was.

Before long, Janet had proof positive. "It hurts, but I like it." Janet was lucky in that her first man, a black gardener in the employ of her parents, was too much of a gentleman to cause her unnecessary pain, and was also gently instructive in the ways of lovemaking. Stella's first, a gigantic boy named Clifford, was clumsy and insensitive; Stella could not decide if she like it or not.

Janet, though, found it absolutely delightful and devoted much time and practice to it.

One day Janet told Stella that she was pregnant; she did not seem particularly worried, although Stella (a fraction more sensible) was distressed. "What are we going to do?"

Janet had wormed information out of the family cook, without the cook ever suspecting that she was being grilled. "It's easy," Janet said. "All we do is this . . ." and she explained.

So it was that one night while Janet's parents were out at a dinner party, the plan was put into action. First of all they rounded up all the pillows in the house and tied them to Janet with some rope Stella had stolen from her father. They bound them to Janet until she was as round as a balloon, a fat white mountain, with just her thirteen-year-old face showing through somewhere near the middle. Then Stella, at Janet's request, pushed her friend down the stairs.

And the worst by far of Stella's memories is the sight of the fat-with-pillows girl bouncing down the stairs and cracking her head open on a small table at the bottom.

Stella can hardly remember what happened after that—she went for help, the doctor came, Janet was taken away. Sometime after that she was talked to by Janet's father, who told her that no one must ever know how this thing happened (and no one ever did).

Janet died four days later, and Stella (in a secret message from Janet's father) was forbidden to attend the funeral unless she wanted to face a criminal charge of manslaughter.

But Stella found that from the hillock, the hillock where Janet had once been queen, she could see the cemetery. She watched from there.

And Mrs. Stinton, alarmed at the sight of her frail and despondent daughter, said, "Eat, *Liebchen*, eat."

Stella ate.

Chapter 4

THE NEXT MORNING, Nathanael awoke, horribly hungover, in a damp bed. The bed was damp both from tears and the sweat that comes from troubled dreams. His mouth was dry and lined with fungus, his head pounded—involuntarily he reached for the bottle of whisky. It was empty. He found another, a quarter of it gone, and drained a long shot down his throat. Then he rose from the bed. Being as he was already dressed, Nathanael had no reason to linger. His intention was to hit the road as soon as possible. Isbister put the bottle of whisky into his pocket, grabbed his travelling bag, and left the caravan.

"A problem, Mr. Isbister! A rebus! A sticky wicket! A most illaqueating situation!" Dr. Sinister stood directly outside. Nathanael heard the low hum coming from the big-top and realized that a show was in progress.

"Doctor—" Nathanael began.

"I am in a phrenesis, and I shall tell you why. In the cursitatic excitement of these past few days, I neglected to alter the advertisement so that it might convey with more verisimilitude the content of our extravaganza. To wit, I left erected a billboard proclaiming the participation of a man with elastic skeletal propensities, in the vernacular referred to as a Rubber Man. Alas, we do not have one; we have a paralipomenon. Whereas the greater part of the general populace would allow the oversight to pass by unchallenged, the crowd today contains an egregious lout who claims to be a connoisseur of this aberration. He has demanded a full refund, and the rest of the crowd has espied an opportunity to retrieve their funds by claiming umbrage to this same deficit."

"Doctor—" began Nathanael again.

"I recall that the Major once exclaimed thus: 'You can bend your finger to touch the back of your hand!', the second person singular referring to your good self. He concluded that you were a Rubber Man, if he had ever seen one, which he has. So although it

136

reflects a parvanimity as regards your talents, it behooves me to concur with the Major in this observation. Yes."

"Doctor—"

"Therefore, if you would be so kind as to perform this feat before our disgruntled audience, you would save the daily intake of funds, which, as ever, is sorely needed."

Soft touch Crybaby Isbister put up little argument. True, he had resolved to leave directly, but he did owe these people something. He followed the little Doctor to the big top. The little man led him through a gap in the back that led to stairs. These led to the portion of the stage that was hidden by the curtain. There he found most of the members (including Major Mite, who had returned) in a profound state of agitation.

"The boogers is getting restless!" exclaimed the midget. "They say they're gonna get the police and god-knows-what-all!"

Listening to the noise from the other side of the curtain, Isbister recognized it immediately. He had heard the sound before, when crowds figured that a boxing match had been rigged, or that the odds had been fiddled with after the gates went up at the races.

Daisy Hisslop touched his shoulder lightly. "Please help us, Mr. Isbister."

Dr. Sinister raced through the curtains. They had to strain to hear his voice above the crowd's rumble.

"Ladies and gentlemen! Ladies and gentlemen! I am not a man that is easily insulted, but this time I feel the true pangs of hurt! To think I would proclaim the existence of something that did not exist—oh, I am cut! I am cut!"

As he listened, Nathanael felt a tug on his trouser leg. He looked down and saw the Major. The little man's face was collapsed in wrinkles to form a wide grin. "It's okay, Nate," he said, "I got Angus—I saved the team."

Isbister had no chance to respond, being as the next words he heard from the Doctor were, "The Amazing Rubber Man!" And then there was silence.

He parted the curtains like a virgin peeking out from the bathroom on her wedding night. He could see little in the darkness. Zap sat in his little cage—he, too, was expectantly quiet, training his uneven eyes on Nathanael. Dr. Sinister was extending a hand to him, motioning for him to come forward. Nathanael took short, hesitant steps until he stood near the front of the stage.

As his eyes adjusted to the gloom, he began to see eyes—like stars at dusk, they brightened one by one, until there was a sky full of them. Nathanael suddenly felt spellbound, hypnotized.

He was nudged by Dr. Sinister, and a small portion of his senses returned. His "gulp" as he swallowed was plainly audible in the quiet. Then he raised his left hand, extended his forefinger, and with his right, bent the digit back until it lay flat along the back of his hand.

The crowd burst into cheers and applause, and Nathanael took the opportunity to mutter, "*Damn* that hurts!" under his breath. He smiled weakly to acknowledge the ovation, and fled the stage. He noticed that Zap, with a grave expression on his hairy face that hadn't been seen before, was bringing his hands together steadily and evenly.

Behind the curtain, the other members were grinning broadly. Daisy and Violet jumped to embrace him, and Nathanael had the pleasant sensation of having four pert breasts pressed against his chest at the same time. Many voices congratulated him—one from high above, one from down below. One—Bobby Merrill's—was an unintelligible groan, but its tone was unmistakable. Dr. Sinister joined them and pumped Nathanael's hand enthusiastically.

Despite himself, Crybaby began to grin. With a double-edged yawp, Janus flung himself up into Isbister's arms and began to lick his face with two long, wet tongues. Despite himself, Crybaby began to laugh and allowed himself to be borne outside the tent, within their circle, like a hero.

Isbister looked over toward Stella's little tent. He saw, heading toward it, the young stone-faced man in the black leather jacket. The young man kept his head lowered to the ground, and worked methodically at flipping a small rock ahead with the point of his boot.

The Major ran up to Nathanael and pulled insistently on his sleeve and trouser leg. "Hey, Nate!" he shouted. "You gotta come meet Angus! He's in my caravan resting up!"

"Hey, okay," said Crybaby, grinning broadly. He was feeling good for the first time in a long while. "I've heard a lot about him."

He followed the midget to one of the caravans, one that was smaller than the rest of them. Major Mite raced ahead, threw open the door and shouted, "Hey, Angus, you awake?!"

"Aye, Donny!" came the answer.

Nathanael followed the Major up the tiny stairs.

The whole of the caravan's interior had been scaled down to suit the Major. The bed was small, and the chairs were miniscule.

Nathanael saw, on a tiny bedside table, a framed picture of a lady's face—the face was rounded and smiling, appealingly female. The walls were covered with broadsides and posters advertising the Major at various stages in his long career.

But Isbister had little time to notice anything, for what gripped his attention most was the giant. He occupied the whole of the caravan's interior, where, hunched over, he was executing a Highland Fling.

Although seven feet two inches is almost two feet shorter than Davey Goliath, Angus McCallister presented a much more awesome sight. He was bigness personified. Every part of him was big, but big with strength and muscle. As Angus danced, he swung his arms around loosely. Crybaby gasped as the mammoth mitts flew about, hands that dwarfed even Davey's. And as Angus's booted feet hit the floor, they made thunder-like booms and crashes.

The giant's face was mostly hidden by shoulder-length white hair and a beard that rolled almost to his waist. What could be seen was a pair of grey eyes and a long, grinning mouth. From this mouth, hummed softly and melodically, came the accompaniment for the fling.

Angus stopped his dance when he noticed that the Major was not alone. He then stepped backwards and sat down upon the bed, which served him like a foot stool. He slammed his hands upon his knees and said, "So this must be Nate Isbister."

The Major motioned Crybaby forward. "This is him, Angus."

Angus McCallister tilted his head and looked at Nathanael. His grin stretched even longer then, and he reached forward, seeming to span the length of the caravan. Nathanael put his hand into the giant's, feeling like a five-year-old shaking with a full-grown man. He realized, in a panicked flash, that if Angus chose to he could crush his hand to a pulp. But the giant's grip, although assuredly firm, did not hurt a bit.

"I've long wanted t' meet ye," announced Angus. His voice, rough-edged with age, was a majestic boom that filled the air. "An' I won't ask what became of ye, neither, for summit became of me, and it's nobody's business but mine." He then glanced over to the midget. "Ah, Donny! How went the show?"

The Major sat himself down in a tiny rocking chair that sat in the corner. Nathanael saw the faded bunny rabbits on the back, and realized that the chair had been made for a child. "It went okay," said the Major. "Some rube started complaining on account of we didn't got no Rubber Man, but then Nate here got up and bent his finger back and did real good." The midget smiled at Nathanael.

"What ye should have done," said the Giant from Cape Breton, "was come fetch me. I could have settled matters reet easily enough." For the purposes of demonstration, Angus drove a fist into the palm of his hand. There was a slap as loud as twenty belly-flops. Angus then winked impishly at Nathanael.

"Hey, Angus, guess what?" asked the Major.

"Reet!" shouted the giant merrily. "I'll guess. Uh—theer's twenty-five harlots lined up withoot, an' they've amassed their total fortune of four thousand dollars, twenty-five cent, and are beggin' to give it to me if only I'll lay with them, all at the same time!" Angus laughed, with a jolly Ho! Ho! Ho!, looking like some sort of super Santa Claus.

"Naw, you addled nimrod!" countered the Major. "That ain't it."

"Aye?—not it, eh? Well, then—I guess that ye've been elected President of the United States."

"Naw, you brawny baboon—and you don't got no more guesses. We're having a party for you tonight."

"A party? For little me?" Angus feigned wonderment. "Ah, it's lovely," he sighed. "Tell me, Donny, will there be any girls there?"

"Well, you ain't met the Hisslop sisters yet. They're gonna be there."

"Ah—I've heerd of 'em. An' they're lookers, if ye ken my meaning?"

"Real good-lookin'," said the Major. "Ain't they, Nate?"

Nathanael nodded. "Real nice," he said.

"An' I get two fer the price of one?" asked Angus. "What grand fun. Or did ye want one, an' I'll have t'other, Donny?"

"Naw, I don't do that stuff no more. 'Sides which, they're in the show."

"How 'bout ye, Natty? What say, I take one, ye can have t'other—an' we'll switch halfway through, in case there's any difference twixt the two."

"No thanks, Angus."

"Suit yourselves, I'll have the both of 'em, then. Oh, I've just thought of summit—s'posin' one of 'em takes a fancy t'me, but t'other wunt to use me head for a cobblestone. What then?" Angus laughed joyously. "That'd be a fix, that would!"

"I think they'll both like you, Angus," said the Major. "They're kinda hot-to-trot."

"Outstanding!" shouted Angus, and in his enthusiasm he stood up. With a crunch, he ran his head through the roof of Major Mite's caravan.

"You ape!" shrieked the Major, jumping from his little rocking chair. "Look what you done!"

Angus's "Ho! Ho! ho!" chimed down through the hole in the roof.

Major Mite circled around the giant's legs, hitting at them with his tiny fists. "And you did it right over my bed, too—if it rains it'll fall right on me!"

Angus's laughter continued, unaffected by the blows being showered upon his legs.

"You galoof!" shouted the Major, and then he too began to laugh. Soon he was rolling on the ground and clutching his side. Whenever his high-pitched laughter began to wane he would glance up at the hole and commence anew.

Crybaby was laughing too—some of it at Angus, his head out of view, some of it at the sight of the tiny man on the ground.

Soon the Major's laughter turned to painful coughing—at that point the Ho-ho-ho stopped, and Angus descended until he was seated again on the bed. "All right, Donny," he said quietly. "Ye'll hurt yerself."

Major Mite struggled to compose himself, and then the three men found themselves silent, except for the occasional exhausted giggle.

Then Dr. Sinister came into the caravan. "Mr. Isbister," he said, "I was undergoing ratiocination as to the likelihood of your whereabouts, and here I find you. By my calculation, it would be advantageous to begin practice now, to maximize usage of the sun's beatific light, which as we all know, is not everlasting."

"Goddam it, Doctor!" shouted Angus. "When are ye going to learn to talk *English?*"

"I'm sorry, Doc—I forgot," said Nathanael. "We'll start right now. Come along, gentlemen." He smiled at the Major and Angus.

"Come on, Angus!" chirped the Major happily. "Let's see you bat a ball all the way to Hell and Honolulu!"

"Aye . . ." The giant's voice was surprisingly quiet. "Well, truth t' be told, Donny lad, I've jest now begun t' feel a wee bit tired after the long haul here."

"Aw, come on, Angus—you never get tired."

"Not true, not true. 'Sides which, I want t' conserve me energy fer the evenin' sport that we were discussin'." He winked slyly.

"But we gotta practise," said the Major. "We gotta show those religious freaks a thing or two."

"I ken how t' play baseball," said Angus, almost angrily. "I was playin' it afore ye learnt how not t' beshit yerself."

The Doctor interrupted. "I feel Angus's fatigue is understandable. Perhaps it would be best if he remained here, where things are discubitory, and joined us tomorrow."

"Aye! Tomorrow fer sure!" said the giant. "I'll stay here, where things is whatever the hell the Doc said, an' then t'morrow, Donny, I'll hit that ball so hard it'll burst jest like a balloon. I promise ye."

"Well, okay—you go to sleep, then."

"Aye, Donny lad, reet t' sleep is where I'm gone. You go practise."

"Okay." The Major walked slowly out of the caravan, followed by Dr. Sinister. Nathanael turned back to say, "Nice meeting you, Angus."

The giant, for the moment, was staring ahead. Isbister noticed that his face, unsmiling, was a bed of slack wrinkles. His eyes were dull and unfocused. But then the grin came springing back, along with the grey twinkling.

"Aye, nice t' meet ye, Nathanael," Angus said. "Now, go practise. I'm restin' up, fer the Horselip girls." He winked again, and Nathanael left the caravan.

So that day there was almost a full turnout for the practice. Davey Goliath came; the Major was there. Everyone came except Angus who, as we know, was resting in the Major's caravan.

(Actually, though, he was doing no such thing—as soon as McCallister found himself alone, he bounded up on to his feet and started his fling again.)

Not only was it a really good turnout, but they were beginning to look like a team. Everyone had a glove, and there were numerous baseballs and bats lying about.

Nathanael shouted, "Okay! Now yesterday we did catching. Right?"

They shouted, "Right!" in enthusiastic chorus.

"Today, then," said Crybaby, "we're gonna start on batting." Nathanael took off his coat and folded it until it resembled the pentagon of home plate. Setting it on the ground, he told the members, "Okay? This here is home plate. Now everyone line up here."

And he showed them to file out along one side of the folded, flat coat. They did so.

"Now, I'm gonna pitch to you. And you're gonna try to hit 'em. Now in baseball you got balls and strikes and fouls and all like that, but we're not gonna bother with it today. Today you're gonna try to hit everything. Got it?"

"Got it!" they answered.

"Okay, then. Now, there's a great big pile of bats there. Some weigh more than others, some are longer. When it's your turn, search through until you find one that feels comfortable. Now, who's first?"

Nathanael ignored Janus's double-edged bark and Zap's loud shriek. The only other voice was a rough, high-pitched, "Me!" that came from Major Mite.

"Okay, Major," said Isbister.

As the midget searched through the bats, picking them up and swinging them ("Naw, too heavy . . . naw, too heavy . . . naw, too heavy . . ."), Nathanael motioned Dr. Sinister to come over.

"Yes, my good man?" said the Doc.

"Now, you watch how I pitch. It ain't a matter of just throwing the ball, there's a lot of leg leverage and stuff. Stand beside me and watch the way I grip the ball."

"Right-o," said the Doctor. He backed away a foot or two and squinted in order to scrutinize Nathanael more closely.

Eventually Major Mite found the smallest, lightest bat. He put it over his shoulder and walked over to the coat/plate.

Nathanael realized, with a silent chuckle, that it would be virtually impossible to throw a strike against the Major, being as the official strike zone lies between the batter's knees and armpits. Then he realized that this was offset by both Angus and Davey—even a blind man could throw a strike against them. Crybaby shrugged and threw the ball.

The Major swung with a loud, "Oooof!" and ticked the ball high up into the air. "Shee-it!" he screamed.

"No, that's good, Major. At least you're making contact."

"You wanna see contact, Crybaby? Throw that boogerish ball again!" shouted the Major. Ally picked up the ball and returned it to Nathanael.

Crybaby threw the ball again—a good, fast pitch that fell right in the Major's zone—and the midget swung. There was a "pop", and the ball dribbled out along what would have been the third baseline.

The other troupe members applauded and cheered. Nathanael thought, an easy out, but he said nothing.

"I'm gonna whap tar outta that thing!" shrieked the little Major. "Throw that booger at me, Crybaby!" Major Mite swung his tiny bat menacingly, making it whistle in the air.

Nathanael's third pitch curved to the outside; the Major's swing missed completely. There came an uneasy silence, accompanied by the shuffling of feet, while Major Mite began to colour crimson. "One more time," he muttered softly. "Just one more, that's all I want."

The pitch came, and this time there was a loud "crack!" The ball flew up into the air, a long, graceful pop fly into centre field. The troupe members yelled, "Hooray!" and jumped to congratulate the Major. The midget, squinting into the air with his aged eyes, watched the flight of the ball and seemed satisfied. He threw away the bat and walked over to sit on the grass.

"Okay, Major," said Nathanael, "you did real good. Who's next?" Again he had to ignore the bark and the grunt. No other voice came, however. "Tanya," said Nathanael, "you're up."

The bearded lady was seated a few paces away, removed from the rest. She gave Isbister a sour look and lumbered to her feet. Pulling up the bat that lay on the top of the pile, she approached the plate with it dragging behind her. Spreading her legs far apart, she assumed a good batter's crouch and menacingly hiked the bat skyward. Her dark eyes, half-closed against the sunlight, stared hard at Crybaby.

She hit the first ball—and not just lightly, either, but with what seemed to be every ounce of strength she had. It sailed away into the empty fields. Tanya dropped the bat, turned away, and picked up the hem of her skirt so that it wouldn't drag in the dirt. She went to where she had been sitting and plopped down. The ball was just landing, far away.

The other members cheered, and Nathanael called to her, "Tanya! That would have been a home run! A goddam home run!"

"Bully-bully," muttered Tanya, and she lay down. Her breasts rolled lazily to either side of her.

Robert Merrill, sticking his hand up into the air, indicated that he wished to go next. Nathanael said, "Okay, Bobby," and the Hippopotamus Boy walked (his huge head cradled in the special neck-brace) to the pile of bats. He sifted through them for a short time, coming up with a mid-weight.

As Bobby Merrill loomed over the plate, Isbister thought, "This should throw off Ambrose's technique a little." It would be hard to pitch to somebody whose head looked as though it had been made in plasticine by a moron. Bobby Merrill's own thoughts were concentrated only on hitting the ball, which he had determined to do.

And he sure gave it a try, too. He missed the first couple of throws by a full foot, but gradually he narrowed it until his bat was whistling only an inch or two away from the ball. But by the end of fifteen minutes he had missed them all.

"Okay, Bobby," said Nathanael. "You're getting the hang of it. Go rest up."

Because the huge lumps of his face buried his eyes into black and unseen caves, it was impossible to tell that the Hippopotamus Boy was crying. He let the bat drop to his feet and then wandered away from the plate.

Little Zapper ran to the pile of bats, wrestled with them for a moment or two, and came up with the biggest one, which he dragged over to the plate. He pulled it up into the air and began to thrash with it, emitting a long series of grunts and squeals.

"Doctor?" asked Nathanael.

The little man was still intently watching Nathanael's pitching style, so he merely shrugged distractedly.

"I may as well give her a whirl," decided Nathanael. He waited a moment for Zap to stop his mindless flailing, but the hairy man seemed to have no intention of doing so. Isbister lobbed the ball slowly toward the plate.

There was no break in the thrashing, but somehow the bat connected with a "pop", and the ball rolled forward some twenty feet. Zap immediately took out after it, hitting it again, croquet-style. He pursued the ball throughout the field, cracking it ahead with the bat. The other members called out to him imploringly, but he paid no attention. He screamed and yowled, thrashing the ball ruthlessly. Finally, the Doctor, Ally, and Isbister lit out in pursuit.

Because the hairy man's battings took him in a mindless circle, the three men spread out. But whenever Zapper came close to one of them he would look up, yowl, and swing the bat high, forcing them to take evasive action. Dr. Sinister talked to him soothingly, Ally shouted, and Nathanael waited patiently.

One of Zap's hits popped the ball into the air—without thinking, Isbister took off after it. He jumped up, grabbed the ball with an outstretched hand, and then collapsed to the ground, screaming painfully.

Through his tear-filled eyes, Nathanael made out the form of
Zap standing above him. His little head was tilted out of curiosity,
and he made grunts that had the tone of concern.

"Legs," explained Nathanael—it was an anguished shout that
just barely made it out between the sobs.

The Alligator Man and Dr. Sinister came over and helped Nathanael to his feet.

"Are you all right?" asked the little Doctor.

"Fine," said Crybaby from between clenched teeth. "I don't
need no help." He threw off their supporting arms rudely, and
took short pained steps away from them. "I'll be fine," he muttered,
calmer now. "Leave me alone," to no one in particular. "Fuckin'
legs."

The Alligator Man came up beside him, a curious expression on
his face. "Nate—" he said softly.

"What?" Isbister wasn't going anywhere specific; he was simply
walking a crooked line, staring down at his feet.

The Alligator Man brought his face closer and spoke in a whisper.
"Nate—I never seen anyone run that fast in my life."

Nathanael swung around—the Alligator Man was smiling. It was
a shy smile, not used to being seen. It trembled, wanting to vanish,
but Ally forced it to remain while he looked at Isbister. Nathanael
watched the smile and thought hard, trying to find something to
say. This is what he came up with: "You're up to bat, buddy."

Ally then allowed the smile to drop and said, "Okay, Nate."

The Alligator Man hit three out of five balls thrown at him—he
would have got a couple of singles, maybe a double. Nathanael
knew that Ally would become one of the team's best hitters,
though, once he'd learned some of the finer points, some of the
tricks.

Between pitches the Alligator Man would turn his head slightly,
looking at the Hisslop girls. At one point Daisy caught his gaze
and called out, "Hit it good, Ally!" The Alligator Man's blush was
made even more obvious by the contrasting green of his neck.

When he was finished, the Alligator Man dropped the bat on the
pile and went over to stand beside the girls.

"You're gonna be our star," said Daisy, brushing him lightly on
the shoulder. Ally turned his head quickly to look where she had
touched.

"Yes, indeed," agreed Violet.

"Did you see Nate run?" asked Ally.

"It hurt him," said Daisy; Violet added, "He said he wouldn't
play, anyway."

"He's gotta play," murmured the Alligator Man.

The conversation (which, incidentally, was a rarity—the Alligator Man hadn't really spoken to the Hisslop sisters for weeks and weeks; even he didn't know why he was in such a good, outgoing mood) was cut short by Nathanael's yelling, "Ladies?" and pointing at the pile of bats. The two girls, a flurry of giggles, danced over to it and sorted through, each coming up with a bat. Then they walked over to the plate; Violet, the right-sided sister, wanted to approach the plate from the left, Daisy from the right. They talked about it in hushed tones for a minute—then the hushes quickly grew into whispered shouts.

Nathanael intervened, and told them that they were a switch-hitter. The girls turned their lovely (slightly glazed) eyes toward him. "A what?" they asked in unison.

"You're a switch-hitter—a guy who can hit from either the right or the left. A guy like that can really screw up a pitcher. So we'll practise Violet from the left, Daisy from the right. Okay?"

They agreed, and Violet picked up her bat. As her sister practised swinging, Daisy ducked down low to avoid getting hit in the head. Violet missed the first pitch and said something under her breath that made Daisy down below go beet red and cover her ears in shame. The second pitch Violet ticked for a foul. The third she drove along first base into shallow right field.

"Little practice and you're gonna be okay!" said Nathanael. "Let's have a look at Daisy."

As they crossed to the other side of the plate, Violet suggested something that made Daisy giggle very loudly. Then, Violet crouching over, Daisy practised a bit—her results were about the same as her sibling's although she seemed a bit more pleased with herself.

The Hisslop sisters walked back to their spot beside the Alligator Man—he acknowledged their return with his shy half-smile and a quick nod of his head.

"Who's left?" demanded Nathanael.

Although Davey Goliath said, "I," Isbister was sure that no one had answered. "Who's next?" he repeated loudly.

Davey increased his voice level until it was just barely audible. "I am left, sir," he said.

"Okay, Davey," said Isbister.

Davey Goliath let his canes drop to the ground and walked slowly to the pile. He stared down at the bats, swaying slightly, for a long time before he asked, "Would someone please pick up for me the one that has 'Mudville Special' written on it?"

"Sure thing, Dave," said the Alligator Man—he ran to the pile and plucked it out. It was a mammoth bat, long and thick, but in Davey's hands it seemed as miniscule and fragile as a toothpick. Cradling the bat as if it were a baby, Davey walked over to the makeshift plate. He raised the bat, staring through his thick glasses at Nathanael, and said, "I am prepared, sir."

Isbister pitched a slowball that cruised almost leisurely through Davey's strike zone. Davey did nothing.

"Davey—" Isbister had started speaking at exactly the same moment that Davey started his swing. He brought the bat around slowly, weakly, but when the swing was through, Davey bolted forward. Everyone realized in a horrible moment that he was about to fall over, but no one could get to him in time. With a weak groan, like the last ounce of air from a flat tire, Davey Goliath pitched forward and fell to the ground. He toppled from almost nine feet, flat on to his face.

Nathanael rushed over and rolled him (not an easy task by any means) on to his back. One of the coke-bottle-bottom lenses was cracked and there was a trickle of blood from his lip. "I missed," announced Davey—and then he passed out.

Listen. This is the author. Sneaking out of his bed late at night, carrying the typewriter into the bathroom, muffling the cracks around the door with towels, and picking out the letters very gingerly so as not to wake up the old bastard in the next room.

Haha, you say, he's come to tell us all about Nathanael Crybaby Goldenlegs Isbister's background. Whatever happened to him.

Unfortunately, that's not why I'm here. I promise you information about Crybaby, but not right now.

I have two novels under my belt, and in each case, I bogged down some hundred and a half pages in. It's crap, I tell myself—then I throw the pages around, screaming, "If the wine is bad, throw it out!" (That's what Charlton Heston, playing Michelangelo, says in *The Agony and the Ecstasy*.) After this comes a period of spiritual cleansing—Charlton/Michelangelo wanders around some mountains and God hurls a bunch of beautiful, cloudy vistas at him. Myself, I just mill around and get drunk and hang out with my buddies, stuff like that. After about a month, I resume work.

But this time—

Just after Davey passed out, I tore the page from the typer and told the geezer, "That's it for now, geezer. I'm going out."

"Whaddaya mean?" the geezer demanded, sitting up on the couch and scratching himself violently. "Next, they takes Davey to his caravan."

I stuck a yellow piece of paper into the machine and petulantly banged out: THEY TAKES DAVEY TO HIS CARAVAN. I tore it out and showed it to the geezer, who took about a minute to read it.

"That's good," he decided. "That's good writing."

"I give up!" I screamed. "I can't take it!" I began to throw around the pages. "If the wine is bad, throw it out!"

The geezer scrambled around on his hands and knees, gathering the pages up, clutching them to his frail and wheezing chest. "Knock it off, asshole!" he shouted. "You're mixing them up!"

"It's crap!" I hollered. "Crap, crap, crap!" Soon all the pages had been the route—from my hands to the floor, from the floor to my grandfather's chest. I stood in the middle of the room, exhausted by my Charlton Heston impersonation. The geezer, protecting the pages like a lioness protecting her cubs, went back to his couch and sat there staring at me. "What's crap about it?" he demanded after a long while.

"Everything! Look, I don't know anything about this place, Burton's Harbor. I don't know anything about carnival freaks or about the House of Jonah. I don't know anything about baseball!!"

"That all that's bothering you?"

"What do you mean, 'That all that's bothering you?' That's enough, isn't it? I mean, I've got a reputation at stake. My job as a writer is to see the world for exactly what it is. To see it, dissect it, and explain it. To pinpoint with devastating precision its strengths and weaknesses."

"Uh-ya," nodded the old geezer, and he dwelt on it for a bit. "What's your point?"

"My point!?" By this time I was screaming rather insanely. "My point is that this stuff reads like a fairy tale! Who's gonna believe this dumb baseball business? And even if people believe it—what the hell difference does it make? WHO CARES?!"

"Everybody cares," he said slowly. "Just no one cares all the time, that's all."

"Look, we'll start at the beginning. First of all there's Nathanael Isbister, right?"

"The late, great Nate Isbister."

"Now he's an interesting character—but you won't let me say a word about him."

"You said whole bunches about him."

"But nothing *meaty*. Nothing . . . real, or gutsy. Like what he did."

"Forget what he did."

"I want to write it!"

"He's dead now. It don't matter what he did. Only thing that matters is the baseball game."

"The baseball game doesn't matter!"

"Of course it matters! If it didn't matter, I wouldn't be making you write about it, now would I?"

"Okay, okay, okay, forget Isbister. Take all the others. Now, how much do I really know about them?"

"What I tell you."

"You don't tell me anything . . . meaty."

"Told you the Hisslops was hot-to-trot."

"Yeah, yeah. So what?"

"Well, how much more meatier do you want it boy? That's four tits, four buns, two—"

"I am perfectly capable of doing the arithmetic involved . . . geezer."

"Watch who you're callin' a geezer!" cried the geezer.

"You don't understand. The book is crap."

"It ain't crap. I think she's real nice. Lookee this page here . . ." He shuffled through the papers and drew one out. Then he groped around the coffee table until he found his reading glasses. Sitting them on the end of his bulbous nose, he read aloud, " 'Zap be . . . gan to rise . . . fing . . . ers . . . (whew, here comes one long as a cat's tail) . . . lab . . . or . . . ee . . . us . . . lee . . . laboreeusly . . . bitting . . . at . . . his . . . his . . .' "

"His tongue, you fool, his tongue!"

"Yeah, his tongue. Now that's real nice writing."

"What was the last novel you read?" I demanded.

"The last novel I read was called *The Fisherman's Folly*, by Willy Wodon. So there!"

"Do you know that there are great works of literature out there? Tough, gutsy stuff that says something about life? Hard-hitting, no-holds-barred, teeth-sunk-in-flesh-type realism?"

"That's what Willy Wodon writes! He had this one part where the girl gets gang-banged by one hundred and three dockworkers."

"You don't understand!" I screamed—then I went back to my desk and sat down. I was on the verge of tears, I'll admit.

My grandfather took off his reading glasses and stared at me. After a long silence, he said, "Oncet, I was walking along the beach, and I saw an open clam shell. And I looked down, and there in the middle of it was a pearl. A perfect white little pearl. So I took that pearl, and I carried it around with me, and when I'd meet a body, I'd say, 'Lookee what I found.' 'How'd you find it?' they'd say. 'Walkin' along the beach. It was sitting in a open clam shell.' Then they'd say, 'Bullshit.' But you know what I found? I found that if I told them that I found an old dead fish on the beach, and that I'd tore its guts open, and that the pearl come spillin' out along with a can-opener and an eight-by-ten of Vivien Leigh, they'd scratch their heads and say, 'Imagine that.' "

"What's your point?"

"My point is, finish the book or I'll nail you to the wall."

"If the wine is bad, throw—"

"If the wine is bad," said the geezer, "get so drunk you can't taste it."

Chapter 5

"IF THE WINE is bad," commented Poindexter Sinister, "it's because it is of my own distillation—conspissate of wild dandelions."

Angus McCallister, who was pulling at a bottle of the stuff, said, "No such thing as bad wine, Doctor, only bad drinkers." Then he turned with a suspicious look to Major Mite beside him. "Ye donna like it, Donny?"

The Major scowled irritably. "It's okay, Angus—I just don't . . ." He let the sentence hang in the air for a moment, then he walked over to the table that held the food.

They were partying in the main tent—Poindexter Sinister had laden two long tables with cold cuts and meats. He had also provided many bottles of his homemade wine. There was an old, crank-em-up Victrola in the corner that sent forth various types of music—now a J.P. Sousa march, next a strange work by Charles Ives, weird discords, insane melodies.

The Hisslop sisters, already well into their cups, danced to it all. They twisted like ancient Egyptian deities, slowly, their eyes closed. Violet held a flask of gin in one hand, which she put, now and then, to her own lips and to her sister's.

Their dancing had diverse effects on the men. Dr. Sinister clucked his tongue and shook his head wistfully, with a small half-smile beneath his walrus moustache. The Alligator Man also shook his head, but his look was grim—he immediately attacked a bottle of dandelion wine with great vigour. Angus McCallister obviously found the performance delightful. He stomped with one huge booted foot and made thunderous clapping sounds. He whistled and shouted, "Bravo!" at the top of his voice. Bobby Merrill rocked his enormous head slowly back and forth. Davey Goliath sat stone-still in a corner, and, although it was hard to make out his eyes beneath the thick glasses (especially with the one now cracked lens), he was obviously training them on the Hisslops. Zap, off to one side, was mimicking the girls, but his movements were grotesquely lurid. The Hisslops' movements were lurid, it's true, but not without an easy and beautiful grace.

Only two of the men seemed totally disinterested—Major Mite, who busied himself at the food table, preparing a huge sandwich, and Nate Isbister.

Crybaby was standing beside the doctor, a glass of wine in his hand, staring at his feet. His look was perplexed.

Dr. Sinister noticed the look and after a moment asked, "Do you like the wine, Mr. Isbister?"

Nathanael's head bolted up with a "hmmm?"

"Do you like the wine?"

Isbister said absently, not knowing where he'd heard it, "No such thing as bad wine, only . . ." He let the sentence fade.

Stella and Tanya sat over to one corner, talking in hushed tones. Tanya had put on a party dress, one bright with polka dots, with a neckline that swooped low. She had trimmed her beard for the occasion, too. Of her appearance, she told Stella, "I hate it."

"You look wonderful, Tanya," said Stella. She reached out with a hand and stroked the bearded lady's coarse bobbed hair.

"I look like a fool," murmured Tanya, and then she too looked at the dancing Hisslop sisters.

"No. No, you don't," said Stella, almost to herself.

By this time, Major Mite's sandwich was almost a foot tall. He had engrossed himself with piling things upon it, but now, as he capped it with a piece of bread, he turned away, leaving his creation, and walked over to Angus. The giant and the midget stared at each other for several seconds until Major Mite said, "So maybe I do."

Angus nodded. "I'm afraid ye do indeed, Donny." He held out his wine bottle. Major Mite, reaching up, took it from him and began to drink.

"We all do," said Angus.

On his little notepad, Bobby Merrill had written:

They dance like the wind,
Their bodies twirl and spin.
With the beauty of a tree . . .

He was stuck for a finishing line.

The music changed to a polka, but the Hisslops continued to twist their bodies slowly.

"Did you know," Stella asked of Tanya, "that Nate is very famous?"

" 'Nate'?" asked Tanya.

"Nathanael. Mr. Isbister. He's very famous."

"No, I didn't know," said Tanya, and that put an end to the conversation.

"Mr. Isbister," said Dr. Sinister, with a nose that shone a little ruddily, "as you are aware, Mr. Isbister . . . I have two goals in life. One is to perform Magic with a majisculity. The other is to find the ultimate entertainment. Yes. Toward this latter end of refocillation, I am always on the perusal for additions and alterations. One source of inspiration to me has long been an encyclopedia, which was a wedding gift presented at the nuptial festivities in honour of my sanctified cohabitation with Loretta, she being my third spouse. Er, my fourth. I digress, due to this muriatic beverage. This encyclopedia, or rather set of same, being as it is comprised of—hic!—one volume for every character in the Roman alphabet, except the couples P and Q, and X, Y, and Z which share housing in the same volume—hic!—where was I? Oh, yes. Just today, in my searches, I unearthed a most interesting fact, which demands feneration, although I do not yet know to what it will lead. Being as you are a sportsman, I shall henceforth report it to you, in the spirit of good-natured, idle, party-type mussitation. More wine?"

Nathanael extended his empty glass, and Dr. Sinister filled it to the brim. Before continuing, both men glanced about them.

Angus McCallister had joined the Hisslop sisters in the middle of the tent and was waltzing with them. Their faces were pressed into the lower regions of his stomach, and he seemed to span both of their backs with a single hand. Davey Goliath had pulled himself up on to his canes and was slowly making his way toward Madame Tanya. (To ask her to dance—she was strong enough to hold him up.) Zap was tormenting Bobby Merrill by doing an imitation of him. As the Hippopotamus Boy sat, his huge head rocking slowly in the neck-brace, working on a piece of paper, Zap, with a sheet of newsprint and a hunk of charcoal, pretended to be doing the same. Ally and Major Mite were talking over in one corner:

The Alligator Man said, "You see how fast Nate ran this afternoon?"

"Fast as a snowball in hell," muttered Major Mite, his eyes swimming dreamily in his head. "Know what Angus is gonna do? Sleep with Daisy and Violet."

"*Says who?*" demanded Ally.

"Says himself, which is good enough for me. He wanted I should take one, but I says no, on account of them being in the show and all. I wouldn't mind, come to think—"

"Couple of dirty old men," muttered Ally. "That Angus must be ninety years old."

Major Mite grabbed for another bottle of the dandelion wine. "Old, old, old, old!!" he shouted. "Everyone around here got a limited vocabulary. Seems like that's the only word I ever hear is 'old'. Old, shit!" He put the bottle to his mouth, holding it up with both of his tiny hands.

"There is an island named Crete, which lies off the coast of Greece," said Dr. Sinister.

Nathanael saw that Stella was sitting by herself in one corner, Tanya having left to dance with Davey. He wanted to go sit with her, but Dr. Sinister was talking—besides which, Stella didn't look particularly unhappy. Her face was smiling, as she took in all that happened around her.

"Long, long ago," continued the Doctor, "they practised a most peculiar sport, named bull-leaping. Picture the stadium, a bombilious and cacaphonous sound rising from the populace. In the middle of a ring, stands the orgulous athlete. The bull is released into this sanctum. Put into a bad humour by his incarceration, the bull—hic!—would charge the man. Still the man would stand still. Still the man would stand, at any rate, as the bull came charging at him, venomous rage steaming from his nostrils. Hee." (The "hee" was a little laugh that the Doctor produced out of delight for his turn of phrase.) "Picture this refragation! When the bull finally bore down full upon the man, the athlete would leap into the air with a herculean nisus, grabbing the beast's horns. With extreme eucrasy, the man would execute a somersault, which would carry him the length of the animal's back, landing him ultimately in the dust of the charge's wake. What," finished the Doctor, "do you think of that?"

Nathanael pondered it momentarily. He had a little bit of wine in him, quite a little bit, really, that was impishly urging him to say, "Bring me a bull!" But what he said was, "Ain't that something?"

"Doesn't it strike you as somewhat barbaric? According to my researches, even the best bull-leapers were not one hundred percent successful."

Nathanael took another long pull at his wine. "I don't figure it's barbaric, Doc. It's like what I was saying about Mother Nature the

other day. It's man against nature. A bull is pure bull, if you see
what I mean."

"Indeed, I do. A bull—hic!—is, in its very bullness, nothing other,
nor could it ever be."

"Yeah. So jumping over one, is—I dunno. It ain't barbaric, at
any rate. 'Least, I don't think it is. You know, when I was a kid,
I thought I had sports figured out. It was all I ever wanted to do.
Of course, my old man, he used to make me work at it, but still, I
wanted to."

"Why do you suppose your father wanted you to be a sportsman?" asked Dr. Sinister, who was pleased that Nathanael was
being talkative.

"He wanted me to be—the *best* at something. I couldn't really
tell you why. When he found out that I had some natural ability—I
started running real fast when I was about two and a half—he just
kept pushing me at it. He used to train me. Even when I was three
or four, my old man'd have me running around fields, and he'd be
standing there with a stopwatch, and he's scream, 'Don't be fifty-
seventh again, you bastard, be number *one!*' "

"Why fifty-seventh?"

"Search me. But, anyway, as I was saying, I liked sports real
well myself. And when I was about thirteen, I thought I knew why.
I looked at it this way. God put you in a body, and He made that
body subject to a lot of natural laws, you know? Like gravity and
stuff. You see, Doc, I was brought up very religious, and I believed
in God. And I believed in a soul. And I got to thinking that maybe
the soul was like a prisoner in the body. Maybe the soul was too
big for the body and was always trying to get out. And sports was
—well, according to natural laws, you should only be able to run
so fast, right? I mean, you get your legs working, you get your
muscles churning as fast as they can go, you take into account the
wind against you, stuff like that, all natural and scientific, and
then you know just how fast you can go. You see? But me, I figured that there was something inside you, inside your *soul*, that
could make you go just a little bit faster. Just a little bit faster,
and it didn't have anything to do with muscles or nature or anything. It was your soul doing it. And when your soul made you go
just that little bit faster, well then, for that moment, you were free.
Does that make any sense?"

"Indeed! Oblectatively! It is precisely analogous to my search
for the capital M. Everything I do, everything that I bid hither
from nothingness and render back to the same, all that—hic!—can

be accounted for in mechanical terms, i.e., I do it with my fingers. Therefore, when finally it happens, and I am not doing it mechanically, then, as you say, in that moment I shall be free."

"You got it, Doc. I figure almost everybody's got their different ways. For me, it was sports. But like, you take the Hisslop girls playing their saxophones. Now that's mechanical, right? Fingers opening and closing little holes. But when they played, I felt something that didn't have anything to do with the holes."

"Yes, yes!" shouted Dr. Sinister. "Have a tad more wine. But, Nathanael, I cannot but notice that you have eschewed sports for quite some time. What of the soul's struggle to be free?"

Nathanael drained his glass and accepted the refill. "Okay. So, I practised and practised, and baseball was my game, and I made the big leagues. I had my talent, and I had my theory about the soul. And back then, I still had my God. Okay." Nathanael let a silence sit in the air. Music poured from the big Victrola, an old, classical tune. "In professional baseball, Doc, they got something called the purpose pitch. That's where a good batter comes up, and you don't want to risk him hitting anything. So the pitcher throws a purpose pitch. He aims for behind the batter's head. Well, what happens, naturally enough, is that the batter jerks his head back, just out of instinct, and the ball hits him square in the side of the face. I knew guys who got their jaws broken so bad they couldn't speak right for the rest of their lives."

"Indeed?"

"Then I had my accident, and I got out of baseball, but I still had a name, so my agent gets me work as a reporter, and on the radio. Swell. So I do a lot of fight broadcasts, because that's really popular. Doc, you ever been to a fight?"

"No, afraid not."

"If you got the stomach, you should go. Go and see how much of man against nature it is. Watch a fight and try to believe in a thirteen-year-old's theory about man and his soul struggling to be free. Those boxers are trying to kill each other. Both of them have got their conks rocked so many times they're little better than idiots. All they want to do is hit the other guy harder than they're getting hit. I saw a guy get killed in the ring." Nathanael felt a lump grow in his throat.

"When?"

"That was just before I quit . . ." Isbister realized that he was beginning to experience hyperventilation, and the reflex action would produce the embarrassing result of tears. So he said, "I'm gonna go talk to Stella."

"Yes—hic!—do. Myself, I think I shall try to teach young Zapper to execute a small terpsichore. Have a cigar." The doctor reached forward and the cigar, already lit, appeared between his fingers.

Nathanael raised his eyebrows inquisitively.

"Mechanics," muttered Dr. Sinister. "Damned mechanics."

The tiny Major Mite stood in the middle of the tent, brandishing a near-empty wine bottle high over his head. He spoke loudly, but to no one in particular. "If I was old," he said, as a J.P. Sousa march came drumming out from the Victrola, "if I was old, could I do this?"

The troupe members watched as Major Mite flew into a dance, his limbs waving about madly. After thirty seconds or so, he fell over on his bottom with a soft "bimp". He sat there and put the bottle to his lips.

Angus McCallister came over from where he stood with the Hisslops and gingerly picked up the Major, cradling him like a baby. "Nay, f'sure," he said softly. "If ye were old, Donny, ye sure couldna do that."

"Effing correct," muttered the Major angrily, putting the bottle back to his lips.

Tanya and Davey were still dancing off to one corner, a slow dance that never varied with the speed of the music. Tanya was inwardly cursing herself, for every third step it seemed she stepped upon the giant's toes. But, then again, she knew that he could feel nothing. He stared straight ahead, through the thick and cracked glasses, dignified and solemn.

Beside them were Zap and Dr. Sinister. "You put your right foot in, you put your left foot out," chimed the doctor musically, holding the Wild Man from Borneo in his arms. The hairy little man's feet were doing what looked like a complicated soft-shoe.

"Who's that guy I see sometimes?" asked Nathanael, supping his wine, sitting at Stella's feet.

"Which?"

"He's just a young kid. Wears a black leather jacket and boots."

"Oh! Edmund."

"Edmund."

"He's in love with me."

Nathanael searched quickly for something to say.

"Of course," continued Stella, "I'm just assuming he's in love with me. He's never spoken to me. All I know is, every day as sure as clockwork he comes to my little blow-off and hides himself in the shadows and stares at me."

"Maybe he's not a right guy," suggested Nathanael.

"He's very quiet, that's for sure. The only reason I know his name is that one particularly hot day he was carrying his jacket, and it had a little name tag sewn inside that said 'Edmund'. I don't know if it's his first name or his last."

The Hisslop sisters excused themselves, as they both had to use the facilities. (Their systems were pretty much synchronized, although there was no reason why they should be.)

"Ladies," boomed Angus, still holding the Major, "I hope ye're not gonna attempt t' make yerselves any lovelier—me poor heart jest couldna stand it!"

Daisy and Violet giggled and withdrew.

Ally, who had been moping around by himself, approached Angus. He was feeling pretty much fortified by the dandelion wine and some whisky he carried in a flask.

"Hey!" he said to the giant from Cape Breton. "I wouldn't get any ideas about them two if I were you."

"Aye?" asked Angus. "For what reason, me friend?"

The Alligator Man stared hard. "On account of you might get—" He let the sentence hang menacingly.

Angus McCallister stared back for a tiny while, set the Major down on to his feet. Angus pulled up his shirt-sleeves and took a deep breath of air. (His chest, still the world record-holder at seventy-plus inches, puffed out magnificently.) Ally took a quick step back, then held his ground defiantly.

Angus laughed lightly. "Aye!" he shouted suddenly. "I ken yer meaning now. Ye're right, lad, I donna think I'm man enough for the pair of 'em. But Donny says he won't take t'other, and same fer young Isbister. But how about ye? Ye look the picture o' health t' me. What say we both have our choose—ye can go first."

Ally clenched his mouth tightly. "You're disgusting," he hissed.

Major Mite rushed to him. "Ally, you don't know what you're doing."

"It's all right, Donny," said Angus, pulling his fingers through his long white beard. "Son," he addressed the Alligator Man, "no one told me those ladies was spoken fer—and they sure ne'er mentioned it."

"I'm telling you," stated Ally.

"Well, that's well an' good, laddy. But hadn't ye ought t' tell them?"

"It's no business of yours," said Ally.

Angus fell into intense contemplation. His brow wrinkled deeply. Finally he said, "Well, laddy, what are ye tellin' me?"

"You leave them alone."

Angus nodded. "An' ye're gonna attend t' them?"

"Ain't none of your concern what I'm gonna do," said Ally.

"All right, laddy. Here's how it boils down. Fer any wrongdoing on my part, I'm sore ashamed. Me ol' friend Donny and I shall now withdraw t' the side here, an' happily drink ourselves senseless. Ye, on t'other hand, shall proceed t' woo those lassies. I donna care if ye're successful or no. But ye're gonna try. 'Cause if ye donna, ye'll get the scrap ye've been hankerin' after." Angus smiled angelically. "Donald, lad, let's get to it."

"You're on," chirped the Major. "Womens is no good, no how." And as they walked away, the Major expounded on this theme. "You remember how Alvira used to tear me apart?"

"Now that was a girl with spirit!" laughed Angus.

"Spirit, my arse!" shouted the Major. "She was hot-to-trot, plain and simple!"

"Nathanael," said Stella—she had never called him that before, and Isbister realized that Nathanael was to be his name if she wanted to talk about anything serious.

"Yes?"

"Look at Bobby," she urged him quietly.

The Hippopotamus Boy sat on a chair, still working on his papers. His huge head, a grotesque construction of flesh and bone, rocked back and forth gently. Spittle spilled from the corners of his always-open mouth.

"Yeah?" said Isbister.

"He's just a young boy, you know. And he's never had a family. I guess they threw him away when he was a baby. Nate, the men around here . . . well, the Major and Pointy and Angus, they're all very nice, but they're older men. Ally's young, but he's always grim-faced and all. See, I think Bobby needs someone to be like a father to him—and he likes you an awful lot."

"Yeah?"

"He looks so lonely there. Why don't you go talk to him?"

Nathanael found himself wishing to do anything to please Stella, so he stood up. "Sure," he said. First of all, though, he went to get himself another drink. He exchanged his glass for a full bottle and went over to the Hippopotamus Boy.

"Hoddo, Bobby, how's it going?"

Bobby Merrill's head came jerking up suddenly, and its great weight threatened to throw both him and his chair over backwards. Nathanael quickly brought his hands down on the boy's shoulders, steadying him.

Bobby Merrill tore off the sheet he was working on and began scribbling madly on the one underneath it. After a minute or so, he handed a sheet to Nathanael that read:

Hello, Mr. Isbister! It is a very fine party. Isn't Mr. McCallister big? Aren't the Hisslop sisters pretty? Do you think I'm old enough to drink wine? Did you ever read a book entitled "The Mountains Are High", written by Heinrich Muffton? Do you think we will win the baseball game?

Nathanael read the note and chuckled lightly. "Well, let's see here," he said. "Hi, Bobby. Yeah, it's a great party. Angus is the biggest goomer I ever saw, and I've seen some monsters. The Hisslop girls are certainly pretty. Sure, I think you could have some wine. Never read the book. And as for the ball game, I think we'll win if we put everything we got into it."

Bobby Merrill wrote:

If you could ask Dr. Sinister for a straw, I could try the wine. As for putting everything we have into the baseball game, I fear I don't have that much to put.

"Hey, Doc!" shouted Nathanael, having read the note.

The Doctor had abandoned his attempt to teach Zap to dance and was sitting exhausted across the tent.

"Have you got a straw for Bobby here?"

The little man's eyes lit up, and he waved his hand in the air. A straw materialized, and he crossed over to give it to Nathanael.

"Hic!" he said. "Mechnics. Er, mechanics." He smiled and went off in search of Zap.

(Look under the table, Doc. You'll find Zap with a bottle of dandelion wine stuck in his mouth.)

Nathanael put the straw into his own bottle and aided Bobby in guiding the end into his huge drooling mouth. Bobby sucked laboriously, and a little bit of wine went into his mouth.

"Now, Bobby," said Crybaby, "I don't want to hear you talk like that again. You got a lot, but you don't know where it is inside of you, 'cause no one ever asked you to find it before."

Bobby gave the bottle back and turned to his writing pad:

In baseball, is a man ever called upon to be noble and courageous?

The question took Isbister aback; he stared at the paper and pulled at his chin. He said, "Sure," and then thought for a bit.

"The way I see it, Bob, noble and courageous men are few and far between. But the men that are always get called upon to be noble and courageous, just in life. And baseball's just a part of life. Christ, I dunno, Bobby."

Bobby scribbled this:

> You must be very brave, Mr. Isbister.

"Me? Naw, I ain't brave. What makes you think I'm brave?" Bobby, after another sip of wine, wrote a long answer.

> I have read a great many books about brave men. You are the first person I've ever met who fits the description. You are tall, well built, broadshouldered, tanned, and weather-beaten. Your eyes sing of a lazy self-confidence and your mouth breaks gently into a grin that conjures up romance and adventure.

"And in case you never noticed," answered Nathanael, "I got a nose that looks like something you'd grow in a garden."

> I suppose,

wrote Bobby,

> that during your countless adventures you have been in many fights. Some men may have been lucky enough to land a punch. But that was just before you mangled them to morsels.

"Bobby," said Isbister softly, "you got me all wrong. Me, I'm a bum. Oh, yeah, people have heard of me and everything, but I'm just a bum. Fights? Sure, I been in loads of fights. In barrooms, fighting over cheap women, stuff like that."

According to Bobby,

> Truly brave men are always overwhelmingly modest.

"Jesus," muttered Nathanael. "Gimme back that wine."

The Hisslop sisters came back into the tent. They had gone to the john, and then to their caravan, where they loaded themselves up with pills. Their four eyes shone slightly and seemed pried open very wide. They glanced around and were surprised to see Angus sitting down on the floor, the tiny Major Mite beside him. The two men were surrounded by a number of bottles, some less empty than others.

"That Alvira," the Major was saying, "was a whore."

"Agh, get on with ye, Donny," laughed Angus. "I suppose that in all yer born days, ye would have been satisfied with jest one woman."

"Ain't the same."

" 'Ain't the same,' " mimicked the giant from Cape Breton. "Donny, ye spent all yer life in carnival shows, and still ye ken nothing."

"You bastard," muttered the Major. "You *had* her, didn't you? You diddled Alvira, right behind my back!"

This accusation brought from Angus a loud thunderclap of laughter.

Violet said, "It looks like he lost interest in us."

"That's a shame," said Daisy. "Still, he hasn't seen the Major in so long."

"I was interested in seeing—" began Violet; but Daisy, very well acquainted with her sister's interests, giggled and slapped her on the behind before she could finish.

"Daisy, Violet."

The girls turned around to find Ally. He was staring down at his scaly green hands, seemingly preoccupied with a hangnail. "Would you care to dance?" he asked quietly.

The ladies exchanged a curious glance. "Sure," said Violet. "Thank you," said Daisy, and the Alligator Man gingerly took both of them into his arms.

Dr. Sinister had indeed thought to look for Zap underneath the table. But instead of getting Zap out from under there, the little Doctor had grabbed another bottle of wine and climbed in beside him.

"I'll tell you, Zap, boyo," said Dr. Sinister, "Theodosia was so insanely jealous!"

Zap looked outraged and emitted a small yelp.

"Oh yes, indeed, indeed! All I need do—hic!—was glance at another woman, merely espy one by the purest chance, totally unculpable of any transgression, and her wrath would be upon me. And she was not one for verbal wrath, either, my tiny hirsute companion. No—hic!—indeed. For, as she stood a head taller than myself, she found it little problem to beat me to a pulverulence! Hic!''

Zap screamed and began to beat the floor with his palms. He broke off suddenly and took the bottle to his lips, guzzling at it like a baby at a breast.

"Well, of course, the whole situation called for a clear view and massive ratiocination. To myself I said, Self—hee!—hic!—it seems you are being punished for infidelity. Have you committed said infidelity? Nay, a thousand times nay! Does this alter the verity that you are being punished for it? Nay, a thousand times nay! Ergo, says I, there is but one recourse. To wit—commit said infidelity, thereby rendering the punishment justified!'' Dr. Sinister said this with such dramatic effect that Zap immediately broke into hearty applause.

"Ally,'' said Daisy, "could you not hold us quite so tightly?''

The Alligator Man, whose eyes were screwed shut, was pulling the girls hard against him, flattening their breasts upon his chest. At Daisy's request he loosened up a little, but not much, and not for long.

"In ever' man's life,'' said Angus, "there's one woman who gets to him. That's what I've learned in me time, Donny. Ye can love any number of 'em, f'sure—but there's just one who gets such a grip on ye, there's nothing ye can do. Fer me, as ye know, it was Penelope. Or Penny I called her, doesn't sound quite so high.''

"You think she ever screwed around on you, Angus?'' asked Major Mite.

"Now that I'm old, Donny, I don' know. When I was younger, I was sure she did, but now—I don' know. It donna make a hair of difference.''

"You're not starting with that 'old' stuff, too, are you?''

"Oh no, Donny! I just meant, now that I'm more—mature.''

"Effing correct,'' stated Major Mite.

"That greenie fella is like t' squeeze the air right oot of them Hisslops,'' noted Angus—Ally had resumed his clutch at full strength as the three waltzed about the room.

Major Mite brought up a finger and pointed at the dancing trio. He opened his mouth to say something, forgot what it was, and pointed at them for a moment longer. Then he said, "They're his Penny. His Alvira. They got such a grip on him, you wouldn't believe it.''

"Oh, I believe it, Donny. He was willin' t' fight me.'' Angus laughed—then he took the tiny Major into his arms and pulled him to his chest in a bear hug. And, lightly, Angus kissed the top of the Major's balding head.

Stella had suggested a game of cards, and five of them were now playing, sitting in a circle in the sawdust. There were Stella, Nathanael, Bobby, Tanya, and Davey. Isbister had suggested poker (the suggestion seconded by Tanya), but the other three didn't know the game. All but Isbister knew how to play a game called Hearts, and that is what they were playing. Isbister had just received the dreaded queen of spades for the third time running.

He closed his mouth up tight and hit the ground beneath him savagely. He let a small "Shit . . ." leak out from between his lips.

"Oh, Nate," said Stella, "you've got to learn to guard against it."

"I know, I know, I know! But Tanya kept leading spades, and there was nothing I could do!"

A quiet voice came from above him, namely Davey's. "When Robert led out the diamond, you shouldn't have played the ace, because you knew I had the other high diamonds and no hearts, and then I should have had the lead, and you could have dropped the high spade." Davey's hands worked clumsily at holding the cards up to his thick glasses.

"How in hell was I supposed to know you had the other high diamonds?" snapped Isbister.

Davey shrugged, as if it were common knowledge. "No one else did," he muttered as the cards were dealt out again.

At the first break in the music, Daisy and Violet pushed themselves away from Ally and thanked him with a small, double curtsy.

"Don't you wanna dance no more?" asked the Alligator Man, remembering that the sisters had never seemed to tire of waltzing around the floor with Angus.

"No," said Violet, "I think we're going to sit down for a while."

"That's a good idea," agreed Ally, and he followed them off to one side.

"Oh!" noted Angus. "He's losing 'em."

"It's too bad," said the Major, "on account of it makes him mean. Just like Alvira used to make me mean. You remember that, Angus?"

"Aye, fer sure. Three feet of livin' hell ye were."

The description delighted the midget Major Mite.

"Now—hic!—Edna is a case in point," said Dr. Sinister.

Zap cradled his head in his hands and stifled a yawn. Both were still sitting underneath the refreshments table.

"From a vicarious viewpoint, if such phrase is not both redundant and repetitive, she was not, to coin the current colloquial, so hot. Deficient of mammary and curvature, and a visage of a not wholly pleasing nature. Hic! But when that woman was in bed, and in the throes of physical embrace—hee, hee, hee!—she knew no pudicity!" Then the doctor sighed. "Ah, the bittersweet outcome of a mulierose disposition."

Meanwhile, Nathanael Crybaby Isbister had just succeeded in dropping the Queen of Spades on a trick won by Bobby Merrill. He did so with a great flourish and a loud laugh. "There you go, you little so-and-so!" He clapped his hands together merrily.

The other four players regarded him in silence, and the hands were dealt out again.

"I didn't want to get stuck with it," mumbled Nathanael in protest.

Off to one side, the Major and Angus were sitting with their arms around one another—or as close to that as possible. Angus, gesticulating with his free arm, was singing this song:

> *Oh, here's a health unto all true lovers,*
> *And unto mine, wher'er she be.*
> *This vera night, love, I mean to be with you,*
> *It's many's a long mile she is from me.*

"She's dead now," whispered the Major.

"I know. Now silence, for it's a lovely air." Angus resumed his song.

> *It's let this night be as dark as dungeons*
> *And there no gay light all to appear.*
> *My arms shall guide thee without a stumble*
> *All in the arrums of you, my dear.*

Angus's last note was long and mellow; he held it gingerly, and then it went away, the dying of a small fire.

Dr. Sinister had progressed chronologically, and was now discussing a woman named Tyoko, who, it seemed, had been more than a little promiscuous. Zap appeared to have fallen asleep, although every five or so minutes he would pop up with a start and lunge for the wine bottle.

The Hisslop sisters sat beside the Alligator Man on a small bench. The three had not exchanged any words. Instead, they were working earnestly on getting drunk.

One evening for recreation all down by the seaside,
I spied a pretty maiden as she moved along the tide,
I spied a pretty maiden as she moved along the shore,
Like two blooming rosies was the cheeks of Janey on the moor.

In Hearts, you must avoid taking tricks that contain either hearts or the queen of spades, for there are twenty-six points to count against you. However, if you get *all* twenty-six, then these points are deducted; this is known as "control".

Nate Isbister was losing pretty badly: Davey Goliath had 6 points, the other three players hovered in the twenties while Nate had 63. So Nathanael was endeavouring to get control. He had 25 of the points needed and was attempting to get the last with a nine of spades that he was sure would take the trick. However, Davey Goliath had the ten.

For the first little moment, Isbister just stared at the card—his face shook slightly. Davey's card had just added 25 to Nate's score, instead of letting him deduct 26 as he had hoped. Finally, Isbister exploded. "Where the hell did that card come from!? I saw it go, I swear! It was already played!"

"Nathanael—" started Stella.

"It wasn't played," stated Davey evenly. "I kept it back in case you were going to control."

"Why don't you mind your own business?" snarled Nathanael. Then he took a large sip of wine and attempted to control himself. "All right, all right, I'm sorry. Let's go."

"You know what, Violet?" asked Daisy. "I'm tired."

"So am I. Let's go to bed."

The Hisslop sisters, feeling the combined effects of certain pills and beverages, were indeed tired. They said good-night to the Alligator Man, bussed him on the cheek, and left.

Ally sat there on the bench, full of hateful thoughts. He had seen the men come and go in the Hisslop's bed, and in his opinion, not one was as handsome as he, despite his green skin. Why wouldn't they have him? He glanced over at the singing Angus, thinking that the girls would have taken that decrepit giant home if he'd kept up his advances.

(Actually, though, Ally was wrong. When the Hisslop sisters were genuinely tired, which was rare, they tried to get as much sleep in as possible. Another night they might have taken Angus— that's true enough, Ally—but another night they might have taken you.)

It's a shame that the Alligator Man didn't have the benefit of my parentheses, for he just sat there full of hateful thoughts.

Nathanael's last hope was this: the first person over one hundred loses; *however* (Hearts is a great game, there are always "howevers"), if one hits 100 points *exactly* he goes back down to zero again and almost assuredly wins the game. When Nathanael found himself at 96 he tried to exploit this loophole, and by means of spectacular luck he managed to do so.

"Hooray!" he shouted. "I win, I win, I win!" He jumped to his feet, elated beyond the point of even wincing at the pain it produced. "Egg-sucking card game thought it had me beat! I win!"

Although Bobby Merrill scribbled out, "Heartiest congratulations!", the other people were oddly silent.

"Whattsa matter?" asked Nathanael.

"We're just tired," Stella answered. "Tanya, could you wheel me home?"

"I'll take you home," offered Nathanael.

"No, no—you're enjoying yourself at the party. You stay here."

Nathanael stared as Tanya assisted Stella into her wheelbarrow and departed.

Davey Goliath was just beginning to struggle to his feet with his canes. Isbister went over and helped him up. Despite Nathanael's strength, the task was quite strenuous.

"Hey, Dave," Nate said, when the giant was fully eight feet eleven and one half inches erect, "you're one hell of a card player."

"I was on the interstate bridge team at my university," answered Davey.

"Boy, you must be good. I was just lucky."

"Yes," agreed Davey in his quiet, even tone. "You were very lucky indeed."

"You should maybe play some local tournaments around here."

Davey nodded but seemed uncertain. "There is a man," he said finally, "who I do not wish to see. He is also an avid card player, and I want to avoid him at all costs."

"Oh, Dr. Hunter," said Nathanael—and later he would add 'without thinking'.

Davey's face was instantly lined with fear. "You know him?"

"Oh, hell, no, I don't know him at all, I just—"

"*I knew it!!*" bellowed Davey, and he turned away quickly, racing with his canes. He headed straight for the table that Dr. Sinister was under. "Doctor! Isbister is one of Hunter's men!!"

Poindexter Frip popped out in a flash. "Now, David, let's not be silly . . ."

"He is! He is!" Davey Goliath was outside the big tent now, hurrying to lock himself into his caravan.

Nathanael went to follow, but Dr. Sinister stopped him. "Not to worry, Mr. Isbister. The episode will be forgotten by morning."

"I sure am making a mess of things tonight," muttered Nathanael. "Davey's mad at me, Stella's mad at me—"

"Stella? Whatever for?"

"I dunno. For losing my temper at cards, I think."

"Ah, yes. One mustn't do that."

Zap, aroused from his slumber by Davey's departure, came up from underneath the table and immediately proceeded to tear off his Tarzan outfit. Naked and hairy from head to toe, he pissed into the tent's sawdust.

"Fortunately for you, my lad," said Dr. Sinister, "there are just us males remaining."

"Well done, son!" boomed Angus, and then he finished his song:

It's when this long night was passed and over,
And then the cocks they began to crow,
We kissed, shook hands, I in sorrow parted,
I took my leave and from her did go.

"Will you knock off that damn singing?" snapped the Alligator Man from his seat on the bench. "It's enough to drive a guy out of his mind!"

"Ah, it's you, laddy," said Angus. "I take it ye weren't one hundred percent successful."

"Shaddup," snarled the Alligator Man.

"Gentlemen," said the little Doctor, "in many countries of this huge world, when this point in a *fête* has been achieved, i.e., the men sitting about, the women having departed—hic!—a custom of grandevity is enacted, one of great oblectativity, whereby we gather in a circle and offer various and sundry toasts. After which we drink copiously to them. What—hic!—do you say to that?"

"In Cape Breton, I've heard of men toasting themselves reet into the grave!" said Angus. "It's a lovely thing. Let's sit ourselves doon here an' get to it!"

And so they made a circle: Angus, the Major, Nathanael, the Doctor, Bobby Merrill, the Alligator Man, and Zap. They each held a full bottle of dandelion wine ("Quite depleting the existing stock," said the Doctor).

"I'll be first," said Angus. "Gentlemen—and friends, I wish to call ye all—I'd like t' give a toast to that type of people what has had me and Donny here all lumpy-throated and singing. Gentlemen—here's t' women."

And they drank.

The Major was next: "Well, Angus, if we're gonna have one to women, I say let's have one to men, too."

And they drank.

Nathanael spent a moment thinking. "It seems to me that when you toast men and women, you're toasting something that sometimes you love and sometimes you hate. So I want to toast baseball."

And they drank.

Dr. Sinister was next. "If we persist in toasting such generalities as men and women, we shall soon find ourselves out of toasts but with an excess of wine. I, therefore, shall proceed by taking the first plunge into the particular, by giving you, gentlemen, a toast to Mrs. Edna Logan, whose culinary feats had no rival upon the face of this earth."

And they drank.

Bobby Merrill wrote his out, and the Doctor read it aloud. "Bobby's toast is to 'men of courage and valour, who fight for their beliefs and fear naught'. Well put!"

And they drank.

"I want to toast the great American people!" said Ally, for he hoped it might insult Angus. But the giant drank to the toast heartily.

And they all drank to the toast heartily.

Angus assumed it was his turn again, but Zap climbed to his feet.

"What's the li'l monkey doin'?" asked the giant from Cape Breton.

"He wishes to make a toast, I presume," said Dr. Sinister. "To what, Zap?"

Zap took his penis into his hands.

"Here, here!" said Angus.

And they drank.

They completed the circle five more times before all the wine bottles were empty. Angus toasted the Major, three women (including Penelope), and a mule that he owned; the Major toasted Alvira, Angus, Dr. Sinister, Morris M-for-Magnus Mulcher, and the institution of motherhood (he was running low at that point on inspiration); Nathanael toasted Babe Ruth, Lou Gehrig, Goose Goslin, Ty Cobb, and Stella; the Doctor toasted five ladies of his acquaintance, for reasons ranging from "loveliness of visage" to "pertliness of mammaries"; Bobby Merrill toasted the Doctor, Nathanael, Lieut. Henry Granger, John Bolt, and Red Weston (the last three being fictitious characters in books he had read); the Alligator Man toasted the French, the Monarchy, the Protestant Church, and the hope that one day all the Americas would be united under one flag; and Zap toasted his penis five more times.

And then they went to bed.

Chapter 6

MEANWHILE, WHEN NATE Isbister is practising his team hard and for long stretches of time, Tekel Ambrose has not altered his life style, or that of his Brethren, one iota. The House of Jonah has reached a level of perfection that cannot be improved upon, and not one of them is about to let himself get out of shape. Thus, the three weeks before game time are the same as any other three weeks for Tekel—with this one curious exception.

He was in the fields one day, gathering up the crop (for autumn is hard upon us), when a woman of the House came out, calling his name. "Brother Tekel Ambrose!" she yelled. "Brother Tekel Ambrose!"

Tekel stood up—he didn't bother to answer vocally, he merely stood up, stern and rigid, and allowed himself to be seen by the woman.

"Brother Tekel Ambrose," she told him, "there is a man at the House who wishes to meet thee."

Again without a word, Tekel marched forth.

He found, in the House's Common Prayer and Meeting Room, a small man busying himself with a careful inspection of the baseball memorabilia and paraphernalia. The little man was dressed in a sombre grey suit and wore tiny spectacles. His hair was thinning, and he exuded timidity, twisting a homburg nervously in his pale hands.

"Yes?" demanded Tekel, and the little man, startled, seemed to jump some four feet in the air.

"Oh . . ." The little man's voice was extremely quiet, almost a whisper. "You are Tekel Ambrose?"

"I am that man," said that man, and he motioned the other to one of many wooden chairs.

"I," said the other, hurrying to plant his little bottom down, "am Dustin Doubleday."

Tekel, without changing a line on his dark face, looked questioning.

"My grandfather was Abner Doubleday," explained the little man.

Tekel Ambrose did not know the name; he had no knowledge of the history of baseball, or even of his most famous contemporaries. For instance, he didn't know the name Nate Isbister, despite his warning at the carnival. He had merely recognized him from a game, long ago.

"It was my grandfather," explained Dustin Doubleday, "who developed and set the official rules to that game which you and your team have taken to such levels of grace and beauty."

Now this was certainly news to Tekel Ambrose. It hadn't occurred to him that anyone had developed the game of baseball. I suppose that deep down he thought it had existed always. But Tekel was never one to look like a fool, so he extended his hand, saying, "I am truly honoured to meet one of such famous lineage."

"It is I," said the little one, accepting the hand eagerly, "who am honoured. It is sad that my dear grandfather could not be here to meet you, surely the game's most accomplished player."

Tekel knew when to be modest, although he didn't have the slightest hint of it in his makeup. "I merely play as well as I can."

"As the eagle takes no pride in its achievement of flight, so you take no pride in doing what to you is natural, although to the rest of us mere mortals, it is surely miraculous."

Tekel shrugged modestly.

Dustin Doubleday said, "I am writing a book about the sport and am accordingly travelling about the land compiling information."

"How long do you intend to remain in Burton's Harbor?" asked Tekel politely.

"Oh, it is hard to say. I should think about . . . oh . . . three weeks."

"Do you, yourself, play?" queried Tekel.

"As a younger man, of course. But in my waning years, I content myself with time spent on the Official Rules and Regulations Committee, as well as serving, whenever called, as an umpire."

"Indeed?"

"Indeed."

Tekel surveyed, with his black and shadowed eyes, the little man. The small one had a face that was childlike in its innocence.

"In a little less than three weeks," said Tekel, remembering the letter he had received, "we shall be playing a game for which, at this point, we have no umpire. It is a most unusual game."

"Indeed?"

"Indeed. We are playing a troupe of social outcasts. Carnival people. Unusual people."

"I see." Dustin Doubleday pondered for a bit. "Whatever for?" he asked.

"It is of no importance. The game has been set. Would you umpire?"

If you had been in the room, you could have read the consternation upon Dustin Doubleday's face: Will I have time, with all my research duties? I don't think I'll be able to manage, really . . . but then, it's only the one game. Why not? Still . . .

It took him many moments before he told Tekel, "I think I should be able to see my way clear."

How my grandfather managed to contain himself for those "many moments" is a complete mystery to me.

Speaking of you-know-who, he just made an interruption that was very strange. As I sat there typing, he remained quiet and perplexed. Which is odd at any time, but even more so in this case, considering I was typing about his own cagey and geezerish self. And then, out of the blue, he said, "Boy, if you're around when I . . . when I . . ."

"When you die?" I suggested helpfully.

"Yeah," he nodded. "When they bury me, will you make sure I'm wearing a baseball mitt?"

I chuckled. "What do you think, that they're going to be playing ball up in Heaven?"

My grandfather shrugged—but that was obviously and exactly what he thought.

"Angus!" yelled Major Mite. The day's show was over, and the midget stood outside his own caravan, wherein the giant from Cape Breton lay in bed (wide awake).

"What say, Donny?" came the voice from within. It seemed to shake the little caravan back and forth.

"It's time for baseball practice! Everyone's out in the field already!"

"Oh! Well, run along an' I'll catch ye up!"

"Naw, naw." The midget sat down on the steps. "I'll wait for you."

"No, go on! I'm movin' slow, Donny, me head's a ton of achin' fat."

"You don't get hangovers. Hurry it up."

"I donna usually get hangovers, no—but there were summit in that vile brew ol' Sinister whipped up is makin' me sore ill!"

"Come on!"

"I'll be there shortly!" The giant's voice was edged with temper. "Now, ye go on ahead!"

Reluctantly, the tiny Major moved away from the caravan. At one point, he spun around and opened his mouth, but he let it fall silently shut, and continued on.

In the field, Nathanael Isbister (despite a sore body and pounding head—he was sometimes quite susceptible to hangovers) was going over some of the finer points of batting. How to place your feet, how to pull the ball, stuff like that. The rest of the troupe members listened intently, with concentration.

Nathanael paused long enough to ask, "Hey, Major, where's Angus?"

Major Mite took his place glumly. "I don't think he's coming. He's got a real bad hangover."

Dr. Sinister asked, "Angus has a hangover?" with a certain amount of disbelief.

"Yeah!" snapped the midget. "That's what I said."

Isbister shrugged and continued. "See, if you swing sooner, you're gonna hit the ball sooner, and it's gonna go in a different direction."

The troupe members nodded. Even Zap and Janus nodded.

The second stage of Poindexter Frip's life lasts from the ages of fifteen through twenty. At the age of fifteen he was fully developed (that is, as much as he would ever be), had a mind full of facts and ideas, and was a practising practitioner of magic with a miniscule. He considered the disgusting Merlin to be his best friend and his only teacher. And when they parted, Merlin cried freely, tears dripping from his asshole of an eye.

Poindexter Frip had joined the military and was promptly shipped to China, where he and other soldiers would quell tiny peasant skirmishes and uprisings. And while I would love to tell you that the young man's bayonet was never spotted with blood, such is simply not the case. Frip took no delight in his job, but, when faced with a foe upon the battlefield, he did what he had to do.

All this while, he kept up his reading; also, at this point in his career(s) he first tried his hand at the writing of fiction, producing a romantic novel about fighting in China entitled *Beneath the Yellow Sun*. It was published under the pseudonym James Featherstonwaugh, and Bobby Merrill counts it among the best of its genre, although he has no idea that the little Doctor is the author.

There is only one Chinese incident that my grandfather and I feel has relevance to Frip's development. He found himself stationed, one year, underneath a mountain that rose high into the clouds. Upon that mountain was a monastery of the most ascetic order. The monks wore burlap sacks when they wore anything at all, even though the mountain was forever snow-capped. Village legend had it that no man had ever seen one of these monks eat, sleep, or defecate, and it was speculated that their lungs took in no air, their hearts pumped no blood.

One of Lieutenant (for he rose to such rank early on) Frip's duties was reconnaissance. He was small, spry, and agile, and found it easy to sneak about the hills and forests in search of peasant insurgents. And it was while performing this duty that he came upon one of the monks.

The monk sat, quite naked, in the centre of a clearing. He had not a hair on his body. His eyes were screwed shut, and he held his arms outright. His legs were twisted beneath him in a fashion that looked horribly painful.

It was impossible to tell the monk's age. His skin seemed as tough as leather, but was faultlessly smooth. His face, totally relaxed and yet as rigid as carved stone, gave no clue.

If he heard Frip's approach, he gave no sign. Neither did he react as the young soldier came over to stand quite near, staring. For a while, Lieut. Frip was not even sure if the man was alive—even after a long and close scrutiny of the naked chest, he couldn't say definitely that he had seen a breath taken.

Lieut. Frip demanded, in Chinese, an account of the monk's presence.

He received, for an answer, a silence as deep as death.

Lieut. Frip repeated his demand, changing dialects to see if that made a difference. It did not.

Frip finally left, and told the story at the evening's mess. One of the older men laughed. " 'E were tryin' to levitate hisself, 'e were."

"Levitate himself?"

"Sure. You know, 'ocus-pocus, up we go, grand swami, up into the air, all like that."

The next day, the monk was still there. Indeed, as far as Frip could tell, he had not moved. His outstretched arms seemed exactly as they had been. This day, Lieut. Frip did not attempt conversation. Rather, he sat down directly across from the man and spent an hour (which was as much time as he could afford) trying to catch the monk in the act of movement. He was not successful.

In the days that followed, Lieut. Frip never missed a chance to scrutinize the monk. He took blades of grass and set them near the monk, memorizing their exact position and distance from him. When he checked them the next day, no change had taken place. Once, having built up his courage, Frip gave the man a little tickle in his left armpit. It had the same effect as upon a brick wall. Lieut. Frip tried dancing in front of the monk, he tried farting near the monk, he tried every source of distraction he could think of short of pissing all over the monk, and he was seriously considering doing that one day when . . .

The monk opened his eyes and turned to him.

Frip jumped back, alarmed.

The monk smiled and shook his head wistfully, as if to say, "This is harder than I thought." Then he shrugged his shoulders, and an instant later was frozen once more into his former state.

While the others were practising batting, Nathanael took Poindexter Frip aside and started tutelage in the art of pitching. And as Dr. Sinister listened and watched, his face was both serene and lined with concentration.

The Alligator Man was pitching for the practising batters. He was happy that Nate had given him this responsibility, but not happy enough to make up for the bitter bile left in him from the previous night's fiasco.

Tanya disdainfully hit a ball way out to centre field. Janus, the two-headed, five-legged wonderdog was there—"Fido" grabbed the ball in his mouth, and trotted it back.

Bobby Merrill could not connect.

Violet Hisslop discovered within herself the secret of meeting the ball, and described in detail the physical sensation to her sister Daisy. Before long, Daisy was hitting the ball too.

Major Mite, sullen today, swung with all his strength at every pitch—those he connected with went quite a way, considering his size.

"Hey, Major," said Nathanael, "why don't you try choking up on that bat a little?"

"Why don't you try a boiling chicken-fat bubble bath, muleface?" snapped the Major—and then to Ally, "Throw me another one, boy, and watch me clobber that booger!!"

All the while, a soft voice sang encouragement from the side— Stella, in her wheelbarrow. "That a boy, Major! Good hit!"

Zap pulled a bat behind him, sometimes raising it and thrashing through the air mindlessly. Because of his behavior at the last batting practice, they would not let him have a turn.

Davey Goliath found that by starting his swing as soon as he saw the windup for the pitch he could almost hit the ball. Not quite, mind you, but almost. He was afraid to put too much effort into the swing, lest the force topple him over once more. Next to Dr. Hunter, Davey Goliath's greatest fear was falling over.

That is our team.

We stink.

And that's exactly what Nathanael Isbister told Stella as they sat that night in her little blow-off tent. He said, "Stel, we stink."

"I wouldn't say that," answered the fat lady. "Most of us were hitting the ball."

"You don't know what these House of Jonah guys are like," protested Nathanael. "When we played them—geez. I was up to bat, right? Now, I was okay. I mean, I could pull a hit pretty much any way I wanted. So that Tekel guy pitches one at me—and Christ, he can pitch—and I lace it down between him and third. It must have been fifteen feet away from him, I swear. But that goomer caught it, just as easy as pie, and lobs it over to first. I wasn't halfway down the line, and I was out."

"But what did you do to him?" asked Stella, with a twinkle in her eye.

Nathanael's eyes started to twinkle, too. "He hit one, way out to the right of centre field, was headed clear over the fence. But I ran after it, and damn if I didn't run up that wall and catch that ball just before it went out of the park. And then, see, all those brothers were running, 'cause they didn't figure there was a chance in hell of me catching that sucker. So that meant they had to get back to their base. So I threw it straight to second—we get a man out there, right?—and Paine, on second base, throws it to first—three men out! Goddam triple play! Ha!"

"That must have got old Tekel's dander up."

"Not so's you'd notice, Stel. He just stayed as cool as can be. And the next time he was up to bat, he . . ." Nathanael's voice took on a quiet tone. "He cleared that wall."

"But what did you do to him?" asked Stella again.

"You know what I did? You know?" The volume came up again. "I stole every egg-sucking base on him, that's what I did! Including goddam home plate!" Nathanael drove his fist into his palm. "That's what *I* did!"

"You have to play with us, Nate," said Stella.

"Can't. You know I can't. Goddam legs."

"You will play with us, though," Stella murmured quietly . . . but Nathanael didn't seem to hear. He was lost in some sort of reverie; every few moments he would whisper, "Goddam legs."

And what, pray tell, are our other characters up to that evening after baseball practice?

Doctor Poindexter Sinister (né Frip) is sitting in his caravan. Although, as we have seen, he has numerous activities ongoing, he has abandoned them all. Until such time as the game has been played, he has decided to stop work on *The Sorcerer* (his thirty-fifth novel), *The Glorioski* (his fortieth orchestral piece), and *Girl Getting Into Bath* (his one hundred and sixty-eighth painting). Replacing these activities is a very strange new one. Dr. Sinister is sitting at his desk, staring at something. He has stared at it for more than an hour already, and he will stare at it for three hours more before fatigue sends him unwillingly to bed.

He is staring at a baseball.

Daisy and Violet Hisslop are not in very good moods. The reason is that the party the night before has depleted their supply of gin and most of their pills. What little they had left was enough to induce a dull sort of drowsiness—nowhere near what was needed to guide them quickly and easily to slumberland. And to make matters worse, they are marooned for the night at the carnival site, so that no young men are to be had. Like all show people, they are reluctant to start intimate relationships with fellow performers. Reluctant, but because of the circumstances, not totally unwilling.

Timidly, Daisy says, "You know what? We haven't really ever talked to Mr. Isbister."

"That's true," agrees Violet.

"We could go visit him."

"I suppose we could. But—"

"But—?" responds Daisy.

"He's sort of a queer duck, isn't he?"

"How so?"

"Well, he's never really tried to talk to us, has he? I don't think he's interested to us."

"I was merely suggesting that we pay him a social visit!" protests Daisy, a little testily.

"I know, I know."

The sisters sit in silence for a time. Both are pulling ebony-handled brushes through their hair.

"We could go visit Ally," suggests Daisy, almost in a whisper.

"That stick-in-the-mud?"

"He's really very nice," says Daisy. "I think he likes us."

"I always thought he didn't like us."

"No," says Daisy. "I think he acts that way sometimes because he really does like us."

"If he likes us," asks Violet, "why hasn't he ever come to visit us?"

"He's shy."

"Shy?"

"Of course he's shy—because he has green skin."

Violet starts laughing. Daisy looks at her for a while, questioning. "What's funny?" she asks.

"Here *we* are, stuck together, and he's shy because of his green skin."

Daisy sees the humour, and allows a little chuckle. But when the laughter is gone it leaves a sad silence.

"I know who we can visit!" says Violet suddenly and energetically, aware of her sister's despondency.

"Who?"

"Angus!"

"Angus!"

They rise without speaking another word and begin to change into some nice clothes.

In the caravan across from them, the Alligator Man responds quickly, thinking the Hisslops are about to go to bed. He is crouched by his window, and in his caravan all the candles have been blown out so that he won't be seen.

In a few seconds, both of the Hisslops are naked, and Ally is in a strange state of ecstasy—strange in that it contains a large portion of self-hatred and a good dollop of unfocused, free-flying rage.

Then the Hisslops begin to pull on good clothes, their nicest, and Ally realizes they are dressing to go out somewhere. When he has realized this, he leaves his business at hand unfinished and crawls slowly into his bed.

Through his mind race the vilest curses.

In Major Mite's tiny caravan there is a heavy silence. The Major himself sits in the rabbit-covered rocking chair, bolting back and forth at a great clip. Angus sits on the bed, hunched over, his huge hands gripping one another hard enough to turn the knuckles white. He stares at the ground.

Finally, though, Major Mite clears his throat, and his voice (like a nine-year-old with bronchitis holding his nose) shatters the quiet into a million pieces. "Anything botherin' you, Angus?"

The giant shakes his head. "Nay. Reet as rain, Donny."

The silence threatens to take over again, but the Major quickly asks, "So how 'bout these baseball practices?"

Angus leaps to his feet—and believe me, there are few things so frightening as a giant leaping to his feet in a caravan designed for a midget. "Fer the sake of Henry, mon! There I be, mindin' me own business quite peaceable in Cape Breton, an ye come an' scream about baseball an' half drag me here agin' me will, an' there I be all tuckered out, and ye take me to a party an' try to poison me with the vilest brew this side of Hell, an' then 'cause I miss a couple of reet stupid practices, ye start actin' all queer—quite fergettin', I might add, that I am the strongest man that e'er lived, an' hardly need concern myself with such a thing as practisin', but nay, ye start actin' all queer, an' sittin' in yer little chair and starin' at me like I had consumption or summit, jest fer the sake of one or two wee practices, quite fergettin', I might add, that I am the STRONG-EST MAN THAT EVER LIVED!!!' "

Angus sits down on the bed again, with a loud creak that threatens to reduce it to splinters.

"What I wanna know," demands the Major, "is why didn't you just stay up in Cape Breton?"

This time Angus's answer is spoken softly. " 'Cause I owe ye, Donny. I owe ye me life many times o'er, I owe ye a great deal of me happiness."

"You don't owe me shit, Angus."

"I do, an' ye know it. Same as you owe me."

The Major thinks about it momentarily and decides it is the truth. "If you owe me, Angus, why don't you come to a practice? That's all I want from you. We got to beat the hellish tar out of them boogers, comin' around and saying as how we should be pitied and likewise similar horse droppings!"

The giant nods. "Aye, Donny—they deserve as good as they're gonna get." Angus pauses and then stands up. "All right. All right, me friend, I'm a-goin' t' tell ye the truth. When I left here, it was because—"

Through the window comes a soft and musical, "Yooo-hooo!" The giant tilts his head. It comes again, "Yooo-hooo!", and the giant's long mouth breaks into a grin. "There is a God!" he shouts. "It's the Horslops come t' get me!" He runs to the door and swings it open, bending over to almost half his size to put his head through the opening. "Ladies!" he says. "Ye look as if Heaven has opened a beauty salon. Step in, step in!" And as they are coming up the stairs, Angus turns to Donny and whispers, "Ye'll get the truth, Donny, believe me." (Though the Major never did, not from Angus.)

Bobby Merrill has very few moments of self-pity. He never considers his ugliness, being as it is so very far removed from the realm of human appearance. He looks like a totally different species, and as the only member of said species, the question of ugliness never arises, for it is based on comparison. But at the moment Bobby is addressing himself to what he feels is the ugliest thing about him. He knows why, now, when a baseball is flying through the air towards him, his attempt at catching it is so miserable. It is because he is afraid of the ball hitting him.

He has known it deep down for a day or two, but only on this night has it risen to be vocalized—or, at least, written. Bobby Merrill has a diary that is reserved for his deepest, most private thoughts, and he has filled one page of it in this manner:

> This day I know I am a coward. I have feared it all my life, but only upon this eve has the truth struck me with such force and clarity. Many might say it takes a moment of vital significance to bring this conclusion, but I dis-agree. Consider as example the novice upon the field of battle. Should he turn and run, shall he be called a cow-ard? I think not. He shall certainly never be called brave, but to save one's hide from almost-certain death is not, in my opinion, one iota so low and contemptible as my own case. I am afraid to be hit by a baseball. This is cowardice in its purest, most loathsome form. When the ball is coming toward me I close my eyes and hold the glove up to protect myself—inwardly I quake with appre-hension—all the while, I know the ball is more than ten feet away from me. I believe that the rest, including Mr. Isbister, feel that my ineptitude is due to my infirmity. I dread the day that they should know the terrible truth; particularly Mr. Isbister, who knows courage as a real thing. I would consider suicide except that as a coward I should never be able to bring it off.

He lays down the pen and lets his head sink to rest upon the table. His head is so very heavy.

And our poor little Zap is sleeping in his cage. He is not forced into his cage at nighttime—indeed, he runs to it eagerly, flipping up the latch and leaping in before Dr. Sinister is anywhere near.

Dr. Sinister has offered Zapper any number of blankets, quilts, and pillows, only to find them discarded in a corner come morning. The hairy little man prefers to sleep naked on the hard floor, curled up tight against the bars.

Zap's normal position is with his knees tucked up against his belly and his hands covering up his face, as if to block out all noise and vision.

Tonight he is having a troubled dream. His legs kick out spasmodically, and his hands press harder against his face.

If you could look over Tanya's shoulder—over her shoulder and into the volume of greyish purple photographs—you would see the story of a little girl.

The setting for the photographs is a rural area of some Slavic country. The fields have a gentle lilt to them; yolked oxen and cows meander lazily across them.

The farmhouse that is shown most often is a small, modest one, the home of a poor family, but it is solid and strongly built, dependable. Two adults turn up again and again. One is a thin man with countless wrinkles lining his face, always in need of a shave. He assumes the same position for all the photographs, standing sternly erect and tucking both arms behind his back. He stares dead into the camera's mechanisms. The other adult is a stout woman who never seems aware that her picture is being taken—she is always going about her business, carting pails, wiping the faces of various children.

There are many, many children, including several boys ranging from a little toddler to a tall, lanky youth who assumes the same stance as the adult male. There are many little girls as well.

The photographs record the growth of one little girl from the ages of one through nine. Her face in the later pictures looks to be out of focus, but closer examination will show that this effect is caused by a fine layer of peach fuzz that covers most of her jaw. For one or two photographs this peach fuzz can be seen to darken. And then the photographs end abruptly.

David Gray Goliat, in his caravan, pursues many diverse interests. Although he was forced to give up his scholastic career, he still keeps many volumes—mostly law, which was his main interest—and spends hours reading them. He also works at bridge problems and is learning chess. He was very interested in the oriental game of *go* (which Dr. Sinister, himself a keen player, taught him) but found that the effort of picking up the little tiles in his mammoth hands was too great.

Mostly, though, he addresses himself to the problem of the Hunter-proof coffin. His new inspiration is to have a lead coffin lowered into the mouth of an active volcano. Thus, he is presently writing up a legal document that will ensure that this is done for him.

Suddenly, though, a thought occurs to him—a frightful thought that makes him break out into a cold sweat. He goes to the book-case and withdraws the biggest volume, staring at its antique cover with a mixture of awe and horror. The book is *The Life and Works of John Hunter, King's Surgeon*, written by Cyril Ossington, pub-lished in 1812. The pages are yellowed and ready to disintegrate. One section of the book has been torn out—the section concerning an Irish giant named Byrne.

With his foot-long fingers working awkwardly, Davey flips through the index until he gets to the Vs. Then he lets out a long sigh of relief—Hunter had no interest in volcanoes, thank God. For if he did, thought Davey Goliath, he would surely know how to turn them off.

Janus is waiting by Nathanael's caravan. It is near midnight when Isbister arrives; Janus greets him by leaping up into the air and smashing him to the ground. Then both tongues get to work at licking his face.

"Stop it!!" shouts Isbister, giggling, and he finally manages to throw the dog off him. He leaps to his feet and marches into the caravan—the dog follows him quickly.

"Well, Fido, Rover," says Isbister, walking to his whisky bottle and pulling off the top, "you did very well at practice today."

"Yawp," answered both heads in unison.

"I told you guys to knock that off," mutters Nathanael, taking a long nip at the liquor. "But, guys, I got some bad news. I'm afraid that dogs aren't allowed to play baseball."

When he turns around to question the silence, Nathanael sees that Janus has pushed the door open and disappeared.

Meanwhile my grandpappy is busy spreading a rumour. Spread-ing rumours is one of his strongest talents. He lays them out every bit as meticulously as a spider constructs a web—and with the same intentions. The rumour he is spreading is this: impossible as it may seem (it's enough to make you laugh—I don't believe it, but I heard a guy *swear* it was true) . . . well, you know how the House of Jonah is gonna play ball with the freaks? Yeah. Well—like I say, I don't believe this myself—there's a fellow willing to bet money on the freaks! Fellow by the name of Brassiere—*the* Brassiere, the guy who makes 'em—staying over to the Fulton Arms.

Tekel Ambrose is writing a letter to Dr. Sinister, informing him that Dustin Doubleday is willing to act as umpire for the game. Mene and Peres stand behind him, glancing over his shoulder, occasionally nodding in silence at something he has written.

Of the other characters (the ones we may term "minor", although it seems to me this is something of a mistake):

Beatrice the Bovine Beauty is chewing cud and reflecting on the unusual amount of activity she has witnessed in the useless and sterile field that she calls home. (N.B., she is *not* wallowing in self-pity.)

The hobos encountered by Nathanael on page three are getting zonkered on lord-knows-what. They have recently fallen in with another band of hobos and are relating this story.

"Know who we met? Only Crybaby Goldenlegs Nathanael Isbister!"

"I thought he was dead."

"Emphatically not so. Alive and kicking. We met and he even cried, no less."

"What about?"

"Rosewood-Forster fight."

"Ha, ha! You ever hear about the time he cried 'cause Cobb busted his ankle sliding into home?"

"Nope. But I heard him cry oncet 'cause a spectator took a ball on the head and needed stitches."

Every hobo recounts in turn an occasion on which Nathanael Isbister was reduced to tears while making a radio broadcast.

"He said it's 'cause he breathes too fast and hyperventilates hisself."

"*I* say it's on account of he's a *crybaby!*"

The truck driver, sitting in his truck, suddenly snaps his fingers and mutters, "A doggy ain't the right answer. Summabitch."

The other characters are either dead or I don't know about. Except for me, whom you may or may not consider a character without the slightest fear of hurting my feelings. I am far from being born.

But in case you're interested, I haven't been outside now for three weeks, except for excursions to Becker's to buy food. I used to have a girlfriend, but she has become convinced that I am shacked up with another. When I tell her that my grandfather won't let me go out she produces a variety of strange noises and hangs up the telephone. As for my other friends, they're convinced that I have snapped, gone to Flip City. Most of them felt I wasn't far from it to begin with.

So my plan is to get this damn book finished as quickly as possible and then turf the old codger out on his bony little ass. If I work day and night, I can get it done in two weeks, tops. I'm going to tear off the pages so fast the feeble old fool won't be able to keep track of me. You ought to hear my typer right now, clickety-clacking like a train. I am filled with a strange sense of exhilaration, knowing that, because I am producing reams and reams, I can write whatever I want to. The geezer can't possibly keep up. I could tell you all about Nathanael Isbister if I wanted to. And I want to. Do you want to know what happened to his legs? I'll tell you. It happened in a motel room.

That's that. I'm trapped. The incomplete sentence above is the result of a shillelagh being brought down heavily across my hands. I've got three broken fingers, and my hams are wrapped in bandages, with splinters made of popsicle sticks. My typing speed has accordingly been reduced to the rate of a very amateurish hunt-and-peck. I resign myself to my fate. It's new-chapter time.

(One note: Angus, after making a heated and excited show of undressing the Hisslops and fondling their breasts and buns, has fallen soundly asleep. There is no room for the girls on the bed, so they have laid out a blanket on the floor and are trying hard to beat each other to sleep.)

Chapter 7

J.M.M. BRASSIERE and Dustin Doubleday did not resemble each other in the least. Brassiere was a man of average height and build, with stern and rigid features. He had beady little eyes that the aimed at whomever he happened to be talking to, as if he meant to curse him to the grave. He was well into his middle age, but seemed extremely healthy and active. Dustin Doubleday, on the other hand, was a very diminutive man whose features lacked any distinctive qualities to speak of. He had milky eyes that floated dreamily and focused on nothing. He was younger than Brassiere by a good many years, but seemed to be in far worse shape physically.

I suppose it was hard on my grandfather in his younger days keeping such characters separate and different. Now his face has surrendered, and collapsed into a senseless sea of wrinkles.

The reason I'm pointing this out is because both men—Brassiere and Doubleday—became well known to the people of Burton's Harbor, and no one ever suspected they were one and the same. At least, no one did for a very long time.

As an example, we will select Gregory Haines, a dairy farmer who lived on the outskirts of that town. While drinking in the Fulton Arms, he caught wind of the rumour . . .

"Hey, Greg," asked one of his friends, "you hear about the game between the House of Jonah and the freaks?"

"Yeah, the wife said something about it. Stupitest thing I ever heard." Greg Haines was a sullen man, or else a little thick—at any rate, he concentrated only upon the glass of beer in front of him.

"Ain't the stupitest thing *I* ever heard," commented his friend. "I heard something stupiter. Namely, there's a fellow who's willing to bet money that the freaks are gonna win."

It took a full minute for this news to penetrate, but when it did Greg Haines set down his glass and whispered, "Got-*damn!*"

"He don't even want odds," continued the friend, "just even money says the freaks'll win."

"Who is the guy?" asked Haines.

"It's the guy who keeps your wife's tits from hanging down around her knees," joked the friend. Greg Haines turned quickly toward him and roared, "What?!"

The man explained quickly, "It's Mr. Brassiere, the guy who makes brassieres."

"Uh-yeah," nodded Haines. He let the insult to his wife pass unchallenged, mostly because he allowed as it was true. "And where can I find this guy?

"He's here, right here, staying at the hotel. Room 312."

Haines stood up slowly, finishing his beer as he rose. Then he walked up the stairs to the rooms, studying doors until he found the one marked 312. He rapped on it with his swollen knuckles.

A voice riddled through the door like machine-gun fire. "What is it?"

"Mr. Brassiere?" asked Haines softly, intimidated by the voice.

"That is my name," it snapped. "What is yours?"

"Haines. Greg Haines. You don't know me."

"Of course I do not know you!! I do not know a soul in this backwater town, and that is by choice! Please state your business."

"Well, it's about a . . . bet."

"Enter."

Greg Haines did so, and found the man sitting behind a desk covered with papers. He was dressed in a paisley smoking jacket and smoked a huge cigar. With his right hand he jotted furiously on various sheets in front of him, but his look was aimed inquisitively at Haines. Finally he pointed with his pen to a seat in front of the desk. "Sit," he commanded, and Haines sat. "Now," said Brassiere, "if I could just ask a moment's indulgence, sir, I must finish these reports for the shareholders."

"Sure thing," said Haines. While Brassiere worked, Gregory looked around the hotel room as if extremely interested in it. Brassiere's voice snapped his concentration. "You, sir, wouldn't happen to be in the position of being able to exert influence on the people at the train station?"

It took Haines a moment to figure out it was a question. "Uh, well, lemme see. I know Sam Knowles, he works down there, but I don't think I do, no, not really. Sir."

"Pity. I am trying to secure the use of a presidential car to transport me back to Chicago—but the loggerheads down at the train station are under the imbecilic notion that said cars are expressly for the use of the President! Have you ever heard such utter hogwash?"

"Nope, I haven't," confessed Haines.

"Not bloody likely," said J.M.M. Brassiere. He threw down his pen in disgust and folded his hands over his chest. "Well, sir. I believe you mentioned a bet. You make reference, of course, to a baseball game."

"Yessir. The House of Jonah and Sinister's carnival people."

"Which did you wish to wager would win?"

"Well, sir, I think the House of Jonah's gonna win."

"Hmm! A great many of your townspeople share this opinion. How much did you wish to wager?"

"I dunno. Twenty bucks?"

Brassiere let a snort of disdain whistle through his nose. "Twenty dollars, eh? Very well, if it's all you can afford—" He pulled a sheet of paper towards him.

"I could afford more," protested Haines. "I could bet fifty bucks. A hundred bucks."

Brassiere looked up at him slowly.

"Two hundred bucks!" shouted Greg Haines. "Yessiree-bob! I want to bet two hundred bucks on the House of Jonah!"

"Right then. What I suggest is this. I will now write up a promissory note to the effect that the wager has been waged. On the morning of the baseball game, you must show up at this hotel room with the money in cash. I will match it, and the money will be held here in this room, under guard of a man from Pinkerton's —I shall handle that—until the game has been played and a victor decided. Does this sound agreeable?"

"Yeah, sure," grunted Haines, already starting to wonder where in hell he was going to get two hundred bucks in cash.

In a flowery hand, Brassiere wrote out the agreement. Then he and Haines signed it.

"Well, sir," said Brassiere, "I suppose that concludes our business. If you would do me the kindness of mentioning to that man you know at the train station—Knowles, I believe you said his name was—that I am interested in a presidential car, I would be deeply indebted."

"I'll mention it," said Haines, and then, quickly, he left the room.

The next morning, Greg Haines woke up with a sick feeling in the pit of his stomach. This was the result of a notion that had been with him ever since he had left Brassiere's room. The notion was simply this—Brassiere knew something that he didn't.

He moved to the window and saw, silhouetted against the rising sun, his cows. He muttered, "Stupit cows," but what he really thought was stupid was his idea of hurrying through the chores and then driving out to see the freak show. He knew it was stupid— but he also knew that he had already made up his mind to do it.

He considered telling his wife what he was going to do, but finally decided that was *too* stupid.

So, early afternoon found Greg Haines in his truck hurrying along the highway toward the freak show. He arrived there just in time to hear Dr. Sinister shout, "Showtime, ladies and gentlemen, showtime!" He listened to the little Doctor list the attractions and then stood in line, fifty cents clutched in his ham, waiting to buy his ticket.

The line inched forward, and at one point Greg Haines, his mind elsewhere, trod down firmly on the heel of the man in front of him. The man turned around and said, "Excuse me," very politely. He was a small man, timid, clutching a homburg nervously in his hands.

"My fault," muttered Haines.

"I was dawdling," said the little man, and then he turned around again, proffering his fifty cents to Dr. Sinister.

The little man was, naturally, Dustin Doubleday, Abner's grandson. Greg Haines dismissed him entirely as soon as he turned around, and soon found himself inside the big tent.

The sick feeling in Greg Haines's stomach vanished quickly. What a fool that Brassiere was! Betting on a team that consisted of two girls stuck together, an old midget, a giant who could barely walk, an ugly, hairy pinhead, a *really* ugly guy with a great big head, a woman with a beard—*one* guy, the green guy, looked like he might be able to play. But the House of Jonah had a great team! Goddam Tekel Ambrose, arguably the best baseball player that ever lived!

Greg Haines was jubilant as he leaped into his pickup truck and roared away, already feeling himself two hundred dollars richer.

The sick feeling had not really vanished. It was merely no longer in Greg Haines's stomach, having found new lodgings in my grandfather's little gut.

As the people filed out of the big tent—some to check out the fattest woman alive, some to check out Madame Tanya—Dr. Sinister busied himself with clearing away some things on the stage, mostly the debris left behind by his magic act. A little man approached him, a little man who exuded timidity. Poindexter Sinis-

ter caught him out of the corner of his eye and spun around quickly, saying, "I'm sorry, we do not issue refunds."

The other little man looked baffled. "Refunds?" he repeated.

"Yes. No." The Doctor studied the newcomer. "Did you wish
to have a refund issued?"

"No. I am Dustin Doubleday. I was wondering if you have received any correspondence from Mr. Ambrose?"

Dr. Sinister dove deep into his tuxedo pockets. "Indeed!" he
exclaimed. "Indeed, I have!" He raced his eyes over the letter, re-
viewing its contents, and then jumped from the stage, holding out
his hand. "Delighted to meet you, Mr. Doubleday!" The two little
men shook hands. "The confustication was due to the fact that we
have notices outside proclaiming the participation of (a) a Rubber
Man and (b) a Wonderdog, and have not exhibited either, as the
Rubber Man is no longer in our employ, and the Wonderdog is
God-only-knows-where, and I was concerned that it was this in-
exactitude that you wished to make me cognizant of."

"I was extremely satisfied with the show," said Dustin Doubleday. "My grandfather was a great one for exhibitions of the *extraordinaire*, did you know that?"

"No. In fact, I find it somewhat startlesome, given what I have
become familiar with, re: the rules of the game as he set them down."

Dr. Sinister's conduct did little to assuage the sick feeling in my
grandfather's stomach—but nothing showed on the face of Dustin
Doubleday, who said, "I thought that since I had made the acquaintance of Mr. Ambrose, I should come meet you, lest there be accusations of bias. Also, you might not be satisfied with myself as
umpire."

"Not at all—you strike me as a man of the highest moral integrity."

"I have studied baseball, as you know, and cannot remember
any reference to your team."

"That is not to be unexpected. Until one week ago we had no
team."

Dustin Doubleday raised his eyebrows with slight surprise, despite
the fact that my ol' granddaddy was in danger of losing his breakfast. "Really? Why are you playing, then?"

"The explication is rather long and convoluted, and ultimately
of no importance. The match has been set, the match will be played.
In fact, this eventitude is what forces me to quit our present locus,
being as we must practise. Would you care to witness our team in
action?"

The idea terrified my grandfather, but, being a masochist at heart, he accepted.

"What's that?" asks the old geezer, pointing over my shoulder. "Maze-o-chist?"

I shrug, waving my (heavily-bandaged) hands in the air. "A 'maze-o-chist' is simply someone who loves baseball."

"Yeah? Maze-o-chist, maze-o-chist. Anyway, see, I followed the little Doctor goom out into the fields. And all the time as we walked, he kept talking on and on, and the way he talked you couldn't hang on to a word he said. But anyway, we get to the fields, and things is way worse than I thought. That giant Davey is trying to hit balls, and he's missing them by a mile each time. The Hippopotamus Boy and the Hisslops are playing catch, only no one's catching nothing. That hairy goom Zap is racing around, scratching at his balls and that's all. The green guy is throwing for the batters, and he ain't too bad—but no match for Tekel. But then I seen a guy I ain't seen before, a guy coaching all the others. And he looks familiar, so I stare at him for a long time, and then it hits me. All of a sudden, I don't feel so sick. 'Cause it was the late, great Nate Isbister!"

"Don't be so dramatic, fool!" I shout. "I know damn well who it was!"

"If this book bombs, it ain't gonna be my fault!" he responds in kind. "I try to add a little colour, and you don't care. I'm beginning to think I should have gone somewhere else to get this damn book writ. You *stink!* You put a whole sex scene in two dumb lines, what with Angus and the Hisslops!"

(This is something my grandfather cannot bring himself to forgive me for. I've tried to explain that with my hands bound up and throbbing with intolerable pain, I've had to make my prose a little more sparse than normal. He will not be convinced.)

I remain calm. "There is a bookstore, dear old grandfather mine, downtown. It is quite a nice little bookstore—they sell used books, you know." (I am enunciating my words overclearly, as if addressing an idiot.) "They have such a huge number of used books that they have set up a stand of books that they give away for free. The only stipulation is that each customer is entitled to just one. Now, grandpapa, three or four miles away from the bookstore is the Harbor Light Mission, wherein we find all the drunks, winos, and derelicts. Every week these drunks, winos, and derelicts select one of their ranks. This drunk, wino, and/or derelict then makes the three-or-four-mile trek to the bookstore to get his one free book. He never selects it, you understand, he merely grabs the closest book and then makes his lonely way back to the Mission. The drunks, winos, and derelicts then take turns reading this book aloud. It is my prediction, gramps, that this book shall eventually find its way to those drunks, winos, and derelicts."

"You think so?" he asks, rubbing at his grizzled chin. "Myself, I ain't so optimistic."

You have noticed that Janus has gone missing. He has done this sort of thing before, but the occurrence still worries everybody. They fear that the two-headed, five-legged wonderdog could well meet an untimely end at the hands of people who consider him the Devil's work.

As Nathanael showed the Doctor how to throw a knuckle ball, the little man asked, "Mr. Isbister, have you any hypothesis as to why Janus might have absconded?"

For some reason the question seemed to irritate Nathanael. Instead of answering he asked, "Who's that rubbernecker watching us?"

"That is none other than Dustin Doubleday, grandson of the illustrious Abner, and officiate of our own impending contest."

"Dustin Doubleday, huh?" Nathanael eyed the little man carefully. "Never heard of him."

"How . . ." muttered the Doctor, hurling another one, "heteroclitic. Am I doing this correctly?" He wound up again and threw the ball, all in a blurred flurry. It meandered its way to the Major's waiting glove.

"Yeah, that's real good." Nathanael's thoughts seemed elsewhere.

"The Knuckle Ball," muttered the Doctor, mentally adding it to his pitching repertoire. "I wonder why the wonderdog has left us. At such a propentious time, it is unlike him."

"Oh, for Christ's sake, Doc, he's just a dog! Dogs wander off all the time, there ain't no *reason*. Try another pitch."

"Right-o!" He threw the ball; this one's path was a little askew. "There is a reason for everything," he muttered quietly.

Nathanael eyed the field, and yelled, "Daisy and Violet, you're still shying away from that goddam ball! You too, Bobby! Now let's see some catching. Tanya, get up off your fat rear and practise a little bit, now come on! Major, where's that damned Angus today?"

"Got the gout," murmured the Major.

"The gout?" asked Dr. Sinister.

"That's what I said, the gout! You want me to spell it? You want me to send a telegram what says it? You want me to rent out a skywriter and get it written up in the sky? You want me—"

The Doctor raised his hand. "I see," he said—and then he spoke confidentally to Nathanael. "I fear things are turning out badly. The Major is not himself, nor is Ally, and now Janus, for some unknown reason, has decided—"

"All right, all right!" shouted Nathanael. "The reason Janus went away is on account of I told him he couldn't play baseball."

"I thought he showed a certain adroitness."

"Come on, come on—I told him he wasn't allowed to."

"Why did you tell him that?"

"Why? Why? Because he isn't! He's a goddam *dog!*"

"He is, in fact, a wonderdog, but you have circumvented the issue. Nowhere in the official rulings does it say that dogs, i.e., canines, wonder- or otherwise, are not allowed to play."

"You're being crazy, Doc. Listen, okay, it may not say that dogs can't play, but it does say that every player on the field has got to take a turn at bat. It says *that.*"

"Not necessarily."

"What are you talking about?"

"I am entitled to change said rules, don't overlook that."

"So you figured Janus was gonna play, huh?"

"I 'figured' nothing of the sort! It is up to you, as coach, to decide that. All I 'figured' was that any opprobrium to his inclusion should not be based on the fact that he is a dog."

"That's crazy."

"Is it true, Mr. Isbister, that professionally there are two separate baseball leagues, one for white men, t'other for black?"

"Yeah, so what?"

"*That* is crazy."

"So you think it's my fault that Janus left, eh?"

"Not your fault, my friend—Janus can be very headstrong. Just a misunderstanding."

"Okay." Isbister spun around toward his players. "Ally, you practise these guys at hitting for a while. I want everybody working hard!" He looked back at Sinister. "You go take batting for a bit, Doc; I'll be back when I find him."

Nathanael walked off into the surrounding fields, his bad legs spinning awkwardly but quickly. The little man Dustin Doubleday hurried after him.

☯

Now, as my ol' granddad hurried after Isbister, something within him came to a decision, namely, that for the purposes of communicating with Nathanael he would drop all pretences and simply appear as the middle-aged shyster he was. Had he known the impression he makes as himself, I'm sure he would have reconsidered. As for why he did it, the old man himself can offer no illumination, or at least not much. I quote:

"Well, boy, most people got their own little facets[1] and masks to hide behind. So I never felt that I shouldn't, too. Just because I had a bunch of 'em doesn't make no difference. But there was something about Isbister. I mean, you could tell he was just being him. Some of it weren't too pleasant, either, but at least it was *him*. And that's where you plant carrots![2]"

So instead of attracting Nathanael with Dustin's barely audible, "Excuse me," or J.M.M.'s imposing, "I say, there! *You!*", my grandfather merely said, "Hey, wait up."

Nathanael turned around. "What? Oh. You're Dustin Doubleday."

"No, I ain't. Keep walkin'."

Nathanael did so. "The Doc told me you were Abner Doubleday's grandson."

"That's what he thinks," explained my grampa. "Where are we going?"

"We're going to find a dog. A stupid, ugly dog that thinks he can understand everything I say."

"Uh-yeah," nodded the geezer. "What's he look like?"

"Looks like any other mutt," said Nathanael, "except for he's got two heads and five legs."

"You're kidding."

"No, I'm not. Now what's this business about the Doctor just thinking you're Dustin Doubleday?"

---

[1] I believe the goomer means "facades".

[2] The geezer has lately come up with these quaint, rural aphorisms—I believe he wishes to be portrayed as some kind of homespun philosopher. As you can see, they are at best sub-literate.

My grandfather explained, bluntly and truthfully, the events that had led to the creation of Doubleday.

Isbister held back a chuckle. "So you're gonna ump the game?"

"You bet. We gotta win."

"So what are you gonna do? Make a lot of bad calls against the House of Jonah?"

"Yeah, I thought I might," announced my grandfather. "Hey, there's a dog!—naw, it's just a stupid cow."

(The four-legged creature in the distance moved away uneasily.)

Nathanael was silent for a good many moments. "What's stopping me from telling Ambrose that you're not Dustin Doubleday?"

My granddad stopped dead in his tracks. "Why the hell would you do that?!"

"Because I happen to believe in fair play," Isbister said—the corniness of it made him wince, but he let the statement stand.

"Well," argued the geezer, "I ain't gonna make bum calls just to hear the sound of my voice, you know. Only when I have to. And with *you* playing, maybe I won't have to make any."

"Who do you think I am?"

"I *know* who you are. You're Nate Isbister, good old Goldenlegs, arguably the best baseball player that ever lived."

"Well, I'm Isbister, but I'm not playing."

"*Not playing?*"

"I got bum legs—or didn't you hear?"

"Oh, sure, I heard about it. But in case you ain't noticed, I'm trotting to keep up with you. Your legs move a bit funny, but, Christ, they move."

"I ain't playing."

"So you're gonna let your friends get turfed out of town without lifting a finger?"

"I knew it! I knew it! I knew this was all gonna land on my shoulders, as if I'm some kind of saviour. Now it's all my fault if they have to leave town—and they want to leave town in the first place! But all this shit is gonna come land on me! Just because I happen to be Nathanael fucking Isbister—"

"Goldenlegs Isbister."

"Goldenlegs! I hate that fucking name! Run, Nathanael, run, Goldenlegs! Don't never slow down, just keep running! Don't be fifty-seventh again, you bastard! Just run!"

"Huh?"

"I'm not playing."

"Why are they playing if they don't mind leaving town?"

"Aw, I don't know. They got pride or something."

"Don't you have pride?"

Isbister thought about it briefly. As he answered, quietly, he kept his eyes moving about the land in search of the wonderdog. "Naw, I ain't got pride. I ain't got anything in the world. I gave it all up."

My grandfather repeated stupidly, "Gave it all up?"

"Yep. Just chucked everything in. Now I don't have a thing."

These words perplexed my grandfather. He spent several seconds wrinkling his forehead, and when he finally said something, he said it angrily. He said, "What gives you the fucking right?!"

"What gives *you* the right to even ask me about it?"

"There's billions of people on this earth, you know!"

"So what? There's only one me."

"There's billions of me's, you idiot!" snapped my grandfather. "You can't just decide not to have anything to do with them!"

"What do *you* have to do with them? I know your type—always looking to make a fast buck. Your specialty is probably old ladies, right? Hustling old ladies, ain't I right?"

"That's right! Old ladies!" yelled my grandfather. "But at least . . . at least I . . . have something to do with them!"

"Okay, Doubleday, or whatever the hell your name is, I think you better just get lost. I think you better clear right out of town. I'm telling Doc Sinister about you, and I'm telling Ambrose about you. And I ain't gonna play no baseball game."

"Now you listen to me, Mr. Isbister, while I tell you a few things. And I ain't just doing this to save my own neck, because I don't happen to feel that my own personal neck is worth it! Now if you think I don't know about you, you're wrong. And if you think I believe that Nathanael Crybaby Isbister has chucked in his connection with the human race, you're wrong again. Anybody who'd cry because a little boy in the stands caught a pop fly and some bigger kids stole it away—which you did, Mr. Isbister, in a Giants-Dodgers game a few years back, on coast-to-coast radio no less—can't chuck it in so easy. So maybe that's what *you* believe—maybe that's what you want to believe—but myself, I ain't buying it.

"And if you think you don't owe those people anything, you're wrong there, too. I mean those people back to the show. I don't know how you fell in with them, and I don't need to know. You're in with them, and you owe them."

Here Nathanael said something rude.

"I'm gonna tell you a story," said my grandfather craftily. "I was in the Great War, you know. I enlisted the day it was declared, because, bygod!, I was gonna help rid the world of the threat of tyranny. So I went to shoot the Huns, and dammit I shot 'em, and in the process I got shot myself. I'd show you the scar, but it's situated where I'm modest about. Anyway, I'll tell you what the fighting was like, 'cause you would have been just a kid. It was all done in trenches and foxholes, little muddy caves—you were crawling around underground, mostly at night, while they shot at you and dropped bombs on top of you.

"So you gotta understand—all the time I was fighting, a little voice keeps running through my head, a little song, like this:

> *Dirty Germans, rotten Krauts,*
> *Kill the bastards, wipe 'em out!*

Like that, right? You gotta understand how much I hated them.

"One night I'm out there doing my best to rid the world of Germans and I get blasted. Kaaa-baaam!—that's all she wrote, lights out. When I wake up, I'm in a foxhole, and my wound is being bandaged up all nice—by a German boy. That's right. Why he did it, I got no idea. I couldn't talk German, he couldn't sprechen me no anglais. He was just an ordinary-looking, blond-type German boy, and that's all I ever was to know about him.

"I spent a few hours in that foxhole with him—all that time, the kid and I didn't even try to smile at each other, let alone talk. I could tell, by listening to the sounds around me, that the fighting had moved ahead a few hundred yards, and that we weren't in the middle of it no more. But then I heard something else, and I took a gander over top of the foxhole. It was a couple of Americans on patrol, checking for to see who was alive. That's when I got hit by an idea that's stuck with me for the rest of my life—and you wanna know what I did? I took out my rifle, and I blasted those two Americans.

"No shittin', Isbister, that is exactly what I did. And I didn't do it just because the German had saved my life, either. I did it because . . . well, loving freedom and hating tyranny and all like that is fine high-flying ideas, but an idea ain't worth as much as a man. And I happened to be in a trench with one perticular man, so he was worth more than men that I didn't happen to be in the same trench with. *Because*, Mr. Isbister, we are all more or less the same sort of assholes on this planet, so all you have to go by is who you happen to fall in with! And *that's* why I shot those Americans." My grandfather levelled his eyes at Nathanael. "And that's why you're gonna end up playing baseball." And with that, my grandfather started to walk away from Isbister.

"And what," Nathanael called after him, "is stopping me from letting the cat out of the bag about you?"

"You won't!" answered the little man, and he hurried off into the fields.

"How did you know he wouldn't?" I ask the geezer.

"I didn't," he admits. "But I figured if I said it certain enough, ol' Isbister would study on it until he came up with a good reason not to."

"I see. One last question. That story about the German and everything—is that true?"

The geezer is tired, stretched out on the sofa. After this, I myself am allowed to sleep. My last typed sentence tonight is the geezer's answer.

"Don't be ridickallus."

Chapter 8

WHEN NATHANAEL ARRIVED back at the caravan grounds, it was nearly eleven o'clock. He could tell at a glance which of the troupe members were still awake. Angus and the Major were; a light came through the tiny window—the two men were apparently talking. From a distance it sounded like a duet between piccolo and sousaphone. Dr. Sinister was up, but his caravan issued only silence. (Incidentally, be sure not to miss the next and concluding instalment of Pointy Frip's remarkable formative existence ... COMING SOON!) And, oddly enough, Stella was still awake. Nathanael had spent enough time with the fat lady to know pretty much what her schedule was. She tended to rise very early in the morning, and by nine or ten at night she was invariably yawning and ready to nod off. At this point she would lower the back of her throne, so that she was more or less reclining, and drift off to slumberland.

So Nathanael looked at Janus and asked, "You wanna go visit Stella?" It had occurred to him that she might be waiting up for his own return, worried. The idea pleased him.

The two-headed, five-legged wonderdog yelped, "Yawp!"

Nathanael grumbled under his breath, but he had given up telling Janus to stop that sort of thing.

Isbister had come across the mutt after hours of searching. He had finally spotted Janus perched high upon a hill, its two heads raised sternly erect, baying at the moon. The surrounding countryside had been filled with an eerie, double-edged howl.

Crybaby had walked up very close to the dog and then, snapping his fingers, he called out, "Come on, Janus! Come here, boy! Nice doggy! Attaboy! Come on home!" This had no effect. Janus kept its two heads raised and called out a mournful "Awooo-oooooo!" Nathanael, being by nature a very stubborn person, persisted in his, "Hey, boy! Come on, boy! Good dog! Good ol' feller!" After a few minutes of this, Isbister gave up. He said, "Excuse me, Janus," and there was a sudden silence. The wonderdog lowered its heads and turned them toward Crybaby.

Isbister shuffled on his feet nervously and said, "It seems I made a little mistake. I was talking to the Doc, and it turns out that in this particular instance, you *are* allowed to play baseball. Understand, I'm not saying that you're definitely gonna play, 'cause I don't know how good you are. But you are allowed to play, technically. So quit feeling sorry for yourself and come on. Come on home." Nathanael had turned and marched off. Soon the dog was trotting beside him.

On their way home, Nathanael said (more to himself, he would have liked to believe), "I was talking to a little shyster today. Telling him about how I'd given up being part of the human race. He said I was full of shit." Nathanael was silent for a bit. "But when I decided not to have anything to do with anybody, if I'd known I was still gonna get in trouble with goddam *dogs*, I never would have done it."

Janus disappeared into the sparse greenery and returned with a stick, plopping it down in front of Nathanael's feet.

"Oh, fetch, eh?" said the ex-baseball star, ex-reporter, ex-radio personality, ex-homo sapien (ha!). "I'll play a little fetch." Isbister picked up the stick and raised it over his head. Just before he tossed it, Janus growled a warning through two sets of bared teeth.

"Jeez, you never let a guy forget, do you?" snapped Crybaby. "I ain't gonna pull no tricks."

Janus was silent, and went into his fetching stance. The game began. They played it through the hills, across the lonely fields, and into the little circle of caravans. Which is where we find them now, headed toward Stella's little blow-off.

When they reached the little staircase the flap of the doorway was pulled away, and the young man Edmund emerged. He was dressed, as always, in a black leather jacket, blue jeans, and pointed boots. Edmund kept his eyes down and pushed past Isbister as if unaware that the man was there. He marched off into the darkness.

Isbister confided to Janus, "That guy, he ain't a right guy. Gives you the willies, don't he?" Janus tilted its heads quizzically, and Nathanael was quick to point a finger at him. "Didn't understand, eh? Dumb doggy." The two went up into Stella's caravan.

"Nate!" said the fat lady happily. She was busy devouring a box of chocolates.

"Hoddo," said Isbister. "That guy was here, huh?" He jerked a thumb toward the night outside.

"Oh, yes, he was here all right." Stella had a mischievous air about her, knowing more than she was saying. She popped a choco- into her tiny mouth.

"And?" gestured Nathanael irritably.

"And—he brought along a bottle of whisky to bolster his cour- age. And—wonder of wonders, the boy finally talked."

"So what did he say?"

"Asked me to marry him." Stella smiled and popped in another chocolate.

"It's no wonder you're fat, eating those things like that." Cry- baby waved a hand at the box of chocolates and then said more quietly, "Asked you to marry him, did he? What did you say?"

"I told him I'd have to think about it. Which I will."

"You're gonna think about it? Stella, I don't know about that guy. He gives me the willies. He kind of looks like a . . . a . . . mur- derer or something. Like a sick murderer type."

Stella laughed lightly. "Edmund? He's just a boy."

"Yeah! He's a lot younger than you are. And you never talked to him at all before tonight."

"True. But he looks nice."

"Stel, I don't think he's a right guy. Something about him." Isbister shrugged.

"You don't think he's a right guy because a right guy wouldn't want to marry a fat pig like me." She punctuated her sentence with a sharp period, popping a chocolate into her mouth.

"That's not true. And you know, you wouldn't be fat if you didn't eat like that—"

"Do you think I should go on a diet, Nathanael?" The sarcasm in her voice was as heavy as herself.

Isbister was quiet for a long moment, thinking. Then he said, "It's your life. Do what you want." Then after another moment, "I found the dog." He pointed to where Janus sat at his feet.

"So I see. Where was he?"

"To hell and gone, sitting on a hill, baying at the moon like a fool . . . and feeling sorry for himself."

Stella studied Nate's brooding face closely. It was a face she'd been attracted to at first sight, though there was nothing at all handsome about it. Nathanael's brow pushed forth heavily and unevenly, and his nose was almost formless, it had been so often broken. Yet for all his hardened, tough-guy looks, when Isbister brooded Stella thought of a poet, and when he smiled she saw a little child.

"Something on your mind, Nathanael?" she asked quietly.

"Yeah," he nodded. "Lots of stuff." He tried to smile but it didn't work—he went back to his brooding.

"How do you expect to become close to people if you keep your whole life a secret?" she asked.

"It works if you don't . . . fall in with people."

"Fall in with people," she repeated.

"It's an expression that the little shyster . . . that Dustin Doubleday uses."

"Have you fallen in with people?"

"Well, I don't know. All I know is that I spent all goddam day looking for this ugly freak dog here, and that I don't think—" his words slowed down, grinding to a halt "—that you should marry Edmund."

"I'll take that into consideration."

Nathanael nodded, then shook his head violently. "It's your life. Do what you want. I'm leaving anyway. Soon as you guys are ready to play a reasonable game of ball, I'll be gone. I been doing just fine up till now. Just me." He nodded once more.

"Just you. Have you ever been married, Nathanael?"

"Naw. I almost got married once."

"What happened?"

"I don't know. I'm pretty hard to get along with sometimes. I was younger then. She just decided at the last minute that it wasn't such a good idea . . ." He shrugged. "See, Stel, marriage is something that you got to take pretty serious."

"Is that your secret?"

"That? Hell, no. That's a long time ago, that is. Water under the bridge. Besides, I don't have any secret."

"Except what happened to your legs and why you're bumming around pretending you don't have anything to do with the human race."

"I'm a bum. That's why I'm bumming around."

"One of the greatest baseball players of all time, and a famous news personality to boot. Pretty unique combination for a bum."

Nathanael muttered, "Takes all kinds . . ."

Stella spoke, almost irritably, "Nate, I want to know you, but you won't let me."

Isbister stared sternly ahead for a long time, twisting his mouth, chewing on the inside of his gums. He rocked back and forth on his feet and, removing from his pockets his calloused hams, he drove his right forefinger into the palm of his left hand. Crybaby remained in this agitated state for several long moments, occasionally looking over at Stella. The fat lady sat unmoving upon her throne in the air. Finally, Nathanael seemed to make up his mind about something—he reached into his pants and took out a bent and flattened cigarette. He lit it, took a long drag, and then spoke.

"The doctors called it a 'nervous breakdown', but that doesn't say much."

She looked at him, a strange expression on her face. It wasn't a look to put him at ease, but he continued.

"See, Stel, a lot of things get me excited. When bad stuff happens, I get all excited, and I start to hyperventilate. I don't know if you're aware of this, but hyperventilation triggers the tearing reflex. That's how actors make themselves cry, you know, they hyperventilate. So a lot of times when I was doing the radio broadcasts, it would *sound* as if I was crying. Well, the audiences got a chuckle out of this, the way it *sounded* as if I was crying. They used to call me Crybaby. I got real popular on the radio—maybe even more popular than when I played ball. If a football player would bust his ankle, then I'd get excited, and the hyperventilation would start, and it would *sound* like I was crying, and the people used to like to listen to it."

He looked over to her to see what effect his speech had had thus far. Stella's expression, intense and mysterious, had not changed.

"About a year and a half ago," Isbister continued, "they sent me to cover a fight. Not a very important fight, either, just a couple of local bruisers. Tyrone Hutt was one guy, and the other was the Great Tom T., a big black guy. Well, this Hutt fellow, he was nowhere near a match for the Great Tom T. The fight should never have been held. But the fans were out to see blood, and that's what they saw." Nathanael cleared his throat. "The Great Tom T.," (he spoke the name bitterly), "the Great Tom T. bounced this guy Hutt all over the mat, and I kept saying, 'They should stop the fight, they should stop the fight, they should stop the fight!' " Nathanael stopped suddenly and looked at Stella. She could see a tear beginning to flow from the corner of one of his dark eyes—he pointed at it. "See? See what hyperventilation does to me?" Then he had to stop and regain his breath. "They never stopped the fight," Crybaby muttered. "And I—I got excited. Really excited. Because Hutt got killed. And I . . . kind of went a little crazy. And I started screaming, I was screaming into the microphone, 'Why didn't they stop the fight!? Why didn't they stop . . . the . . . goddam . . . fight . . . ' " Nathanael then gave way completely to sobbing, and buried his face in his hands.

Stella said softly, "And that's why—?"

Isbister raised his head—through his tears she was hazy and seemed distant. "No," he said. "That's not why." He wiped at his face with the back of his sleeves and struggled to compose himself; after a few minutes he was ready to continue. "Well, I guess that when I went . . . when I got *really* excited . . . I guess I might have scared some people. So the radio station says, why . . ." An attack of hyperventilation threatened to send him back to his sobs, but Nathanael fought against it violently. "They said, why didn't I take a breather from doing sports? Something easier. So they sent me to cover a social event. This big . . . social event." He started to cry again, quietly, and did not go on.

"What social event?" asked Stella.

"It was May the sixth, 1937 . . . Lakehurst, New Jersey," announced Nathanael. "The landing of the *Hindenburg.*"

He stood erect and spoke the words evenly and calmly, although tears streamed down his cheeks, and his whole body trembled. Then he exploded and ran to embrace Stella. Crybaby hugged her with all his might, bawling unabashedly. "All those people got killed, Stella, they all got killed dead, and the night was filled up with fire and with people screaming because they were burning, and . . . and . . ." He abandoned his attempt at speech and merely held on to Stella the Fat Lady, and struggled to push his body against her, and cried until his tears were spent.

You have probably heard the voice of Nathanael Crybaby Isbister. A recording of his coverage of the *Hindenburg* landing still exists and is played frequently. It is a frightening thing to listen to. It is the voice of a man who has no control over the hell that is pouring out of him, no control over the absolute terror that has engulfed him. At the end of the recording he announces, from the bottom of his raw, naked, and very human soul, that he cannot continue.

Many of you might be wondering how this last section found its way into the book, being as my grandfather has been, up to now, adamant about keeping Isbister's past shrouded in mystery. I myself was shocked, but did not question it. My grandfather, however, gives me an unbidden explanation.

"I got to thinking," he says, "about what it was like back then. A lot of fellas were on the bum just like Nate—but they were different. They were on the bum mostly because they *hated* other people. They figured they'd been stepped on, trampled, and drug through manure all their lives, so they finally just said, 'Fuck you guys, I ain't having nothing more to do with you!' But Isbister, he didn't hate other people at all. Farthest thing from it. But I guess sometimes he was . . . *angry* with us."

"Angry with us?" I ask, half listening, half typing out Nathanael's conversation with Stella.

"Yeah . . . 'cause sometimes we do such . . . *stupid* things." The next words I hear from my grandfather have a strange sound to them—somewhere within lies a moan. He says, "Look at your hands."

I do look at my hands, resting on the typewriter's keys. Where they are not bandaged the skin is beginning to shine a brilliant purple; many of the joints have swollen to twice their normal size. I turn to my grandfather—he sombrely lifts his gaze from my hands to my eyes. I see how old he is, my grandfather, how many wrinkles line his face. "They'll heal," I tell him, and get back to my typing. He says nothing and is motionless. "Remember," I ask him, "how Major Mite used to get into McCallister's trousers and then they'd go to a whorehouse?" I wait for the laugh. It starts off slowly, a couple of silent chuckles, but soon my grandfather is wheezing and coughing and rolling about on the ground. When he is through laughing, my grandfather starts in again with animated conversation about Isbister. "Yeah, he didn't hate us at all," he states.

I suggest, "Maybe there wasn't an ounce of hate in the man."

"Don't be stupid, boy!" he says, and bats me on the head. (It does not hurt.) "That man had more hate than anyone I ever met!"

"But you just said—"

"For *himself*, boy. He hated himself."

It hadn't occurred to me, stated as simply as that, but I begin to dwell on it. "I wonder why?"

"Lots of reasons, I suppose. But probably the main thing is that he couldn't really hate anybody or anything else. And there's some hateful stuff goes on in this world, boy. Sometimes a lot, sometimes not so much, but always some. And Nathanael could only take it out on himself."

We are beginning to uncover a small bit of what is Isbister, and it seems to me that my grandfather is warming to the subject. I realize that he has spent many hours trying to unravel the mystery himself, despite his frequent and violent assertions that Isbister's past does not matter. So I ask, "Are you going to let me write what happened to his legs?"

After a moment he says, "I dunno. Maybe. Not likely, though. It would ruin the consistency."

There is hope for us yet.

Chapter 9

AS ADVERTISED, HERE is the next instalment in the Life and Times of Poindexter Wilhelm Frip, a.k.a. Dr. Sinister.

When his term of duty was over, young Frip was twenty years of age. He had determined some time back to become an artist, although he was unsure which field to make his specialty. Initially, though, he thought to become a painter; with that in mind, he went to Gay Paree.

Paris in the late nineteenth century was a grand and glorious place for young artists. They formed a closely knit community and exchanged with one another all they had. They shared ideas, food, lodgings, and love. Young Frip had been frugal with his money while in the army, and came to Paris with quite a little bundle. He immediately rented a spacious apartment that contained a brightly lit studio. He equipped himself with pigment, oil, and brushes, and got down to work.

It wasn't long before he became a very important part of the Parisian artistic community. He was important because he was the only guy who had any money. Within a month his spacious apartment was no longer spacious—it was chockablock with people. In his own studio he was constantly knocking elbows with other painters. These others borrowed vast sums of money from him, spent it on drink, came to his apartment thoroughly plastered, broke things, raped his models, and lord-knows-what-all. And while they told Poindexter to his face that his work was good, behind his back they chuckled and jeered.

Frip, though, was still an innocent, and it never occurred to him that he was being taken advantage of.

Enter Marie.

Marie was a painter's model, the most beautiful one in the city. She had long red hair, full lips, and oddly vacant eyes. Her body was perfect—the first time she disrobed in Poindexter's studio, his hands shook so violently at her wonderful nudity that he was forced to dismiss her until the following day.

Now this may surprise you, but the name Poindexter W. Frip is not without a place in the annals of the history of modern art. True, one would have to be an historian of extensive knowledge to have come across it, but the fact remains that it is there. There are two periods in his career when Frip turned out work of lasting value. The first was when he was painting Marie.

Dear readers, you should see some of these paintings. My grandfather has, in his old seafarer's trunk, various reproductions, mostly postcard size. Even so small, they are majestic. Marie is always naked; in one she is reclining on a bed, staring at you with eyes that are oddly vacant but full of mystery. In another she is testing bath water with a big toe and looks so innocent that you initially feel a pang of guilt for seeing her nude—but the sheer glory of the nudity glues your eyes to the canvas and you cannot tear yourself away. All in all, they are wonderful. In the geezer's words, "They give you a chubb the size of a baseball bat." Even his contemporaries were forced to admit that Frip's paintings of Marie were "surprisingly passable".

The reason they are so good, as you might have guessed, is that young Poindexter Frip was hopelessly in love with Marie.

She was an odd girl and extremely quiet; when she did speak, it was often hard to make out what she meant. Mostly she would stare out into space, her eyes oddly vacant. Much of this rather curious person can be explained by a fact that young Frip was never cognizant of, that is, that Marie was an opium addict.

But, oh! he loved her. He painted her, he wrote poems about her, he dreamt about her. And in fact, his love was not unrequited. She seemed to prefer his company to that of all the others. When there were parties she would always go to be beside him, and she would not move from his side until the festivities were ended. Saying goodbye, she would kiss him softly on the mouth and squeeze his little hand. At other times, though, she seemed to be entirely unaware of him. Many times she passed him in the street without a flicker of recognition in her eyes. When this sort of thing happened young Poindexter was beside himself and could not be consoled. He would drink himself violently drunk and pass out senseless in the gutters of Gay Paree.

This went on for a couple of years and near drove Frip out of his mind. When Marie liked him, he was joyful and bursting with life; when she appeared not to, he was morose, glum, and almost suicidal.

Then two things happened. One was: thanks to his buddies, his bundle of money ran out completely, leaving Frip penniless. Exit his buddies.

The other was: the night before he was to vacate his spacious apartment (to take up lodgings in a squalid garret that he could just barely afford), he returned home to find Marie and one of the other painters rutting joyfully in the middle of the floor.

So begins the next period in which Frip's paintings are considered valuable. Alone in his tiny garret, never venturing out-of-doors, and drinking incredible quantities of absinthe, Poindexter painted some of the harshest and ugliest pictures that the world has seen. He painted Hell—dying drunkards, syphilitic whores, and starving children. He painted men that had the very hearts torn out of them. The absinthe produced in him unbelievable nightmares of cruelty and chaos, which he splashed across the canvases. These paintings have a power that almost bowls you right off your feet. In the geezer's words, "They turn your goddam stomach."

Frip's consumption of absinthe was an attempt to commit suicide. Unfortunately, absinthe poisoning often takes a few years and Pointy decided one day that his sad life should end right then and there. On that moonless night he went to a bridge and tied an anvil around his neck. Without a second's hesitation, he leapt towards the Seine below.

Frip was in a state of delirium from the early stages of absinthe poisoning, but what happened to him seemed as real as anything ever could. First of all he felt fingers working at the knot around his neck: deft, cold fingers. The rope fell away, and he was no longer bound to the anvil. And then, just before he hit the river, he heard a familiar voice whispering into his ear.

And the voice said, "Nobody can't hold on to nuffin'."

Poindexter Frip landed in the water, came up for air, and started heading for the bank.

As he pulled himself out he had resolved that (a) painting was not his cup of tea and (b) he had to leave Paris. In the grandest tradition he left the city that very instant, on foot. He marched off in the direction in which he happened to be headed.

Hearing Merlin's ragged, boozy voice had surprised him, but not unpleasantly. While he walked, he began to think back on his years of tutelage with that man. Frip stopped to pick up a stone from the road and, tentatively, sent it into nothingness and brought it back. He had not kept up practice for the past five years, so his first few passes were clumsy and amateurish. But by the time he had walked a few miles it began to come back. He practised with all manner of objects he found littered about the road—stones, coins, bottles, buttons, etc.

He was doing his magic, quite absentmindedly, when he reached his first village. He didn't notice that behind him was a throng of ragged children running along and laughing delightedly at his every sleight-of-hand. Hearing (and subsequently seeing) them, Poindexter stopped and allowed a small circle to form around him. Then he pulled stones and buttons from their hair, ears, and noses. After a few minutes he went to take his leave.

The adults had seen him amusing the children, and as he went by their modest homes they called to him coyly, offering various food and drink. No one family could afford to give him very much, but by the time he reached the other side of the tiny village he was stuffed and pleasantly pickled. For the first time in years, Frip felt happiness; upon the open road he laughed frequently, for no good reason.

And that is how he made his way across Europe.

It was as he went through Brussels that he saw a sign on a door advertising the need for a highly versatile translator. It was the door of a large newspaper. Although Poindexter looked like a tramp after his long and arduous journey (it had taken weeks and weeks —he had been walking with no true direction, so that an outline of his trip would look like tangled fishing twine), he resolved to apply for the position. He marched in and impressed them immediately with his knowledge of foreign languages. He was given the job, along with an advance so that he could clean himself up.

Poindexter Frip decided that his real artistic bent lay along the lines of literature. So once he was settled into an apartment, he equipped himself with a typewriting machine and got down to it. His days he spent translating, and his nights he spent writing novels.

Although he produced eleven novels during this time, only one achieved acclaim. It was extremely popular, and the critics felt it was the best novel published that year. It was entitled *In My Eyes* and chronicled the love between a starving young painter living in Paris and a beautiful red-haired model with oddly vacant eyes. In the end both commit suicide.

During this period Frip married. His bride was a lovely young lady named Jeanne—she worked as a pianist for a ballet school. She was a high-spirited girl, quick to laugh and quick to cry, and she loved Poindexter very much. And he loved her just as much. She taught him to play the piano, and he taught her to speak fluent

English. They had one child, a boy, that they named Charles in honour of Jeanne's father.

Poindexter Frip's story might have ended here, the two of them living happily ever after. Although his other novels could never match the success of *In My Eyes*, they sold modestly well, and he might have spent a contented life writing them. Jeanne made a decent salary working at the ballet school, and it was work that she enjoyed. So the story might have ended here, and I'm sorry that it didn't.

But the sad fact of it is that Jeanne and the three-year-old Charles were among the victims of a horrible train wreck. They had been going to visit her parents for the weekend; Poindexter had remained behind in order to meet a publisher's deadline.

There you have it. Frip disappears for two years and is not heard of. When next we see him it is in the United States of America. He has a caravan and an old horse named Floyd. He performs magic. He has changed his name so that it contains a duality, so that it represents opposites. He has known good and evil; he is Poindexter Sinister. We call him Doctor.

"Hey, Doc!" exclaimed Crybaby Isbister. "You really got that one down good!"

"Indeed?" was Dr. Sinister's response. He threw another pitch, and Nathanael watched as it broke down and to the left, crossing the makeshift plate.

"That's great!" shouted Crybaby happily.

"Mechanics," announced the little man. "Simple, damned mechanics."

"Okay, you guys," screamed Nathanael to the other players, "let's throw that ball around a little bit!"

I have allowed a couple of days to slip by in the narrative, mostly because not much has happened. Nathanael has been in rare good spirits lately; every day he works the team hard and enthusiastically. He shows up for practices grinning broadly, pushing Stella along in her custom-made wheelbarrow. Stella herself sits by the side and sings out encouragement.

Janus has also been in good spirits because he is allowed to play with the team. The two-headed, five-legged wonderdog races about, catching baseballs with the greatest of ease. Then he runs them back to the infield so quickly that Isbister has begun to think that Janus's inability to throw is not so much of a handicap after all.

Zapper, the hairy little pinhead, has started to show distinct signs of understanding the game. Although he gets confused from time to time (he has been spotted standing far out in centre field, a bat in his hand, crouched down and waiting for a pitch), for the most part he gets it right. If a ball comes toward him, he endeavours to catch it, although he rarely succeeds. If he does, he will throw it to another player, although he rarely succeeds here either.

Ally (as Nathanael predicted) shows great promise as a hitter. His distance is not remarkable, but he almost always makes contact. Isbister has taught him well how to place a ball, how to find a hole in the field and send it there. Ally's catching and throwing are also very strong. (It should be noted that the Alligator Man is in a good mood when, and only when, he is practising with the team. Otherwise, he is his same sullen, brooding self, if not slightly more so than before.)

The Hisslop girls have acquired all the basic skills of baseball, although they can do nothing particularly well. They manage to hit one out of every three or four balls, and some go far enough that they might, with luck, be base hits. The sisters catch fairly well; Violet has the stronger throwing arm, and she returns them.

Tanya has all the basic talents, and in practice has done some astounding things. She has walloped a ball to hell with very little effort, and has hurled one to home plate from deep centre field. Her problem, though, is her lethargy, her not caring one iota about the task at hand. (Nathanael has asked Stella to have a talk with her about it.)

Davey Goliath has come *so close* to doing things right that it makes Crybaby want to scream. He misses hitting balls by a fraction of an inch, and he misses catching them by the same fraction. There seems to be something missing, some small thing that is preventing Davey from clicking. Isbister has often wondered what it could be.

With Bobby Merrill, things are not going so well. He has become positively obsessed with the idea that he is a coward, and is so sure of it that he has started to do cowardly things that he never would have done before. Any crack of the bat will send him running for cover. He avoids situations that will bring him close to a baseball. He has declined to take batting practice, scribbling in his little book:

My arm is extremely sore. Might I sit this one out?

Angus McCallister has yet to show up for a workout. His excuses have been varied and imaginative, ranging from, "I canna teday— 'tis the anniversary o' the death o' me dear mother, and Cape custom has it, ye can *not* play baseball," to, "Because o' the rain that is a-comin', the bunion on me third toe, left foot, has begun achin' t' kill the deevil, so I canna." At dinner, however, he seems to be healthy enough, eating as much as the other troupe members combined (excepting Stella). He laughs and tells filthy stories, and winks nonstop at the Hisslop girls.

Major Mite has been unendurably irritable. The members of the carnival have long since given up trying to talk with him, being as every question or statement is answered by a high-pitched, snarling insult.

That's how things are going. I choose to come back to this particular day of practice because something out of the ordinary happens. After all the players have taken a turn at bat, Nathanael Crybaby Isbister walks up to the plate and tells the doctor to try that fancy pitch on him. Nathanael hikes the bat up to his shoulder and crouches. Dr. Sinister winds up unceremoniously and drills the ball forward. Isbister hits it—it sails like the American Eagle into the air and almost disappears from sight before dropping to the ground.

On the faces of all the players—including Crybaby's—there are smiles.

Chapter 10

OUTSIDE THE WIND was howling, and a cold rain pelted on the roof. Inside the caravan that served as their kitchen and mess-hall, the troupe members drank an after-dinner coffee, keeping warm beside the stove. No one was in a hurry to leave.

"Nathanael," said Dr. Sinister as he prepared Zap's coffee (five heaping spoonfuls of sugar, a large dollop of cream), "I was strolling out along by the highway today, which is, in sooth, quotidian, being as I have a rigid and prescribed route for my perambulatory constitutional that necessitates walking out alongside the high—" He was interrupted by little Zap who, having taken a sip of his coffee, spat it out across the table, narrowly missing Isbister's left shoulder. Dr. Sinister added another heaping teaspoonful of sugar to the hairy man's cup and then proceeded. "—way. I happened to notice that these were posted every hundred or so yards, although it was hardly a porscrutation on my part." The Doctor reached inside his old tuxedo jacket and withdrew a handbill, which he passed to Nathanael. Isbister read it through quickly and muttered, "Tomorrow, huh?"

"What is it then?" demanded Angus. He had been topping up his coffee with whisky, and now had far more liquor in his cup than caffeine.

Nathanael handed the handbill to Angus absentmindedly. McCallister accepted it with a slight scowl. The giant then stared at it for a while and every so often he would mutter under his breath, "How's that?" or "Do tell . . ." or "The deevil . . ."

For the first time in many days, Major Mite laughed. He erupted into a high-pitched giggle and pointed his tiny finger at Angus. "What a faker!" he shouted, delighted. "He don't know how to read!"

Angus laid the handbill down sheepishly. "It's just that I donna have me specs with me . . ." he muttered. Then he shoved the paper across to the Major. "Here smart feller, ye give it a go."

Major Mite stopped laughing abruptly and reached for the hand-bill. He put on some miniature spectacles and gazed at the printing for some long moments. He then announced, "Yep, it's tomorrow."

"Ach, mon, ye've jest now heared Natty say that!" shouted Angus. "Tell us what's tomorrow!"

"What's tomorrow?" responded the Major. "What's tomorrow? Why, the . . . uh . . ."

The Alligator Man reached over irritably and snapped the hand-bill out of the Major's hand. He read it quickly. "The House of Jonah are playing the Alexandria Athletics. Price of admission, fifty cents." He threw the handbill on to the table, muttering something about "stupid old geezers."

Nathanael seemed to have reached a decision. "We're going," he told the people. "It might scare you to see the House play, but I figure it's better to get scared now than on the day when we play them."

His suggestion was met, for the most part, by an uneasy silence. The troupe members exchanged rapid glances, then looked down at the table below.

Isbister searched their faces one by one. "What's the matter?" he asked.

Violet Hisslop said quietly, "Well, we have a show to do tomor-row."

"You can cancel one show, can't you? Eh, Doc?"

Dr. Sinister nodded. "Indeed we can. Indeed we will."

The troupe members looked at the Doctor fleetingly and then returned their glances downward.

Angus McCallister stood up and slammed a massive foot on to the floor, shaking the caravan. "What grand fun!" he shouted. "We'll go t' the game, me friends, and have us a good time!" Then his voice got quiet. "There won't be no trouble."

Tanya asked sullenly, "Do we *all* have to go?"

"Aye!" said Angus. "We're all going. It's the coach's say-so."

"I'm not afraid to go to a ballgame," said the Alligator Man. " I got just as much a right to go to a ballgame as the next guy."

"Damn reet, lad," stated Angus.

"The only problem is that of mobility," said Dr. Sinister. "The lorry might well prove Lilliputian."

Angus wrinkled his brow, confused.

"The pickup might not hold us all," said Dr. Sinister.

"Sure an' it will!" shouted Angus. "We just gotta snuggle up, that's all." He then used one of his grey eyes to wink at the Hisslops, the other to wink at Tanya. The troupe members laughed loudly, but finished their coffee in silence.

After a while the rain stopped. Nathanael helped Stella into her wheelbarrow and pushed her across to the little blow-off tent. Soon they were in their usual position, Stella seated high upon her throne, Nate squatting below on the ground.

"So what was it, Stel?" asked Isbister. "They were all afraid to go into town."

"Well, Nate, that's not exactly true. Most of them will go into Burton's Harbor if need be. Daisy and Vi go in all the time. It's just that Alexandria is a strange town—and what with us all going together, it's bound to start some sort of commotion."

"Are you afraid to go into town?" Crybaby asked quietly.

She nodded.

Just then the sound of bootheels could be heard on the steps. The flap of the tent opened, and Edmund came in. He had the collar of his black leather jacket turned up against the bite of the wind, and looked steadfastly at the ground. In his right hand he held a bouquet of flowers. The weather had been cruel to them—most of the petals had been lost, and the stems were bent and broken.

"Hello, Edmund," said Stella.

Edmund noticed Nathanael; the two men looked at each other. In a flash it became a staring contest, neither man wanting to avert his gaze lest it should be taken as a sign of weakness.

Stella made introductions. "Edmund, Nate. Nate, Edmund."

Isbister responded with a quick and almost imperceptible nod. Edmund grunted, a short hoarse sound. And still the men glared at each other.

"Did you bring me flowers, Edmund?" Stella prodded.

Without looking, Edmund thrust them out to her, almost smacking her in the face with his fisted hand.

"They're beautiful," she said as she accepted them.

With those words, something in Edmund's manner changed. He turned immediately from Isbister and looked at Stella with a shy smile.

Even though it was Edmund who had broken eye contact, Nathanael felt defeated. He rose slowly to his feet. "I'm going now, Stel," he said quietly, hoping she would bid him stay.

"All right," she answered almost absentmindedly. She was still busy with a close inspection of the ruined flowers.

Dejectedly, Nathanael walked from her tent.

Nathanael wept.

When Isbister emerged from his caravan the following morning, the site was a scene of great activity. The troupe members ran excitedly to and fro, engaged in various and sundry enterprises.

The little Dr. Sinister was hammering a sign into the ground. It read, "Spectacle Cancelled—Dreadfully Sorry!" He finished just as Isbister came up beside him.

"Good morning, Nathanael, dear boy," he said quietly. "I had feared that the sporting would prove dispanurgic due to inclimate precipitation, but as you see, my qualms had no basis." The doctor threw his arms up to the sky, where a bright sun sat alone in the cloudless blue.

"It sure is a nice day," agreed Nathanael, although that fact did little to cheer him up.

"Yes, indeedy-deedy-do!" said the Doc, giving the sign another little tap with his hammer.

The Alligator Man was leaning inside the open hood of the pickup truck, fiddling with assorted gadgets. His green hands were coated with grease, and he was whistling. He was in a good mood because (a) going to a baseball game was a change from the regular daily routine and (b) the Hisslops had dressed up very nicely, which required great time and trouble, and meant that they had stayed naked longer than usual that morning. He called out to Nathanael, "Hey, Nate! You know anything about motors?"

Nathanael shook his head glumly.

The door to the mess caravan flew open, and the Hisslop girls stuck out their heads. They did look remarkably beautiful this morning, and even Isbister could not stop a smile from drifting across his face.

"Yoo-hooo! Nathanael!" they called in unison.

"Yes, ladies?"

"Do you like mayonnaise on ham sandwiches?" asked Violet.

"Or mustard?" asked Daisy.

"Mustard," muttered Crybaby.

Daisy turned to her sister with an impish giggle. "I told you so!" They disappeared into the caravan.

Angus McCallister came striding into sight. He boomed out, "Meself, I like *ham* on ham sammiches! Don't you lassies go giving me no piece o' meat that's so thin I'm like to blow me hooter in't!" He laughed loudly.

"All right, Angus!" yelled the Hisslop sisters from within the caravan.

Major Mite trotted alongside Angus. He, too, seemed to have been caught up in the excitement of the day and was grinning broadly.

"Donny," said Angus, "ye take the high harmony. Ye recollect that we used ta sing this vera tune when ol' Morris M-for-Magnus signed us with that big show in Tulsa. Alrighty— 'Take me out to the ball game, take me out to the crowd—' " The two began a duet —a distance of about three octaves separated the voices.

"Knock it off, you guys!" yelled Ally, but it was obvious from his tone that he didn't mean it, and the two old friends continued singing merrily.

Zap appeared sheepishly from behind one of the caravans. He was sheepish for a very good reason—instead of his usual loincloth *cum* Tarzan outfit, he was dressed in a checkered shirt and shorts. His feet had been stockinged and put into running shoes. Upon the pin of his hairy head sat a baseball cap.

"Doesn't the dapper Zapper look the epitome of sartorial splendour?" asked Dr. Sinister.

Zap screamed loudly.

Janus ran up to sniff at Zap inquisitively. It occurred to Nathanael that the two-headed dog was making a joke, treating the well-dressed Zap as a total stranger. He dismissed the idea as foolish. Zap, for his own part, spied an opportunity to mess up his clothes, so he pounced on Janus, and the two began fighting in the dirt. Dr. Sinister hastened to intervene.

Davey Goliath hobbled out. He was dressed in a severe grey suit, and his shoes were brightly polished. Because his head was so far above everyone else's, no one really noticed the troubled expression on his face. Davey Goliath was concerned because Dr. Hunter could well be lurking in the crowd at the baseball game.

That is, no one noticed but Angus. He marched over to Davey and leaned toward him confidentially.

"Davey," he said, almost in a whisper, "ye ken this man Hunter?"

Davey started at the mention of the name but managed to control himself. He nodded slowly.

"What does he look like?" asked Angus.

"He is small," answered Davey Goliath, "but do not let his size fool you. He more than makes up for it by evil cunning. He has tiny eyes like a fox and oversized ears like a wolf. His hair is white," he concluded. "But all this means nothing, as he is a master of disguise."

"Can ye not think of anythin' else, lad?" pressed Angus.

"Yes," said Davey quietly. "Wherever he goes, he takes with him a cauldron full of boiling water. He means to use this to strip the flesh from my bones."

Angus nodded decisively. "Aye. He should be easy t' spot. If I spy him, Davey me lad, that little mon is as good as dead."

Davey was visibly relieved.

Bobby Merrill was dressed the same as always, his huge head supported in the neck-brace. He had considered wearing his monk's cowl so that the hood could hide his misshapen face but he eventually forgot about the idea. For one thing, a monk's cowl at a ball game would be almost as conspicuous as he himself was. For another, he was a coward, afraid of a baseball hitting him, and didn't feel he had the right to try concealing his shame. He avoided going near Mr. Isbister, and instead drifted over to stand beside Tanya.

Madame Tanya, alone of all the troupe members, looked unexcited. In fact, she looked downright bored and was continually stifling yawns as she watched the preparations.

Bobby Merrill scribbled out a note and handed it to her. It said:

Didn't you sleep well, Miss Tanya?

She read the note and smiled. "Yes, Bobby," she answered. Bobby wrote:

I think this should be grand fun, going to a baseball game. I've never been to one in all my life. Have you ever been to one, Miss Tanya?

"No," she responded; she looked at the Hippopotamus Boy's horribly ugly face, and smiled once more. Finally she said, "Yes, I suppose it might be fun at that."

Bobby Merrill grinned, although it was impossible to tell by looking at him.

Isbister looked around for Stella and saw that she wasn't there. He realized that no one had gone to fetch her yet, being as caught up as they were. He hurried off to her tent.

"Finally!" she exclaimed as he poked his head through the blow-off's opening. "I was beginning to think I was going to be left behind!"

Nathanael had a strange and burning desire to ask what had happened the night before, how long Edmund had stayed, what they had talked about, etc., but he shoved it all from his mind. He tried his best to smile warmly. "We wouldn't leave you behind, Stel," he said.

Stella giggled lightly. "That's good, Nate." Her voice was soft and as tender as she was. "Very good, indeed."

Nathanael had the impression that what was "very good, indeed" was not the fact that Stella wouldn't be left behind, so he asked, "What's good?"

" 'We'," she answered.

"Huh?"

"You said 'we'. 'We wouldn't leave you behind,' you said."

"I guess I did," mused Nathanael. "I'll go get your barrow."

He ran around to the other side of the tent and drew the contraption up to the rent in the rear of Stella's home. He parted the canvas and touched her shoulder lightly. She fell backwards, into his arms, and he helped her settle into the cushions of the wheelbarrow. As Nathanael pushed her towards the others, Stella said, offhandedly, "That Edmund surely does want to marry me."

Despite the fact that moments before Isbister had struggled hard not to ask about it, now he didn't care to know. He changed the subject quickly by saying, "You should see Zap. The Doc's got him all dressed up in regular clothes. Funniest thing you ever saw."

As if on cue, Zap came running up to the wheelbarrow and threw himself in on top of Stella with a few contented grunts.

"Don't you look nice, Zapper?" asked the fat lady rhetorically. The hairy little man nestled into the folds of her flesh and promptly went to sleep.

Janus followed quickly behind. Apparently he was not through tormenting the Wild Man from Borneo. Janus began to bark with the strange doubled echo, attempting to rouse Zap from his slumber.

Isbister hushed him sternly. "You guys be quiet," he said. "If you like Zap's clothes so much, I'm sure the Doc could rig up some fancy duds for you."

Janus went instantly silent and crept alongside the wheelbarrow shamefacedly.

Dr. Sinister sang out, "With the advent of the lovely Stella our number is complete and our embarkation at hand!"

Their embarkation wasn't really all that close at hand, seeing as they had still to figure out how to fit all thirteen of them into the fairly small pickup truck.

"I," said Dr. Sinister, taking charge (although in practical matters of this sort his taking charge usually proved quite ineffectual), "shall sit in the back along with hale males such as Angus, Ally, Nathanael—wait! Wait, wait, wait! I've made a ludibrious error. Ally is the only one capable of operating the lorry. Therefore he must sit up front. In addition to . . ." He twitched his nose back and forth, trying to decide who would sit in the cab of the truck.

Angus completed the thought for him. "I'm thinkin' that Violet and Daisy should sit up front with Al, an' the rest of us all into the back."

"We don't mind sitting in the back," announced the Hisslops.

(A dark look clouded Ally's face as he considered the possibility that the girls didn't *want* to sit up front with him.)

"No," said Dr. Sinister. "Mr. McCallister's logic would seem to me ineluctable. Violet and Daisy shall ride with Ally. Now, first of all . . ." Again his nose twitched as he tried to think what should be done first of all.

Again it was Angus who finished the sentence. "First of all, let's put Miss Stelly up theer. The little 'un can stay with her." But instead of waiting for assistance, Angus bent down and enveloped the wheelbarrow in his massive arms. He raised it from the ground and placed it gingerly on to the truck—he did this so smoothly that Zap never even stirred in his slumber.

Isbister silently calculated the combined weight of the barrow, Stella, and Zapper. After that he stared, awestruck, at the giant from Cape Breton.

Dr. Sinister said, "I espy toward the rear a raised section, designed no doubt with some applicability, although I would be hard put to offer a suggestion as to what that might be, *however*, it seems to me that it would serve commodiously as a *seat*. Perhaps for Miss Tanya."

Everyone chuckled at Dr. Sinister. They were delighted with his uncontained excitement.

Tanya was about to jump into the truck when Angus stepped forward and gallantly offered his hand. She climbed up daintily.

"And now," said Dr. Sinister, with a twitching nose.

"And now," said McCallister, "let's pile in it!!"

Davey Goliath stepped up into the truck as if it were a single step. He remained standing, supported by his thick canes, until

Angus was up also, and then he asked the giant to help him sit down. Angus grinned heartily and did so. "It be a mite of a long way doon fer us, ain't it, laddie?" Nathanael assisted Bobby Merrill into the back and then climbed in himself. Major Mite pulled himself up with a few low grunts and curses, Janus sprang up eagerly and that left only Dr. Sinister remaining on the ground. Unfortunately, there did not appear to be a square inch of free space remaining.

The little Doctor took great pains to disguise the sad frown on his face. "Oh, dear," he murmured. "Well, this might prove both a boon and a benison—I've plenty of work to occupy myself . . ."

Nathanael said, "We can make room, Doc. We just gotta squeeze together, that's all."

"But Alexandria is somewhat transpontine, and I fear it may be a discomforting journey."

The men in the truck had already shoved themselves tightly together so that there was ample room for Dr. Sinister's tiny bottom. His grin returning instantly, the little man climbed in, drew up the back, secured it, and sat down. Then they were away.

In the cab of the truck, Violet Hisslop was going over in her mind her sister's theory that the Alligator Man liked them. Being the right half of the pair, she was sitting by the door, well away from him. Mischievously she shifted over until the length of Daisy's thigh touched Ally's. He jerked his leg away instantly, and his hand flew out to work the stick shift.

Violet leaned over to look at him. The Alligator Man, she decided, was really very handsome. He was a fool to think that skin with a greenish tinge made any difference to two girls who had spent their entire lives in freak shows.

Ally, for his own part, was being sullen and silent. His hard eyes rested on the road; his jaw was clenched tightly as he concentrated on driving. He was madly going through his memory for some conversational gambit but was having no luck at all.

"Ally," said Violet (he responded with a quick and eager "Yeah?"), "why don't you ever come visit us?"

Daisy, in the middle, stared straight ahead, reddening.

The Alligator Man was obviously stuck for an answer. "Why? Uh . . . I don't know. Busy. Why . . ." He then drew a deep breath and said, "I'd like to."

"Well, then," concluded Violet, "you're very welcome to."
They drove to Alexandria in silence.

In the back of the truck, Angus was leading the others in a sing-song.

They arrived at the ballpark and spilled out of the truck. Dr. Sinister, who carried the money, instructed the others to follow him. He went to a wicket and purchased thirteen tickets, which he then presented to a man beside a turnstile.

The man at the turnstile had become very bored over the past hour. He stared blankly with absolutely no expression or thought. He accepted the tickets and nodded curtly to the voice that announced, "Thirteen."

By the time the thirteenth admission had walked by he was extremely agitated and badly in need of a drink.

Despite the excitement of the troupe members, the day did not turn out to be a good one.

There was no "trouble" of the sort they had feared. There were hushed whispers and pointed fingers, but they had all long grown used to that sort of thing. They sat by themselves in their section of the bleachers, aware that at any one time twenty or so people were staring at them open-mouthed, but they had grown used to that sort of thing as well.

What was depressing to them was the show that Tekel Ambrose and his Brethren put on.

The other team, the Alexandria Athletics, were ranked second in their league. The next step for their better players would be the majors. They trotted on to the diamond to a thundering applause from the nine hundred (or so) spectators.

Then came the House of Jonah.

Simply put, they looked ridiculous. They were all cast from the same mould—their hair fell freely to their shoulders, and their long, immaculately cared-for beards came to their waists. This did not harmonize with the light pinstriped baseball uniforms they were wearing.

Instead of charging from the dugout enthusiastically, the Brethren marched in a ridiculous single file that would have been more appropriate at a funeral. All of them were looking steadfastly at the ground below them; they were at prayer.

At first this spectacle brought on titters and chuckles from the stands. Tekel Ambrose raised his head and scanned the audience with his black eyes. There was quiet.

The national anthem was played on an old organ somewhere. One or two of the notes were horribly out of tune.

The umpire shouted, "Play ball!"

The Brethren of the House of Jonah went up to bat first, being as the Alexandria Athletics (or the Alex A's, as they were known locally) were on home turf.

The first batter was Mene Ambrose. He very quietly entered the box, hiked up his bat, and waited.

The pitcher for the Alex A's was a young man named Knowles. His first name was Sebastian, but around the county he was called "Knuckle" Knowles because he threw such a mean knuckle ball. Scattered about the bleachers were various scouts from the major leagues, who had been told to pay special attention to Knowles.

Isbister pointed them out to Stella, who was sitting beside him. "See those guys with little notebooks, Stel?" he asked. "Scouts from the big leagues. I guess these Alexandria Athletics got them some pretty good ballplayers."

"I hope they win!" exclaimed Stella.

"Yeah," nodded Nathanael—but he seemed uneasy.

Knuckle Knowles leaned forward and pasted on to his face a most intimidating glare. He swung his arms behind his back and toyed with the ball inside the glove.

Mene Ambrose remained serene. There wasn't the slightest hint of agitation upon his calm features.

Suddenly Knuckle Knowles's arm shot forward, and a baseball was speeding toward home plate.

Mene Ambrose appeared to be performing a sort of ballet. First of all the bat described a slow and graceful arc through the air. Instantly the ball was headed in the other direction. Mene Ambrose let the bat drop gently and began what looked like a trot to first base.

The shortstop for the Alex A's scooped the ball from the ground and shot it without hesitation to first. It was a perfect throw, right into the glove of his teammate.

Incredibly, Mene Ambrose was already there. His hands were folded in front of him, and his face still wore the same serene expression.

Nathanael Crybaby Isbister muttered, "Jesus . . ." under his breath.

This performance was repeated, with minor variations, by Peres Ambrose. He allowed one pitch to sail by him, one that was called a ball by the umpire. Peres hit the next one in a line drive near third base. Again, the opposing player had to make a spectacular catch and an instantaneous throw—but again, it made no difference. Mene now stood calmly on second, Peres on first.

The next batter for the Brethren was one whose name we don't know, although I guess if I were a thorough researcher I could dig it out. But what, really, does it matter? He looked the same as the rest of them and conducted himself in precisely the same manner— i.e., calmly and methodically driving a ball just to the left of first base.

The bases were loaded.

Then came Tekel.

Had our friends bothered to look around, they would have seen that for the first time since their arrival no one was staring at them. But our friends were too busy looking at Tekel, just like everybody else.

Knuckle Knowles assumed a most menacing look. He shoved his lower jaw forward and formed his eyes into a round and evil glare.

Tekel Ambrose's face darkened as if a rain cloud had passed above it.

The expression on Knuckle Knowles's face began slipping, like a cat trying to cling to a brick wall—finally it fell off altogether.

The pitch came—it was Knuckle's best pitch, a crazy, meandering ball that seemed possessed by demons and madmen, whirling like a dervish.

Tekel Ambrose drove the bat forward and connected with a resounding "thwack". The ball flew from the park like a bird, easily clearing the fences of deepest centre field.

The Brethren, without emotion, trotted past home plate, and signs were changed so that the score read "Home-0, Visitors-4".

Nathanael Isbister knew that he had just witnessed two things: first, a spectacular display of baseball. He remembered that the House of Jonah had been good, but he had forgotten just how good. The second thing he had witnessed was the end of Knuckle Knowles's professional baseball career. The scouts were all getting up from their places, slipping their notebooks into their pockets, and hurrying off to other games.

(Here, safe within my parentheses, I could really hit old Tekel below the belt, and spell out the extent to which he and his Brethren ruined Knowles's life. Oh, it's a sad tale! But, then again, Tekel *et al.* were just doing what they did best, so it wouldn't be fair to blame Knuckle's pitifully tragic life on them. True, it ended in suicide not long after this very game, but we can never be sure that this game had anything to do with it, can we? Therefore, guided by my overwhelming sense of fair play, I will not say a thing about it.)

The other Brethren were not quite as good as the Ambrose brothers, with the result that the half-inning finally ended. One of them hit a fly, which was caught, to left field. Another was thrown out at first. Another was struck out by Knuckle Knowles, who really was an exceptional pitcher. (But too late, Knuckle: the scouts have left the stands.) When the Alex A's came up to bat, the score was 11-0.

As we know, the pitcher for the House of Jonah was none other than Tekel. He stepped onto the mound almost daintily and shot in conference. Tekel nodded and directed his gaze at the first batter. He did not alter his expression perceptibly, but again the rain cloud passed above him; great shadows flew over his gaunt face, full of darkness. His eyes seemed to glow with a kind of black light.

The batter did his best to return the look, but to no avail. Within a few seconds his knees were trembling slightly.

Surprisingly, Tekel's pitching style was silly-looking. It's hard to imagine anything being silly about Tekel, but this is true. His arm flew forward with elaborate dips and curves, as if it were made of rubber. He did not throw the ball so much as push it along its way. Still, the pitch flew across the plate before the batter had time to react.

The umpire called out a loud, "Steeeeeeerike!"

Peres Ambrose, who was the backcatcher, returned the ball to his brother.

Nathanael Isbister was astounded by the variety of pitches that Tekel could deliver flawlessly. They came fast and slow, dipping and dropping, changing direction constantly. The best that either of the first two batters could get off him was a foul pop-up into the stands.

Meanwhile, the fielding Brethren stayed crouched and unmoving in their positions, ready in case, by some miracle, a batter should connect with one of Tekel's pitches.

The miracle did happen. Gordon Mackay, third up and one of the best batters for the Alex A's, belted one out of the park. Although the left field player did a noble job of trying to catch it, it was simply not within the range of human capabilities.

Gordon Mackay rounded the bases jubilantly, his arms held above his head, his chest puffed with glory.

Isolated upon his mound and unable to do a thing, Tekel Ambrose's face turned a dark shade of midnight. He was mad.

The next batter was struck out mercilessly. Three rapid pitches screamed over the plate, defying the man to do so much as nick one. The first inning was over, and the score was 11-1.

Nathanael Isbister looked over his team to see the effect the game had on them thus far. He was saddened.

From left to right along the bench: Angus McCallister, unwilling to show signs of a faltering spirit, was feigning sleep; Major Mite was muttering, "Alexandria Assholes if you ask me. . ." under his breath; Madame Tanya was looking even more bored than usual, which one would have thought impossible; Janus was asleep (or maybe just pretending, like Angus—who knows?); Bobby Merrill, although his ugly face was untelling, was making nervous motions with his hands to signal his distress; Davey Goliath, bolt upright and towering, was as grim-faced as a child taking cod-liver oil; Zap (who had no idea what was going on anyway) was throwing around some peanuts that the doctor had bought for him; the Doctor himself was issuing forth a series of philosophical sighs and "Ah, me"s; Stella was chewing a fingernail and looking up occasionally at Nathanael from the corner of her eyes; (here is where Nathanael sat); the Alligator Man, with the profoundest of scowls, was enunciating the single word "Shit," with great relish; and the Hisslop sisters, in whispers, were making comments about the rear ends of some of the Alex A's, as if, though they were being beaten severely, this could be compensated for by their far cuter bums.

Investigative research of the most thorough and diligent sort has uncovered this information about Tekel Ambrose.

As a lad of twelve, he was not a remarkable baseball player. He was, of course, in the best of physical condition owing to the regimen of the House of Jonah, and could execute all of the necessary plays flawlessly. But there was nothing remarkable about

Tekel. It seemed at the time that his younger brothers, Mene and Peres, would be far better. Those two played with zeal and enthusiasm, eager to gain the praise of their elders. Tekel, coldly aloof, did not seem to crave this praise — and so he would play baseball, rarely making mistakes, but never showing a sign that he would one day become superhumanly good.

The boys of the House of Jonah spent a good deal of time playing the game. When they played, there was no laughter. There were no joyous and jeering catcalls. The boys had already learned that baseball was Work—they played with the sullen silence of assembly-line workers.

Their practice fields were constantly changing, owing to the fact that the Brethren worked their fields on a rotating basis. After a few weeks of practice at one location, the men would appear with farming implements and the youngsters, nodding, would march off to another. So it was that one day they found a field that dropped off sharply on one side into a thickly weeded gully.

Because he was fairly good (but far from extraordinary), Tekel Ambrose played the outfield in those days. This day he was in left field, which meant that the drop into the gully was directly behind him.

The practice began; the boys had divided into two teams, Mene heading one, Peres the other. When the teams were chosen, neither one had selected Tekel until he alone was left unpicked—then Peres, with a distinct look of annoyance, had claimed him. This did not both Tekel. Indeed, he found it admirable in his brothers that they could so easily discard familial bonds in favour of that most perfect thing, Work.

Peres had marched his team out into the field, indicating to Tekel the left field. Tekel accepted, although he saw immediately that he was being punished. Should he miss a ball (which he did from time to time from a lack of concentration), it would be lost in the thickets and weeds below. He would have to find it, and in doing so his legs and arms would be scratched by thorns. Mene and Peres were constantly doing this sort of thing to their older brother, angry that he was not as good at baseball as they were.

Tekel went to this position obediently. He crouched and waited. The first ball that came in his direction he caught. He caught the second as well. However, the third sailed high overhead. He had simply miscalculated its path, expecting it to drop sooner than it did. Tekel heard the soft crackling of twigs as the ball landed in the gully behind him. He spun around, removed his glove, and climbed down after it.

The House of Jonah had always preached a stoic indifference to pain, and the twelve-year-old Tekel did his best to ignore the scratches of the thorns.

The gully was a foot deep in dead bushes and thick weeds, and Tekel saw that the task of finding the baseball was a formidable one. It was, in fact, next to impossible; it was, however, likewise impossible for him to abandon the search. Such an act would be unthinkable. Dropping to his hands and knees, he began to cover the ground inch by inch.

The pain of the scratches grew as his naked forearms and calves became crosshatched with fine red lines. Tekel realized that what he wanted most to do was cry out in agony; with this horrible realization came a torrent of tears that streamed, hot and burning, down his face. He brushed the tears away one by one as they came, and they came for a few moments and then no more.

Tekel pulled apart the tangled clumps of brown and brittle branches, peering between them in hopes of spotting the lost baseball. He knew that by now the boys had resumed practice without him.

As he pulled apart one clump, Tekel was started to see, not the black brown darkness he had grown used to, but a bright white. He dug further, and chiselled words appeared in the white— chiselled words that read:

HERE LIES MORRIS UPCHURCH
1804 — 1867
MAY GOD TAKE HIS SOUL

With a terror that he was never to know again, Tekel Ambrose realized that the weeded gully hid a graveyard. He became frantic then, wanting to run away, knowing that he couldn't until the baseball was found. He tore away at the weeds, this time sincerely unmindful of the pain. Blood began to flow freely from his hands, and thorns stuck him so deeply that they became imbedded in his skin.

More and more gravestones were uncovered, and each one increased the terror. Most of Tekel's mind was by this time irrationally horrified, but some small part of it, a part full of morbid curiosity, made him note each name:

WALLACE BEARD
1812 — 1880
GOD HAVE MERCY

ELIZABETH ASH BEARD
1850 — 1872

This small part of his mind drove him to do the subtraction, to figure out how old each person had been. When Elizabeth Ash Beard turned out to have been twenty-two when she died he flung himself away from her, tearing at a clump with renewed vigour and terror.

TRENTON BRACE GORDON
1841 — 1876
IF GOD IS MERCIFUL,
HE WILL HAVE THIS
WRETCHED SOUL.

Some stones, like this one, instantly filled Tekel's mind with stories. He could clearly see Trenton Gordon, fool and imbecile, always getting into trouble for touching little girls, for burning stray cats, for fornicating with farm animals. Where the stories came from, Tekel didn't know—he knew only that they were not welcome.

Every marker mentioned God; most assumed He would take the soul with no questions asked. Others were less sure, and seemed to be making appeals to His mercy and love. This one put it most strangely:

CHARLES T. BROOKMAN
1802 — 1877
MAY GOD TAKE THIS SOUL:
AS CHARLES WOULD DO IF
HE WERE GOD, AND GOD WERE
CHARLIE T. BROOKMAN.

Years later—many, many years later—Tekel Ambrose would think back to this stone and allow himself a smile. When he was twelve, though, and bleeding and scared and doubting that he would ever find the baseball, it was merely chillingly incomprehensible, as irrational as the terror that engulfed him.

He found the baseball.

It lay, innocently, in front of a gravestone. Allowing himself a cry of joy, Tekel lunged at the ball, sprawling down on the ground.

He read:

> HENRY WELLS GOLIGHTLY
> AGE — 2 MOS.
> KNOW THEE, GOD,
> HE HAD NO SIN. . .

There were two more lines of poetry chisselled into the stone, but Tekel did not read them. He was running from the gully, hoping to regain the higher ground before the tears came once more.

He emerged on to the field a sorry sight. He had been gone for less than five minutes, but he now stood, bloody and trembling, his uniform a collection of tatters.

Tekel Ambrose tried not to—but he could not help thinking of Henry Wells Golightly. Through his tear-brimmed eyes, the baseball in his hands looked like the head of a tiny, dead baby.

He threw it all the way to home plate. That was the first extraordinary thing he did, and it was the first of many. From that day forward Tekel Ambrose applied his every energy and thought to the playing of baseball. To watch him practise and play you might think he was. . .well, possibly running from something. As a recently divorced man, running from that heartbreak, might throw himself into his work with a monomaniacal passion. But then you would reconsider. Tekel Ambrose wasn't running from anything. He was confronting something, doing mortal combat with it—fighting invisible demons that were with him wherever he went.

And after you were through all these ruminations, you would do just one thing: stand in awe of Tekel Ambrose.

The Brethren of the House of Jonah beat the Alexandria Athletics 21-4. Tekel Ambrose had done many extraordinary things. He had hit two home runs, two doubles, and was walked once. His pitching had yielded exactly five hits, he had gone the entire game without a sign of fatigue.

Once a ball had been driven by a batter right over top of him. It looked to be clearing his head by a distance of about nine feet, but Tekel Ambrose caught it, jumping and twirling about in midair.

Major Mite quoted W.C. Fields at this point, although he didn't know it. The Major said of Tekel Ambrose what Fields said of Charlie Chaplin: "The guy's a fuckin' ballet dancer."

Chapter 11

SO THEY WENT home.

They sat around the dining table amid an awkward silence. Angus alone made a sound, and this was but a soft and melodic humming that came like a breeze from many miles away.

Dr. Sinister prepared the meal very hurriedly and methodically, as if impatient to be doing something else. He ladled the food on to the plates and set them in front of the troupe members with whispered admonitions: "Eat. Eat." And when all were served, he spoon-fed Zap at such a clip that the Wild Man from Borneo was unable to get up to any mischief. He merely sat there, his eyes crossed and quizzical, and swallowed obediently every time a heaping load was shoved into his mouth. The others, caught up in the little Doctor's haste, began to ram their food down quickly, and the dinner was finished in record time.

"Ah!" beamed Dr. Sinister when he saw that all the plates were clean. "I'm pleased to see the repast dispatched with such celerity."

"Ach," muttered Angus, "if there was celerity in that salad, I'd no time fer tastin' it."

"An excellent quibble," said Dr. Sinister, although he didn't really seem to notice it. "Down to business," he announced, and cleared his throat. "We witnessed this day a demonstration not unlike the extravaganzas of ancient Rome, to wit, a puny minikin is pitted against gargantuans and prides of lions. . ." He furrowed his brow. "Actually, you know," he said confidentially, "the analogy is tenuous, being as in the one case the minikin referred to is a Christian, while in our analogue it is the gargantuan factor who are representative of a spiritual. . ." In a thoroughly uncharacteristic move, Dr. Sinister hit himself on the head and pulled at his hair with exasperation. "What tripe I spout!!" he screamed. "Right, then," he said, and a tinge of his old cockney accent crept back into his voice. "We all saw it. What are we going to do?"

All of the heads (even Zap's; even Janus's) swung around to look at Nathanael Crybaby Isbister. He began to shuffle his feet beneath the table; he brought up his right forefinger and drove it into the palm of his left hand. "Well," he began, and then realized that he hadn't the slightest idea. His hand flew up to tug on his chin, and he muttered, "Goddam." He finally said, "See, I think those Alex A's played way too defensively. I mean, all they could think about was stopping Tekel and the boys. It's like they were hypnotized or something. Yeah! Tekel would just give 'em the evil eye and they started thinking, 'Oh, God, we gotta stop them.' And, deep down, I don't think they thought they could do it. It's like they had a hex on them. They never started thinking, 'Hell, we're just as good as them! If they're gonna rack up ten runs, we're gonna go get us eleven!' And that's why they lost. I mean, *shit!* . . . excuse me, ladies. . . those Alex A's were good ball players. There is no way in the world they should have lost that bad."

Major Mite muttered morosely, "Goddam right."

"But what," asked an unexpected voice, namely Davey Goliath's, "can *we* do about it? If a semi-professional baseball team does not have sufficient self-confidence, how could *we*?" He pointed to all assembled with his foot-long finger, unwilling to vocalize what they were thinking.

Nathanael knew that an easy answer would be "leadership". But he was afraid to say it, knowing that the mantle would be placed on his shoulders. Then a thought occurred to him—the troupe members had all lacked the self-confidence to go into Alexandria, until. . . The thought hit him with such force that he bolted up angrily from the table. "*God damn you!*" he bellowed at Angus McCallister. "Why the hell won't you play baseball?"

Angus feigned incomprehension. "What do ye mean, 'won't', Natty? I sure as the deevil will! Tomorrow."

Nathanael remained angry. "Tomorrow, tomorrow, tomorrow. It's always tomorrow."

"Sure, an it is fer sure. . ." started Angus.

"And then tomorrow you'll have some malarkey cooked up about it's being St. Aloysius' Day, or about your bunions, or—"

"Jest because I've strong religious convictions and certain medical disorders, don't be makin' a case that I'm, fer some strange reason, avoiding the practices."

"And don't you play us for fools, McCallister!" shouted Nathanael.

"D'ye wish t' come t' blows with me, Isbister?" challenged Angus, half-rising from the table and forming a fist as big as an anvil.

Nathanael's first impulse was to jerk back quickly; then, after a moment's reflection, he leaned forward and thrust his jaw out at the giant from Cape Breton. "You bet." He snapped off the words like twigs of wood. "I'll come to blows with ye, alrighty, boyo," Nathanael said, mimicking Angus's thick accent.

Major Mite squeaked out, "Nate, don't be stupid!"

"I ain't being stupid at all! You just watch." Isbister stood up and pulled off his jacket. He began to roll up his shirt-sleeves with quick and precise turns. "Okay, gooney," he said casually, "let's go."

"*Gooney!*" bellowed Angus, and he grabbed for Major Mite's tiny shoulder. "Donny, tell him what I done in New Orleans."

"Nate," pleaded the Major, "one time in New Orleans he took apart twenty guys, no crap!"

"Oh, did he? Did he, now?" Isbister had a drunkard's manner to him, arrogant and goading. "I don't care. New Orleans is an awful long way from here. Come on, Angus, let's go." He hooked a finger at him impishly, as one would do to a child.

"Ye'd think he didn't need his head!" shouted McCallister.

The other members were staring at this scene with disbelief.

"I shall be waiting outside," announced Nathanael with a smile, strutting toward the door of the caravan.

"Ye're not serious?" demanded Angus.

"Oh, yes!" chirped Isbister.

"Look, Natty, jest sit back doon an' we'll talk this all out sensible."

"No, Angus," Crybaby said. "No. I'm waiting outside for you." Then he was gone.

Major Mite was the first to break the silence. He leaned across to the giant Angus, whose expression, if it had to be named, was one of bewilderment. "Well," said the Major, "I guess he's asked for it."

"Aye," whispered McCallister.

"What's gotten into him?" Stella wondered aloud.

The Alligator Man said, "He's a pretty tough guy, Crybaby is. He can handle himself."

"Against Angus?" asked Dr. Sinister.

"He's got it comin' in spades, Angus," said the Major. "You got to go out there."

"Aye," whispered the giant from Cape Breton.

"Yoo-hoooo!" came Nathanael's voice from outside.

"Brother!" said the Major. "He's itchin' for it!"

Angus sat stock-still, looking down at his folded hands.

"I know you don't *want* to," said the Major, "but I don't see as you got any choice."

"Aye," repeated McCallister in a hoarse whisper.

"Go on," said the Major.

The giant Angus cleared his throat and shook his head. "I'm not goin'," he muttered.

"You gotta!" screamed Major Mite. "He called you 'gooney'."

" 'Gooney'," mused Angus quietly. "I've been called worse."

Major Mite was dumbstruck. "I don't believe my ears."

Nathanael Isbister came back into the caravan; he didn't seem at all surprised to see the silent Angus still seated at the table. Without a word, Crybaby sat down and reached for his coffee.

In an evening full of awkward periods of quiet, this was the quietest, the longest, and by far the most awkward. The troupe members looked alternately at Angus and Nathanael. From Nathanael they received an inscrutable shrug; Angus refused to raise his eyes.

Bobby Merrill silently broke the silence, by writing out a note and passing it to the centre of the table where all eyes could read it. He wrote:

I don't understand.

Nathanael nodded. "He's afraid."

The tiny Major Mite was outraged. "Angus ain't afraid of nothing or nobody! He could have torn you to ribbons, buster!"

Isbister nodded again. "Absolutely. I'm no match for him."

"So what the hell do you mean, he's afraid?"

"He's not afraid that he won't beat me, Major. He's just afraid that you won't have any stories to tell. You won't be able to say, 'Angus ripped apart Isbister in four seconds flat,' because he wouldn't have. I'd land a couple of punches—"

"What kind of crap is that?" demanded the Major.

"It's—" started Nathanael, but Angus suddenly reared himself and completed the statement for him. "True. It's true, Donny. I amn't no superman no more. It's jest what I've been wantin' t' tell ye. I amn't a superman. Jest a man."

"You're the strongest man alive."

"Nay," stated Angus. "Sure an' I'm strong, Donny. But there's many as strong—many stronger. I'm just. . . a man."

"And that's why you haven't been practising," said Nathanael. "Because you couldn't bash a ball all the way to hell like the Major says you could."

"Aw, how could ye understand?" asked the giant quietly. "Ye donna understand, ye donna know what it's like. I was the strongest man on this earth. The verra strongest. There wasn't a single man who could tangle with me." Angus smiled at his reverie. "But then. . . I started gettin' old. An' I lost a bit o' the strength. Donny, before I left the show I started gettin' tired. Why, my God, I'd never got tired in me life! But I'd lift those weights, and damn me if I weren't a-sweatin' an' tryin' t' catch me breath. Well. . ." He stopped for a moment's reflection. "I'm jest a man, now. Jest a ordinary man."

"There are people here," snarled Nathanael, "who would give anything to say that, and you act as if it's an insult to be an 'ordinary man'." The disdain in Crybaby's voice was unmistakable.

Angus rose up from the table. "Who in hell are *you* t' say that t' me?! Ye who *cry* for ordinary folk but won't have a thing t' do with 'em? At least I did summit! I was the strongest man alive!"

"Okay, okay," muttered Nathanael. "We both drew a little blood. I'm sorry."

"Aye—I be sorry, too," said Angus.

"Angus," Isbister said, after a long moment, "do you remember when we were loading up the truck to go to the game?"

"Aye? What of it?"

"You lifted Stella's wheelbarrow into the truck."

"Aye. . ."

"Like it was nothing."

"Aye. . ."

"Do you realize how much that weighs?"

The troupe members watched as a broad grin flowered across Angus's face; they all joined him in smiling.

Angus stood up from the table; he had to stoop his shoulders slightly to prevent his head from bumping into the ceiling. Then he said, "I want ever'one t' go get a good night's sleep, as we've a lot o' work t' do tomorra. Natty, I think thee an' me should go t' yer caravan an' discuss general tactics an' plans an' such like. What say?"

"You're on, Angus."

"Reet. Doc, ye can come also—providin' ye promise t' speak the King's English an' none other."

Dr. Sinister said, "Angus, my usage of the sesquipedalian shall hereafter be replaced by terse and laconic elocution."

"Reet, Natty," said Angus, "we'll leave him behind."

Now, what exactly was discussed by those three men will never be known exactly. From that day forward, however, Angus, the Doctor, and Crybaby Isbister were always seen together, talking in a hushed, conspiratorial manner. The trio would eye various troupe members and then whisper hurriedly, arguing for a few seconds but quickly coming to an agreement, signified by vigorous nods of their heads.

The other members quickly accepted that they were being led by a triumvirate, a triumvirate that worked remarkably well, particularly at team practices.

Crybaby Isbister was the technician and tactician. He spoke quietly and methodically of various strategies and techniques, demonstrating them to the assembled members.

The giant from Cape Breton now took up the other aspect of a coach's work, that of cajoling his players into doing their best. He could be alternately gentle and harsh; yet his gentleness was never construed as softness, nor his harshness as cruelty. He showed no favouritism, although he was likely to pat the Hisslop girls on their firm buttocks for little or no reason.

The Doctor's role was less clear-cut. Basically, he served as an example. Should Isbister's explanations be hard to follow, the Doctor would understand first and then explain it in other terms to anyone still in the dark. Dr. Sinister was the first to obey Angus's orders, doing so quickly and happily.

During practices, the other players felt secure and confident under the leadership of the three men.

On the other hand, when they weren't practising, they couldn't help a vague sense of misgiving. The triumvirate, with their stares and whispers and pointing fingers, were up to something. What they were doing, in fact, was considering each player's problems individually and trying to arrive at possible solutions.

Some were simple—or at least, simple in that there was little they could do. Such was the case with Zapper. Although the Doctor said he would spend extra time with the Wild Man from Borneo in an attempt to get him to understand the game, no one felt this would bear much fruit. (Lately, Zap's most immediate response to the sight of a baseball was to pop it into his mouth. His glove he liked to insert into his pants so that it covered his crotch. As for the bat, Zap still seemed to think that its purpose was to play a spirited and freewheeling game of solitaire croquet.)

Of course, some players didn't constitute much of a problem. The Major was one; since Angus' mood had turned, so had the Major's. He was now his old self once more, foul-mouthed and jubilant.

The Hisslop sisters also presented little problem. They were playing, the two of them, rather well. The triumvirate, though, all agreed that the girls had to give just a little bit more if the freak team was to win the game. This came up during a discussion of the Alligator Man.

Stella was no problem, as she was not actually going to play. In fact With her cheery smiles and sideline enthusiasm, she was a whole line of cheerleaders rolled into one.

The three did come up with what they thought might be the answer to the question of David Gray Goliat; unfortunately, it was a plan that could not be implemented until the day of the game (less than a week away!)

Janus didn't have any emotional problems, of course, and was always in good spirits. His only shortcoming was that he was a dog. Crybaby still felt that Janus's caninism prohibited his participating, although he had to admit that the wonderdog would be an asset in the field. As noted previously, Janus's lack of a throwing arm was made up for by his ability to run amazingly quickly. And when he came within ten feet of a teammate he would snap his two heads back quickly, which more often than not resulted in a perfect lob towards his fellow's glove. Also (although Nathanael attributed this more to his imagination), Janus seemed to have a good grasp of the rules and strategies involved in baseball. Crybaby's attitude was, basically, "Too bad Fido and Rover is a dog." Angus agreed with him, arguing with Dr. Sinister. "Bejaysus, Doc, it's a mutt! A mastiff! A hoond!! How in hell can it play baseball?" "Well," responded the Doctor, "aside from his batting average, I'd say he can play rather well."

This left, problematically speaking, Tanya and Bobby Merrill. They were the biggest problems because they both had deep-rooted and very personal blocks about playing the game. Angus seemed to know what to do about Tanya, or at least he thought he did. He refused to tell the others, however. "I'll not tell ye, fer it don't work all the time. Meself, I've known it to do wonders."

No matter how much he was pressed, Angus would not tell—in fact, the whole question seemed to embarrass him.

Bobby Merrill was perhaps the biggest problem of all. There was no doubt that something was bothering the boy, and bothering him badly. No one could offer any idea whatsoever as to what it might be.

Thus the triumvirate decided that it was time to go and talk to the grotesque Hippopotamus Boy.

On the very evening that the trio went to visit Bobby Merrill, the Alligator Man went to visit the Hisslop sisters. His preparation was very elaborate. It included bathing, pressing his trousers, shining his shoes, covering himself in after-shave lotion, shaving (I've got the order right, trust me), brushing his hair, and drinking a twenty-sixer of whisky. And then, with what he thought to be a confident and debonair swagger, he left his caravan and walked across to the Hisslop girls'.

Bobby Merrill's trailer was extremely neat and orderly. Its four walls were mostly taken up by bookshelves, full of large volumes of poetry and romantic novels, arranged alphabetically and never out of order.

The furnishing was sparse, that is, it was comprised of three items. The first was a small bed, one end covered with a hill of pillows. Bobby slept in a position that was more sitting up than lying down, his swollen head raised high on the pile of cushions. The second piece of furniture was a rocking chair; the back had been cut in half to accommodate Bobby's head. The last item was a large desk with a secretaire top that rolled down to reveal numerous filing slots, all jammed with sheaves of paper. This was Bobby's poetry; the papers were sorted according to subject. One slot, for example, might be given over entirely to odes concerning *Nature*. Another might be labelled *The Fairer Sex*. In a drawer, usually kept locked, was Bobby's dairy.

I say the drawer was "usually" kept locked because at this specific time it was not. It was open, the diary was out, and Bobby (his neck-brace supporting his balloon head) was writing in it:

Cowardice takes many forms and not all are recognized as such. As well, ofttimes an action may be designated "cowardice" that in reality is nothing at all like that foul failing. Angus's reluctance to play: is that cowardice? I think not. This is merely loyalty to his dear friend Major Mite—this is laudable. He did not want the Major to be disappointed in him and thusly hid the fact that he had fallen from his former heights. However, to be afraid of being hit by a baseball. . .

At this point there was a knocking at his door. Bobby liked to leave no thought unfinished, so, although he was going to think up something along the lines of "the lowest, most swinish and despicable, the uttermost *loathsomest*," etc., etc., he had time enough only to scribble "STINKS" before going to answer the door.

Bobby hid the diary in the drawer and locked it tight.

He was expecting no one, but upon hearing the knock he assumed that it was Davey Goliath. David and Bobby were fairly close friends, and it was not unusual for the giant to hobble across once every two weeks or so. On these occasions the two would play a card game called Railroad which is, in my opinion, a great cardgame, and I'd like to take the time to explain how it's played, but I can't.

Instead of finding David Gray Goliat, however, Bobby found the threesome. Instantly he was terrified. They had come to throw him off the baseball team—no! no! to throw him out of the show! Somehow they had discovered his vile secret.

"Hoddo, Bobby," said Nathanael, nodding his head a bit and smiling.

Bobby stared back—he had no idea what to do.

"All hail, Robert," chirped little Dr. Sinister. "Would you very much resent us stepping inside?"

Bobby took two or three steps backward to allow them entry; anyone watching would have thought he was backing away from axe murderers.

Angus McCallister came in last of the three. He tried to put Bobby at ease with a soft tongue-clucking, a large wink, and a friendly "What say, Robby?" It didn't work.

"Sit down, Bobby," motioned Nathanael.

Robert Merrill managed to shake his huge head once from side to side, a strenuous task that would have left him exhausted had he not been so upset by the visit.

The triumvirate exchanged rapid glances; they had not expected Bobby to be quite this distraught.

"Well, Robert, you're probably thrown on your beam ends as to why we've come," said Dr. Sinister suddenly.

"No real special reason," said Nathanael.

"Jest a social call, like," put in Angus—and then, to prove that it was a social call, Angus did something sociable. He said to Bobby, "An' how're ye feelin'?"

"An excellent query!" said Poindexter Sinister by way of seconding the motion.

All this was interpreted by Bobby as cruelty of the greatest magnitude. Why, he wondered, did they keep up this masquerade of social niceties? Why didn't they just come out with it and accuse him of cowardice?

"Bobby," said Nathanael finally, seeing that Angus's tack had not worked, "We couldn't help noticing that lately something's been bothering you a little bit."

Now, Nathanael Isbister may have been capable of a good many things, one thing he was not capable of, however, was deceit. Bobby Merrill saw instantly that his secret was still exclusively his own, and while he was relieved, he was also a little disappointed. Quite a weight had actually been lifted from his chest when he thought the trio knew. Now he was trying to decide whether or not he should tell. . . and after a few moments of intense and heated inner debate, he decided he would. He dashed for his little notebook.

His first written answer was scrawled rapidly and thrust into Dr. Sinister's hands. Bobby took a step backwards and waited expectantly. The little Doctor perused the paper for a long time and finally took a guess with, " 'I am a canard' ?"

Bobby snatched another piece of paper and made great big block letters that spelled out:

C O W A R D

The three men made a circle around the paper. They stared hard for many long moments until Angus asked, "What's it say?" in a soft, embarrassed whisper. For the first time in his life, Bobby Merrill wished that he could scream, so that he might bellow the answer once and for all and be done with it.

The little Doctor answered Angus. " 'Coward'," he said.

"Coward?" repeated the giant.

Bobby Merrill, the grotesque Hippopotamus Boy, lunged for yet another piece of paper and scrawled furiously for some moments. He was crying so profusely that the tears managed to find their way free, out of the deep and black caves that hid his eyes. They dropped on to the paper and made the words blur.

When he was through, he handed the paper to Dr. Sinister. This was simply out of habit—he was far too distraught to be thinking clearly.

Poindexter Sinister had some trouble making out the wet and runny words, but in time the message was read:

> Yes, I am a coward. A *coward*. Have you not noticed me cowering on the baseball diamond? Have you not noticed me cringing and quacking* with fear whenever a baseball is even remotely close to me? The simple truth of the matter is that I am a coward, fearful to my marrow lest the ball should strike me.

The Doctor had supplied the punctuation.

The three men were quiet. Then Angus said, "Well, fer crissakes, laddy, *I'm* feared t' be hit by a baseball! I think it'd reet smart."

This had no effect on Bobby. He had, of course, assumed that everybody was reluctant to be hit by a baseball. However, the words he assigned to this were along the lines of "trepidatious" and "cautious". The label "cowardice" he applied only to himself.

Dr. Sinister tried this approach: "Robert, perhaps it is because you have yet to make contact, body-to-projectile-wise, with a baseball. You may find it merely a short-lived grate, hardly lethiferous, easily overcome."

Robert Merrill responded to this by scribbling, "Once bitten, twice shy," on a piece of paper.

Nathanael Isbister had been thinking hard for a long time. He then asked a question that was not expected by anyone in that caravan. "Bobby," he asked, "do you hate people?"

There was no need to wait for an answer—Bobby did not.

Nathanael proceeded. "Bob, I don't like to be cruel, but... what with the way you look, and the life you've led, and the way you get treated sometimes, it'd be understandable if you did. Goddamit, you should! You should hate all mankind, and hate them with a passion. But you don't."

* "Quaking" is likely what is meant.

Isbister hadn't touched another man for many, many years, but at this point he crossed over to the Hippopotamus Boy and put his arm around his shoulder. Nathanael didn't notice either the monumental ugliness or the stench.

"To me," Crybaby said, "that's bravery. All that other stuff, not being afraid of fights or pain, stuff like that, that doesn't amount to nothing. I knew a man would fight anything in a second—that's cause he hated everybody. But you don't.

"Bobby," Nathanael concluded, "I figure you're the bravest guy I ever met."

It took Robert Merrill, the Hippopotamus Boy, almost an hour to fully understand what Isbister had said. For it had never occurred to him that hatred was an option open to him.

Such was the greatness of that young man Merrill.

How many of you out there are familiar with the state of drunkenness? Considering that this book will likely be read only by those derelicts mentioned in Book II, Chapter 7, and my own personal friends, I should think the answer hovers very close to one hundred percent (the only exception being my girlfriend and, seeing as she's convinced I'm shacked up with someone else, I'm not sure she counts).

Therefore I shall proceed along this course.

Do you know this feeling? You go into a barroom, sit down, and begin to drink. You down possibly half a dozen bottles of beer while keeping up a fairly intelligent conversation with your companions, whoever they may be. I am not drunk, you tell yourself . . . not drunk at all. Then you stand up in order to go to the can. Your first attempted step is a long lurch sideways that sends you into a neighbouring table. Your next step, a hasty effort to regain lost territory, results in your kicking yourself in the ankle. Thereupon follow five or six quick stumbles, and finally you are doing something that nearly resembles perambulation. I am, you realize, thoroughly pissed.

My point being that this truth is accepted only once you have tried something that you have not attempted since commencing consumption.

While the Alligator Man prepared to visit the Hisslops, he did much walking; this took the form of nervous pacing, circling the interior of his caravan like a caged lion. He had not done any talking.

The Hisslop girls opened their door and gave Ally quite a shock, for they had not finished dressing. (The Alligator Man had been so caught up with his own preparations that he hadn't even peeked through the window toward the girls' caravan.) They were dressed in flannel dressing gowns (modified to permit their bonding) that were very modest—but with bodies like those of the Hisslops, nothing could hide the fact that under those dressing gowns was wonderful nakedness.

(Now here is why the barroom scenario above is significant.)

The Alligator Man opened his mouth; the following was his first attempt at speech: "Shreezegeist, youse guys grot gate tits!"

You drunks out there may know that even while the mouth behaves like this, the inner workings of the mind can remain relatively cogent. Ally's mind went, Oh, my God, I'm drunk—I gotta be sober. To this end, the Alligator Man proffered the bouquet of flowers he had brought them. When he saw his empty green hand, he realized that he had left them back in his caravan. He then opened his hand and pretended that his intention all along had been to shake in greeting.

"Oh, Ally," laughed Violet, "we're old friends. We don't have to shake hands."

"You don't hafta if you don't wanna," snarled Ally defensively. It was hard for him to break the habit of being nasty—but as soon as he realized that was what he was being, he said, "How'reya?" in as friendly a tone as he could muster.

"Fine," the girls answered in unison. Then they motioned that he should move out of the doorway where he had been standing for the past moments, weaving like a blade of grass blown by a strong wind.

The Alligator Man lurched forward, heading for a chair he had spotted in the centre of the room. Unfortunately, besotten as he was, Ally had forgotten that the Hisslop girls were Siamese twins. He headed straight for them, assuming they would separate to allow him passage. He ended up with his arms wrapped around the sisters, his head caught between their shoulders.

"Ally," said Daisy, "what are you doing?" Then the girls caught a whiff of the Alligator Man's breath and realized that they had a drunk on their hands.

"Come on, Ally," said Violet, "you'd better sit down."

Although there was nothing he wanted more in the world, Ally pulled himself away angrily. "Nope!" he shouted. "I'm okay. I don't need to siddown." He looked at their faces. "Youse guys are real goo'-lookin'," he announced, and then his head began to swim. "I gotta siddown."

The girls pulled off to one side and let the Alligator Man stumble on across the room. He threw himself down into the chair, falling like a crumpled newspaper.

The Alligator Man grabbed the arms of the chair and squeezed until his knuckles blanched under the strain. While he did this, he presented various facial expressions to Daisy and Violet. Talking about it later, the sisters decided that these were, for the most part, meant to be smiles. They didn't look much like smiles, though. They looked as if an invisible imbecile had hooked his fingers into Ally's mouth and was stretching the lips in various directions.

"Well," said Violet, "it's about time you came to visit us, Ally. We've always wondered why you've never come to visit us."

The Alligator Man did not seem to feel that this was a statement that required a response. He gave another try at smiling.

"Would you like something to drink?" asked Daisy.

"What do you got?" asked Ally, leaning forward excitedly.

"Oh!" Daisy was startled. "Oh. Well, we have everything. Gin, whisky, beer. . ."

"That's it!" shouted the Alligator Man. He had decided to try to sober up. "Beer."

Daisy and Violet didn't drink beer themselves, but they usually had a few bottles around for the young men that came to share their bed. They rose and went to the icebox.

Because Ally's vision was blurring, he was able to watch not two but *four* sets of buttocks swaying beneath the flannel material. And as the Hisslops bent down, it was *eight* half-moons that strained hard against it.

The Alligator Man began to get excited—indeed, he imagined that he was the proud possessor of a large and throbbing erection. Such was not the case, but it's true that Ally was extremely horny. He rose and flexed his fingers in imitation of an eagle's talons. Then he rushed at those four lovely bottoms. Only his left hand met real flesh; the other grabbed at thin air. The Alligator Man fell to the ground then, making contact first with his jaw. There was a sickening crunch.

Daisy and Violet stared at the form on their floor. It was Violet that had been goosed, and she was rubbing her flesh slowly and gently. "Kind of excitable, isn't he?" she said; her sister nodded in agreement.

Suddenly, with many gurgling sounds, the Alligator Man was all motion. He struggled up from the floor and bolted through their door. And then there came violent retchings. Daisy and Violet stood motionless and listened to Ally's suffering until they heard him stumble into his own caravan.

With many sighs, they went to bed.

That same night, Crybaby Isbister went out for a little stroll around the caravans. The air was raw and biting but the night itself felt somehow peaceful. Nathanael simply wandered about aimlessly, leisurely smoking cigarettes and taking moderate pulls from a hip-flask. Every now and again he would take a baseball from his pocket and flip it into the air. He'd let it roll down his arm and then snap when the ball hit his bicep, bouncing it back to his hand. He would spin it over his head and then trap it behind his back. For all intents and purposes, Crybaby appeared to be farting around.

But Nathanael was a man with a mission, and very shortly he saw something that made him stop his tomfoolery. He saw a caravan door open and a large figure emerge. The figure was obscure in the night, wrapped in a dark cloak and huddled against the wind. The person, whoever it was, walked with a quick, determined stride, but after a few moments it became obvious that he was going nowhere, simply making the circle of trailers as Crybaby had.

Nathanael followed, ducking behind caravans in secret agent style, although the figure up ahead never gave a backward glance. And as soon as Crybaby had established firmly just how quick the pace was, he cut through the ring of trailers and stood in the shadows, waiting.

When the cloaked figure was about twenty feet away, Crybaby jumped out from his hiding spot and shouted, "Hey! You!" The baseball was already in his hand, and he fired it along the ground. The pill shot forward quickly, taking short, erratic bounces off the ground. The other person reacted instantly, turning the lower half of the body sideways and dropping down on one knee. The figure barehanded the baseball and shot back up, and in the same instant the throwing arm was cocked and then released.

Nathanael Isbister thanked his lucky stars that he had thought to duck beforehand. The ball missed his scalp by about an inch, a throw that whistled in the night.

The two people stood and stared at each other. Both were wrapped in shadows and silence for a long, long moment.

And then Crybaby spoke. "You know, I played bush-league ball, anyway half a season's worth, with an outfit name of the Queen City Cowboys. There was this outfielder name of Tommy Drivotch that we sometimes played against. Nice fellow, kind of quiet. He was an adequate fielder, had a so-so arm, but he could hit real well. I always wondered whatever happened to old Tommy Drivotch. It seemed like all of a sudden he just disappeared."

"I suppose you think *I* might be this Drivotch."

Crybaby shrugged. "The notion crossed my mind. You look like him. And you've played a lot more ball than you let on. I shot a grounder at you just now and you fielded it like a pro, and I've never shown anyone on the team how to catch like that."

"It is ridiculous to think that I am Tommy Drivotch."

"Oh yeah? Now, suppose you tell me just why it's so ridiculous."

"Because," said Madame Tanya, "Drivotch could not hit a curve."

Nathanael laughed lightly. "That's true enough."

"Mr. Isbister," the bearded lady went on, "they say you have a drinking problem. That would mean that you very likely have something to drink back at your caravan."

Crybaby nodded. "Right on both counts."

"Why don't you offer a lady a drink, and we'll have a nice long talk, man to man."

Madame Tanya said, "My father believed in dybbuks and golems. He believed that elves lived inside mirrors. He believed that the dead could rise up from the ground, and he believed that God was good. He believed all that, but he could not believe that a girl could grow hair on her face.

"So, when the beard came, my father took the family to America. We stood for hours in the line at Ellis Island and when our turn came, the man asked my father what my name was.

" 'Tony,' said my father.

"It was the first I'd heard of it. My mother had dressed me for the voyage in overalls but I thought that was just so my dresses would not be spoiled. But then I understood that I had been dressed like a boy. My hair had always been cut short. I was to be this boy, Tony. My father found it easier to believe that a boy could have a cunt than that a girl could have a beard."

Tanya laughed without joy and reached for the bottle of whisky. She put it to her lips and drank a long pull. After she put the bottle down, Tanya patted her lips lightly with a handkerchief.

"I had liked very much being a girl. Where I come from, you learn very early about the mysteries of life. You learn to feel that women know what life is about, that we share the secret of the world, and that it's something men could never understand. I'll tell you the truth, Mr. Isbister—"

"Nathanael," corrected Crybaby.

"—Nathanael, you learn that men are, in a way, stupid. And as for boys—" Tanya waved her enormous, manicured hand disdainfully through the air, completing the thought. "But I was to be this stupid young boy Tony. As if that wasn't bad enough, I had to be this boy near Trenton, New Jersey."

As Tanya took another drink, Nathanael reflected on her tale. Sometimes, he thought, she had to try hard to infuse her voice with bitterness. There was an impish quality just barely hidden beneath the surface, like an elf in a mirror.

"And what is there to being a boy in America?" asked Madame Tanya. "There are silly movies on Saturday afternoon. There is fighting for no good reason. There is making fun of everything that is strange. There is reading nickel novels about cowboys and Indians and then pretending to be these same idiots. But most of all, there is—" Madame Tanya raised her eyebrows like a school-marm.

"Most of all," responded Crybaby obediently, "there's base-ball."

"Exactly. So Tony played baseball. That is, indeed, just about all that Tony did do. I don't know why it appealed so much to Tony. I suppose it was because in baseball you are a part of something, the team, but at the same time you are alone. No one can get close to you, everyone is at his specific position on the field. Mostly, Tony liked to hit. That's what baseball is all about, finally—one person with one stick of wood finding that one spot on the baseball that makes everything connect. Everything. Not just the bat and the ball. It makes *everything* connect." Tanya tilted her head and raised her eyebrows. "Do you know what I mean?"

Crybaby nodded violently—he'd had a few nips at the bottle himself. "A guy I played with called it 'the sweet spot'. Oh boy, do I know what you mean! Sometimes you could smack that ball and everything would make sense. As long as that ball was up in the air, everything would make sense. I used to have a dream, when I was younger, that one day I'd pop one, and it'd go up in the air and over the infield and over the outfield and out of the park and just keep going. Around and around the world, just like the moon. And everything would make sense." Crybaby grabbed for the whisky bottle with a grin on his face.

Tanya, looking at Nathanael oddly, said, "If anyone could do it, it would be you." The bearded lady continued her own story, or rather Tony's, after a moment. "Young Tony was a pretty fair baseball player. He was signed when he was sixteen by Jocko Dunn—" (Nathanael raised his eyebrows, impressed by the mention of the Chicago Cubs' top scout) "—and he played double-A ball in Danville. That was Tony's dream come true, except that he fell in love with the third-string catcher. Then, suddenly, there was no more Tony, there was Tanya again, but Tanya in a baseball uniform pretending to love baseball when all she really loved was this boy. And the really silly thing was, Tanya stood a better chance of making the big leagues than this boy did. I suppose it was obvious to everyone that I loved this boy, so they called me a fairy. Even my own father! That was easier for him to accept—'Tony is a *fagele*,' he'd say.

"But then I was eighteen, something happened. Namely—" Tanya touched her breasts. "So goodbye to Tony. Of course, I tried everything to get rid of the beard. Shaving, depilatories, all sorts of quack remedies, but nothing worked. So I am a freak. That is why I joined a freak show. If you are a baseball player, you join a baseball team. If you are a freak, you join a freak show. But I am also a woman, Nathanael, my whiskers notwithstanding. What you discovered tonight was the ghost of a boy named Tony who played ball for a Chicago double-A farm club. I realize that he might have helped your baseball team, but he no longer exists. I am a woman named Tanya. And "—the bearded lady rose to leave—"baseball is a silly game."

Chapter 12

MY GRANDFATHER ALSO went to see the Alexandria A's get soundly trounced by the House of Jonah's baseball team. Like the troupe members, he regarded it as a thoroughly disgusting spectacle. It put the fear of God into him. Already his promissory notes totalled nearly seven thousand dollars, and there was still almost a week left before the game was actually played. His bets would likely amount to ten thousand or so, which was, incidentally, $9,997.00 more than he had in his pocket. With that last three dollars, my grandfather resolved to find himself an accomplice.

My grandfather had a long list of diversified talents, most of them useless. One of the big ones was finding accomplices. Even when he was without a scheme, if he had nothing better to do he would find an accomplice. Finding accomplices was almost an avocation with him.

The first thing in finding accomplices is knowing where to look. My grandfather's strategy here was simple. He would take his (then, young, but still geezerish) self down to the seamiest, seediest part of town. Then he would slowly walk the skids past the bars. He walked until he heard the tinkle of breaking glass, and then, spinning about, he would determine exactly which bar it was that a patron had just been thrown through the plate glass window of. And that was the place.

On this specific occasion the bar happened to be called The Sailor's Wife. My grandfather walked in, delighted to find that a mug of draught would cost him only a nickel. Quickly he calculated that his three dollars allowed him no fewer than sixty mugs of draught. But always wary of doing himself too great damage with the evil brew, he altered this to fifty-eight mugs of draught and a pickled egg, which he allowed would satisfy most of his nutritional requirements. Climbing up on a barstool, he demanded three glasses of beer. The pickled egg, he told himself, could wait.

The bartender, a slender and effeminate man, served him, and scowled when he received absolutely zip for a tip.

My grandfather downed the first draught, and with the second began a very intense scrutiny of the establishment. The glass was still three-quarters full when he found his accomplice.

The man sat in the room's farthest corner.

He looked like he had been sucked out, as if some beast had fastened his mouth around the man's big toe and sucked until nothing—neither meat nor marrow—was left inside the skin. The skin itself was covered with tattoos—but as the insides had been sucked out, the words and bright colours had begun to fade and shrivel away. The man was now a collection of illegible scribblings and indeterminate designs. Most of his face consisted of his bottom lip; it was large and loose, and someone seemed to have pulled it up until it reached just below the man's eyes. The eyes themselves were as blue as the sea—and, as if to further this nautical impression, the man was constantly pitching them from side to side, creating the illusion of waves. There was a little sailor's cap perched upon his head, looking as if it was a pelican that had, for some reason, decided to roost there.

The man, although solitary, was far from silent. Most of his vocalizations, however, were of this nature: "Yaaaargh! Friggirig-gidiggihiggy—yaargh!" I hesitate to write down the words that *were* intelligible, for fear that you wouldn't believe me—but if you're still disbelieving things at *this* point, there's no hope for you. His words were mostly nouns, hollered out by themselves and for no good reason. "Icebox!!" or "Bedspread!!" or "Yuc-catan!"

This man, according to my grandfather, was possessed of the most beatific smile. Despite the wrinkled, mostly-lower-lip face, this old man had a grin to make Paul Newman's look like a half-hearted scowl.

My grandfather grabbed his remaining beer from the bar and walked over to this man's table. Without asking permission, he pulled up a chair and sat down.

The man regarded him indignantly. In order to do this, he pulled up his lower lip even further and closed one eye. At this point the lower lip, the one eye, and ten thousand wrinkles were all that made up his face. You might expect a three-year-old child to draw this face with a crayon. The man raised a bony fist (covered with tattoos that could no longer be read) and said, "Wanna fight?"

"Naw," said my grandfather, taking absolutely no umbrage at the challenge. "Just want to buy you a few drinks."

It took quite a while for this piece of information to make itself known within the workings of the sucked-out sailor's mind. But when it did, he smiled. His smile was like the sun coming out after a dismally long thunderstorm. "Okey-dokey!" he chirped happily. "Yuccatan!"

My grandfather loaded the little table with mugs of draught, and the two began to drink in silence. That is, near-silence. Between mugs of draught the sucked-out sailor man would say, "Yuccatan." It took about six beer and as many repetitions before my grandfather realized that Yuccatan was, in fact, the man's name.

Once the initial batch of beer had been done with, they loaded up the table again, and this time they drank more slowly. They began a kind of conversation. It was freewheeling and illogical, with Yuccatan carrying the ball most of the time.

"Used to work for the undertaker," said Yuccatan. "Sewed up the mouths. Got a bottle of wine a day. Got fired."

"For what?" asked my grandfather.

"Drank the embalming fluid." And then, after a long silence, "Damn near killed me."

My grandfather, never one to be outdone, countered with a long and complicated tale about having his toe bitten off by a rabid wolf in the backwoods of British Columbia. When Yuccatan failed to be impressed, my grandfather came up with the *coup de grace.* "And do you know what?!" he demanded dramatically. "The damned toe grew back!"

Yuccatan refused to believe it. "Show me!"

Gramps pulled off his boot and displayed a full set of withered toes. Yuccatan gasped and was satisfied.

To the sucked-out sailor, two stories occurred. One was that his teeth were always falling out and growing back. The other was that he had once been bitten by a rattlesnake.

"What did ya do?" asked my grandfather. "Did you cut open the wound with a knife and suck out the poison and spit it on the ground?"

Yuccatan listened to this with a child's wonder, but when it was done he waved it away as if irritated and said, "Nope."

"So what did you do?"

"Told the snake to fuck off," said Yuccatan.

My grandfather then claimed to have himself bitten a rattlesnake.

Etc., etc.

This sort of thing kept up all through the night. At last call my granddad took the dime that was meant to buy a pickled egg and ordered two more glasses of beer. Yuccatan applauded this course of action, being as pickled eggs had been known to "make people's goonads wrinkle and fall off."

Yuccatan became my grandfather's accomplice just like that. When they were finally thrown out of the Sailor's Wife, they stumbled merrily through the streets, their outrageous lies following merrily behind like a pack of stray dogs.

Gramps sneaked Yuccatan up to his room at the Fulton Arms and told the sucked-out sailor that he was welcome to sleep on the floor. Yuccatan collapsed on it like a puppet whose strings had been cut, and began a loud and off-beat snoring.

Later that night my grandfather was awakened by the sound of that same snoring coming from right beside him in the bed.

In the morning, after drinking an emergency supply of whisky that my grandfather kept hidden away, Yuccatan was made knowledgeable of the scheme. The plan delighted him—it produced a long and glorious smile on the old man's face.

My grandfather told Yuccatan what it was he had to do, and what he would need for it.

Yuccatan said, "I know where to get one. Now, let's go borry some money from my sister."

The young reporter woke up, snapped upright, and wondered where the hell he was. He was used to this sort of thing, so he experienced no panic, no terror. It was a hotel room, obviously. He had booked himself into a hotel. And then, calmly, he began to wonder where the washroom was; he had a violent need to be sick.

He was lying naked on top of the sheets. His body was flabby and pale; it seemed older than his face, which looked like a baby's. The young reporter swung his legs around, groaning, and felt for his trousers with the big toe of his left foot—he was unwilling to open his eyes until it was absolutely necessary. His foot hit the cold metal of the belt buckle, and he reached for the pants and drew them on, still with his eyes screwed shut. . . but he was forced to open them, for something was wrong.

Somebody (maybe himself) had cut his trousers off just above the knee so that they had become ragged schoolboy's shorts. He cast his aching mind back, hoping for a blurred flash that might give him some clue to this mystery. Nothing was forthcoming. Groaning once more, he pitched himself toward the door and wandered out into the hall.

The bile was leaping up into his gorge like a bunch of kids on pogo-sticks, but the young reporter did not hurry. He looked slowly down the row of doors until he saw the one that said "CONVENIENCE", and he began to make his way toward it. There was a quick grey flash in the corner of his eye—it looked like a rat. The young reporter knew it was no such thing and paid it no mind.

Halfway to the washroom, another door opened, and the two men came out. One was a short, wiry man, just entering middle age. The other was an ancient man who looked as if everything had been sucked out of him. The two men were talking loudly, and the young reporter hoped they did not notice him.

They did. The ancient one stopped him with a hand that was almost transparent. With a mouth that rippled like an imbecilic ocean, the old man said, "Oncet, I died. My heart stopped for seven minutes. I seen the Pearly Gates. The angels were playing the trumpet."

The young reporter did not blink. What he did do was deposit a large pool of liquid vomit at the feet of the two men.

The men shrugged and continued past.

Angus McCallister did not resent old age. But it had to be dignified. His one regret was that his own life had been a series of sleazy sideshows. When he cast his mind back it filled like a bucket with warm and happy thoughts, but sometimes irritating images came back as well. He remembered, for example, little men in ramshackle barns, making bets that he could pick up a horse. He remembered executing this feat, seemingly without effort. Mostly he remembered the look in the eyes of the horse, a sad and defeated look that emphasized the cruelty and stupidity of the whole thing.

On his farm in Cape Breton, Angus was dignified. He worked with his massive hands from dawn until dark, until they were crimson and calloused and lined with dirt. The men in town respected him as a knowledgeable and worldly elder, and any argument was settled finally by taking the matter to "Mr. McCallister". Of course, the townspeople still revelled in his legends, feasting over them lustily, but always when the giant was well out of earshot. That was dignity.

And now, Angus sighed, here I be once moor.

He was making his way toward Tanya's caravan, stuffed into a grey suit that before this had seen only the inside of a Cape Breton church. In his hand there was a bunch of flowers that looked ridiculously miniscule.

But then agin, the giant thought, dignity ain't everythin'. Some of the best times he'd had with Donny were things like wandering naked through busy streets, lordly drunk and singing tunes. Not much dignity to that. I dunno, Angus challenged himself, there be summit like dignity there. I dunno, he concluded.

He did not climb the four steps that led to Tanya's caravan; rather he stayed on the ground and rapped gently on the door.

Tanya's voice, the husky mid-range, shot out sharply, "Who is it?"

"Angus, ma'am. McCallister."

"What do you want?" Tanya demanded.

"Ah, well, ma'am, it be a social call," was his answer.

"What do you want?!"

Seeing an open window further along, Angus went to it and stuck his head through.

Tanya was standing near the door, naked. She swung around to face Angus and made no move to cover herself. Placing her hands on her hips, she stared menacingly and repeated, "What do you want?"

Angus, always a gentleman, jerked his head back quickly, but not before he'd had a look at Tanya's body. He was relieved, because from the neck down she was definitely a woman.

"I'll come back later, ma'am," he announced.

Tanya yelled out, "What do you want?", but the giant was already far away.

And long after he was gone, Tanya was still whispering, "What do you want?", and every part of her was longing for the answer.

It did not bother her that she had been seen naked. In her little blow-off tent she had often shown her body to disbelievers

who threatened police action unless they were one hundred percent satisfied that she was a woman. Her usual routine was simply
to undress to her underthings—but if a rube persisted, she would
pull off her pants without emotion.

She looked down at her womanhood now.

Once, as a little girl, she had found an apple in the corner of
a closet. It had been there for months and months, and it was so
shrivelled that the smell alone indicated what it once had been.

Tanya thought of that apple now.

What did he want?

In a flash, Tanya decided that she did not like Angus. He was
everything she disliked about men. He was loud and lecherous,
insensitive and brash. Tanya did not like men very much, neither
did she like women.

She was confused and could not rid her mind of the picture of
the apple. For the first time in many years, she began to cry.

Tanya put on a nightgown that made her white and formless,
then climbed into her bed. Out of habit her left hand went underneath the sheets. Tanya withdrew it violently and spent an hour
trying to get to sleep.

The little girl giggled and blushed as Dr. Sinister continued to
pass the coins from nothingness to somethingness and back again.
Hesitant and shy, she would reach out with her tiny hand whenever the little man proffered them. Then they would vanish, and
she would exclaim and begin to giggle.

Beside her was a man who could have been either her father
or her grandfather. He was old and fattish and warted, and was
delighted with the child. He and Dr. Sinister exchanged a series
of glances that expressed this delight totally. The fat man laughed
from deep within his throat at all the girl's fruitless attempts to
retrieve the money.

Behind this little group was Nathanael Crybaby Isbister, also
delighted. He was standing with his hands in his pockets and
chuckling loudly, offering such advice as "Don't let the old guy
flim-flam ya, princess."

Crybaby was going to attend the freak show at the behest of
the Hisslop girls—they were trying out a new tune in today's
show, one that they'd written themselves, and they wanted
Nathanael's opinion of it. So, being a soft touch, he'd said, "Okay."

This was his first time at the show since the day after his arrival. He was, somehow, afraid of it. (Being an insomniac, he wouldn't sleep until near dawn—then he would slumber through the show and wake up when it was over, safe in his caravan. Dr. Sinister had taken down the Rubber Boy sign, so Nathanael was never again called upon to fulfil that role.)

But this day seemed to rest easier with him, starting as it did with the laughter of the young child. Hell, he reasoned, if it gets too rough in there I can always leave after the Hisslops play.

Finally Dr. Sinister allowed the little girl to take the money from him (plus an extra quarter which she'd find when she got home), and her father led her into the big top.

Isbister stepped up next. "No hablo fifty centimes," Crybaby said, pulling out the linings of his pockets for dramatic effect.

"Quite all right," responded Dr. Sinister. "All in the family and all that." His hand went out for the money of the people behind Crybaby.

Inside the tent there was a middling crowd, most of which was now huddled around Zap's tiny cage. As usual, the Wild Man from Borneo was screaming loudly and fashioning horribly grotesque faces. He reached through the bars of his cage with his hairy hands and tried to grab hold of people—they would jump back, terrified.

Nathanael had walked toward the outside of the little crowd, and found himself standing behind the father and daughter. The girl was taking short leaps into the air, attempting to see above the heads of the adults. Nathanael wondered why the man did not lift her. Looking closer he came up with the answer. The man had an empty shirt-sleeve that was pinned to his side.

Isbister tapped his shoulder. "Hey, Mac," he said, "you want I should pick up the girl so's she can see?"

The man regarded him suspiciously and said nothing.

"It's okay," Nathanael assured him. "I work here. That's my job, making sure everyone can see okay."

"Oh!" said the man. "That would be very kind of you then."

"Hey, princess," said Nathanael to the little girl, "you wanna see Zap?"

"Yes, please," she said, and grabbing hold of Isbister's neck she was lifted high.

At her first sight of Zap, her grip tightened until Nathanael thought he might choke.

"It's all right, princess," said Crybaby, "he ain't as bad as all that. He just gets excited by all the people, that's all."

"Why does he do that?" demanded the little girl in her six-year-old voice.

"I dunno," muttered Nathanael—the girl had turned her head away so that she was hugging Isbister and not looking at the Wild Man from Borneo.

"Hey, Zapper, calm down, boy!" Crybaby was afraid of living up to his nickname (what, again?) if this little girl didn't stop being scared.

Zap looked up in the middle of her ferocious antics and saw Nathanael and the child. He toppled over backwards, and when he rose again he had a foot-long, silly grin upon his face.

"Now look at him, princess," urged Nathanael. Slowly the girl turned, and when she saw Zap, she giggled. Lightly and reluctantly at first, and then freely and loudly.

Zap began to "monkey-see, monkey-do" with a boy near the cage who was sticking out his tongue at him. The boy scratched his ear, Zap scratched his ear. The boy crossed his eyes, and Zap crossed his even further than they were already. The boy lifted both his arms high in the air, so did Zap. The boy (with a wink at his friends) brought a fist down hard upon his own skull, and so did Zap. That is, Zap, reaching through the bars of his cage, brought a fist down hard upon the boy's skull.

"Why does he pretend to be so mean?" the little girl asked of Nathanael.

Isbister sighed, knowing the difficulty of explaining it to the little girl. "He doesn't pretend, princess. See, he ain't smart like your old man. He doesn't know what he's doing."

"No," said the little girl, and she turned back to the wooden platform.

Dr. Sinister appeared beside the cage and hushed the audience with a wave of his arms.

"The magician," whispered the little girl, naming the new things in her world.

"Ladies and gentlemen!" shouted the Doctor. "Please do not taunt the Wild Man from Borneo; we do not wish a re-eventuation of last year's unfortunate occurrence!!"

Nathanael chuckled, and so did a good many other people. Zap was sitting down, grinning at the little girl, and sucking his thumb, looking like a harmless, if hairy, baby.

Dr. Sinister regarded him. "Ah!" he said. "You've not been taunting the Wild Man from Borneo. Very good. Excellent. Indeed." He looked momentarily puzzled, and shook his head quickly. "Ladies and gentlemen, the jungles of pestilential Borneo are peopled by creatures exactly similar to this specimen. . ." Etc., etc.

When the Doctor told the audience to ask simple arithmetic problems of little Zapper, the girl would whisper the answers into Nathanael's ear quietly. Today no one posed anything that demanded more than Zap's ten digits to solve, so he went through five or six questions at good speed and was awarded with a healthy round of applause. Zapper turned away almost bashfully. The little girl mysteriously whispered, "See?" into Nathanael's ear. Isbister, not understanding, merely nodded, and turned her so that she had a better view of Major Mite.

While the Major did his soft-shoe, the little girl sang a skipping song that went:

> *Little Major Mite jumped in,*
> *And tried to jump the rope.*
> *But when the rope was near the ground,*
> *It caught him by the throat.*

Nathanael chuckled.

At question-and-answer time, someone asked of Major Mite, "Whatever happened to that great big goomer, what's-his-name, Mango or something?"

"You re-fer, my good man," intoned the Major, "to none oth-er than An-gus Mac-Cal-i-ster, who is at this ver-y mom-ent farm-ing a piece of land in beaut-eous Cape—"

"Here I be!" shouted Angus from behind the curtain that served to make a backstage, and he strutted out, his footsteps boomed and made the wood creak painfully.

"Hoooo!" said the little girl.

"You think he's tall," said Isbister, "wait till you get a load of Davey."

Angus's appearance on stage was greeted by applause; most of it, however, came from the other troupe members.

Under his breath, Major Mite joked, "Always tryin' t' hog the spotlight, ain't ya?"

"An' here I thought we was a team, Donny," chuckled the giant, and then he addressed the crowd. "Ho, theer!" he boomed. "What the Major said be true enough, folks. I'm a farmer now, jest like some o' yerselves. I may well have a coupla feet on most of ye, but still, I'm jest a farmer, an' damned proud o' that. What I come out here t' say is that in jest under a week, come Sa'urday, we're goin' t' have a bit o' sport 'round here. Might be ye heerd about it. Us at Doc Sinister's is gonna be playin' baseball with the House of Joner lads. An' I jest wanted to say that ye all should come, fer ye'll see summit ye'll not likely see agin. 'Cause we're a-goin' ta win.''

And then he winked, a long one that involved the whole audience in a mischievous secret. They applauded.

"An' noo," Angus went on, "if the Doc would be so kine as t' pump thet wheezer back theer," indicating the old organ near the rear, "the Major an' me would lief sing ye our ol' stan'-by, 'Wild Mountain Thyme'."

When the Major sang his own song ("Oh, I am the Major, the minute Major Mite"), his voice had been worn and had wandered off-key. For this song it lay upon Angus's like a lover:

> *Oh, the summertime is gone,*
> *And the leaves are softly turning—*
> *And the wild mountain thyme*
> *Blooms across the purple heather. . .*
> *Will ye go, lassie, go?*
> *And we'll all go together*
> *To pull wild mountain thyme,*
> *All across the purple heather. . .*

The little girl hummed sweetly under her breath and turned her head toward Zap's cage. The Wild Man from Borneo was fast asleep, lullabied by the song of the giant and the midget. The girl tapped Isbister's shoulder to show him. "See?" she asked again.

Next was the Alligator Man, and out he came, glowing with the colour of dollar bills.

The little girl's eyebrows rose high on her head. "He's all green," she stated to Nathanael, full of wonder. "All like grass."

"Ain't that something?" said Nathanael.

Because the Alligator Man's act consisted solely of his standing stock-still and being stared at, the child soon grew bored with him, and amused herself by trying to think of all the things he was as green as. "Green as a frog. Green as the water in a pond. Green as. . ." She bit her tongue, thinking.

"A cow?" suggested Nathanael.

"A cow!?" shrieked the little girl.

"Yeah—a sick cow."

The girl, with a slight twisting of her face, showed Nathanael that she didn't feel this was a good joke.

The next introduction contained the word "Brobdingnagian" which Nathanael remembered from the first time. "Hey, princess, this is Davey. He is the *goddamdest*—er, the tallest guy you could ever see."

Out hobbled Davey. Nathanael noticed two things that were different on this occasion. One was that the giant was hobbling much more quickly than he had before, and the other was that he was making a concerted effort not to use his canes. From time to time Davey was forced to rely on them for support, but mostly he held the tips off the ground.

The little girl wondered aloud whether Davey was the tallest man in the world. Before Nathanael could opine, she said, "I bet." When Dr. Sinister called upon any member of the audience to measure Davey Goliath, a young man dressed in army garb leaped on to the stage and up the stepladder eagerly. For some reason, Davey kept smiling and didn't seem the least bit nervous. He even got a bit cocky—when the soldier announced, "Eight foot, eleven and a half inches!", Davey, with as wide a grin as he could muster, said, "It's because I drank my milk."

Nathanael was impressed. Perhaps, he thought, some of Angus's self-confidence has rubbed off on young Davey.

(Well, Nate, you're a little off the track there. It's true that Davey has come to idolize Angus, but the main reason he is so calm is that he has unearthed a hitherto unknown fact. That is, Dr. John Hunter could not abide the smell of garlic. Davey is laced with it. As the young sailor will report to his girlfriend, "He may be tall, but he sure smells bad!")

In silence, Dr. Sinister began his magic. Isbister watched the reaction of the little girl; her mouth hung open, and her eyes would not move from the prestidigitator. At the end of his act, Dr. Sinister produced a bunch of flowers and threw them into the audience. Nathanael struck out with his arm and caught them. "Here, princess," he said. "From the Doc."

"From the magician," she said—and before taking them from Crybaby she applauded the tiny man upon the stage.

"And now," said Dr. Sinister, "a phenome ne'er before witnessed in the canine world—"

"This is Fido and Rover," whispered Nathanael. "They're really stupid, but they think they can understand everything you say." Then, after a pause, "They're one hell of a ballplayer, though, considering."

"—Janus!" concluded Dr. Sinister, and out trotted the wonder-dog.

"Janus is what they call them," said Nathanael with disdain. "Sounds like a girl's name to me."

The child was bewildered by the dog's appearance. "Two heads," she noted, "and five legs."

"Just a stupid dog like any other dog, that's all they are," commented Crybaby.

"Who does he belong to?" asked the little girl.

"Everybody," answered Mister Isbister, and he could not prevent a note of pride from creeping into his voice.

Something was bothering the little girl. She thought it through in her mind before finally asking, "When he eats, does he have one bowl they both share from, or two different bowls?"

"Two bowls," answered Nathanael (and he considered for a moment printing FIDO on one and ROVER on the other).

"Next," sang out Dr. Sinister, "the rarest of sibling relationships, first personified by Chang and Eng, born in 1911 in pestilential Siam, whenceforth we derive the appellation 'Siamese Twins', the lovely Hisslop sisters, Daisy and Violet. By the way, today the ladies will favour us with a tune of their own composition, entitled, I believe, 'The Source'."

But first the girls had to take down their skirt to prove that they were not gaffed, that is, faked. Then they were given their saxophones, and they began to play.

Daisy began solo, drawing out a high and graceful melody. It was made up of long, held notes, played almost in silence, as slow as honey. When Daisy had stated this theme once, Violet came in.

Violet's part was a dissonant harmony that slammed against the tune like a sledgehammer. Most of the crowd visibly disliked it—their faces screwed up as though they were tasting poison.

Isbister and the little girl listened, transfixed.

Daisy's beautiful melody finally could no longer take the battering Violet's was giving it, and it began to fight back. If Violet should hit with a half-tone separation, Daisy would counter with a quarter-tone. The intervals screamed at each other like cornered cats. Then they began to pick up speed, the girls' fingers running up and down their horns, the contest obviously becoming one that entailed nail-scratching, hair-pulling, biting, and blows below the belt.

By this time the people were covering their ears and laughing nervously. All but Isbister and the little girl.

When the battle seemed at its most frenzied, the transformation began. The two opposing melodies would now and again find themselves in unison, or romping in playful harmony. Instantly they would be at odds once more, but it was never long before they found themselves together. As quickly as the tunes had agreed to fight, they agreed to make peace. Up and down they went together, stating themes and answering them, inverting each other, each the other's logical extension. It was still odd, though, as if the two tunes were escapees from Johann Sebastian Bach's Insane Asylum.

The coupling reached a high-pitched, almost squeaky, conclusion, and then drifted gently back to earth.

The song finished with Daisy's original tune stated once more, but this time Violet played a gentle accompaniment, giving the melody a leisurely massage.

The music ended in silence.

Isbister and the girl applauded loudly. Someone else booed.

The Hisslops ran quickly from the stage, always embarrassed by their abandonment to the music.

"We should now," said Dr. Sinister, "like to introduce to you Robert Merrill—"

Uh-oh, thought Nathanael Crybaby Isbister. This could be rough going for the kid.

The gasps came loudly and all at once as Bobby emerged from behind the curtain.

"Don't be scared, princess," whispered Nate.

She turned so that their faces were inches apart and gave him a quizzical look. "I'm not scared," she returned. "Are you?"

"Naw."

"How come?"

Isbister thought about it momentarily. "He's a friend of mine," he said.

Some of the other people were scared, though; when the murmurings reached a high point Bobby Merrill turned and left the stage. (Nathanael felt his eyes well up, but drew strength from the little girl that he held in his arms.)

Madame Tanya was introduced and promptly declared gaffed by about half the audience. Dr. Sinister told them about the blow-offs ("that cost only twenty-five, two-five, cents, two bits, one quarter of a dollar. . .") and then he said, "But first, let us hear Madame Tanya tell us how she keeps her whiskers so very resplendent."

This is what started it all, mused Nathanael. This dumb crack about the House of Jonah.

"You should never. . ." began Madame Tanya, and then she seemed to lose the thread of it. "You should never. . ." she repeated, but it vanished again. "You should never!" Then Madame Tanya burst into tears. She covered her face and ran blindly back to her caravan.

The Author (not me, I'm the *author*) also happened to be in the audience that day. When Madame Tanya ran from the stage he felt his legs start to move after her almost instinctively; he stopped them when he realized that he had no idea where she might go.

He did not stop them in time to prevent himself from running into a large man holding a child. The large man shot forward, surprised, and had to circle around to avoid falling over. His legs moved awkwardly as he did so, almost spastically, and his face filled with pain. The Author hurried to steady him by the arms.

"I'm sorry, bud," said the Author.

Isbister set the little girl on the ground as soon as it was safe to do so. With a light "bye-bye" she ran to take her father's hand, and together they left the big top.

Isbister regarded the Author. Ugly-lookin' cuss, he decided.

"A crowded place ain't the best for runnin' around in," said Crybaby.

"Yeah," said the Author. "I'm sorry."

The two men were about the same age (the Author was, in fact, two years younger), about the same size, and had both had faces that were hard and beaten. They had both decided that the other was an ugly-lookin' cuss.

Isbister muttered, "It's okay," and turned away. The Author saw that he was heading for the stage, so he called out, "Hey, buddy, you work here?"

Isbister swung around suspiciously. The two were like dogs, circling and sniffing. "Maybe," Nathanael said.

"I wonder what was buggin' the bearded lady," said the Author.

"Me, too. Ain't like her."

"No, huh?"

"Nope."

Isbister and the Author stared at each other. Both had the feeling they had seen the other somewhere—but instead of trying to pinpoint the origin of this feeling, they simply assumed it was due to their both belonging to the Fraternity of Ugly-Lookin' Cusses.

"Hey," said the Author, "what's all this about a baseball game?"

"I guess you don't come from around here."

"Nope. California."

"California?"

"Yep."

"Well," said Isbister, and he went to sit on the stage, taking the weight off his recently pained legs. "They got this group of religious guys here, the House of Jonah."

"I heard of them," said the Author, and he went to sit on the stage beside Nathanael. "They got a ball team, right?"

"Right. Well, they don't like us very much."

"How come?"

Isbister shrugged. "I guess on account of we're a bunch of ugly-lookin' cusses."

The Author laughed loudly.

"So," continued Nathanael, "they come in here one day, and they say they wanna play us baseball, and if we lose we gotta leave town, right? So the Doc—that's Dr. Sinister—he says okay, 'cause he wants to get out of here anyway, and the House says they're gonna play all handicapped so that we *maybe* stand a chance." Isbister took a deep breath of air. "But then the Major chases after them and tells them to stuff playing handicapped, and so now we gotta play the whole team, and everyone in this loony-bin here figures we're gonna win." Crybaby shrugged again, his favourite mannerism (next to drilling his finger into his palm and, of course, crying).

"Maybe I'll stick around for that," said the Author. "I'm supposed to be on my way back to California, but I'm taking my own sweet time about it."

"Yeah?"

"Yeah."

"Suit yourself," said Isbister, dropping to the sawdust floor. "It's Saturday, about a mile or so that way." He pointed. "And, hey, there's a rumour going around that some guy in Burton's Harbor is making book we're gonna win. Might be you get into that action."

The Author also jumped down. "I ain't interested," he said.

"Not a gambling man, huh?"

The Author was walking toward the exit. "I'm a gambling man, all right," he called back over his shoulder. "I just don't like to throw my money away."

Chapter 13

IN STELLA'S LITTLE blow-off tent, there is a cold silence, made even colder by the wind that howls without. Nathanael, sitting cross-legged (ouch!) in front of Stella's throne, is tearing apart the butt of a cigarette he has just smoked, playing with the flakes of tobacco, making from them a design with his thick and calloused forefinger. Upon the throne Stella sits, the white mountain of woman, trying to decide on a tactful way of asking Nathanael to leave. She is not expecting Edmund—he has told her that he would not be coming for a couple of days, as he has to work overtime at the garage. But, Stella thinks, ever since Nate entered the tent a cold silence has reigned, and she does not like it.

The reason for the silence is simple and sad. Sad because the two people involved are beginning to feel awkward and unfriendly, when the fact is that they like each other very much. The silence grew this way:

Nathanael entered with his standard, "Hoddo," and took his place near her plump feet.

Stella said, "Hi."

Neither had anything else to say at the time, and both attributed the other's taciturnity to a problem of some kind. Nathanael, hoping to glean some clue, looked up at Stella sideways.

To Stella, Isbister's look was mysterious and foreboding, the look of a spy peering out from shadows. She glared back intensely, searching his face for an answer.

What's she starin' at like that, wondered Nathanael, and his own look became even more mysterious.

Stella glared all the more, her eyes like searchlights upon Crybaby's face.

So both went for the easy answers. Stella: He doesn't like me because of this thing with Edmund. And then, defiantly: Well, to hell with him, it's none of his business. Nathanael: She doesn't

like me because she thinks I'm mad about that Edmund weirdo.
And also defiantly: Well, I told her I thought it was her business,
not mine—to hell with her if she don't believe it.

Finally Stella said, "Well, Nathanael, I'm getting pretty tired."
She yawned to lend it authenticity, stretching out both arms, the
fat dangling down almost a foot below.

"Yeah," said Isbister, standing up. He winced a couple of times
but hid it, unwilling to let Stella see him show any kind of weakness.

Look at him going for sympathy, thought Stella.

"See ya sometime, huh?" said Nathanael, thinking, tired my
fat keester—she's waiting for that Edmund, as if I give a tinker's
cuss.

"Goodbye," answered Stella, thinking, he thinks I'm waiting
for Edmund! She became quite insulted that Nate didn't believe
she was just tired, even though she wasn't.

"Goodbye," said Nathanael; he spun around and raced down
the four rickety stairs.

Nathanael Crybaby Isbister gathered together the material of
his coat to help protect his neck from the wind. Then he took a
long look at the caravans around him. Which one of these freaks,
he thought, which one of these deformed, ugly freaks has got any
booze?

The young reporter, down in the bar of the Fulton Arms Hotel,
was trying to think his way out of a problem. Oh, was he in
trouble! He had taken a train heading for Gilbertsville, Tennessee,
his pockets brimming with expense money from the nation's
biggest magazine, and somewhere between the bottle and the bar-
car he had arrived, penniless, in Burton's Harbor, Upper Peninsula,
Michigan.

He let his head drop on the table in front of him.

He felt like crying. The story he was supposed to be covering
was as juicy as a peach. It dealt with the Tennessee Valley Authority, who were spending the government's money like nobody's business. One hundred and twelve million for the dam in
Gilbertsville! Hooey! Spending money like it grew on trees, and
everything fucking up on them. The young reporter giggled,
drunkenly. And then—oh, this was priceless!—the chairman,
Arthur Morgan, had accused his two colleagues, Harcourt Morgan

and David Lilienthal, of "moral and ethical lapses"! Moral and ethical lapses! When the young reporter had first heard that he could not contain himself—right there in his editor's office he jumped to his feet, launched into a soft-shoe, and sang at the top of his voice, "Moral and ethical lapses, moral and ethical lapses! Best of all the crapses, is moral and ethical lapses!"

Even now, drunk and on the verge of blubbering, he whispered gaily, "Moral. . .and. . .ethical. . .lapses. . ." He blacked out for a moment or two.

Then he came to and thought, well as long as I'm here, I better do something. His groin shrivelled as he envisaged the telephone call to his editor (which he would have to make collect, no less):

"Hello, Mr. King?"

"Yes?"

"What's the most newsworthy story happening in Burton's Harbor, Michigan?"

The young reporter broke down then and cried shamelessly.

And through his drunken brain danced snippets of conversation. All around him, it seemed, people were talking about brassieres. Who cares about brassieres, the young reporter thought, unless they are littered about a trail that leads to moral and ethical lapses? No, wait. . .they weren't talking about brassieres, they were talking about *a* brassiere. . .maybe the biggest one in the world or something. Maybe that was his story. "Hello, Mr. King, I've got a lead on the biggest damn bra. . ." He cried a little bit more. No, it wasn't even *a* brassiere, it was a *Mr.* Brassiere. What a stupid name, thought the young reporter. Still, every single person in the bar was talking about him.

With a reporter's instinct he pricked up his reporter's ears.

"No bullshit, he's willing to bet on the freaks. Any money you want."

Freaks! thought the young reporter.

"Against the House of Jonah, no less. Goddam Tekel Ambrose!"

Tekel Ambrose, House of Jonah = baseball. The young reporter bolted upright in his seat, muttering, "The great American pastime."

"Have you ever been out to the show?" demanded Greg Haines at a not-too-distant table. "Lemme tell you what they got. A tall guy what can barely walk. Major Mite, he ain't as big as my arm. Two little girls stuck together. What else, lemme see. A gotdamn dog! Lady with a beard. Um. . . a hairy little guy what's an idiot. Lemme see. Oh, the ugliest guy in the world, looks like a hippotamus. Er, hippopotamus. Lemme see. . ."

The young reporter sprang to his feet with a "Yahooooo!" It silenced the place. Then, with a small grin, he said, "Human interest."

The Author (not me, of course, I'm the author, and sick and tired of it) wandered along the road, his hands thrust deeply into his pockets, taking long and boyish sweeps with his legs. He felt delightfully perverse, because his pockets were at that moment chockablock full of money, yet he was behaving the same way he always did. He liked walking anyway, particularly in new country. The land around him was unlike any he'd seen before. Immediately beside him were small squares of farmland, like patches torn brutally from a head of hair. Beside those rose tall and unruly trees, now red and yellow and half-naked. Behind the trees lay the line of sharp white sparkles that indicated water.

So the Author walked happily. He caught a stone on the toe of his workboot and shot it up into the air.

He was coming from Chicago, where his east-coast publishers had just given him the money that he carried now in his pocket. The Author was becoming famous. His collection of short stories had received universally good reviews—"the finest work to date of this young writer", etc., etc. The Author, though, was unsatisfied. He knew that he was rapidly getting a reputation as a crafter of little marvels, miniatures—short stories and small novels that were nice, certainly, and touching, but in the long run inconsequential. What he really wanted to write was something big, as big as life (a phrase the publishers threw about—idiotically, in the Author's opinion), something that mattered. He had an idea, a story about the displaced Okies of the depression. The Author was letting the idea ferment in his brain, letting it become a full-grown vision. To this end, as he told Isbister, he was taking his own sweet time about getting back to California. How he wound up in Burton's Harbor, Michigan, was something of a mystery to him—it had been an accident. But still, he did not regret it. The sideshow had been interesting, although the Author did not like to see people exhibit themselves in any way. These particular freaks, he reflected, were not lacking in dignity. The Author let the conflict slip away—he had no real interest in understanding life in that way. He didn't want to analyse it, he didn't want to set up a table of cause and effect and make sure that the whole thing balanced up.

The Author merely wanted to *know* it, to know the whole of it, without exception.

The Okies were like freaks, he reflected, at least in the eyes of the monied people back in California. He remembered sadly the exchange he had witnessed at a gas station. (The Author was fascinated somehow by garages and gas stations, and would often hang around them for hours on end.) A truckload of Okies had just filled up their old crate and were about to drive across the Mojave Desert. One of the garage attendants had remarked, sarcastically, that it took a lot of courage to attempt such a feat, especially in an old heap like that. The young Okie, his cap pulled down over his eyes, had shrugged. "Don't take much courage to do somethin' when you don't got no choice but to do it." The attendant had shared a chuckle with his co-worker, thinking the young Okie stupid. (That, even now, made the Author angry.) As the family drove away, the two attendants had talked. One asked, "How can they live like that?" "They ain't human," responded the other. "They're more like animals. A human being couldn't live that way."

The Author kicked another stone, with all his force.

Speaking of gas stations—here's one now. The Author walked over to it, circling around in the lot with no particular purpose.

A truck was being filled at the pumps. The driver stood beside the cab, his head nestled on the hood. He was snoring loudly, his eyes covered up by a baseball cap. The Author walked over to him and tapped his shoulder lightly. The truck driver awoke with starts and sputters, confused. It took him several long moments to compose himself (during which he tried to adjust his baseball cap, placing it first backwards, then front-, then back-, over and over), and then the truck driver said, "Huh?"

"Need a ride into town," said the Author.

The driver had a boyish face that was heavy with slack lines. He was still too muddled to attempt speech, so he merely pointed to a little sticker on his windshield that read, "NO RIDERS".

"Aww," smiled the Author. "A good guy don't do something just because some yahoo puts a sticker on his window telling him to."

The driver thought about it, tugging on the brim of his baseball cap. "Okay," he at last resolved. "But you got to crouch down low on the running board till we're out of sight of the station."

"Sure, Mac," said the Author, and up he climbed. They drove around the corner, and the Author climbed inside the cab without waiting for the driver to slow or stop. He was a bit of an old hand in such matters.

The driver said, "Know any riddles?" as soon as the Author was comfortable.

"Lemme think about it. I know lots of riddles, I guess, but I can't think of one I could ask you."

"How about, what has. . . ummm. . . three arms, and two heads, and six toes?"

"What does?"

"Search me. Got to think about it." The driver furrowed his brow and worked the stick shift. "This is a tough one."

"Yup," agreed the Author.

"I keep making them tougher and tougher," said the driver, " 'cause I've been riddle-solving for a long time. The easy ones ain't much of a challenge anymore."

"Well, you got me on this one."

"Yeah, it takes practice." Something occurred to the driver. "You know, I picked up a guy a couple of weeks back, and he had a whamdoozle of a riddle. All about, what walks on four legs in the morning, two legs in the afternoon, and then three legs at night?"

"A man," answered the Author.

"Yeah!" the driver exclaimed. "A man. I figured it out about a week ago. The answer's a man, on account of he crawls when he's a baby, and then he walks when he's a man, and when he gets old he uses a cane. At first I figured the answer was a dog, but that's not as good as a man. Sheeee-it, that's a good riddle! I sure wish I knew more good ones like that."

"There aren't too many that are as good as that," said the Author.

Yuccatan and my grandfather were treated royally at the home of the sucked-out sailor's sister. She was an immensely fat and jolly woman who took an immediate liking to that old geezer grand-daddy of mine. She fed them, gave them a loan, and then forced upon them various items which she had recently relegated to the garbage dump. These included many clothes left behind by an erstwhile lover, seven shoes, a mirror with a crack in it, and a radio.

In the Fulton Arms Hotel room, Yuccatan and my grandfather were having a whale of a time with this last item, an old beat-up thing that gave off as much static as real sound. They were beating each other up to get at the tuner, racing it up and down the spectrum.

My grandfather had just managed, by means of pulling Yuccatan's trousers down and binding his ankles with them, to gain control of the knob. He was searching frantically for a sporting event. No sooner had he found some minor league football game when Yuccatan employed one of the seven shoes to crack the geezer over the head. When my grandfather came to, Yuccatan was beaming his beatific smile. "Mex'can music," he explained. From the radio came the strains of "La Cumparsita". Yuccatan, pretending he possessed castanets, was doing a crude imitation of the hat dance, his ankles still bound by his pants. His naked legs shone a pale blue, almost transparent.

The music stopped suddenly, and both men said, "What the hell?"

"Ladies and gentlemen, we interrupt our programme of dance music to bring you a special bulletin from the Intercontinental Radio News. At twenty minutes before eight, central time, Professor Farrell of the Mount Jennings Observatory, Chicago, Illinois, reports observing several explosions of incandescent gas, occurring at regular intervals on the planet Mars."

"Get me back that football game!" screamed my grandfather, and he lunged toward the radio. Yuccatan, still dancing the hat dance, dealt him a stern one in the gobbles. "Here come the music again," the sailor explained.

They introduced the ever-popular "Stardust", Ramon Raquello and his Orchestra. . .

Yuccatan, exhibiting extraordinary strength considering his lack of substance, pulled my grandfather from the floor and began to fox-trot with him. It was not long before they were interrupted again. . .

"Due to the unusual nature of this occurrence, we have arranged an interview with the noted astronomer, Professor Pierson. . ."

My grandfather made another attempt to bring back the football, but Yuccatan held him off. "They're talking about Mars," explained Yuccatan.

The thrust of Professor Pierson's interview was that the explosion of gas on the planet Mars was a natural occurrence; he then dispelled the theory that the planet was inhabited.

Yuccatan looked disgusted—but then came some swing music, and the sucked-out sailor was off dancing again. This time it lasted but twenty seconds.

Then they broke in once more, this time to say that an object of unknown origin had been found near Grovers Mill, New Jersey.

We know today what panic all this caused, for it was, of course, Orson Welles' famous broadcast, *War of the Worlds*. Its effect was truly remarkable—people fled from their homes, highways were jammed, and more than one person tried to commit suicide.

What was the effect in the Fulton Arms Hotel room?

When it became perfectly clear that the Martians were invading, Yuccatan shouted, "Hooray! They've come back to get me!" He then launched into a lengthy tale concerning his visit to the planet Mars, how they treated him like a god (mistaking his tattoos for special markings that figured prominently in their mythology), how they finally returned him to Earth with a promise to collect him when the civil wars that tore their world apart were resolved. "I must get ready for them," said Yuccatan. He went to the middle of the room and pulled off his clothes. "They don't wear them on Mars," he explained. " 'Mars' is just what we call it. They call it 'Jkght'." "Jkght" was exactly how he pronounced it, one of the few sounds that his toothless mouth and phlegm-filled throat could produce easily. "I will now sing," he announced, "the Jkghtian song of welcome, 'Pfry jk Fdy'." And sing he did, combining gurgling noises, gasps, and many sounds like a drunkard heaving.

My grandfather, seeing that Yuccatan was totally involved with his "song" reached for the radio's knob. "If Earth is gonna be destroyed by Mars," he said quietly, "I'm listening to the goddam football game first."

So, this gives us an historical pinpoint. That radio show was broadcast on October 30, 1938. It was a Sunday night show. Thirty days has September, April, June, etc., Monday, Tuesday, etc.; therefore, I conclude, the baseball game between the House of Jonah and Dr. Sinister's Exhibition of Extraordinary Eccentricities was played on Saturday, November 5, 1938.

Hmmm?

This is very strange. Burton's Harbor is north of Sault Ste. Marie and Thessalon, hardly known for moderate climes.

My grandfather is sleeping on the couch. I cross over and wake him up rudely. "Pray tell," I query, "just exactly what were they doing playing baseball on November the fifth?"

"I'm sleeping," he tells me.

"Why were they playing baseball on a bitterly cold fall day, namely, November the fucking fifth?"

My grandfather snores loudly—I know he's pretending.

"November the fifth!?" I scream.

"Could be," he mutters at last, "that I got my dates wrong."

Chapter 14

WELL, THERE AIN'T gonna be no more screwing up of dates.

What we need, I yell, is *simultaneity!*

The old geezer tries to interrupt, but I cut him off with an ear-slicing "SHHHHHH!" He shhhhhhes.

All right, you old dilapidated sack of debris, if you say it was November the fifth, it was. They better wear thermal underwear, though. I begin to laugh, hysterically, at my own non-joke, in a serious attempt to terrorize the old man. It's time for simultaneity! And the time is November the *fourth!* That's right, I tell him. You're not getting another chance to screw up. We're going to have one last look at everyone before the game, and then, that's it!

"But," he begins, "stuff happened—"

"SILENCE!" I bellow, and the geezer is silent.

(Magic, I marvel. Just like Tekel and Dr. Sinister, I too have become a wizard, capable of the grandest of miracles—I have silenced my grandfather.)

"Where do you want to start?" I demand.

"What, you mean *now*?" he sputters. "I was sleeping."

"We'll sleep before the game like everyone else."

"Bucko-boy, you are getting cocky!" He tries to regain a bit of his former bravado, searching for his shillelagh. But his eyes are sleep-blurred, his brain foggy.

"With whom do you wish to commence?" I repeat, menacingly calm.

"Well. . ."

"We shall start with that new lad, the young reporter."

So, here is what our characters were up to that night. That night being Friday, November 4, 1938.

The young reporter was, quite simply, getting drunk. But this time he didn't have any big problems that might force his drunkeness down morbid and self-pitying corridors. He was as happy as a lark. He had received one hundred dollars in the mail from his editor. He had managed to sell him on a story about the ball game. "It's a natural, Mr. King, a natural. I've been out to see the freak show. Do you know who's there? Major Mite. Sure, *the* Major Mite. You know, 'You must always comb your hair. . .' and all that? That's it. And the Hisslop Sisters, you know, they were in that movie that got banned*. Not to mention the tallest man alive, the *ugliest* man alive. . . Hey, that reminds me, you better get Walker up here right away. No one's going to believe these guys without photographs."

Mr. King said, in his basso profundo monotone, "Walker is not here."

"Well," asked the young reporter, "where the hell is he?"

"He is in Gilbertsville, Tennessee," responded Mr. King. "He went there to meet you."

"Oh, yeah. Heh-heh-heh." (The young reporter could not fake a laugh worth beans.) "So who?"

"Lambert."

(That, if the young reporter were not feeling so good, would be a damp spot. Lambert was young and brash, his specialty capturing on film accidentally-exposed portions of female anatomy. He had so many photographs of derrieres exposed by wind-lifted skirts that one might think he and the wind were in cahoots. The young reporter was much fonder of Walker, even though Walker was sullen and silent, as cold as ice. Walker wore spectacles that made his eyes look like a fish's; the glass was tinted a deep brown-yellow from the cigarettes that he smoked nonstop. Still—Lambert could take a picture of a lady's breast, and it would look like a girl giggling because her tit was showing. Walker could take the same picture, and it would be an image of a woman displaying her breast proudly, this wonderfully soft and rounded thing that meant life. Lambert would score with the girl afterwards, sure; Walker would be dismissed with a sneer. That did not affect the photographs.)

"Not to mention Tekel Ambrose, Mr. King. You know, some people figure him to be the best ballplayer in the world."

Mr. King was silent—the young reporter wondered what his *faux pas* might have been. Of course! It came in a flash. Mr. King was one of those who years ago had assigned the best-player

---

*The girls had a small part in Tod Browning's *Freaks*, 1932.

pedestal to that kid, Isbister. All Isbister fans were stubborn and unwilling to entertain contrary notions.

"Next to Nate Isbister, naturally," said the young reporter.

"Oh, yes. I've heard that Ambrose is very good."

"And religious! Sir, something *big* is happening here in Burton's Harbor, Michigan. That's why I came here instead of going off to Gilbertsville. After all, sir, you know what they say—ethical lapses absolutely pale in comparison to *human interest!* (The young reporter said "human interest" the way a pervert might say "moist beaver".)

"That's all very well," said Mr. King. "But why didn't you tell Walker that you had changed your plans?"

"Oh. . .heh-heh-heh. Well, sir, I got so excited, sir, by the prospect of this human interest story, that I. . .well, I *plum forgot!*" (The young reporter was a country boy at heart. Though he was responsible for wonderfully written phrases like "the men gentle and silent, each snail-like withdrawn into the quietude of what he singly is doing", he was also given to exclaiming "Plum forgot!" and "Gee whillikers!".)

Mr. King had reluctantly sent one hundred dollars and Lambert.

The young reporter was getting drunk in the Fulton Arms barroom. Across the table from him was Lambert, who was paying for all the drinks. "Didn't King give you any money?" Lambert asked, peeling off some dollars for two double whiskies. "He gave me fifty dollars in expense money!"

"Fifty dollars?" whispered the young reporter, awestruck, grabbing for his drink.

Lambert leaned back slowly, his eyes scanning the room for young women. There was a decided dearth of them in the bar. He resignedly began to ogle a woman of forty-odd years who was sitting in a corner, dead drunk, singing Finnish folksongs.

Lambert indicated with a jerked thumb. "What do you think?"

The young reporter was hopelessly in love with a girl far away, in a distant town. He shrugged and said, "Okay, I guess," but he never looked at the woman in question.

"Hey!" said Lambert. "Did you make any book with that Brassiere guy?"

"Naw," said the young reporter irritably. (Irritably? Yes, indeed—any reference to women made him think of the faraway girl. He was headed down a morbid and self-pitying corridor.)

"I did. Ten bucks worth," Lambert announced. "You know, that guy is *the* Brassiere, the guy who invented and manufactures brassieres."

"What?" The young reporter was anything but stupid. "You got that wrong, Lambert. See, brassieres were invented by a guy named Titzling."

"Hey, I get it!" chortled Lambert. "That's pretty good. Titsling."

"Yes, well, I realize there is humour inherent in it, Lambert, but that is the truth of the matter. Titzling invented brassieres."

"Well, all I know is, that's what this guy told me."

"*He* personally told you that he was responsible for the brassiere?" inquired the young reporter. He waved at the waiter, demanding more drinks. Then, to remind Lambert, "Mr. King gave you *fifty* dollars? Geez. . ."

Lambert smiled proudly and reached for his wallet.

"He personally told you that?" the young reporter continued.

"Yeah. I went up to his room to make a bet, and while I was there I showed him my private stock to see if he wanted to buy any." (Lambert's private stock was, naturally, a battery of incredibly lewd pictures.) "So he says something like, 'You obviously love bared chests, sir—it must pain you to meet the man that harnessed them!' So I say 'Huh?' and he says how he invented the brassiere. Get it?" Lambert paid for the drinks.

The young reporter's eyes narrowed suspiciously.

The Hisslop sisters tossed a coin into the air, their purpose being to decide whether to go to the Fulton Arms or the Sailor's Wife. Daisy favoured the former, Violet the latter, and this was the only way of deciding.

"Heads!" sang out Violet, catching the coin herself and slapping it on to the back of her wrist. She then raised her hand a quarter of an inch and peeked craftily. "Shit," she said.

They began to walk toward the Fulton Arms Hotel.

"Now remember," cautioned Daisy, "we're not to get drunk tonight. We've got to be in our best shape for tomorrow."

"Don't you remember what Mr. Isbister said about Babe Ruth?" responded Violet. (She was being a little troublesome, irked at not being able to go to the Sailor's Wife where, she felt, the company was more colourful.)

"Mister Isbister. Mizzderizzbizzder," mumbled Daisy—then, abruptly, "I wonder what Ally's up to tonight?"

(Since that ill-fated night Ally had shown up for practice only. The rest of the time he spent sequestered in his caravan, not even taking meals.)

"He was *so* drunk!" laughed Violet. "He must have been so nervous. All on account of thee and me."

Daisy did an imitation of Ally, lurching drunkenly (pulling Violet along with her, of course) and saying, "Cheeze-greist you guys grot gate tits!"

"What should we do about what those three were talking about?" asked Violet, meaning Angus, Isbister, and Doc Sinister.

"We'll see if he's up when we get back," answered Daisy. "I hope he is. I think he's cute. He has a very nice bottom."

"Ally's playing baseball well, anyway. He can hit like anything!"

"That's true. He hits them so hard because he's mad. I wonder how hard he'd hit if he was happy."

Violet thought about it. "Maybe not as hard," she ventured.

"Maybe even harder."

They were silent for a little time then, until Violet said, "I hope we win tomorrow."

"Now, now, remember what Angus said."

(What Angus said, standing up at the dinner table, all seven-foot-two of him, was, "Tomorra will be here soon enough. An' it don' do no one no good to be frettin' o'er it. So, t'night, ever'one relax. Go to a movin' picture. That's what I'm a-goin' ta do," he added impishly. "I'm a-goin' fer a movin' picture.")

The girls walked through the door of the Fulton Arms Hotel and made their way over to the booth they thought of as their own. It was a corner booth; there they could sit inconspicuously and watch all the young men in the place.

That evening's fare was fairly uninspired. The locals tended to be older types, downcast farmers with beer bellies and rough, red hands. The only promising prospect was seated at a distant table—a young man with slick black hair and a pencil-line moustache. He was dressed in a fashionable pinstriped suit and seemed to be made of money (not that the Hisslop girls cared about that particularly). He peeled off bills with great flourish, paying for all the drinks that he and his companion were having.

His companion did not interest the sisters; although handsome, he was a morose-looking young man and seemed to be single-mindedly intent on drinking himself into oblivion. Double whiskies disappeared in a single swallow.

The other man, the one with the moustache, saw the girls looking at him. He smiled slowly and winked.

"Well, he's not what you'd call shy," remarked Daisy; she was not attracted by boldness, although it was by no means what we would today call a "turn-off".

"He certainly isn't," agreed Violet, who liked this trait in men. "Shall we smile back?" she wondered aloud.

Daisy regarded the young man. "Let's do," she decided, and in unison they radiated a winning smile.

The moustachioed man seemed to become very excited. He turned quickly to his companion, very agitated, pointing out the Hisslops. The other man looked up slowly, drunkenly, his eyes lighting upon the girls only after a long period of floating around the barroom's rafters. When finally he saw them he looked momentarily puzzled. Then the look was gone. It wasn't as if he had resolved anything—only that puzzlement seemed very natural to the young man and was easily dismissed.

Daisy and Violet watched as the two men conversed. The situation was obvious—the moustachioed man was gung-ho for joining the ladies, the other man was against it. Their arguments were obvious even from a distance. With a poorly coordinated wave of his arms, the morose one indicated, "If you want to go, *go!*" The other, clutching his hands together, implored, "But there's *two* of them!"

"The small one's a real stick-in-the-mud," muttered Violet.

"Too true," said Daisy. "Leave him on his tod, buddy."

Finally the two came to some kind of agreement; both men rose to their feet and approached the Hisslops' booth. The one with the moustache came with a studied swagger, bouncing lightly on the balls of his feet. The other walked unevenly, his steps sounding loudly with flat-footed plops. He kept his eyes on the ground, but that didn't seem to prevent him from tripping over chair legs and bumping into table corners.

The moustachioed one came to a stop in front of the sisters' table and lit a cigarette. Now, this phrase "lit a cigarette" deserves some expanding. The man removed the packet from an inside jacket pocket and flung it into the air. It did a triple half-gainer. He caught it with his other hand and held it gingerly twixt thumb and pinky. Then, with a finger hidden behind, he gave the package a little tap, and a single cigarette came leaping out of the opening. It too did a triple half-gainer and was caught deftly by the free hand, lodging securely between the first and second fingers. The other hand replaced the cigarette packet, coming from the pocket this time with a gold-plated lighter. With an imperceptible jerk of the man's wrist, the lighter's top flew backwards, exposing the mechanism. The young man slapped at it, popping his fingers, and it came aflame. Then he lit his cigarette.

The morose-looking young man applauded him.

"Hi!" said the moustachioed one, ignoring his companion. "My name's Ernest Lambert, but my friends call me Ernie. Would you mind if me and my little buddy sit with you?"

"Lambert," cautioned the young reporter, "I am by no means your 'little buddy'."

"Come on, little buddy, let's sit down with these two little ladies here. Hey," Lambert said, turning to the girls, "I'll bet you two are sisters, right?"

Their bonding was hidden below table level; even so, both Daisy and Violet were forced to agree with the young reporter, who said, "Christ, Lambert, what a stupid thing to say."

"What do you mean, stupid?"

"Well, they're only the most identical-looking twins I've ever seen—" The young reporter stopped suddenly and looked at the Hisslops. "Oh, yeah," he said.

"Are you two going to join us?" asked Violet.

The young men sat down. Lambert immediately launched into a bit of finger-drumming on the tabletop. The rhythm was either extremely complicated (12/4 in the right hand, 5/8 in the left) or else spastic. As he did so he grinned and swung his head to look alternately at Daisy and Violet. "So, uh, how do they tell you girls apart, anyway?"

Violet answered, "I'm the one on the right."

Lambert nodded until something occurred to him. "Yeah, but I mean, you're not always on the right. Right?"

"Wrong," Violet answered. "I'm on the right all of the time. We're Siamese twins."

"I'm Daisy."

"I'm Violet."

"They play the saxophone, too," said the young reporter. "I saw the show."

"Did you?" asked both girls at once. "Did you like it?"

Before the young reporter could answer, "I liked parts of it," Lambert put in with, "You guys are *Siamese* twins?"

"Yes," they answered.

Quite forgetting himself, Lambert said, "Well, fuck me."

Daisy and Violet shared a mischievous giggle.

Dr. Sinister had come a long way since he was born, a five-and-one-half pound Poindexter Wilhelm Frip, although he hadn't put on that much weight, if the truth be told. But now, sitting in his caravan, indulging in cognac and cigars, he felt as if he had arrived at the end of a journey. There is a feeling one gets, returning home from far away, that a circle has been completed—at times like that, a person almost feels that he could die contentedly. It was this feeling Dr. Sinister had that evening; never before had it been so pronounced and strong.

Poindexter Sinister never reflected on his past. True, he was quite given over to reminiscing about various women with whom he had shared portions of his life, but in his heart these feelings were ongoing and not of the past. He had once written in his journal, "I love them better now than ever I could whilst I resided with them." As far as thinking about his life and trying to assess it, this was something he had never done.

Until now. Now he weighed his existence.

And Poindexter Wilhelm Frip was happy. The cigar tasted good, and the cognac was soothing.

The Sorcerer, his thirty-fifth novel, lay in his desk, a pile of loose-leaf sheets. It was unfinished, his hero marooned on a desert isle with no hope of rescue.

The *Glorioski* manuscript lay on the pump organ, deserted, this chord:

left friendless and solitary.

The naked young girl on the easel stepped into the bath with some undefinable thing amiss with her otherwise perfect left breast.

The cigar tasted good, the cognac was soothing.

They might call me talented, Dr. Sinister thought. Balderdash. I have only one talent, but it is a good one. I can love easily those whom others can love only with difficulty.

I am not a better man for having loved them, and they are no better for my love. Howsomever, he mused, we manage to keep the ball rolling, and I (the cognac having affected him a bit) have giggled a good portion of the way.

I have not written a great novel nor a great symphonic work; I have painted no masterpieces; I have not, alas, performed Magic (note that capital).

Dr. Sinister took a long puff and a deep sip.

I may yet, he announced to himself.

Then again, I may not.

He giggled.

*

Tanya watched as the huge, lumbering frame of Angus McCallister stamped away from her caravan. She noted that he walked almost angrily, his hands stuffed into the trouser pockets of his Sunday suit.

She pulled her fingers through her beard and thought about it.

He had come to her caravan with this invitation: "Would ye care ta go to the movin' picture show. . . with me," he added, as coy as a little boy. Dwarfed in his fist with a massive bouquet of flowers.

She had answered, "Don't bother me anymore, Mr. McCallister." Surprisingly, she had been touched by the look of hurt that swept across his face. Tanya tried to explain herself. "Look, it's you lot who want me to play this silly baseball game tomorrow. I don't want to, but I will. So I need my sleep."

Angus dropped the flowers to the ground and turned away. "Go on an' sleep," he muttered.

Now Angus was a (big) speck on the horizon. Tanya slammed the door shut and shouted at it. "I hate you!" Even though she sincerely believed this statement was true, the voicing of it made Tanya feel sillier than she ever had before. For a moment, the bearded lady was deluged by feelings and impulses. She flung herself on to her bed and cried.

The Wild Man from Borneo happened to be passing Tanya's caravan. He had freed himself from his cage and escaped into the night. In a while he would go to Dr. Sinister's caravan and allow himself to be found. The tiny prestidigitator would carry him off to bed with softly whispered reprimands.

Zap heard the sobs and turned quickly to the point of their origin. Running quickly to the bearded lady's caravan, he clutched the windowsill and pulled himself up.

Tanya, as we know, lay on the bed crying. The pillow case was soaking wet. Zap tilted his head quizzically. The woman's rear end was raised up and exposed, and she was frantically digging at it with her fingers.

Zap dropped back to the ground. He fell and rolled in the dirt. Then he ran away from the circle of caravans, out into the empty fields that surrounded them. There he howled. He had quite a repertoire of howls. There was one regal and triumphant howl. There was a maniacal, senseless howl. There was a howl of outrage. There was a howl of defeat. They followed one after another, constantly changing, no two howls ever quite the same. The Wild Man from Borneo kept up his howling for close to an hour. Finally, however, there were no howls left. And then Zap abandoned himself to the tears that he had seen on Tanya's pillow.

Tiny beads of blood crept up the (very) long leg of David Gray Goliat. He was sitting in his caravan, stripped to his underwear, methodically pressing a needle into his skin. As a drop of blood appeared he would move the needle upward and draw another. His face was passive, mildly interested, as he did this.

After a while he threw down the needle and sat back. He did not bother to wipe the blood from his leg.

There came a knock on his door. Davey did not respond. When it came again he asked, "Who is it?" in his quiet voice.

"Aawhye Wmlx," was the response. It was the Hippopotamus Boy, the bone that shot through his mouth obscuring any attempt at speech.

"I am in my underthings," announced Davey. "But come in if you wish, Robert."

Robert Merrill opened the door and waddled in. He had his notebook in hand and was busy scribbling out a merry message:

> Well, David my friend, tomorrow is the big day! I know
> I should be getting my rest, but I find myself much too excited—

Then the Hippopotamus Boy glanced over at his friend and saw the bloodied leg. A groan escaped him, and he tore off the page he was working on and wrote:

> My god, what has happened to your leg?

He handed this piece of paper to David. The giant obviously knew what was written and crumpled the sheet without reading.

Then he picked up the needle and said, "Watch," to the Hippo-potamus Boy. Slowly he pressed the pin into his thigh. It went in about half an inch, and a ball of bright crimson appeared. Bobby Merrill watched horrified.

Davey withdrew the needle and turned slowly to Bobby. "I," he announced, "cannot feel that."

Bobby wrote:

What does that indicate?

David read the note. Then he answered, "What it means, Robert, is that I am dying."

Bobby began to scribble again, but this time he made an attempt to speak the words as well, so that his writing was accompanied by a long and low moan.

He wrote:

We must get you to a doctor. We must, immediately.
This is horrible—

Even though Bobby was some feet away, the giant found it little problem to reach out and tear the paper away as the Hippo-potamus Boy wrote. Davey crumpled it up, tossing it away into a corner.

"I told you that in the strictest confidence," he said. "No one must know."

Bobby showed that he was distressed and began to write another note, which Davey reached for and crumpled in the same way.

"I want to play that baseball game," said Davey.

Again Bobby tried to write a note; again it was crumpled.

"Bobby, we all knew I was going to die soon," spoke David Goliath. "But I don't want to go to the hospital—at least not until after we've played that baseball game."

My grandfather descended the staircase into the Fulton Arms Hotel barroom, and found it jam-packed with raucous drinkers. The place was filled with smoke and talk, and my grandfather felt at ease. He sat down at a table and smiled pleasantly around him, patiently awaiting his first drink.

(Yuccatan, for the sake of what my grandfather called "security" was sequestered in the hotel room. "Sequestered" is perhaps the wrong word—he was, in fact, bound head to toe with about twenty feet of the strongest rope that could be found. A rag had been jammed into his toothless mouth, and his leg was chained to the bed's headboard.

(My grandfather had explained that, what with it being so close to the day of the game, the two of them could not afford to be seen together. Yuccatan had promised to go wherever my grandfather was not going, but this, for some reason, was not good enough for the geezer; he said that Yuccatan should not be seen at all. I should note that my grandfather did not manage to contain the sucked-out sailor by means of physical strength. As usual, he was diabolical. All he did was mention the name Houdini. Yuccatan's eyes lit up immediately and he announced, "I am twicet the 'scaper that Houdini was!" "Oh, really, is that so?" asked my grandfather. "Let's see.")

My grandfather's reverie was interrupted by an "Excuse me". He turned to see a youngish man (who was shit-faced drunk) weaving over him. The man had a baby's face, but it was smeared with a sneaky and smug grin.

My grandfather panicked—the reason being, he did not know who he was supposed to be. The barroom had given him a sense of security, and he had let down his defences. Instantly he became Dustin Doubleday, but then, fearing that it was wrong, he became J.M.M. Brassiere. In between he became his own geezerish self. Over and over it went, his face undergoing unbelievable spasms as he circled through the personas. The young man watched, bemused. The personalities came faster and faster. Finally the young man asked, "Are you J.M.M. Brassiere?" and my grandfather screamed, "YES!" so loudly that for a moment the barroom was silent. Then the geezer recovered. "Yes, I am. I do not know you."

The young reporter displayed his press card, which my granddaddy sneered at with great disdain. "As per usual," he announced, "I've absolutely nothing to say to you."

The young reporter smiled, canny, and said, "Are you the Brassiere who developed the undergarment of the same name?"

My grandfather hesitated, but it was imperceptible to the naked human eye. He nodded.

"But, brassieres were developed—" began the young reporter.

Here my grandfather displayed (even I am forced to admit) a certain kind of genius. He said, "I assure you, as I have repeated on many occasions, that I did not know the girl prior to that evening. I was certainly unaware that she had a medical condition. How was I to know she was but fourteen? Now, seeing as the highest court in our fair land has exonerated me completely, could you see your way clear to stopping this incessant badgering?"

Now, this is hard to explain, but I will try. I have compared our young reporter with a sexual pervert before. This is helpful here. Say you have a pervert who was approaching a lady with the intention of exposing himself. He sidles up, breathing heavily and grinning. The instant before he whips it out, the seemingly demure girl whirls around and pulls open her coat. Underneath it she is naked. One can easily imagine the pervert turning around, dumbstruck, and wandering away making small sputtering noises. This is exactly what the young reporter did, sputtering his way back to Lambert and the Hisslop sisters.

My grandfather was now J.M.M. through and through, and he turned in his seat testily. "Does one think," he shouted, "it would be possible for me to get service in this slovenly establishment? Garçon! Garçon!!"

The Alligator Man also entered the Fulton Arms Hotel, but he saw the Hisslops sitting with the two young men and whirled on his heels quickly, dashing out before he could be seen. Out on the sidewalk he pronounced "Shit" with great elocution. He began to walk toward the Sailor's Wife then, although for a moment he considered re-entering the Fulton Arms and apologizing to the girls. He ruled it out—why, he did not know. His thoughts, black as they were, stopped for a little bit as the Alligator Man watched a rather interesting event take place beside him.

Beside him was the wall of the Fulton Arms Hotel. Dangling from a window some three stories up was a chain of bedclothes that had been knotted together to form a makeshift rope that hung about eight feet from the sidewalk. Midway down this rope was an old sailor man. He was climbing down slowly, taking fearful glances at the pavement.

Ally laughed lightly under his breath. Even if the man did fall, he wouldn't hurt himself. He so lacked substance that the Alligator Man was certain he would simply float down, circling like a leaf.

"Hey!" Ally called. "Just slide down and I'll catch you at the end!"

The old sailor looked down. Without hesitation he let loose his grip—the Alligator Man had to rush forward to catch him. The old man fell soundlessly into his open arms.

Yuccatan gave the Alligator Man a small peck on the cheek by way of thanks.

"What are you doing?" asked Ally—meaning not the kiss, but the great escape he had just witnessed.

"Being better than Houdini," explained Yuccatan. "Your hands is green," he told his saviour, as if the same mightn't have known. "Knew a guy with red hands, oncet. Turned red 'cause he murdered his mother."

The Alligator Man set the sucked-out sailor down on his feet and began walking again toward the Sailor's Wife. Yuccatan began trotting beside him. " 'Nother guy," he continued, "had one blue hand, one green hand. Not the same shade green as yours, more a yellowy green. He was a Indian. Holy man."

The Alligator Man chuckled. "My whole body's green," he said.

The little sailor waved that one way with a withered hand and a raspberry. "Naw."

The Author was at that very moment sitting at a table at the Sailor's Wife. He was doing his best to nurse the beer that sat in front of him. The Author was a fairly heavy drinker and trying to cut down; he was not, however, doing a very good job of nursing his beer. As slow as he could drink was still pretty fast. Not only that, but there was a little voice nagging him to buy a shot or two of tequila. He could, he knew from experience, ignore that little voice only for so long. Eventually he would have a tequila, and his beer-drinking speed would increase logarithmically. Then another tequila (beer-rate up again), another tequila (etc.). The Author knew, a little sadly, that he would end that evening very drunk.

The Author looked around him at the sad-faced farmers, all sullenly sipping at their brew. He drummed loudly on the tabletop. As true to life as he made his fictional characters, there seemed always to be an immeasurable distance between them and the people he saw. He would give his characters boundless spirits, often as big as he could make them, but never any bigger than he sincerely believed could be found in real life. But then, at times like this, people seemed to be trapped in cocoons. They seemed shrunken, smaller even than their physical beings. He shrugged and drained his beer. Looking around, he told the waiter to bring him a shot of tequila.

Angus McCallister, fresh from his bounce off Tanya's cold shoulder, stood outside Major Mite's caravan and called, "Donny! Let's say ye and I go in to toon! There be a moving picture I'd like ta see."

Major Mite's voice crept out wearily. "We can't, Angus. Ally took the truck in and we got no other way of getting there. So why don't we get our sleep?"

"Sleep, sleep, sleep! Why is it ever'one here want ta sleep their life away?"

"We wanna beat those religious guys, don't we?"

"Aye, t'be sure, we wanna beat them. . . at the baseball game. *But,* they already beat us at a greet deal more than that if we all start climbing inta bed hours afore we wanna go ta sleep, and all snivellin' around like wee boys in short pants without a mind t' havin' no fun, and all the sperit sucked reet ootta us!!"

"What's got your goat, ya big baboon?"

"Ye come oot a'theer, Donald Pe-faff, else I'll come in an' get ye."

Major Mite came to the door and swung it open. He was dressed in a nightshirt, replete with a tiny tassled cap.

"Come on an' get ye dressed noo, Donny, we be goin' inta toon."

"We ain't goin' no place. Ally's got the truck."

"All right, if that's the way ye're goin' ta be."

"That's the way I'm—"

Angus picked up the Major and began to storm away from the caravans.

"Stop! Stop, you imbecile!!" shouted the midget. This had no effect, so the Major yelled at the top of his voice (and the top of his voice is something to hear, believe you me), "NOW LISTEN TO ME McCALLISTER YOU HAD BETTER JUST STOP RIGHT NOW I AM ABSOLUTELY AND SINCERELY SERIOUS NOW YOU HAD BETTER WHOA UP AND STOP!"

So serious was the Major that McCallister gradually slowed his rampaging stomp until he was standing stock-still. "What?"

"Don't ya think," asked the Major, "that we should take a couple of bottles along for the trip?"

Janus trained both sets of eyes on Nathanael Crybaby Isbister. The man was sitting on the bed in his caravan, hunched over, staring hard at the floor. In his right hand there dangled a half-empty bottle of Irish whiskey.

Janus whimpered, which made Nathanael's head jerk up. "Damn dog, the both of you," he muttered. Something occurred drunkenly to Isbister and he stabbed forward a finger. "Okay. You're so smart, you can understand everything I say, right? So tell me, bright-ass, what the hell's a-matter with me? Eh?" Nathanael left no interval for response. "You don't know! You don't know!! Nobody knows but me!" Crybaby stuck the neck of the bottle into his mouth and guzzled. This seemed to make him quiet, and he addressed the floor in a thoughtful manner. "Keep to myself, that's all. No law against it. Keep to myself." With another guzzle he became angry, and Janus was once more forced to shy away from a thick, pointing finger. "Damn dog, the both of you! I hate you, the both of you! Dogs playing ball? *Bullshit!*" Then, of course, Nathanael broke down and cried. Why did he ever think he could hold it off? He cried for many minutes, stopping finally when he realized that Janus (the left head of Janus, that is) was licking his hand lovingly.

Nathanael rose, sucked in his breath, and pretended he was sober. "C'mon, Fido and Rover. Let's go visit Stella. She ain't gonna marry no weird guy like that Edmund."

And now things start coming together, and all these stories start to intermingle, tiny rivulets flowing to the sea. I suspect my grandfather is making all this up, complicating the story out of sheer spite. For the two of us, it is well past five in the A.M., and the dawn is already beginning to bless the horizon.

In case you haven't noticed, I am counterattacking my grandfather's obfuscations and complications with atrociously bad writing, not hesitating one microsecond before typing, "tiny rivulets flowing to the sea". Oh, it is a battle, my friends. If my grandpapa thinks he can frustrate me and make me stop, he doesn't know the type of man I am. Winners never quit, and quitters never win.

My grandfather tells me that all this happened:

Being a particularly randy geezer, especially with one or two double Scotches under his belt, he found his eyes feeding lustily upon the Hisslop sisters. Despite the company they were keeping (i.e., the strange young man who'd tried to blow his cover), he resolved to sit with them.

He did it with some sort of style, however. (Or so he claims.) He raised his fingers into the air and made them snap several times like a Gatling gun. "Boy! Garçon!" he called in his loudest voice. The waiter (a man who was also the most tattooed person in the state of Michigan) demanded, "Yeah, Mac?" from five tables away. My grandfather said, "Do you see the twin visions of loveliness that sit there? The two with alabaster skin and cherry red lips? The two with eyes that sparkle like a night in mid-summer?"

The waiter said, "Yeah."

"Well, find out what would most please them, and give them the same in quantities befitting their regal presences."

All this, naturally, was done at such a volume that everyone in the establishment turned toward the Hisslops, anxious to find out what their favourite beverage might be. Violet, answering for both of them, ordered double gins.

My grandfather flew over to their table, leaping over various personages and chairs that stood in his path. (He didn't really, but what the hell.) He introduced himself with a deep bow from the waist, saying, "J.M.M. Brassiere. Mon pleasure, petits mourceaux."

Then he sat his bony bottom down.

As the Alligator Man and Yuccatan neared the Sailor's Wife, the latter was involved in a long and complicated tale involving a fellow he had once sailed with. The man's name was Squabb, pirate and poet. On one voyage, it seems, Squabb's ship put in at an island that was peopled by apes. If that phrase "peopled by apes" sounds suspect, then it's Yuccatan who's to blame, for that is what he said and meant. These apes had the ability to think, reason, and speak. They had set up a very complicated democratic government, their leader being a particularly large female named, Yuccatan claimed, Mary. One of the apes' customs, should a newcomer arrive, was that he should sleep and mate with Mary. This was that Captain Squabb agreed to do. He spent one long, arduous night in Queen Mary's court, and in the morning. . .

Here Yuccatan could not contain his laughter, and he exploded through the bar's swinging doors, a blur of motion and phlegm. Ally deposited him at a table, and Yuccatan continued.

"In the morning, Mary come out. She was dressed in her most beautiful robes. She looked pretty, even though she's a monkey. Then Squabb comes out, with robes on too. Mary says, 'This is Squabb.' We was silent. Then Mary said, 'Worst lay I ever had.' "

Even Ally could not help laughing at this, the latest in a series of outrageous tales.

"Kicked us off that island!" epilogued Yuccatan. "Ker-boot!"

Their laughter attracted the attention of an ugly-looking cuss seated at the table immediately beside. He was cradling his head in large and rough hands, frowning at it all, but with Yuccatan's crackle he looked up and grinned.

"Hey," he shouted, "can I join you guys?"

"Free country," muttered Ally.

Then came the inevitable, "Yuccatan!"

The Author grabbed his drinks (by this time he was double-fisted, beer and tequila) and plunked himself down. He glanced around the table, nodding at his newfound compansions. He saw Ally's hand and said, "Oh, yeah. I saw your show. Hey, wait a minute—how come you're out drinking? Isn't that ball game tomorrow?"

"Yeah," scowled Ally, and then he thought, what the hell?—he was there all alone, no one from the show would ever see him enjoying himself, so he said, "Yeah, but I figure I should relax. Maybe I shouldn't be boozing, but—"

"Are all of you guys out drinking?"

Ally reflected. "Most of us."

Yuccatan started waving his hands in the air, indicating that something was occurring to him. When something occurred to Yuccatan, it took about thirty seconds. "Baseball game?" he finally shouted. "Twixt the freaks and the bohos?"

Ally chuckled. "The bohos?"

"Religious bohos," explained Yuccatan. "Which side you on?"

"Don't you remember? I got green hands."

"Oh, yeah."

"I'm gonna be there," said the Author. "I wouldn't miss it for the world."

"I'm gonna be there," said Yuccatan, even though he knew he wasn't allowed within ten miles of the site.

"Everybody's gonna be there," said Ally. "Who would have thought it? Have you heard there's some loony making book on *us*?"

For some reason, Yuccatan started chuckling with great mirth.

Several people reported it to the local constabularies, but all were considered either drunk or crazy. The reports differed from person to person, but they all had a common theme. Somewhere along the highways trotted a giant, cradling something in his arms. Many people said it was a child in a nightdress (they all mentioned the nightdress), others said it was a tiny man, and more than one maintained that it was a monkey. The giant, they claimed, was drinking from a large bottle of something and making inhuman, ghastly sounds, filling the night with terror. (What Angus was, in fact, doing was singing—the ghastliness can probably be attributed to Major Mite's attempts at harmony.) All the reports came from motorists, who had seen this apparition as they passed it on the road's shoulder.

"Stella!" screamed Nathanael from outside her tiny blow-off.

"Awoooaahhh!" screamed Janus, but Nathanael hushed him sternly. "I can handle this myself," he said "Stella!!"

"Well, for God's sake, come in!" shouted the fat lady. "What's stopping you?"

"Nuthin', that's what," countered Nathanael, and he stomped up the stairway.

"What's the matter?" asked Stella with concern. She recognized instantly that Isbister was pie-eyed, and knew him well enough to see that anything could happen to him in that state. As she had said before, there was much in that man.

"I don't know," moaned Crybaby, but it was a moan so full of weakness that he couldn't stand it. "Where's that Edmund goomer?" he demanded brutally. "I think I'd like to tear him apart a little bit."

"Oh, shut up, Nate," snapped Stella. "You'd like to do no such thing."

"Lucky for him he's not here, that's for damn sure."

"Why did you come here? Shouldn't you be resting up for the game?"

"Naw! I done all I can for you freaks, you're good enough to lose on your own. Me, I'm leaving." He spun around on Janus. "And don't get any ideas about coming with me, either, you dumb dogs. I wanna be *alone* again."

"Did you come just to hurt me, Nathanael?" asked Stella quietly.

Nathanael stopped and felt the tears welling in his eyes. He pushed them back somehow, and collapsed to the floor. He was too drunk to notice the pain in his legs.

"I don't want to hurt you, Stel. I don't. I. . . I. . ."

"I'm going to marry him, Nate. The day after tomorrow. The day after the game."

"NO!" screamed Isbister, and then the tears came, all in a gush. "Don't," he moaned.

"He's nice. He loves me," explained Stella.

"No, no, no." Nathanael climbed to his knees and crawled over to the fat lady. He placed his hands on her and pulled himself up; his tears wet her dress.

"I—I love you, Stella," said Nathanael. "I'll marry you. Marry me."

"Oh, Nate," she said, "you don't love me."

"I do," he bawled. "I love you. I can talk to you. You're the only one I can talk to. I told you things—I told you about the fight and I'll even tell you about my legs, 'cause you're the only one I can talk to."

"I'm the only one you ever tried to talk to, Nate. You don't love me."

"I do. I don't feel alone when I'm with you. Marry me, Stella, please marry me."

"Don't you understand anything?" shouted Stella. "Edmund *wants* me, Nathanael, he wants to make love to me, he wants to be my husband."

"But I could—"

"You could what, Nathanael? I am grotesque. I am a *freak*. You couldn't stand the sight of me naked, let alone the thought of actually making love to me."

"But I love you."

"If you love me, that's fine. But don't pretend you could ever be a husband to 'me, because you couldn't. Edmund can, and that's why I'll marry him."

Where Crybaby's tears came from I'll never know. There shouldn't have been any left inside him, but they came with renewed force and it seemed like they would never stop.

"Oh, Nate. . ." whispered Stella the fat lady, and she reached forward to put her hand in her curls. She stroked him as gently as she could.

After a while, Nathanael had spent most of his tears and he merely whimpered. Then he broke himself away and stood up.

"Well," he announced, "here's what happened to my legs."

"Why do you want to tell me?"

Nathanael's face had a strange set to it, a kind of half-smile. "Everyone wants to know what happened to Crybaby Isbister's golden legs."

"It's going to hurt me, isn't it, Nathanael?"

Isbister ignored that question. "So, here's young Goldenlegs Isbister out on the field. Everybody loves old Goldenlegs. They scream 'Run, Goldenlegs, run and don't ever stop!' Oh, my, yes. They tell the young lad, 'You're better than anyone, you are, Goldenlegs. Better than Ruth, better than Gehrig, better than fucking Tekel goddam Ambrose, and just twenty-two years old, no less!' And, and, he tries to say, you know, 'Hey, listen to me, I have this problem with my girlfriend, we can't talk, and some-times I just want to—I don't know what I want to do. . .', but they say, 'Don't talk, Goldenlegs, you son-of-a-gun, *run*! Run, run, RUN!!' "

"Stop!" shouted Stella.

"Stop!" shouts my grandfather.

"I'm in charge now, old man. You started it, but it's my ball game now."

"Listen, boy, I want to talk to you serious." And it would appear that he does. His voice is soft, and his manner intent.

"What?" I ask.

"Son, when you come right down to it, all a man's got is one thing—he's got his dignity. His stake in humanity is his dignity. And if you write what Nate did, you might take it away from him. And he don't deserve that. He never did nothing to deserve that."

"But he did tell Stella."

"She was the only one he ever told."

"How is it we come to know?"

Inexplicably, he says, "I don't think you're really my grandson. I'm not proud to have you for a grandson. You don't care about nothing or nobody. I'm sorry I came to you."

"Well, go away."

"What would you do?" he asks.

"I'd finish it. I've got to, now."

"So I might just as well stick around. Go ahead, write. You're a very good writer," he adds sarcastically. "You surely know nice words, and you know how to make a pretty sentence. A hell of a writer."

My fingers hover above the keys, and some force prevents me from pounding down. My grandfather looks at me intently, and I don't know what's on his mind. Finally, all I can say is, "Hey, I bet Angus and the Major are arriving at the bar."

Angus and the Major burst through the door of the Sailor's Wife at about eleven o'clock that night. The giant from Cape Breton was slightly out of breath and sweaty from his five-mile jog. "There be greenie!" he sang out, and he strode to the Alligator Man's table. He sat down at the one available chair, keeping the Major on his lap like a ventriloquist's dummy. Major Mite seemed perfectly satisfied there.

"Who be the company here, lad?" demanded Angus of the Alligator Man. Ally had been drinking a little bit (even laughing), so even though Angus McCallister was not one of his favourite people, he answered cheerfully. "This little guy here," he said, indicating the sucked-out sailor and even planting a friendly hand on that scrawny shoulder, "is called Yuccatan. And he's full of shit."

Yuccatan took umbrage, gesticulating in the air with a withered forefinger. "If I tole a lie, let God strike me dead!"

The other man at the table, the big ugly-looking cuss, shushed him. "He might hear you," he explained.

Ally said, "I didn't catch your name, Mac."

The big guy shrugged. "Most people call me Mac."

Something occurred to Ally. "How'd you guys get here? I got the truck."

Major Mite answered, "Trotted. Leastwise, Angus did."

"Oncet," chimed in Yuccatan, "I ran over a hunnert mile."

"Aha!" boomed Angus. "So that be the way we're playin' the game!"

Yuccatan paused, for the first time, to look at the newly arrived McCallister and Mite. They didn't seem to hold his interest —he dismissed them with a shrug.

Daisy was very attracted to older men, particularly those with charm and wisdom; these qualities were in evidence in J.M.M. Brassiere. (Ha. I feel sick.) So she and Violet had come to an unspoken decision. Daisy was to be with Brassiere, while Violet would make do (not that she minded) with the gallant and mustachioed Lambert. The only problem was the young reporter, who was still in their midst and drunker than the proverbial coot. He was waving glasses in the air and calling out in a kind of low moan, "She was so beautiful! She was so. . ." And then, after a pause that lasted almost a minute, *"Beautiful!"*

"I have found, lad," said J.M.M., "That many of the fairer sex are won over by that quality that is so often wanting in the younger generation: perseverence. Go to her; go to her on your knees, lad!"

Daisy reached over to stroke J.M.M.'s balding pate.

"She hates me," stated the young reporter.

"Yeah!" said Lambert (who was a little more stunned than usual, still upset by the Hisslops' being Siamese twins). "He's right. Go to her. But not on your knees. That stuff's no good. Just go to her and grab her!"

"You are an animal," said Violet with a wink.

"On your knees," reiterated Brassiere.

"Naw," maintained Lambert. "Just grab her!"

"She hates me," moaned the young reporter, and he began to drain all the liquor on the table.

"They hate me," said Ally, although he was nowhere near the condition of the young reporter. In fact, he was in a pretty good mood.

"Sometimes you act kind of strange with them," said the Major.

"They dunna hate ye, lad," said Angus. "They told me that them very selves."

Ally poked with a finger. "I know about you, you son of a gun. You slept with them."

Angus wagged his huge head wistfully. "Would that that were the truth, son. I tried to make a go of it, but—"

The Author pictured the Hisslop sisters in his mind. "They were real good-looking," he pronounced. "I don't see why they'd hate you, Al. You're a regular guy."

"I get mean sometimes, Mac," said Ally, just a little sadly.

The Author said, "There's a world of difference between getting mean and being mean. Who doesn't get mean?"

"Oncet," chimed in Yuccatan, "A girl left me. Left me to go marry the President of the United States. I got so mad that. . ." (You won't believe this one—I mean, of course you won't believe it, but I mean, you won't *believe* it.) "I got so mad that I went up to him. . . it were President Taft. . . and I called him 'Snake in the weeds!' and booted his keester. Booted it so hard that I broke his asshole. Couldn't take a decent crap after that. That's how come he were so fat."

Angus said, "When Alvira were with Donny, he got mad sometimes. I remember one time that he and that lad Gnat come to blows. . . ha, ha! They tussled for near three days."

Major Mite chuckled. "I wonder whatever happened to ol' Commander Gnat."

"Likely passed on," suggested McCallister.

"I'll tell you a secret, Angus," whispered the Major. "That Commander Gnat—he was okay."

"T'be sure, Donny. Ye donna think Alvira would leave ye fer just annabuddy?"

"Maybe they don't hate me," said Ally suddenly. "They invited me over to their caravan one time—but I was scared, and I got drunk and I blew it."

"Give it another shot," said the Author. "Show them that you're interested."

"More drinks!" shouted Ally.

"Well, old-timer," I say quietly, taking a very long time repapering the machine, "continuity and all that, you know."

He's sitting on his sofa, his scrawny arms crossed angrily, his face a perfect example of that abstract expression "miffed". He is not talking to me.

"Nathanael is telling his story," I remind him.

Suddenly he is all motion. "What about ol' Doctor Sinister?" he shouts.

"Gone to bed. Dreaming of his lovely ladies."

"Zapper? You left little Zap out in the fields!"

"No," I say quietly. "I already wrote that he'd turn himself in. He's asleep, too."

"Tanya?"

"Cried herself to sleep."

"But later. With—"

"But that's later. Right now he's in the Sailor's Wife, trying to stir the Alligator Man into action."

He thinks for many long moments. I take the time to relieve myself, unwilling to start in on Nathanael's tale while the geezer is in such a foul mood. When I come back, there is a fox-like smile on his withered face, and he is drumming happily with his fingers.

"What is it?" I ask suspiciously.

"Tekel. Tekel Ambrose. What's he doing?"

I search through my notes. There is no mention of him, and I am forced to ask, "So what was he doing? He was probably just sleeping, and you know it."

"Nope."

No, Tekel Ambrose could not sleep that night. (A likely story.) In a life full of eight hours' worth of slumber every night, no more, no less, on this particular evening, Tekel Ambrose couldn't sleep. He climbed out of his bed and went to the window, throwing it open to gaze at the moon. It sailed in the sky, a thin slice, a ghostly nail-paring covered by cloud.

Tekel, as we know, had never been forced to provide himself with a conscience. That was given to him as a birthright, a strict and rigid conscience that he never had to bend even a little. Possibly this was why he was never troubled with sleeplessness. Until now.

But he only looked at the moon for a minute or two before he yawned a healthy yawn. Then, his mind as clear as a baby's, he climbed back into bed and drifted off to sleep.

"The truck driver! The hobos! Beatrice the Bovine Beauty!"
"No. No, I'm sorry."

Nathanael had covered most of his life. He talked through a stream of tears that left his face dripping wet. Stella listened, her face as still as stone. Only a single tear rolled over the fatty mounds.

"And we played a game down in Peoria. And all I can remember is the people shouting, 'Go, Goldenlegs, go!' And that's when it hit me, Stella. All I was was a pair of legs. I thought, I'm not a human being—I've never been a human being. Just a pair of legs. Nancy said she was going to walk out on me, because I wasn't nice to her sometimes. But I wanted to be nice to her, I wanted to but I couldn't, because I didn't know how. Any other human being in the world would have known how, but not me, because I wasn't a person, just a pair of goddam legs. Goldenlegs. That's all they cared about. That's all I was. And I'd see people in the stands, watching me. All sorts of people—rich people, poor people, mechanics, farmers, whores, pimps, kids—I'd see them all, everybody, and I'd want to. . . I dunno. Love them, maybe. Love them. But I didn't know how. I couldn't reach out to them, because I didn't have any *hands*—just. . . just a pair of stinking *legs*! And after that game in Peoria, Stel, I went out, and I got drunk. My God, I got drunk. Looking for a fight. And I found it. I found the fight of my life."

My grandfather is rolling up his meagre belongings into a blanket, binding it with binder twine. Occasionally he drops things on the floor in order to attract my attention. He is walking toward the front door when I shout, "Continuity, continuity! My, do I love continuity! Things are really happening in good old Burton's Harbor!"

"You know what to do," he says, resting a gnarled stump on the doorknob. "You're a hell of a good writer."

"Sure, you go ahead. I know what to do. Ally and Yuccatan go back to the hotel, and the Major and Angus go back and chew the fat with Dr. Sinister, and you go home with the Hisslops, you sly dog, along with Lambert, and the young reporter goes to bed—"

"That ain't what happened and you know it!" he screams.

"Oh, really? That's what I thought happened."

"You can't do nothing without me, can you?" He tosses down his bumming-bag and comes racing back into the living room. "Now, all those guys in the Sailor's Wife. . ."

My bandaged hands begin typing at a rapid clip.

What all those guys down at the Sailor's Wife had done was convince the Alligator Man to give it one more go. Ally didn't think much of the notion—he kept dismissing it with a wave of his green hand and a "Naw".

The others were persistent.

"Why the deevil not, laddy?" demanded Angus. "It's no as though ye had owt to lose. Ye've said they hate ye."

"Yeah!" shouted the Major. "Where's your spirit?"

"The sperit!" shouted the Author, in imitation of the Okies that he found more and more on his mind these days.

"Oncet," spoke the wrinkled Yuccatan, "I was in love. With Mary Pickford. But she wouldn't give me spit on a sidewalk. 'Cept, I walked over to her, showed her my manly thing. Wanted to divorce Fairbanks, marry me."

"Naw," said Ally again. "Look guys, I can't. I'm—I'll tell you the truth. God's honest truth. I'm afraid of them."

"Never say it!" shouted McCallister imploringly.

"It's true, it's true. Why, when I walked into the Fulton Arms tonight and saw them sitting there with those two guys, I just turned around on my heels and walked straight out again."

This produced a rather dumbstruck silence—until Angus spoke. "D'ye mean to sit theer an' tell us that the ladies is reet this very moment perched on their lovely bottoms over ta the Fulton Arms?"

Ally saw his mistake straight away. "Earlier on. They've probably left by now."

The Author, Angus, Yuccatan, and the Major rose as one and grabbed hold of the Alligator Man. "Let's go," they muttered under their collective breath.

And so it happened that just as the young reporter went down for the last time, all hell broke loose.

Let me first explain about the young reporter. He had, all night long, been allowing his head to drop on the table with loud crashes. It would stay there for several moments and then rise again quickly. The young reporter would explode with something along the lines of, "She's so beautiful, but I love her!" For the Hisslops and their companions this presented a problem. Not only was this guy a fifth wheel, he was also bent horribly out of shape and made for a very bumpy journey. Finally, though, the young reporter's head went down and did not come up again. He began to snore softly, like a child.

The Hisslops looked at the two men, J.M.M. Brassiere and the photographer Ernie Lambert. Violet, always the more forward, voiced the proposal. "Would you two care to accompany us to our home?"

Lambert was still a little upset by (what Dr. Sinister might call) the prodigious bonding of the sisters, but his life's philosophy was basically "broads is broads". "I got a car outside," he offered. "I can drive us."

"My schedule for tomorrow is rather cluttered, what with the wagering and such," announced J.M.M., "and I needs must have my slumber. Howsomever—"

Whatever his "howsomever" was we shall never know, for at that moment the barroom doors flew open and in walked five personages.

Ally said, "Hi, Daisy. Hi, Violet," and then plucked Lambert up from his chair by the collar. He shot a clenched green fist into the photographer's face.

J.M.M. Brassiere, upon catching sight of Yuccatan, ceased to exist. In his place was my geezerish grandfather, who shouted at the sucked-out sailor, "What the hell are *you* doing here?" The ancient mariner, hard put for an answer, dove at my grandfather's ankle and sank his toothless gums into it.

The bar's bouncers, two enormously big men, came charging forward, intent upon stopping the fracas. The Author and Angus, sharing a wink and a grin, made ready to repel all boarders. The four met with an almost sonic "BOOM!"

The Major hollered, "I'll take on any man in the house!" and brandished his microscopic fists. This offer received much response —however, the respondents were not at all sure who had issued it. They stomped past the Major and selected one of the other men. Which sorely angered the Major, until he heard a tiny yapping. Then his eyes lit up. "A dog," he muttered. "They got a goddam dog here." He valiantly went off in search of a fight.

The young reporter snored peacefully through all this, despite the fact that at one point he was picked up and hurled clear across the barroom.

From all accounts it was one hell of a fight.

My grandfather and Yuccatan stopped fighting long enough to go upstairs to their hotel room. There they continued with renewed force and vigour.

The young reporter slumbered in the barroom's corner until a bruised and bloodied Lambert put him to bed.

The rest drove home in the pickup—Violet and Daisy sharing the cab with Ally; the Major, Angus, and the Author sitting in the back, sucking on a bottle of whisky and singing filthy seashanties.

They drove into the campsite.

Dr. Sinister was sound asleep, dreaming of a woman.

David Gray Goliat was simply asleep—as far as the giant could tell, he had never had a dream in his life.

Robert Merrill's dreams were of his friend Davey.

Zap's dreams we shall never know.

Tanya was not asleep at all.

And in Stella's tent, Nathanael was spinning a tale.

"Don't do it!" bellows my grandfather.

"Listen to this," I tell him. "You're going to like this."

The Hisslop girls quickly removed their clothes. Although Ally had seen them naked through their window many times, their disrobing was a new and wondrous thing. They did it with no more self-consciousness than if they had been preparing for a bath, and if they happened to glance up and see Ally looking at a breast with the wide eyes of a schoolboy, they would smile. When they were naked they lay Ally down on the bed and began to take his clothes from his body. He did not do anything—although if a nipple happened to brush lightly over his face he would put his mouth to it and bite gently. He closed his eyes and felt his penis being freed, although stiff and throbbing. Many hands began to stroke it lightly, lips were pressed to its head.

Then suddenly Ally was all motion. He sprang up and grabbed the girls, burrowing his head and hands into them. He explored the whole of their bodies slowly and tenderly, and then with gentle prods he laid them on their backs and kneeled above them. He kissed Daisy's forehead first, then Violet's. Then he kiss Violet hard upon the lips, then Daisy. He feasted upon Daisy's neck, then up on Violet's. Then Violet's breasts, then Daisy's. And so on until he had travelled the length of their beings.

In the darkness of the caravan, Ally's green body was almost iridescent.

And then he pressed his lips to the ugly, scarred flesh that held the girls together. He kissed it lovingly.

Daisy and Violet turned to look at each other and smiled. Their eyes brimmed with tears. No one had ever done that before.

"What is this, a stroke-book?" shouts my grandfather.

"Some people are never satisfied," I say, disgusted—but not really disgusted, you understand, because at least he's being a geezer again.

The Author, Angus and the Major were drinking profusely and talking about women. Angus stood up as if reminded of something. He pointed at the Author. "Ye'll no be goin' back inna toon t'night, laddy. So ye might as well have me place on Donny's floor here."

"Where are you going to sleep, Angus?" asked the Author.

"Me? Oh, I'll find me a place."

And when the knocking came, she knew who it was, although she couldn't be sure it wasn't one of those amazingly lifelike dreams.

And when she opened the door and saw Angus she cried again, clinging to him and soaking her beard and his shirt front with tears.

Angus patted the top of her head. "Theer, theer, Tanya," he whispered. "Ye'll be gettin' yerself inta a state."

"I'm going to sleep now," announces my grandfather before I have a chance to say a word.

"Alrighty," I speak quietly. "I'll just finish up here, then I'll go to bed, too. And tomorrow—we start on the game."

"Whatever you say." He peels off his shirt and pants and lies down on the couch. He looks like a plucked chicken in his BVDs.

I wish him good night. He doesn't respond.

And so I must go it alone. Please try to understand, anybody out there who might be reading. I don't *want* to write what Nate Isbister told Stella. And if I can infer anything from my grandfather's surly sarcasm, the fact that I am going to would indicate some failing on my part. I may well lack a certain compassion; however, it may ue a compassion that comes with advanced years. I am young and caught up in a tale about a baseball game—and for Nate Isbister, baseball, like all of life, was a thing of damnation and redemption.

"So I went out drinking, Stella, like I say, in Peoria. And, well, I was full of this business about hating my legs. So I started to drink. I've always been a big drinker, you know, I could always throw it back. All night long in the bar, I tried to talk to people. I'd say, 'Hey, how's it going?' But they all said, 'That was one hell of a game, Goldenlegs,' and I'd say, 'Goddam it, my name's not fucking Goldenlegs, my name is Nathanael. Ain't that a funny name?' I'd ask them. 'Nathanael is a funny name, so you all me 'Nate.' But no, no, always Goldenlegs. So I drank some more. And then some more. And ladies would come on to me, play with my hair, call me Goldenlegs. And I wanted to hit them, I wanted to tear them apart, but I didn't, because it wasn't their fault. All I was was Goldenlegs.

"And back at the hotel, all the guys were having a party. I wanted to be with them. I wanted to. But when I opened the door, they all shouted 'Goldenlegs!' and then I just came apart.

"They were doing construction to the hotel, adding a wing. I went over to where they were working and hunting around, and I found just the perfect thing. I took it back to my hotel room, and I locked the door.

"Stella, I broke my legs. I did. I did it myself. With a sledge-hammer. I sat down with my legs stretched out in front of me, and I hit them and hit them and kept on hitting those *goddam* legs until they were just pulp, bloody pulp. . ."

"Stop!" shouted Stella, her face wet with tears. "All right, Nathanael, you've done it, you've made me cry. You hurt me. Now leave. Get the hell out of here!!"

Silently, Nathanael left.

BOOK THREE

Chapter 1

NOW, AS WE all know, some half a mile from the show's big top is a large, unbroken patch of field, more than big enough for a baseball game. It is devoid of trees; it is absolutely without mounds or hillocks. Moreover, it has no grass; some time ago there had been a few patches but they have gone down Beatrice's gullet, fuel for her philosophical ruminations. Indeed, here there is nothing, just a large expanse of dirt, blanched by the sun, flat as a board, a grey mixture of clumps and stones and pebbles.

But, now as if magically, a baseball diamond has appeared.

White chalk-lines mark the baselines, there is a batter's on-deck circle, a pitcher's mound has been scraped together. There are four wooden bases securely anchored with foot-long spikes. The most surprising appearance is the tall wooden fence that contains all of this.

What magic has been wrought? None, of course. All this is merely the House of Jonah's way of doing things. For the past two days, the young boys have been working. The young boys with the downy peach fuzz beards. They moved the lumber by mule-power, scorned and laughed at by truck drivers barrelling past. They had assembled enough bleachers to contain, if need be, over one thousand customers. The boys also intend to circulate in the bleachers during the game, making sure that every seat-holder has paid a dollar and a quarter for the privilege.

No one is sure how many people are likely to show up. But it is ten-thirty in the morning (the game is scheduled to begin at 2:00 P.M.), and already two or three trucks have stopped, their owners climbing out and milling around nervously. There has been no poster or broadside advertisement for this game, but it looks as if Word of Mouth has done its stuff again. In fact, because I have an historical perspective, I know that by a quarter to two those bleachers will be jam-packed, rear ends pressed cheek to cheek across every available inch of board. The people will be anxiously awaiting the coming of the rival teams, as we should be too. Except that you and I, dear reader, have a bit of unfinished business to attend to.

This unfinished business is quite a simple matter, really; it takes place in a room at the Fulton Arms Hotel, a room registered under the name of Brassiere. In that room is J.M.M. himself, wearing his paisley smoking jacket, puffing a Havana, and hurling abuse at the railway employees, who have not, as yet, seen fit to let him hire a presidential train. Also in that room is a huge vault-like safe sitting against a wall. This safe is protected by an employee of Pinkerton's Detective Agency. As everyone knows, these are the best law enforcement agents in the world, hand-picked by the famous Mr. Pinkerton. This particular specimen must have been with them for an awful long time, being, shall we say, rather advanced. Decrepit, in fact. Who am I trying to kid, eh? It was our lovely Yuccatan, wrapped up in a uniform that he got by nefarious means.

It's as simple as this: there is, in Burton's Harbor, a small, scrawny man who affects the name of Slick Teddy. Slick Teddy is a compulsive gambler, and a little on the dull side. This is why he has some small importance here. He could, because of previous dullness at the gaming tables, afford to wager only a solitary five dollar bill. My grandfather, disguised as J.M.M. Brassiere, said that this would be all right, and that Slick should show up at nine o'clock *sharp* on the morning of the game. Slick showed up on time, and was instructed to hand the money to the security guard. Slick did. My grandfather then likewise handed a five dollar bill to the security guard (the money was borrowed from Yuccatan's sister). Yuccatan (the Pinkerton man) then put both five dollar bills into the safe. Slick was shown the door. Then Yuccatan went into the washroom, removed from the wall a sheet of plywood, and took out the ten dollars. Which was, coincidentally, what a man named Fermont had wagered. Fermont arrived at nine-oh-five. Twenty dollars went into the safe—which was what a man named Lubert had wagered, scheduled to show up at ten past. You see how it worked? By late morning my grandfather was handling the big bets, the ones in the hundreds.

Now, let's play ball.

Pregame Warm-up

(No Press Passes Allowed)

It seemed as if all our friends, every single one of them, woke up as soon as the day began to dawn. On the average, they had had 2.8 hours of sleep for the night, a figure that would have been all the lower were it not for the fact the ol' Doc Sinister managed to rack up almost nine and a half. So then, awake, they began to drift outside to gather around the pickup truck that would transport them to the field of battle.

The first to show were the Major and the Author. They had talked for hours and hours, the midget reliving his life with Alvira, his legendary feud with the Commander—his conversation sailed drunkenly from these specifics to points of philosophy, eg., "Womens ain't worth frog-shit at the bottom of a dried-out well." Slowly the Major's words had run out, and soon he was fast asleep in his rabbit-covered rocking chair. The Author bunked down in the tiny man's cot, and being as he was a big fellow, it was like trying to make a bed out of a foot-stool. It seemed to the Author that he had slept for twenty minutes when a hand shook him rudely awake.

It was Major Mite. "Wake up, Mac," he said. "Time to get up."

And now, as the two stood beside the pickup truck, the Author looked at the darkened horizon and saw the sun peeking up like a mischievous schoolgirl. "Shit," he muttered, "I *was* only asleep for twenty minutes."

"Naw," insisted the Major. "It's late. I wonder where everyone else is."

"Asleep," suggested the Author.

"Naw," repeated the Major, and he said no more, for today he was not given to talking.

Of course, he was right: the others were not sleeping. The next to arrive were Angus and Tanya. They walked from the dawn hand in hand.

"Mornin'," said the Giant from Cape Breton. "Where's ever'one else?"

"I don't know, Angus," answered Major Mite, genuinely concerned.

"Look, guys," said the Author, and he stabbed a finger toward the east. "Being a writer, I should be able to describe the scene for you. The hills are blanketed by Mother Night, held within her velvet coat. Sprinkled lightly, by the hands of fairies, come the first washes of sunlight. Lo, the dawning—"

"What's he goin' on aboot?" asked Angus.

Tanya spoke. "I guess it is kind of early. . ." She seemed at a loss, somehow, giving half-smiles to Angus, questioning looks to the Major, and avoiding altogether the friendly gazes of the Author.

Major Mite broke the silence with great animation. "Hey, we're gonna whop tar out of them pilgrims!"

"They're not the pilgrims," muttered the Author.

"We all are pilgrims and such is our seity," came a high-pitched tone, and Dr. Sinister arrived on the scene. Immediately he got down to business. "Ah, Mr. McCallister!" he chirped. "How delightful to see your eximious personage. Not, mind, that I am in any way lachrymose in viewing Tanya, Major Mite, and this gentleman, whomsoever he might be. . ." (The good Doctor did not seem particularly interested.) "It is just that I have a herculean endeavour that would best be attended to by Angus. Angus," he addressed the same, "in mine abode you will find a rather large cardboard box. I find its largesse slightly minacious and altogether prohibitive of my fetching it here mineself. Would you be so very kind as to get it?"

"Ach," Angus said as he marched away, "an' if ye could speak the King's English it would ha' been here by now!"

"I'll help Angus," said Madame Tanya, trotting off in her manly way to catch up to him.

"I don't believe I've had the pleasure," said the Author, cocking an eyebrow at the Doctor for Major Mite's benefit.

"Oh, yeah," said the tiny man. "Mac, this here's Doc Sinister. Doc, Mac."

The Author pumped the Doctor's hand effusively, quite alarming the distracted little magician. "Oh," said the Author, "I knew who you were 'cause I've seen a show. I just wanted to be introduced. And let me say that it's a great honour to meet you."

"Indeed?" sputtered Doc Sinister. "If you say so."

"You're going to pitch for the team today?" inquired the Author.

"I am going to do my very utmost to fulfil that rosterial function, yes."

From the dawn came a musical sound, a whistle carried on a bed of giggles. It was Ally and the Hisslops. They said, "Good morning," in unison so that it formed a "Good morning" pyramid, the girls at the bottom, Ally at the top.

"I am *so* nervous," said Violet. "Doctor, if we lose are we really going to have to leave town?"

"Such is the wager."

"Don' neever talk of losin', lass! Ye got t' think oonly of winnin'!" This, not from Angus, but from Ally doing an imitation of the same. The people around him laughed, and the Alligator Man blushed a bit.

"Who's takin' the mickey, then?" This *was* Angus's giant-sized voice, and he came into sight bearing a huge cardboard box. He saw the newcomers and smiled. "How's ever'one?" he asked.

The answer, all around, was "Fine."

"What's in the box, Doc?" asked Major Mite.

"Mayhap we should wait on the others. I shall go fetch Zap."

Tanya said, "I'll go get Stel. I . . . I want to speak to her anyway."

The two went off.

"Yonder comes the big'un," noted Angus, and into their circle came Davey Goliath. He marched sternly erect, grim, but he walked without his canes, and he seemed to make the ground rumble with his determined strides.

Everyone was surprised, and more than a bit alarmed, no one more so than Daisy Hisslop. She called out, "David! You might fall!"

"I might," he agreed calmly. "I trust you would then help me back to my feet."

"Fer sure, David," answered Angus. "That's a good lad."

Davey Goliath smiled a bit.

Robert Merrill, the Hippopotamus Boy, looked like an artistic genius in the grips of an unrelenting and slightly demented muse. He scribbled at his little pad then tore out the page savagely, leaving a trail of them behind him. For the most part, the pages on the ground said things like, "Oh, boy!" and "This is it!" and "Today's the day!" Bobby finally completed one page that seemed to him acceptable, and he handed it to the Alligator Man to read aloud.

" 'Morning all! Today our courage will be tried, and I know you all, and love you all, and believe with every ounce of courage that none among us shall be found wanting!' " Because Bobby's words had come out of the Alligator Man's mouth, it seemed most natural that Ally should make the reply. He cast about momentarily before saying, "We love you too, Bobby."

Janus came then, a blurred flurry of typical canine antics, both heads going after the one tail, emitting sharp double-edged yaps and the occasional growl. He ran around the circle, dizzying the members as they tried to follow him with their eyes.

"Our star outfielder!" shouted the Major, and this had a curious effect on the animal. It was as if both heads thought simultaneously, "Oh, yeah, I'm the star outfielder. What am I acting so crazy for?" And with that, Janus plopped his butt on the ground and began to pant— with great dignity, naturally.

Dr. Sinister arrived with Zap, who alone seemed unexcited. This was because the Wild Man from Borneo was still half-asleep. As soon as he saw the people, though, some sort of cognitive process took place, thoughts jumping over synapses like cripples over hurdles. Zapper let loose a mighty howl then, beating his chest in grand gorilla style. He pounced on Janus in an attempt to wrestle away his excited energy. The dog pulled away with an ill-tempered growl, as if to say, "Cool it."

Their voices seemed to arrive before they did. Stella's, "So how do you feel?"; Tanya's, "I'm not sure. Strange. All right, I think. Good." Then the voices fell away, from fear of being overheard. And Tanya pushed Stella in her wheelbarrow into the circle of friends.

The fat lady smiled. "Well, Doctor, let's show them what we've done."

"What about—" began the little man, but Stella interrupted him. "Open up the box, Poindexter."

Somewhat reluctantly, Dr. Sinister pulled open the top of the cardboard container. Inside were baseball uniforms.

"Stella is the seamstress," explained the Doctor, "and I have done the embroidery."

Everyone agreed they were the most beautiful uniforms in the world.

They were almost pure white, with crimson socks and markings. And on the backs, in a Gothic style of print, were names.

Dr. Sinister handed them out. There was a special two-person pair, of course, for the girls. One jersey read:

VIOLET

HIS

and the other:

DAISY

SLOP

There was also a special double-headed canine jersey, and the name JANUS ran lengthways along the spine. Most of the jerseys had just last names—MITES, McCALLISTER, MERRILL, GOLIATH, SINISTER—although for some this was impossible. There was one MADAME TANYA and another ZAPPER, W.M.F.B. Ally's back was the most decorated, being as his jersey bore the complete

THE ALLIGATOR MAN. Stella was already wearing her sweater, the name STINTON filling up a small part of her very large back.

Dr. Sinister reached sadly into the box. "There is one more," he said quietly, and he pulled out a jersey that read ISBISTER, and underneath this, CAPTAIN. The troupe members stared at this sweater for a long moment.

"You better give it here, then." Nathanael walked into their circle and took it. He looked around at their faces, slowly, examining each set of eyes. Then he shrugged. "How come no one woke me up?"

So, all our friends are here. Here at the baseball game.

(Well, hold on, I tell one small lie—Tekel and the boys have yet to show. This is understandable, however, seeing as the House of Jonah travel by foot. They are always on time, but never early. As well, I suppose, it has to do with Tekel's demonic game plan. He, leading his army, swoops on to the pitch, the king of dark enchantments—and within seconds, the battle has begun. It tends to leave the opposition a trifle unnerved.)

That is, in fact, what we are all doing—waiting for Tekel Ambrose and the Brethren of the House of Jonah, fervent witnesses for the Lord of Salvation, and one hell of a baseball team to boot!

You and I shall take a look around.

I don't know about you, but I have never in my life seem so many people show up for a baseball game that wasn't a major leaguer.

I see that the Author has more or less appointed himself batboy for the freak team. He is strolling among the players, checking equipment, asking their preference in bats, patting rear-ends as he says, "You're gonna do all right." The members of the freak team (I don't like to call it that, but that's what everyone else around here is saying) look glumly nervous. They stare around them, bewildered by the crowd, made uneasy by the alternating rounds of laughter and applause that are directed at them. Nate Isbister is limbering up, doing exercises to stretch the muscles of his twisted legs. His face is slightly pained. Angus McCallister struts to and fro, three or four paces one way, twirling around for three or four paces back. He is covering about twenty feet each way. Of all the freaks, only one is calm: Dr. Sinister. He stands off to one side, a baseball in his hand. Every so often he will flip it into the air, a childlike action. He is waiting.

Let's take a look around the stands. As I say, all of our friends are here.

There is the young reporter. Hoo-boy, is he hungover! He has spent most of the morning spewing up bile, and little green flecks of it still cling to his clothing. His face has a visible greyish tinge to it. Cigarette smoke wraps around him like a straight-jacket. He holds a tiny notebook and is writing quickly. Although he looks, at the moment, incapable of speech, his prose is flowing out in beautiful verbal loops as he describes the scene.

Beside him, lumpy-faced, grumpy, and doubly black-eyed, is Ernie Lambert. He is putting together photographic equipment, looking very industrious and professional. He has realized, of course, that his assailant is THE ALLIGATOR MAN from the freak team, but he bears him no hard feelings. It must be said for Lambert that he never bore grudges. Besides, he had been trying to pick up the guy's girlfriends, and could hardly blame Ally for being mad. Ernie Lambert is about to take the best photographs of his career.

Greg Haines is here; so are all the men from Burton's Harbor. They have all come directly from J.M.M. Brassiere's hotel room where they have matched money with the undergarment prince, dollar for dollar. Greg Haines, along with everyone else, was pleased and relieved to see the Pinkerton guard here—this sight removed any nagging doubts about J.M.M. being on the up and up.

All our friends are here. The baseball-capped truck driver wouldn't have missed it for all the tea in China, and is sitting in the stands with his wife, a pretty young girl of about nineteen. At the moment the truck driver is snoring loudly, his head flopped over on his shoulder. He has left instructions with his wife to wake him up when the game begins.

Sitting underneath the stands, staring at the diamond through wood and legs, is the circle of hobos. They have come all the way from page three, bless their hearts. They are passing around a bottle of lord-knows-what.

One of them remarks, "Lookee. Crybaby Isbister. He's going to play, looks like."

And although this has been something of a running joke among the circle of hobos, this time it is said with a measure of earnestness—"Sure hope he don't start crying."

The ghost of Morris M-for-Magnus Mulcher roams the field, chuckling at the size of the gate. He himself could not have invented a better draw, and is kicking himself in the backside for not coming up with it when he was alive.

Oh, and yes, Beatrice the Bovine Beauty is here, somewhere.

In fact, the only guy who isn't here in some way, shape, or form is Mr. Pfaff, Major Mite's daddy. And, as far as I'm concerned, that's okay, 'cause I never liked the guy.

You-know-who is there. Grandpappy mine. Only he's bespectacled and tiny, wearing a cricket cap and a lumpy chest protector that is almost twice as big as him. He is standing off to one side, thumbing through a huge sheaf of handwritten pages. They are the Doctored (Sinister) Rules of Baseball. Across the first page, in a flowery hand, it says:

I find these acceptable. T. Ambrose.

Yuccatan is here, although this is in direct contradiction of a mandate from his chief. At least he has had the foresight to crawl out of his Pinkerton's uniform, knowing in a hazy way that without it he won't be recognized by any of the men from Burton's Harbor. He is sitting in the stands, dressed as a sailor man, his pelican hat on his wrinkled head, boring the trousers off a fellow whom the Fates obviously have something against. Why else would they have sat him down beside Yuccatan?

"I played baseball only but oncet," the mariner announces, as if this is a logical progression from his last statement, which dealt with his part in the invention of talking motion pictures. "After the game, the Baby comes up to me. 'Who do you play for?' 'Nubiddy. Nothing else to do today.' 'Good,' says Babe. 'If you played regler, I was gonna quit.' "

The man beside him wonders what he has done in his life that has so angered the Fates.

Three things happen all at once.

A cloud passes in front of the sun, and the world is wrapped in shadow. From this shadow, borne out of it, comes a silence. And into this silence come Tekel and the Brethren of the House of Jonah.

Tekel Ambrose marches up to Dustin Doubleday; Nathanael Isbister sucks in a breath of air and does the same. Doubleday nervously lays down the rule book—he is made uneasy, as is everyone else, by the midnight shades that colour Ambrose's face.

Tekel immediately gets down to business. "I stipulated that only members of the entertainment troupe could play," he says, addressing Doubleday but levelling a black look at Nathanael.

"I'm the India Rubber Man," says Isbister, "and I'll bend my finger back to prove it if you don't believe me."

"No matter," snaps Ambrose. He turns to Doubleday. "We are playing on turf foreign to both teams. I suggest we flip a coin to decide who goes up first."

Dustin Doubleday nervously digs into his pocket which provides, by some miracle, a penny. He throws it into the air where it seems to be suspended longer than God would normally allow, twirling like a circus acrobat and sparkling in the sunlight. Tekel Ambrose turns his eyes on it and announces, "Tails." It seems as if this was what God was waiting for—as soon as the word is spoken the copper drops into Doubleday's palm. He slaps it over on to his wrist and reveals it. "Tails it is indeed," he announces.

Tekel says to Doubleday, "We shall have the first at-bat," and turning to Isbister, a kind of half-smile comes to his face. "You are the home team."

"Oh, hell," says Nathanael, "everybody knows that."

(Game Plan. Here is what the three of them—Nate, Angus, and Dr. Sinister—have come up with in terms of who should play what position. Sinister, as we know, is the pitcher. Nate has taught him every pitch in the hurling repertoire; as well, the Doc has come up with a couple of his own. He has a pitch with a lot of top spin that breaks the ball downward. The Doctor calls it the "Dipper", although in a few years it will become more popularly known as a slider. Nate Isbister is going to play centre field, naturally. Some years ago, a sports reporter wrote, "Nathanael Goldenlegs Isbister is the ultimate centre fielder—the man and the position were made for each other." So those two decisions were easy to make. Major Mite is going to be the backcatcher. This seemed logical, seeing as the Major would not have to crouch in the typical style, giving him an edge should he have to throw to a base or catch a pop-up. Ally is assigned to first base by virtue of his overall skill and razor-sharp instincts. Second base goes to the Hisslop sisters because they can handle throws from both directions, Violet should they come from third, Daisy if they come from first. Third base belongs to the Giant from Cape Breton, Angus McCallister. And, although it makes for a sort of absurd joke, Davey Goliath is the shortstop. While he is not quick, his enormous reach allows him to fill quite a gap in the infield. Now, there are too many of our friends for a one-to-one allocation, so left and right field are divided up, two people splitting alternate innings. Left field is divided between Zapper and Janus. Right field is covered by Tanya and Bobby. The only player not playing is Stella, but she is still a very important part of the team.)

"Come on, guys," says Nate Isbister. He doesn't shout it, he doesn't scream it. He speaks in a normal voice, without an echo of emotion. "Tanya, you take right field for now, and we'll start Zapper out in left."

"All right, Nathanael," says Tanya, and she trots out to her position.

"Take your places," instructs Nate, and he takes Zap by the hand and walks out into the field.

The reaction of the crowd is a curious mixture of applause and giggles. Our team is followed out by encouraging hollers, shouts, grunts and barks from Stella, the Author, Bobby and Janus.

— — —   — — —   — — — (House of Jonah)
— — —   — — —   — — — (Exhibition of Eccentricities)

Mene Ambrose is the first batter. Looking slightly ridiculous with his long, tumbling beard and pinstriped baseball uniform, he enters the box, hikes up his bat, and directs his still-as-stone gaze toward the opposing pitcher.

The opposing pitcher, Dr. Poindexter Sinister, smiles at him gently.

Behind Mene Ambrose is a high-pitched and rapid muttering. "Come on, Meanie, ya bearded galoof," says the Major, "let's see you try and hit one. Maybe if you hit one your brother Tickle will let you eat the crust offa a dead bear's ass. What ya think, Meanie?"

Mene, as far as anyone can tell, is doing a very good job of ignoring him.

Suddenly the little Doctor is a blur of motion, and a baseball comes rapidly toward home plate. Mene allows it to pass, and Dustin Doubleday calls the curve outside.

The Major is outraged, tearing off his catcher's mask and spinning around on Doubleday. "*Outside*?! What are ya, blind?! How much money did Tickle give you?"

"One more outburst and I will forbid you to continue," Dustin cautions him.

Frustrated, the Major turns around and returns the ball to the Doctor.

Dr. Sinister, with his curious windup (without the aid of modern day slow-motion, it is impossible to see exactly what this windup entails) sends another one, a fast ball, across the plate. Mene goes for it and connects, but it fouls up into the bleachers behind first base. Mene has a ball and a strike.

Mene stares hard at the Doctor, who smiles once more at him before throwing another ball. The pitch lacks a little stuff, and Mene smacks it, a drive that streaks toward Davey Goliath, beelining at his kneecaps. The giant is too slow to react, and the ball bounces off his leg. Angus scoops it from the ground and hurls it to Ally on first. It is a good throw—Ally snags it easily and goes through the motions of making the tag. It is all for naught, as Mene Ambrose has been standing on the bag for quite a while.

"I'm sorry," says Davey Goliath.

"Ye stopped it, didn't ye, laddie?" answers Angus McCallister.

Next up is Peres Ambrose, whom the Major refers to as Perry, telling him that if he plays well, his brother Tickle might allow him to have sex with a porcupine. The Doc takes a look at first and hurls one that Peres allows to pass. It drops easily through the zone; Dustin Doubleday calls it, "Strike one!" Mene, though, has taken advantage of the situation and is standing on second base. The Hisslop girls, quite forgetting the rules of the game, are trying to tell him to go back to first base.

The Doctor feels it is his fault. He looks over his shoulder at second base, holding Mene to a safe distance, before throwing the next ball.

Peres smacks it hard, and it sails into the air, a pop fly deep into centre field. Nate Isbister arrives underneath it, snapping his glove around the ball. A split-second later he is throwing it—Mene has tagged up a second, and he and the ball are now racing for third. It is a close call—Angus catches the ball and swipes at the sliding Mene.

When the dust settles, Dustin Doubleday calls Mene "Safe!"

Half the crowd denounces the call, the rest seem to think it fair. The Author is the most vocal of the denouncers, marching up to Dustin Doubleday and yelling at the top of his voice, his language spicy as Mexican food. The little umpire listens carefully and then snaps out in a geezerish voice, "Take it easy, buddy—I know what the hell I'm doing." The Author looks at him quizzically and marches away.

The ball game is resumed.

The next batter may or may not be the same as the man who batted third in the game against the Alexandria Athletics. As I have mentioned before, all the players are cast in the same mould, the mould of Tekel Ambrose, and there is not much sense in identifying them.

This one is significant in that he is Dr. Sinister's first strikeout of the day. The Doc draws upon every resource, knowing that the situation is decidedly dicey. There is a runner on third and only one out. The first pitch screams straight toward the plate and then drops suddenly. The batter for the House of Jonah misses the ball. The next pitch, a change-up, the batter ticks for a foul off third base. Dr. Sinister then delivers a knuckle ball, which is ticked for another foul. Then there is an outside pitch, one more foul, and then two balls that sink too low, giving the batter a full count.

Dr. Sinister closes his eyes momentarily, and in his reverie flips the ball idly. After an incredibly fast windup (some spectators swear he twirls around like a dervish), the ball shoots out. The batter swings hard at it, but the ball seems to avoid the bat of its own accord, leaping over it like a horse in a steeplechase. The batter, pulled by the force of his own swing, spins around and ends up on his keester. Even for a Brother of the House of Jonah, it is hard for the man to keep his dignity.

Major Mite is merciless. "You're in trouble now, eh, buddy? Tickle's gonna have your balls for a necktie."

But this is no time for joking around, as even the Major realizes when he sees the next batter. Tekel Ambrose is approaching the batter's box, his face darkened even further by his predecessor's humiliation. He lifts his bat and stares at Dr. Sinister.

Behind him, there is silence from the tiny Major.

The Doctor hurls the ball, and with a seemingly effortless swing, Tekel connects. It is stroked far into left field, Zap's territory, and the Wild Man from Borneo screams loudly. Then he turns around and charges deeper into the outfield. Nate Isbister is beside him and then past him as they head for the boards that fence off the playing area. The ball clears the fence by a foot or so, accompanied by a loud "Crash!", the sound of Nathanael Isbister colliding with the plywood boards. He runs into them with such force that many people are convinced he didn't even know the fence was there. Nate Isbister falls back on to the ground and says, "Shit." Mene and Tekel Ambrose have scored for the House of Jonah.

Isbister dusts himself off as he gets to his feet. Some feet away, Zapper is standing, looking at him anxiously. "Good boy, Zap," nods Nathanael. "We would have had it if it weren't for the egg-sucking fence."

They walk back to their positions.

We end on a bright note, though, top of the first inning. The next batter connects with the Doctor's fourth pitch and grounds it down the third base line. Angus McCallister reaches out with his bare hand, engulfing the ball. He then flings it across the diamond to the Alligator Man. The runner is undeniably out at first. Our team is up to bat.

    2 — — — — — — — — (House of Jonah)
    — — — — — — — — — (Exhibition of Eccentricities)

En route to the dugout, Angus McCallister sidles up to Davey Goliath and nudges the boy gently. "Lad," he says, almost a whisper, "take a good gander at yon Tekel."

David obligingly directs his bespectacled gaze toward Ambrose, who is warming up on the pitcher's mound, hurling balls with his surprisingly silly style.

"Does he remind ye of annabuddy?" asks Angus.

The giant concentrates. "There is something about the darkened eyes," he decides, and then a horror-filled realization descends upon him. "You don't think—?" he gasps.

"Aye, lad," says Angus. "He be a master of disguise, t'be sure, but I think that be the boyo himself."

Davey nods, seeming to shake off the terror. "He won't get me."

Before we get right down to it, let's look at our batting order. Because everyone plays, everyone (except, we hope, Janus) has a turn at bat, giving us a ten-man roster:

1. MAN (The Alligator)
2. HISSLOP (Violet/Daisy)
3. MITE (Major)
4. McCALLISTER (Angus)
5. BORNEO (Zap, the Wild Man from)
6. LADY (Tanya, the Bearded)

When he is through swinging the weighted bat for a warm-up, the Hisslop girls give the Alligator Man a peck on the cheek for luck. He enters the batter's box.

It seems to Ally that the stadium is in total silence, although if he thinks about it, he can hear the hubbub of the crowd. The silence emanates from Tekel Ambrose's eyes, a sort of angry silence. Ally is also conscious of a heavy silence coming from directly behind him, a silence from the crouching backcatcher, Peres Ambrose.

Ally hikes the bat to his shoulder and swings loosely through the strike zone.

Before throwing his first pitch, Tekel raises his eyes heavenward, following this gaze with a slight nod. Then he pushes forward with his arm, and a ball flies in the air. Ally swings at it, missing completely. As soon as this happens, the crowd noise enters like a bronco through the gate, a deafening clash of chuckles and jeers. But when Tekel is ready to throw again the silence returns. Ally misses the second pitch too, and again is crushed by the crowd's roar.

Nathanael Isbister calls Ally out of the box, putting his arm around his shoulders to confer.

"He's getting to you, buddy. You never went for pitches like that when we were practising. They're sucker balls, garbage—what's worse, you're missing them by a mile."

"I don't know what it is," says the sad Alligator Man.

"I know what it is, it's goddam Tekel Ambrose, that's what it is. So forget about him. Just look at the ball. When he's got it behind his back, pretend he's invisible, that you can see clear through him. Look at the ball."

"I'll try," says Ally.

"Now I'll tell you one more thing. He's thrown two big curves, so look out for a fast ball."

"Okay." Ally returns to the box.

The Hisslop girls, in the on-deck circle, have stopped their warming-up to watch Ally. Nathanael notices and shouts, "Forget about him. You guys got your own work to do."

Ally tries to follow Nathanael's advice, visualizing the ball as it rests behind Tekel's back. When it emerges he follows it with his eyes, and is just about to swing when he notices it beginning to drop. Ally jerks his bat back, allowing the ball to pass. Dustin Doubleday calls it a ball.

With a one-two count, Ally patiently awaits the next ball. That's how he refers to it mentally—not as Tekel's next pitch, but as the next ball. When it comes, screaming into the strike zone, he goes for it and connects.

Unfortunately, Mene Ambrose, at shortstop, makes a spectacular play, somersaulting on the ground, trapping the ball, and releasing it to first base even before he is up on his feet. Ally runs with every ounce of his strength, and almost makes it safely to first. The ball gets there before him, though, and he walks sadly back to the dugout.

Nathanael nods to him. "You got it. Next time."

Daisy Hisslop feels the same silent presence and is unnerved by it. She swings madly at Tekel's first pitch, missing it by the proverbial mile.

"Oh, shit," mutters Isbister. "He's really got us."

Daisy looks down at her sister Violet, who is bent over to avoid the bat. "Sing," Daisy demands.

"What?"

"Sing. Sing a song," Daisy implores her, and as the next pitch is thrown, Violet breaks into:

Camptown ladies, sing this song, doo-dah, doo-dah. . .

Daisy hits this one, fouling it up into the stands. But at least she hit it. "Keep singing," she tells Violet. "Just keep singing."

Camptown racetrack four miles long,
All the doo-dah day.

Daisy swings again, ticking for another foul.

"Getting closer," she whispers; Violet keeps singing.

The next pitch, however, is one of Tekel's specialties, a ball that seems possessed of demons, a ball that flies on a course unrelated to the laws of nature. Daisy lets it pass, confused by its meandering. When Peres Ambrose catches it, Dustin Doubleday says a soft, "Strike three". (My grandfather tells me of a great reluctance to make that call, but the pitch found the geometrical centre of the strike zone so exactly that there was little else he could do.)

Daisy drops the bat, and the girls turn away.

Running by them to pick up the bat, the Author gives the girls a broad wink. "Way to go," he says.

The Major is up next, and presents a new problem. He is not, I think, "psyched out" by the Ambrose clan. Indeed, he strides into the batter's box with a tough little swagger, telling Peres, "Better back off there, Perry, or I may knock your block off." And before he hikes his bat to the ready position he points a miniscule finger at Tekel, as much as to say, "Gimme your best one, buddy."

We have stated before that to throw a strike against a midget is extremely difficult, even for the best of pitchers—the strike zone is simply too small. The St. Louis Browns, some years after this story, actually used a pinch-hitting dwarf, as the man was virtually assured of a walk to first base, where a runner could be substituted.

Thus, Major Mite at bat should have been our first bright spot in a rather dismal first inning. This is not the case.

Tekel's first pitch comes, and everyone in the stands can tell that it is sailing well above the Major's shoulder, quite removed from the strike zone. Everyone can tell that this is going to be ball one—everyone, that is, except the diminutive Major Mite, who lifts his bat and swipes at the ball. It coasts through for "Strike one!"

"Lucky for you, Tickle!" the Major shouts in his high-pitched voice. "Try another."

Tekel obliges, and shoots another ball forward. Again, it is sailing too high; again the Major goes for it, swinging the bat above his head, missing cleanly for his second strike.

Nathanael Isbister calls the midget from the box and explains the situation to him, even though Major Mite has heard it all before. The tiny man is disgusted. "You want I should just let the boogers go by, huh?"

"Well, yeah," answers Crybaby. "At least we'd have a man on first."

"Nothing doing, Nate. The idea is to smack the ball, and that's what I aim to do."

The Major re-enters the box. "Don't worry about catching this one, Perry, it's not gonna get to your glove." And then, swinging around, he shouts, "Let's see a better throw, Tickle! I heard you were good!"

Tekel is good, of course, great even, but this third pitch is still not quite low enough. The Major goes for it, however, and that's that for the Major; that's also the end of the first inning.

2 — — — — — — — — — (House of Jonah)
0 — — — — — — — — — (Exhibition of Eccentricities)

As he approaches his dugout, Tekel Ambrose notices something that seems to bother him. He calls to Dustin Doubleday, "Make sure that play does not commence until that grotesque dog-like creature is removed from the playing area." Tekel hooks a thumb toward left field where Janus is romping around playfully, running circles around Nathanael.

Doctor Sinister, approaching the pitching mound, supplies the response. "Are you ephecticizing that we should remove one of our star outfielders?"

"It is a dog," says Tekel, who is given to these simple declarative statements.

"He is a *wonder*dog, in fact," says the Doctor, "but without prefixes he should still be allowed to play. This is stated illucidly in the amended rule book."

"You are making a mockery of this!" shouts Tekel. "Debasing a great thing. Everything you touch is defiled."

Dustin Doubleday settles the issue. "Even in the regulation rules, nowhere does it state that a two-headed dog may *not* play. In our revised edition, it states quite clearly that such a creature *may*."

Tekel thinks for a moment and then says, "But he must go up to bat. That rule is not changed."

Dr. Sinister says, "He shall go up to bat, if you insist with pertinacity."

"I do," says Tekel.

"We shall then morigerate. You realize, I hope, that his strike zone, knee to armpit or their canine counterparts, is less than five inches?"

Tekel turns away. "He does not have to bat," he snarls, and then he hooks a finger at the Doctor. "You shall pay dearly for this, sir."

The House of Jonah have four players to go on the roster before the Ambrose brothers return to bat. These four men are younger than Tekel and the lads, but that's about the only difference. They are all excellent athletes.

The first of them comes up to bat, silent and graceful.

Dr. Sinister, after smiling a warm greeting, throws a rather good pitch, a curve. The batter watches it closely and elects to go for it. It pops up into the stands, a foul—strike one.

For some reason, a performance short of perfection is a source of humiliation for the Brethren of the House of Jonah. They get mad. You can see nothing of this in their faces, though. You can tell only by the way they deal with the next situation, that is, this first batter drills the Doctor's second pitch into right field.

Bobby Merrill, his monstrous head cradled in the neck-brace, runs toward the ball. His "run" is actually more of a penguin-like waddle, but it is fast enough to bring the Hippopotamus Boy underneath the arc of the ball. Bobby holds up his glove—the ball lands quietly on his face, knocking the lad to the ground.

Nate Isbister arrives, scooping up the ball, and he throws it to Angus McCallister. The runner has just passed second base; reluctantly he returns to it.

Nathanael helps Bobby up, dusting him off, talking to him. "Line up the ball and take a step back," he reminds him. "You get hurt?"

Bobby swings his huge head back and forth, groaning what is meant to be, "No."

The next batter for the House of Jonah chooses to let Dr. Sinister's first pitch sail through. Dustin Doubleday calls it, "Strike one!" The batter does the same for the next, but this one is called a ball. Even though the Major argues this call with some conviction, the pitch is undeniably outside. The next is also a ball. The next one, though, is a good one, a change-up that the batter goes for too soon, ticking it off for a foul and a two-two count.

The batter laces into the fifth pitch, a line drive that seems to be ascending into centre field.

It looks like slow motion, the way Davey Goliath is swinging his arm up over his head. It also seems excruciatingly slow the way Davey takes a little hop into the air.

Some of the spectators claim that the ball was at least twenty-five feet in the air when Davey caught it.

Davey Goliath collapses on to the ground with a horrible crash, first crumbling to his knees and then bolting forward. He falls the length of his body and lies still.

The man on second takes a quizzical gander at the immobile giant and starts off for third base.

Angus McCallister is the first to react, leaping over to Davey and plucking the ball from his hand. He spins around to face the runner who has just reached third.

"I'd stay theer if I were ye, son," he calls out, and the man does so.

Flipping the ball to the Doctor, Angus helps Davey to his feet. David Goliath is obviously in great pain, but he denies it vehemently. "I'm fine, Mr. McCallister," he states. "I just fell over, that's all." He forces a thin-lipped smile. "A sense of balance is not my long suit, you know."

Out in right field, Bobby Merrill has scribbled out a note that reads:

We *mustn't* let David play!

Then he remembers his promise, and he crumples the note into a little ball, tossing it away.

"Play it to home! Play it to home!" intones Nathanael from centre field.

Dr. Sinister, perhaps a little rattled by Davey's collapse, throws a pitch that the third batter has no trouble hitting. It soars out to the deep outfield.

Nate Isbister turns and bolts after it. Already some of the spectators are cheering his play—and it is thrilling to see the man run, his awkward legs propelling him forward in a blurred streak. The ball falls over Nate's right shoulder and into his glove like a homing pigeon that has come to roost.

The man on third tags up just as Nathanael spins around. Isbister leans back and then shoots forward, sending the ball toward home plate. Major Mite catches it and jumps on the sliding runner, stopping him just as he is about to touch safely. The man is out.

The crowd applauds wildly—the freak team has managed to hold the House scoreless for an inning, which is a feat very few baseball teams have managed.

2 0 — — — — — — — — (House of Jonah)
0 — — — — — — — — — (Exhibition of Eccentricities)

And now, at the bottom of the second, Nate Crybaby Isbister holds court in his dugout.

"Okay, we're doing okay here. But I'll tell you one thing—it's gonna start getting rough. Those Brothers out there are getting madder and madder, and they're just gonna start playing better and better. So we're gonna get smart."

Nathanael then collars Angus. "Okay, now, you're up. I'll tell you what Tekel's gonna do. He's gonna send you a couple of sinkers—they're gonna cruise at you low and then drop. Okay? Now, you go for them. Don't worry about hitting them—as soon as you go for a couple of them klunkers around your knees, Tekel's gonna figure he's got your number. Then he's gonna send you that fast ball of his. He'll put so much stuff on it it'll look like an airplane taking off. But that's okay, because you're gonna be waiting for it. Okay?"

Angus nods hesitantly. "S'posin' he donna?"

"I'm betting he will," says Nathanael. "That's how he pitched the big guys from the Alex A's. A couple around the knees, then *zoom!*"

"Ach, well, I'll have her a go."

Angus marches up to the plate, acknowledging as he does so the applause of the crowd. It's an impressive sight, the legendary Giant from Cape Breton, his long white hair and beard stirring slightly in the breeze. Just before entering the box, Angus tugs at his whiskers for the benefit of Tekel Ambrose, as if to say, "Mine's nicer than yours." Tekel, of course, glares blackly.

Tekel's first pitch does indeed come low, slicing off the bottom of the giant's strike zone, and sinking even lower afterwards so that Peres is forced to make the catch by trapping the ball 'twixt glove and ground. Angus has taken a swing at it, looking more like a golfer than a baseball player, and he is called for strike one.

The next pitch is the same, although Angus doesn't miss this one completely. He catches a piece of it, popping it high into the stands for a foul and the second strike.

Angus looks over at Nate; Nate nods.

Nathanael knows he is right when Tekel Ambrose hesitates a split-second before going into his delivery. The ball comes out of his hand incredibly fast, so fast that Angus has to start his swing immediately, relying solely on instinct and Nate's prediction. He pulls the bat through the centre of his strike zone with every ounce of his gigantic strength.

And there is a "Pop!!"

Angus didn't get all of it, but he got enough to propel the ball into centre field where it takes a bounce, the fielder unable to get there in time.

Angus charges toward first base.

The fielder for the House of Jonah makes a picture-perfect throw to the first baseman (Lambert doesn't take a picture of it) but Angus, with his long stride, has arrived first. (Lambert does snap Angus McCallister's face as the giant stands on base, a proud, defiant gaze that contains an embarrassed smile.) We have a man on base.

Zapper is up. The freak team wouldn't consider not sending him up, but they are a little concerned. While he seems to know that he should hit the ball, no one is at all sure if he realizes that should he do so he has to run. Dr. Sinister has positioned himself at first base—he is hiding a banana behind his back.

With grunts and squeals, the hairy little pinhead enters the box, the bat resting on his shoulder. He looks around, his face quizzical, searching through the faces in the stands. He appears to have no interest in Mr. Ambrose on the pitcher's mound. However, because Zapper has entered the box with bat ready, he has declared himself able to receive a pitch. Even though Zap isn't looking, Tekel throws one.

It curves inside and Zapper appears to jerk his head quickly to look at something behind him. The ball bounces off the crown of his pointed head, knocking him to the ground.

He is up in a second, thrashing around madly, hurling hoots in every direction.

Isbister goes over; the Wild Man from Borneo embraces Nathanael tightly, like a frightened child.

Nate looks at Doubleday, who says, "Take a base."

Tekel storms off his mound, his face darkened. "Why should he take a base? It was a fair pitch—he moved into its path purposefully."

Isbister screams in grand baseball style. "What the hell do you mean, Ambrose? For one thing, he can't do anything 'purposefully'! For another, you were trying to dust him off and you know it!"

Tekel remains calm but is obviously angry. "Mr. Isbister, I will not stand for that accusation. I do not try to 'dust off' anybody."

"He wasn't even *looking* at you!"

"He was in the box."

Dustin Doubleday steps between them. "Gentlemen, please. I have awarded the player his base. I fail to see why you are having this discussion."

Tekel, who reveres an umpire almost as much as he does God Himself, turns away and starts back to his mound.

Isbister takes Zapper by the hand and walks him down the base line. Nathanael chuckles silently. "Goddam it, Zap," he mutters, "you couldn't have done better if you knew what you were doing."

When they reach first, Nathanael leaves the Wild Man from Borneo in the hands of Dr. Sinister. He then races over to Madame Tanya in the on-deck circle.

"Okay, okay," he snaps. "Look, I know you don't give a tinker's cuss about any of this, but it seems to me that you might as well do it right."

Tanya interrupts gently. "I'll do the best I can."

Nathanael pauses to study her face, and finds something there that he hasn't seen before. He nods.

"Okay, Tanya, listen. I want you to look at his pitches. Just look at them, pick the one you want, and blast it. See, I don't want you swinging at the bad stuff because then Ambrose is gonna see the kind of power you got. This way I'm betting he slacks off a bit to save his arm. So just look and wait. When you see your pitch. . ." Nathanael completes his sentence by swinging his arms through the air and screaming, "*Blam!*"

Tanya chuckles and leaves for the batter's box.

Isbister, hands on hips, spins around to his dugout. "Two men on, nobody out, we're gonna score us some runs off these guys!"

Tekel's first pitch weaves quickly past Madame Tanya. Dustin Doubleday calls it strike one. The next ball curves sharply away and is called a ball. (My grandfather tells me this was one of the few questionable calls he made. It seems to me that the geezer got caught up in being an umpire and tried to call a fair game, quite forgetting about the money in his hotel room.) The third pitch, a fast ball, screams through Tanya's strike zone and is called accordingly. The next pitch, Tanya whacks. It sails over Tekel's head, over Mene's head at shortstop, and then drops to the ground while the left fielder charges at it.

The play for the House of Jonah is to third, but Angus runs halfway there and then dives. His hand touches the bag before the fielder has made the throw.

Tanya is well on her way to first.

And, miraculously, Zap is at second. In all the excitement, no one noticed him doing it, but somehow the little man has arrived safely at his base.

Even the Doctor is bewildered, but he simply shrugs it off.

Well, there we go! The bases are loaded and nobody's out. This, of course, is the worst situation a pitcher can be in. Many begin to crack at this point, and start to throw overcautiously. Tekel Ambrose does not get overcautious; he gets angry.

Coming up for the freak team is the player-coach Nathanael Crybaby Isbister.

During his short but legendary professional career, Nathanael had a reputation as a low-ball hitter. He also tended to go for the first pitch.

The question is, how much of this does Tekel know? The two did meet in play some fifteen years before, but does the bearded man remember? Because of Isbister's size, the obvious way for Tekel to pitch him would be low. This would be a mistake.

Tekel, his face blackened, studies Nathanael closely. Peres, the backcatcher, signals him with a couple of fingers, a suggestion that Tekel keep the ball up.

Tekel Ambrose gives an imperceptible shake of his head. Then he goes into his windup.

The ball is incredibly fast—it is also low.

Goldenlegs Isbister hits it, takes a few steps toward first base and stops dead.

In a silence (but a peaceful silence, not a House of Jonah rager), everyone watches the baseball sail from the park.

In modern day argot, kiss it goodbye.

The crowd applauds and screams loudly. Slowly, almost without their knowing it, they are becoming home team fans.

Stella beams proudly.

The players come home—Angus, Zapper (led by Dr. Sinister), Tanya, and then Nathanael Crybaby Isbister. His teammates embrace him.

The young reporter nudges Lambert. "That's really him, isn't it?"

Lambert nods. "The real thing. Mr. King's gonna love this."

"Did you get a picture of him hitting the ball?"

Lambert shuffles his feet. "No. But I took a picture of him hugging the fat lady."

The young reporter is a little confused, but he returns to his own work.

The truck driver sits back down. He has been up on his feet, waving his baseball cap and bellowing, "Yahooooo!"

The hobos, hidden underneath the stands, all smile the drunken smile of lord-knows-what. One of them vocalizes their collective sentiment—"First we seen him cry, now we seen him *play*."

A certain portion of the crowd has started to grumble. These are the men who have made wagers with J.M.M. Brassiere, unaware that the freak team would contain Goldenlegs Isbister. But they are all consoling themselves with the same thought— "Don't worry about it. Isbister may be great, but Tekel's even better."

Well, we all know that this is a moot point, one best handled by baseball scholars and historians. But I can tell you one thing— Tekel was never as good as he was for the next few innings of that game that day.

The Hippopotamus Boy is the unfortunate first victim of Tekel's wrath. He faces three pitches, screaming fast balls that break every which way. Bobby Merrill takes three useless swipes at them. The first out on strikes.

Then it's Dr. Sinister, the personified object of Tekel's hatred. The little Doctor receives the darkest midnight glare that Tekel can deliver. Tekel receives the most beatific of smiles.

The little Doc gets a piece of the first pitch, but hits it foul off the first base line for the first strike. The next one he misses completely. Dr. Sinister summons all his concentration and lashes out at the third pitch. There is a pop, and the ball rises up.

Tekel Ambrose would have to jump up about ten feet and to his right about six to make the catch. Which is exactly what he does.

Dr. Sinister is a blurry little blotch scurrying along the first base line when he realizes what has happened. He slows down, staring (a little fascinated) at Tekel Ambrose. "I say!" says Doc Sinister. "That was well done!"

No one is ready for what is about to take place.

David Gray Goliath steps forward. It used to be that Davey's great size had a certain pitiful quality to it. That is lacking today; which is odd, because our Davey looks patently ridiculous in his too-small baseball uniform. A cap perches precariously on the top of his head, almost nine feet in the air.

Davey steps into the box, holding a bat which he makes look like a London bobby's billy-club.

His face, as ever, is expressionless. Yet before this, I always found it possible to attach the word "grim" to it. Not so today. His face is utterly without expression.

Except for just before Tekel winds up to pitch. Then Davey's face becomes a storm of black fury, his eyes raging from behind the thick yellowing lenses. Davey stabs out with a foot-long finger at Tekel Ambrose, and although he speaks with his usual soft voice, the giant's words are clearly audible to every set of ears in the place:

"You won't get me."

Each word is equally weighted, somehow, in its defiance. It is, "*You* won't get me", "You *won't* get me", etc., all at the same time.

Lo and behold, our friend Davey Goliath has already done the impossible—for Tekel Ambrose is genuinely nonplussed. He stares at David with great confusion chiselled on his face.

But this is only momentary. Tekel's face clouds over again, and Davey's drains of emotion, and it all happens so quickly that everyone wonders if the scene did indeed occur at all.

Tekel goes into his windup; out sails the ball.

Davey's swing starts, and it starts from the centre of his being; it starts twenty-three years ago, when Mrs. Goliat gave birth to a perfectly normal baby boy; it starts one hundred and sixty years ago, when Dr. John Hunter began to pester James Byrne; and I suppose it starts hundreds of thousands of years ago, when mankind finally got the brain working well enough that it could be screwed up with very little effort.

So it's obvious that the pitched baseball (which started just less that a second ago) stands very little chance.

Ask anybody what the world record for the distance of a batted ball is. They might tell you that the Babe once hit one 587 feet. If they really know their stuff they'll name Roy Edward Carlyle at 618 feet. No one will mention David Gray Goliat, because no one measured his hit. Which is a damn shame, I think, because Davey's encyclopedia listing is a little sparse as it stands:

> Goliat, David Gray, (Davey Goliath) 1915-1938; the tallest man (8' 11¾") that ever lived.

(I suggest we all take a moment to fix up our Britannicas—let's all go scribble in, "He also hit a baseball further than anyone ever did before or since.")

The crowd is standing in a second, gazing at the ball—they are quiet, awestruck, as if watching the takeoff of man's first flight to Heaven. Which they are.

When the ball is well out of sight, beyond the fences of deepest centre field, then come the cheers.

But because all eyes have been trained on the baseball, no one has noticed what has happened to the batter. When they look at him, they find that he is a huge mass sprawling halfway down the first base line.

Nathanael Isbister runs over to him, kneeling down beside the giant's head. Davey Goliath looks at him through pained eyes and manages a smile.

"I did well, didn't I, Mr. Isbister?" he says, his voice a faint whisper. "Captain," he adds.

"Jesus Christ," mutters Crybaby, and what else could I call him at a time like this? "You sure did do good, Davey, but—you got to take the bases."

The giant shakes his head wearily. "I can't. . . Coach. I'm sorry."

A shadow falls across Davey's face; looking up, Isbister sees Tekel Ambrose. "If he cannot take the bases, he is out," says the bearded man.

Frantically, Nathanael looks over to his dugout. "Angus! Ally! Tanya! Get the hell over here!"

"The player is out," repeats Tekel Ambrose quietly, "unless he can round the bases."

"Fuck you, Ambrose," snaps Nate, and as his teammates draw near he yells, "Come on and help me drag Davey around the bases." Then he looks up, puzzled, because they have made no move to help. "*Come on!*" he bellows.

Angus speaks, "Natty, the lad is sore ill. I think we'd better let him be."

"He's gonna be out!" screams Isbister, his gruff voice as hard as nails even though tears stream down his face.

Angus whispers, "But it's just a game."

"Don't you understand!? They'll get him! He'll be out!!" In desperation, Nathanael tries to move Davey by himself, pulling at the giant's shoulders with all his strength.

"You are not allowed to assist," says Tekel Ambrose. "He must round the bases of his own power. He is out."

"He's not out!! He hit a goddam home run!"

Tekel goes over to Dustin Doubleday. "Tell him that the player is out."

Doubleday is searching through the rule book. With a small smile, Tekel takes it away from him and flips the pages, deftly locating the one he wants. He hands the book back, pointing to the pertinent phrase. Sadly, Doubleday walks over—Isbister has managed to drag Davey about ten feet toward first base. The little umpire sends an arm through the air, gently proclaiming Davey Goliath out.

Isbister looks down at Davey's face and then turns his gaze to the dark, bearded man. "You lose this game, Ambrose. I swear to hell you do."

Dustin Doubleday turns to the stands. "A doctor?" he demands of the people there.

(TIME OUT)

A doctor has been found, and he is ministering to Davey behind the crowded bleachers.

In our dugout there is a heavy silence. The Author, having felt it, has left to buy a hotdog. The troupe members stare at Isbister sullenly; that man has turned his back on them all, his arms folded across his chest. Every now and again he will pull a hand across his face, wiping away tears.

It is Stella that speaks to him. "Nathanael," she says, "we realize that baseball is an important game to you, but. . . well, it is just a game. And all of us, because of what we *are*, feel very strongly about each other, and. . ." All this circumambulation is getting her nowhere so, after taking a small breath, Stella proceeds rapid-fire. "We appreciate all the help you've given us, but we cannot forgive you for trying to drag poor Davey around the bases. Don't you realize how serious his condition is?"

"He's dying," mutters Nathanael Crybaby Isbister.

"And yet," says Dr. Sinister, "even though you were cognizant of that fact. . ."

Slowly, Nathanael turns around. And he says, "It's because of what you are that you feel strongly about each other, eh?" He shakes his head with a kind of half-laugh, half-sob, very quietly— but then his voice comes with force. "Then why don't you see what happened? They got him. *He* got him." Nathanael quickly searches their faces and becomes angry when he sees no comprehension. "*Dr. Hunter fucking got Davey!*"

For the silence that follows I have no words. I am probably a pretty shit-poor craftsman with words, but it's difficult to describe things that are very, very human. So I state facts and facts only:

It's Angus McCallister who breaks the silence by saying, "Let's get on with the game."

It is Major Mite who speaks next, saying, "It's time to beat tar out of some bozos in pinstriped pee-jays." Next is Dr. Sinister.

"Indeed, let us resume, and resume without remoration, for we are in the vanguard of the scoring." And Ally says, "Thanks to Nate." Several people then say, as if there might be some confusion about the point, "Our captain."

So they leave the dugout—but as they go, Stella calls out, "Nate," very softly.

He returns to her, crouching down so that they are staring at each other, face to face. Nathanael smiles at her quickly, before she has a chance to speak. "We're doing okay, eh, Stel? Four to two."

"I'm sorry," she begins, but Isbister stops her. "Hey, Stella, maybe you wouldn't mind hugging me, eh, for good luck?"

They hug each other for almost a full minute; when they release, Nathanael hurries to wipe some tears from his face. He laughs, embarrassed. "I cry too damn much," he says.

"Well—" running her hand through his multicoloured locks "—most of us don't cry enough. I guess that's something we've all got to learn, Nate—the right amount of crying we should do in this world."

2 0 — — — — — — — (House of Jonah)
0 4 — — — — — — — (Exhibition of Eccentricities)

Unfortunately, we don't really have time to worry about Davey right now. As I say, there is a doctor looking at him, and we'll find out soon what the situation is.

Isbister has to do a little shuffling around in the field because of Davey's absence. He assigns Bobby Merrill permanent duty in right field and moves Tanya over to third base. Angus McCallister becomes the shortstop, and I'll wager that that particular hole in the field never had such a tight plug.

And so we take our positions. Nathanael Crybaby Isbister walks hands in hand with the gruesome Wild Man from Borneo, leading his little teammate to left field.

(In the dugout, the Author has returned with a couple of footlongs. He sits himself down on the bench, munching away, using his free hand to pat the twin heads of Janus the Wonderdog. He notices two tears streaming over the mounds of Stella's face, and he looks at her for a long moment. The Author nudges her. "Everything okay?" he asks. She nods, smiling.)

So then my geezerish grandpa (disguised as Dustin Doubleday) intones, "Play ball!"

A bearded man walks calmly into the box and assumes his stance. The Major at backstop suggests that he begin packing immediately, seeing as he and his Brethren would most assuredly be leaving town. His answer is silence.

Our little Dr. Sinister seems to have found his pitching stride. (And he's going to need it!) Being an older man, his actual arm cannot send a ball off with extraordinary speed, but you can't be a prestidigitating practitioner of magic with a miniscule for fifty-odd years without developing incredible manual dexterity. This is where the Doctor's talent lies. He controls the break of his balls well, and is a good strategist, breaking them inside to back the man off the plate, and then sending balls that careen to the outside. Most of the time he uses his left arm, saving his right for trouble occasions.

The first bearded batter, after taking a ball and two strikes, sends a line drive toward right field. Ally goes for it, Dr. Sinister coming over to cover first—Ally dives at the ball, trapping it on the ground. He pops to his feet and throws all in one motion. The runner has just rounded first and is barrelling for second base. Dr. Sinister receives a well-thrown baseball and launches it to the Hisslop girls.

The player from the House of Jonah arrives at just about the same time the ball does. He throws himself at the girls, knocking them backwards about ten feet before they are able to make the catch. Having made second, the player jumps up and takes a few steps toward third. Angus McCallister is standing on the base line, holding the ball between his massive fingers. The giant from Cape Breton says, "Let's see ye try tha' stunt with me, boyo."

You might think that a strong wind has just risen, hearing the "oooooo"ing noise in the air. You have to listen closely to realize that it is a soft booing from many of the people in the stands. It is a half-hearted, almost shy, boo; after all, the House of Jonah have a reputation for being absolutely fair at all times, and, of course, what that player did was technically *fair*. . .

Ally runs over to help the girls back to their feet. They are somewhat shaken, but with all parts intact. The Alligator Man then turns on the Brother who is standing peaceably on second base.

"Hey!" Ally demands loudly, even though the man isn't two feet away. "This is a *baseball* game, you know. It ain't no fucking football game!"

The bearded man nods gently, and says, "It is a baseball game." Now where have you heard that before?

Violet Hisslop says, "It's all right, Ally," and propels him back to first base, taking the opportunity to give his backside a quick caress.

Well, the House of Jonah are back at the top of their batting order, which means that the next batter is Mene Ambrose. That man enters the box. The Major is quick to assure Mene that he was just lucky the first time. Dustin Doubleday instructs Major Mite to stop tormenting the batters or be evicted from the game (although my grandfather tells me he was privately quite amused by the Major and still chuckles to think of some of the midget's lines).

Mene takes a full count, three balls and 2 strikes, before lacing into one of the Doctor's dippers. The ball sails into right field, heading for the grotesque Hippopotamus Boy. Bobby Merrill waddles quickly to be beneath it—he stands still for a moment and then takes a full step backward. The baseball lands in his held-out glove.

Nate Isbister is running over. "Throw the ball, Bobby!! The guy's tagging!" Indeed, the Brother is well on his way to third. Awkwardly, Bobby Merrill launches the ball forward, but it is not near anybody or anything. Nathanael Goldenlegs Isbister wheels around quickly—and then collapses to the ground with a shout and a short scream.

The Alligator Man has picked up the ball, throwing it the length of the diamond to Major Mite. The play is close, but not close enough—the House of Jonah have scored again.

Ally then goes over to Nate. (Isbister is picking himself up again. This is the second time he has tried to do so.) Ally knows better than to try and assist Isbister; he is forced to watch the agony that Nate must undergo. Finally, after almost a full minute, Nathanael is erect. He and Ally stare at each other for a long moment.

(And the stands are buzzing as if full of bees—"Did you see that?"

"He fell down." "Just like that. Boom.")

Nathanael says, "Come here, let me lean on you, Al. I can walk it off in no time."

So, with the Alligator Man as support, Nathanael Isbister spins slow circles out in centre field, his gait going from near-crippled to strange but graceful in a short while. Nate gives Ally's back a slap and disengages himself. He trots deep into his territory, as the next batter is Peres Ambrose.

After looking at a ball and a strike, Peres smacks at a pitch; mind you, he doesn't go for the wallop, he merely gives it enough to send the ball over Dr. Sinister's head and toward second base. The Hisslop girls, excited and perhaps still a little shaken from their collision, quickly become a tangle of limbs. The ball, as if with a mind of its own, seems to weave through this tangle, selecting the only course that allows it to pass untouched and land some ten feet behind the bag at second. Angus McCallister has to be quick to grab the ball, holding Peres at first base.

And at first base, Ally grimly watches the next batter enter the box. He moves his mouth only very little, slipping the words out the corner at Peres. "I can see the crummy way you guys are playing. . . pick out all the weak spots on the field. . . smashing up the girls. . . I'm gonna get you guys for that one. . ."

Peres's serene silence is infuriating. Ally continues at a louder pitch, "I wouldn't want my name to be Ambrose if I were you. . . nossiree. . ."

And as Dr. Sinister goes into his windup, Peres Ambrose takes off from first base like a bird from the branch of a tree. "Hey," bellows Ally, "he's going!" Ally gesticulates wildly at the runner, and the Major at backstop is ready. The ball never gets to him, though, for the House batter reaches way out and gets it, sending it toward the Alligator Man. Ally doesn't notice the projectile until the last possible moment, which gives him just enough time to make a fool of himself, lashing out at it uselessly, looking as if he is waving it bye-bye.

The outcome of this particular hit-and-run play (which is finally put to an end by Nate, who comes from the field to grab the ball) is that the House of Jonah now have men at second and third. There is only one out, and the Brethren are just one run behind. Which is too bad, because:

Tekel Ambrose comes out of the dugout. He cleaves the air with a practice swing, and for the short moment of that swing his face is lined with out-and-out viciousness. In a thoroughly uncharacteristic way, he makes a gesture from the box. His gesture is the same one Babe Ruth was known for making, indicating with the bat where the baseball was to be hit. Tekel points at Nathanael Crybaby Isbister. And with that gesture, a gauntlet has been thrown; for these two men the game has become a private contest. Many historians are unaware that this game even happened (which is a large part of the reason why the geezer wanted it written up in the first place) and have spent countless hours pedantically and hypothetically arguing the various merits of Ambrose vs. Isbister. They still do it today, even though many years ago Tekel Ambrose pointed at Nathanael Isbister and said, silently, "Let's settle this once and for all."

This challenge is so strong as to exclude the little Doctor, in the sense that it doesn't matter what kind of pitch he throws. His first is a good, hard curve ball that bends in sharply toward Tekel, but that bearded man doesn't seem to care at all. His swing does not look especially hard or quick, but as soon as that "crack!" comes, it's obvious that the swing was both. Out flies the ball, higher and higher, and it is indeed headed toward Nathanael.

Now the chant is ubiquitous; although no one person in the crowd is saying it loudly, they are all saying it, as if it were a prayer. It can be heard everywhere— "Goldenlegs, Goldenlegs, Goldenlegs. . ." And Goldenlegs is tearing back for the boards, his legs spinning drunken circles that propel him with miraculous speed. This time he doesn't go into the boards, he runs up them; he swings his arm high into the air, taking a leap from the top. The baseball, though, is some twenty feet high; Nathanael is achingly and amazingly close, but the ball eludes him. Isbister flips a somersault and disappears out of sight.

So we are on the shitty end of the stick again. The House are in the lead at the top of the third, 6 to 4, with only one out. The only thing that is the least bit encouraging is that the Ambrose brothers have already played.

Then: the next batter, after taking a ball and a strike, connects with one that the giant from Cape Breton picks out of the air easily. He lobs it over to Ally. Our green first baseman, still stinging with embarrassment, makes sure there is no mistake on the play, catching the ball with two hands, tagging the man out.

The next batter finds a hole between first and second base and sends the ball there. Robert Merrill's waddle couldn't possibly be of any use there, so it is up to Nathanael to sweep in from centre field. This he does, and manages to hold the runner at second.

(He is in no way slowing down, our Nathanael, but now as he runs he finds it harder and harder to keep the pain out of his face.)

With a man on second base and two men out, Dr. Sinister racks up his second out on strikes. This he does mostly with his newfangled dipper. The youngish player is completely baffled by the ball's trajectory—he misses one completely, ticks off another for a foul. Then the little Doctor seals the batter's fate with a change-up, a ball that seems to apply its own brakes as though the plate were a red light.

We're up, at the bottom of the third.

Nathanael Isbister and Dr. Sinister confer as the Brethren take the field.

Nate asks, "Did you hear anything about Davey yet?"

The little Doctor shrugs sadly. "There is no sign of palingenesis."

"Doc?"

"He hasn't come around as yet." The little magician looks up at Nathanael. "When this game is done, much is going to change."

"What do you mean?"

"It's a feeling I have. Much will change; foremost among these changes will be the way that I talk."

Dr. Sinister looks so serious in this proclamation that Nathanael is forced to burst out laughing. He hugs the small man tightly; then, to introduce a note of levity, Nate recalls, "Hey, you know what's out there? Right out there on the other side of the boards where I went over?"

"Yes? She came then? Beatrice?"

Nate looks baffled. "No Beatrice—just a skinny old cow."

"Very good," announces Dr. Sinister—their conversation is cut short, as the Alligator Man is entering the box.

2 0 4 — — —   — — — (House of Jonah)
0 4 — — — —   — — — (Exhibition of Eccentricities)

The Alligator Man, from the outset, refuses to be intimidated by Tekel's glares and concentrates solely on the path of the ball. Nathanael has told him that for all his talent Ambrose is a rather unimaginative pitcher, tending to curve his first two throws and then bomb through a fast ball. Ally looks at the first pitch, which bends outside for a ball. He then thinks that, according to Nate, the next one's going to come in close. When Tekel releases the ball, Ally takes a tiny shuffle backwards and swings the bat around. With a "click", the ball runs down the third base side, between the man there and Mene at shortstop. Both men take lunges at it, ending up on their guts. Finally it is up to the left fielder to scoop up the ball—the Alligator Man has reached first base.

The Hisslop sisters, about to enter the box, jump up laughing, clapping their hands together.

This time it is Violet's turn to try. Daisy crouches down to avoid that bat, and whispers to her twin, "Do you want me to sing?"

Violet is feeling Tekel's unearthly silence and she nods quickly.

Camptown ladies sing this song, doo-dah, doo-dah. . .

Violet waits for the pitch.

(With his hands shielded from all eyes but his brother's, Peres makes a few quick motions; Tekel nods.)

Tekel goes into his windup.

It all happens too quickly. Nathanael Isbister bellows, "Ally!", but to no avail. Tekel has whirled around and fired the ball to first base. The Alligator Man makes a panicked attempt to get back to it from his lead-off, diving as if there is a pool of water there. But after this desperate moment, Ally is sitting on the ground, hurt, embarrassed, filthy, and incontrovertibly out.

Ally has a short tantrum, pulling out two clumps of dirt and flinging them around like a child in a sandbox. He rises to his feet, swipes at the grime on his uniform and, avoiding any eye contact with the Hisslop girls, he trudges back to the dugout. (Muttering "Shit" so's you could smell it, too.)

Daisy and Violet look sadly after him.

Tekel takes that opportunity to whistle a pitch through the strike zone. Somewhat reluctantly, Doubleday calls it as such.

Nathanael Isbister storms out to Tekel's mound, his arms swinging with obvious malicious intent. It must be said of Tekel that there is absolutely no cringe to be found anywhere on his person. He waits in his damnably patient manner.

"Now that's a pretty cheap trick, Ambrose!" yells Isbister.

"Mr. Isbister," says Tekel quietly, "your team is playing much better than I would have anticipated. I can only assume that you have been instructing them. Now, if you neglected to tell them that if they are in the box with the bat raised they have declared themselves ready to receive pitches, then you are to blame."

"Violet wasn't even looking at you."

"She was in the box. The bat was raised. Where she was looking is hardly my concern."

"Did you ever hear of common—" Isbister searches for the right word, finally electing, "—*decency?*"

"You have no right to malign my character."

"What character?" Isbister demands before turning back to join his team.

Violet raises her bat again, and keeps her eyes trained on Tekel Ambrose. Crouching below her is Daisy and her soft, "I bet my money on the bob-tailed mare. . ."

Tekel, using a kind of sarcasm that is the closest he ever got to humour, cocks a shaggy black eyebrow and calls out softly, "Are we ready?"

Violet speaks to her sister, something about Tekel needing a magnifying glass to find his joint. Daisy giggles and blushes.

Tekel Ambrose twirls about on the mound like a prima donna, sending forth a baseball. Violet, by some miracle or maybe magic with a miniscule, whops it for a Texas Leaguer, a pop fly that lands softly between the infield and the outfield.

Violet takes off for first base; however, Daisy, seeing the hit, has taken an excited leap into the air, shouting "Horray!" This causes Violet to fall to the ground—which brings down Daisy on top of her. The girls scramble about and manage to get to their feet, but the Brethren have had plenty of time to play the ball to first.

Red-faced and furious, the girls march back to the dugout, the embarrassed centres of attention.

The Alligator Man is the first to start laughing. Then Nathanael, the Author, Angus, and the Major join in soon they are accompanied by Dr. Sinister's giggle. Even Tanya is guffawing. Eventually (although at first this laughter cause the Hisslop girls to flame a brighter and more furious red), the sisters join in themselves.

And out on his mound, Tekel Ambrose watches like a scientist examining an alien life-form.

The young reporter nudges Ernie Lambert. "You make a picture of that—of them laughing?"

"Got it."

Things are quieting down in the dugout; the girls are hugging Ally, who kisses them both on the lips and whispers, "I love you—but you looked *soooooo* stupid."

Nathanael Isbister takes the opportunity to sidle up to the Major, as the midget is heading out for the batter's box. "Uh, Major," Nate approaches cautiously, "you know how Ambrose has trouble throwing strikes on you?"

The dwarf slices his bat through the empty air. "If you say so."

"So, uh, you'd get a base on balls for sure if you just let them go by."

Major Mite takes another swing, one that causes Nathanael to jump back to avoid further injury to his twisted legs. "Look!" explodes the little man. "I don't wanna talk about this no more! The idea of the game is to hit the ball, and that's what I'm gonna do."

Nate opens his mouth to say something, and the Major stabs with a finger as if he is shoving the words back down Isbister's gullet. "*AND* if you tell me once more about how I'm short, *OR* if you say something stupid like how I shouldn't try to clobber a ball just 'cause I'm a little past my prime, *THEN* I'm gonna take this here bat upside your head, and then whenever anybody asks, 'What the hell ever happened to Nathanael Goldenlegs Crybaby Isbister?', I'll be able to say, 'He got his brains splattered around because he didn't know when to *KEEP HIS MOUTH SHUT!!*' " The midget nods sharply. "Wish me luck, Nate."

With a barely concealed smile, Nathanael mutters, "Luck" and returns to his dugout.

Luck, though, is something the little Major does not have. He suffers the same fate as before; that is, three pitches whistle well above his shoulders, sure-fire balls were it not that three useless swipes on Major Mite's part turn them into strikes, and our team is out.

No word on Davey.

2 0 4 — — — — — — (House of Jonah)
0 4 0 — — — — — — (Exhibition of Eccentricities)

It is Janus's turn in left field. I suppose that his presence still infuriates Tekel Ambrose, because he can be seen in his dugout gesticulating toward that part of the field.

Nathanael looks over to the grotesque two-headed creature and speaks under his breath. "Looks like you're gonna get a chance to shine, kiddo."

His prediction is accurate. The first batter from the House of Jonah takes a strike and a couple of balls and then sends one out to left field.

It can be said of Janus, as of many great athletes, that he never folded under pressure, that he performed in competition better than he ever did in practice. Janus runs for the ball, reaching it easily, and then the right head (Nathanael's Fido) pulls away, allowing Rover to snap the ball gingerly between its teeth. The batter is out.

"Bring it here, Janus, I'll toss it back for you," calls out Nathanael, and the dog turns obediently, trotting over and laying the ball at his feet. Isbister throws it to the infield and then calls out to Tekel in the dugout, "Try that one again, Ambrose! That's some dawgie, eh?"

If his intention is to get Tekel mad, it's working. Tekel turns and burns his eyes into those of his brothers Mene and Peres. They nod.

The next batter for the House of Jonah gets on base by means of lobbing the Doctor's fourth pitch out toward Robert Merrill. The Hippopotamus Boy waddles as quickly as he can to the ball, and throws it close enough to the Alligator Man to hold the player to first.

Uh-oh. . .

Mene Ambrose enters the box. He looks at a strike from the Doctor, watches another one sail through for a ball, and then lashes out at the third. It streaks toward Dr. Sinister and strikes him squarely on the forehead, bouncing a few feet from him. The Doc follows after it, picking it up and tossing it to the Alligator Man so that runners are held at first and second. Dr. Sinister takes a look around, making sure that all is in order. Then he keels over.

Dustin Doubleday calls a time out, and several people (Ally, the Author, and Doubleday himself) converge on the diamond to check on the Doctor. By this time the little man is sitting on the mound, massaging his forehead gingerly.

"Are you all right?" asks Doubleday.

"Well—" The Doctor seems hesistant.

"You're gonna have one heck of a goose-egg there," says the Author.

"Why, yes," agrees the Doctor, still rubbing it slowly.

"Can you hold on?" asks Ally, and those were probably the best possible words he would have used, for something seems to stir in the dazed little Poindexter Frip. "Nobody can't hold on to nuffink," he mutters in a broad accent, and then he pulls himself up on to his feet. "I feel quite chipper now," he says. "Kindly tell Mr. Peres that he can enter the box."

Unfortunately, I suppose the Doctor is still a mite rattled. He lobs a pitifully slow ball toward Peres. That man has ample time to shuffle to his left a tiny bit and take a long swing. There is a loud "curr-rack!!" and the ball sails over the head of Bobby Merrill, well over the boards, and drops out of sight. Three runners come in to score for the House of Jonah, putting them ahead 9 to our 4.

In the words of the future Nobel Prize winning Author, "Oh, shit."

(It is interesting, though, to note the lack of excitement in the stands. True, there is a smattering of applause but this is (a) merely polite and (b) emanating only from those men who have wagered money with J.M.M. Brassiere. Most people are scowling. The truck driver is. The hobos are. Yuccatan is. And the young reporter is writing, "Most of the people around me are scowling." As he writes, there is a scowl on his face.)

Dr. Sinister, though, seems to have shaken off his daze. He sends a nice curve ball at the next batter who ticks it high behind him. Major Mite turns around and charges back, tilting his head to watch the ball. He has to extend his arm to the full of its rather inconsequential length to make the catch, but make the catch he does. Two out for the House of Jonah.

Which brings out Tekel, swiping the empty air with seemingly loose swings that produce an audible whistle.

Again, this is just between Nathanael and Ambrose, a state of affairs that is beginning to tee the Doctor off a bit. Thus Poindexter gives this pitch his all, putting a fiendish spin on it that makes it slither like a side-winder toward the plate. Tekel Ambrose hardly seems to look at the pitch; his black eyes at first seem distant. In fact they are trained on centre field, on Nate, on that point above the wall. When the lunatic baseball finally crosses the plate Tekel takes a poke at it. Pop. Away we go.

The ball is to the right of centre field, high as the heavens. The crowd jumps on the chant the instant the ball is hit— "Goldenlegs, Goldenlegs, Goldenlegs. . ." That crippled streak from the freak team is at it again, his legs churning, his deepset eyes riveted to the sky.

This ball is not going to clear the boards so easily, if at all; unfortunately, there doesn't seem to be any way on God's earth that Crybaby can reach it in time, fast as he may be going. But as the baseball plummets downward, Nathanael leaps headlong into the air, his arm extended. His gloved hand wraps itself around the ball in the instant before Isbister crumples to the ground, squashing up like a one-man head-on collision.

The crowd is on its feet.

Which is more than can be said for Nathanael Isbister. He remains on the ground for a long time. Eventually he raises himself awkwardly and begins a very slow trot toward the dugout. As he passes the stands he notices a small clutch of children, schoolboys, who are following his every step with eyes full of worship. He stops in front of them and tosses the baseball into the air, watching with a smile as they battle for it. Then he says, "Just remember, kids, my name's not Goldenlegs." Just before he turns away he adds, "It's Crybaby."

2 0 4   3 — —   — — — — (House of Jonah)
0 4 0   — — —   — — — — (Exhibition of Eccentricities)

Well, at least we're into the power stretch of our lineup. First at the bottom of the fourth is that grey giant from Cape Breton Island, Angus McCallister. But things ain't going to be so easy this time—Tekel has realized that Isbister has been coaching his hitters, that Isbister has figured out Tekel's usual way of doing things. Therefore Tekel changes. The first pitch to Angus is high and inside; McCallister has to jerk back rapidly to avoid the ball. Then the giant raises the bat again.

Nathanael hollers from the dugout. "He backed you up, Angus! Get back in there!"

McCallister sees that he has unknowingly surrendered some six inches of his claim on the plate. He takes them again.

The next pitch comes low, and Angus goes for it. He manages only to tick it into the stands for a foul and a one-one count.

Then Tekel does something that for him is very uncommon—he feeds the batter. That is, Tekel's third pitch is very slow and deliberate and well within the strike zone, extremely easy for Angus to hit.

Easy for Angus to hit, but not easy for him to hit well, even though he was once the strongest man that ever lived. McCallister smacks the ball away, but it doesn't go out any faster than it came in. It cruises leisurely out to left field and falls into the glove of the player there. Angus's long legs have already propelled him past first base, but he turns abruptly away before reaching second, jogging back to his dugout.

The giant goes to Isbister. "Is it me imagination, Natty, or be I flim-flammed?"

Nate chuckles. "He fed it to you, Angus. Let you hit it."

"An' now why would he do that?"

"He must have figured you couldn't do much to it, Angus. I hate to say it, but he must have figured you were..." Isbister hesitates.

"Old, is it?" asks McCallister.

Nathanael nods.

The giant from Cape Breton scratches at his ear for a while, deep in thought.

Up for us now is the Wild Man from Borneo, dragging the bat behind him into the box. He raises it up and, because Tekel seems to be the focus of all attention, takes a quizzical look at that man.

Tekel throws him a pitch.

Zapper's swing is more vertical than horizontal. That is, he raises the bat up and then hauls it down with both hands as if the bat were a hammer and the plate a giant nail. But somewhere along the line the bat meets the ball with a tiny "click". The baseball rolls out in front of the plate, dribbling toward Tekel.

This, for me, is one of the high points of the game. Tekel takes off from the mound at the same instant Peres Ambrose leaps out of his catcher's crouch. They reach the ball at the same time, both stoop to scoop it up, and their heads meet with a resounding coco-bonk (a wrestling term). The two Ambrose brothers fall backwards on their keesters amid much laughter from the bleachers.

Zapper, meanwhile, is taking a leisurely walk to first base.

Tekel is the first to flip on to his knees and grab for the ball. He flips it over his shoulder, somehow making a perfect throw to first. But the Wild Man from Borneo is already there, standing on the bag, diligently picking at his left nostril.

Tekel and Peres rise to their feet, both furious with each other, both unwilling to show it. Tekel motions his brother back behind the plate irritably, wagging a long finger. Peres swings around, equally irritated, and trudges back. They both ignore a voice that is calling out from somewhere—a voice that sounds like a nine-year-old with bronchitis holding his nose. "Hey, are you guys okay?" (A stifled laugh.) "I think maybe your brains is rattled up a little bit, huh?" (Now the laugh, with no attempt at stifling.)

Madame Tanya is up to bat; as Isbister predicted, now that Tekel has seen her stuff, he's going to be merciless. This is especially true after the humiliation he has just suffered, even though it had nothing to do with our team. Tekel's first pitch screams through the strike zone so fast that Tanya barely has time to react. She misses for strike one.

(Our team is becoming more than a little concerned about Zapper. He seems to be getting excited, emitting small squawking noises and dancing around the base. Even Tekel seems a little perturbed by him. Between pitches Tekel will deliver the typical hold-the-man-at-first squint, but this doesn't stop the hairy man's eccentric circles.)

The second pitch Tanya hits foul for strike two.

(Ambrose raises the ball menacingly, trying to get Zapper to stop. But every time he moves to throw it, Zap's little dance seems to drift safely close to the bag. Somewhat frustrated, Ambrose turns his attention to Tanya.)

The instant he throws there is a loud scream, and Zapper is headed for second. Tekel's pitch is outside, but Tanya goes for it, missing for her third strike. Peres catches the ball and springs out of his crouch, lobbing the ball over Tekel's head to the second baseman. The Wild Man from Borneo leaps skyward, groping forward with his hairy hand. A split-second before he is about to touch the plate the player traps the ball and swings down, brushing Zap's knuckles. It is very close (as one of Ernest Lambert's photographs points out), but it behooves Dustin Doubleday to call the man out at second and the freak team retired at the bottom of the fourth.

Of all our team members, the Alligator Man is the most upset. "We shouldn't never have let that little idiot play!" he shouts.

Zap has reached the dugout, looking decidedly sheepish. Dr. Sinister rushes to console him. "It's all right, Zap," he coos.

"The little idiot," mutters the Alligator Man, loudly enough to have Zapper hear. The Wild Man from Borneo, even if the words are lost on him, understands the tone and looks even more hurt.

Isbister shushes Ally with a wave of his hand. "He was just trying to steal second like he saw Peres do. Lay off him."

"But he doesn't know what the hell he's doing!" protests Ally, giving the Wild Man a cursing look.

"Look, Ally. . ." And Nathanael's voice takes on an authoritative tone, not very loud, but extremely forceful. "First off, we're holding up the game. We gotta take the field. And *second off*," says Crybaby Isbister, "the little guy almost made it. Now, let's go."

2 0 4   3 — —   — — — — (House of Jonah)
0 4 0   0 — —   — — — — (Exhibition of Eccentricities)

The House of Jonah is up to bat at the top of the fifth. Before the Ambrose boys can get up again there are five younger, more inexperienced lads—five as yet imperfect copies of Tekel.

The first of these hits the ball down the third base line. Tanya grabs it and heaves it across the diamond to the waiting glove of the Alligator Man.

The next one fares better, popping one over the heads of the Hisslop sisters. Nathanael comes ripping in from centre field, trapping the ball, but the player has arrived safely on first.

"Let's get going!" bellows Nathanael as he trots back to his terrain.

The next man hits the Doctor's fifth pitch, a line drive that is out of anybody's reach. The closest to it is Angus as shortstop; he flings himself sideways, reaching out with his enormous reach, but the ball screams by him. Again it is up to Isbister to get the thing, and he makes a play to second. Unfortunately, the Hisslop girls in their excitement get themselves tangled up again, the ball bouncing from them to the ground. The player rounds second and heads for third. Angus McCallister has just about raised himself to his feet—now he is forced to fling himself earthward once more, pulling the ball in and spinning around so that he is sitting on his keester. This stops the action, but the runners are at first and third, with only one man out.

These facts are repeated in a loud voice from centre field. "We can't let them score anymore!"

Our little Dr. Sinister seems to perform best under pressure. His pitches baffle the next batter. The first one takes a drop and curves outside, so that the man misses it by what looks like a good foot. The next pitch is hit foul, strikes two. The Doc now heaves a couple of called balls. With a two-two count, Dr. Sinister seals the batter's fate with the dipper, and that is the second out.

The situation, though, is still serious. Nathanael intones from centre field, "They got runs that could come in, now we gotta be careful! They're beating us bad enough as it is, we gotta make damn sure they don't score!" It's hard to say whose benefit this is for—the only player who could really hear him is little Zapper, who, despite his recent failure, is playing his alternate inning in left field.

The next batter takes a ball and a strike before hitting the big one; a pop fly that is gone toward the boards in left field. Nate wheels about and charges toward it, realizing that this could mean one run for sure, possibly as many as three. He therefore puts everything into his crippled legs, and boy, does he go fast! Again the crowd is chanting, "Goldenlegs! Goldenlegs! Goldenlegs!" With a quick backward flick of his head, Nathanael catches a glimpse of the ball and then looks ahead, his brain working instinctively with a computer-like accuracy, calculating where the ball will fall. He looks at the spot as he charges forward—and sees the Wild Man from Borneo standing there, his glove stuck high in the air.

"Get out of the way, Zap! Get out of the way!" bellows Isbister, hoping that at least something in this tone will communicate with the hairy little pinhead.

And then something causes Nathanael Isbister to stop dead in his tracks, his jaw hung stupidly open.

It is a voice we have never heard before.

"I got it!"

The ball falls almost gently into the Wild Man from Borneo's glove, making the third out.

Zap looks at Nathanael, an odd expression on his furry face, half-pleased, half-disgusted. Then the little man shrugs. "Well," he says, "I fooled everybody for a good long time."

TIME OUT

Our team has asked for another break in the action.

The members are huddled around Zapper in the dugout, none of them quite believing what has just taken place.

Zap sits in the middle of their astounded circle, a scowl on his ugly face. Occasionally he will glance upwards to meet a pair of eyes, but he will meet them for only a short instant before staring once more at the ground.

Dr. Sinister breaks the silence first, his single word full of wonder. "Why?"

Zap waves a hand in frustration, and gives off one his orangutan-like howls. Then he resigns himself and speaks. "You wouldn't understan'." His newly heard voice is a squeaky, nasal one, heavily-laden with a Brooklyn accent.

"Try us," urges Stella.

"Well. . ." starts Zapper, and jumps to his feet. "Just look at me! What da hell am I now?" he demands. "I'll tell ya what I am. I'm ugly! And dat's all. Just ugly. Da same as anybody else except ugly." Then his face laces with a small grin. "But before. . . jeez. I was da Wild Man from Borneo. What is it, Doc? 'Not quite human, not quite simian, straddlin' a fine line between da two—' " Zap laughs. "Not only dat, but it was kind of fun."

Daisy Hisslop says, "I don't see how you could stand it, never talking to anybody."

"Wan't so bad," says Zapper. "Like, most of youse guys talk to me, even dough ya don't wait around for no answers. Jeez, ol' Doc dere talks to me all da time. Sometimes I couldn't get da guy to shut up."

Dr. Sinister smiles sheepishly, and Zap grins back warmly. "An' I'd like ta t'ank ya for dat, Doc. A lot."

Zap sits back down on the bench. "An' if I wanted ta talk, I'd just bend Janus's ears a little bit. He's pretty smart for a mutt." Then something occurs to Zap and he smiles up at Ally. "Da only time it gets rough is if someone's callin' me a idiot an' like dat."

Ally says, "Sorry about that."

"All this time. . ." muses Stella, "Our little Zapper."

"Yeah." Zapper shrugs. "I guess now it's all over. I fooled ya for a long time. Now it's over. Ya still wanna call me Zap?"

"What else?" Dr. Sinister asks.

"I dunno," the Wild Man shrugs. "Ya could call me Hoiman." (Herman.) "Dat's my real name, Hoiman Shepps. I'm t'irty-t'ree years old."

The Author has been included in their circle, and he speaks now for the first time. "I don't think you look like a Herman. Zap suits you better."

The people in the dugout nod agreement.

Zap climbs to his feet once more. "So, let's get on wit' dis baseball game. We'll talk later. Actually, it's just as well youse found out about me now, 'cause I wanna tell youse somet'in'. Wit de obvious exception of Isbister, you guys is pretty bad. Now you're talkin' to a guy here who practically grew up in Ebbets Field. An' I was runnin' out of sneaky ways ta get on base."

The people around him laugh.

"An' also, I t'ink dat if da goils play at second base everyt'in' happens too fast. If dey played field, dey could say like, 'Daisy, you get dis' and 'Violet, you get dat.' I'll play second base—if dey don't mind."

"Fine with us," says the Hisslop girls in perfect unison.

"Also," asks Zap, "how's Davey?"

"We don't know yet," they answer.

Zapper nods slowly. "I t'ink we gotta win dis game."

2 0 4 3 0 — — — — (House of Jonah)

0 4 0 0 — — — — — (Exhibition of Eccentricities)

Now that Zap is talking, there seems to be very little chance of getting him to shut up. Even though he is fully eloquent, he retains many of his Wild Man mannerisms, emphasizing and under-scoring by jumping up and down, pounding on his chest. At this moment he is pointing at Nathanael Isbister—Nate is swinging a weighted bat, about to enter the batter's box. "Jeez," says Zap, "I seen him play whole lots of times when he was young. Hoooeey!!" (That hoooeey was actually a long drawn-out bellow, something you'd think was for summoning elephants to their graveyard.)

Nathanael Isbister picks up the bat and enters the box. His entrance throws a blanket of silence over the stadium, and for what seems like much more than a moment the two men, Ambrose and Isbister, glare at each other through dark deepset eyes. Isbister rhythmically slices the air with his bat, pulling it with a whistle, jerking it back. Tekel grinds the ball into the pocket of his glove, his shoulders spinning slow circles.

Nate hikes the bat over his shoulder and waits.

Tekel, in a blinding flurry, pulls his arm back and then launches forward.

Nathanael initially goes for it, but then he sees its curve. Nate brings the bat back, the tension causing a visible bend in the hard wood. Dustin Doubleday motions outside for ball one.

Tekel throws another, this an incredibly fast one—Isbister pulls the bat with every ounce of strength, but the ball eludes him. Nathanael spins around, ending in an awkward kneeling position on the ground.

"Strike one," says Dustin Doubleday.

Nathanael climbs back to his feet, using a strange kind of half-smile to prohibit any emotion from lining his face.

The next ball is so close to Nathanael's face that only superb reflexes prevent his jaw from being broken into a thousand pieces. Isbister's first reaction is to drop the bat and take one or two charging steps toward the offender, Tekel Ambrose—but he stops, takes some deep breaths, and enters the box once more.

(And again, very low, like a gentle wind, comes the booooing sound. . .)

Tekel rips off another, but this is his one and only bad pitch of the day, a ball that hits the ground far short of home plate, a ball that eludes even the glove of his brother Peres. If we had had a man on base he could have taken another—but enough of these ifs, right? However, if we might at this point allow a tiny conjecture—is it possible that with those two charging steps Isbister managed to rattle our Tekel a little bit?

Tekel Ambrose throws a pitch, one that seems relatively slow. Nathanael swipes at it gleefully, thinking that maybe Tekel's on the decline. Then Isbister hears a sickly "fwop" and watches the ball flip behind him for a foul and a second strike. Peres Ambrose scrambles urgently after it.

"Lemme see the ball," says Nathanael.

But Peres has it in his glove already. "You cannot ask to see the ball; only the umpire may."

Nate waves wildly at Doubleday. "For Christ's sake, ask to see the ball before he's got it all wiped off!"

Peres Ambrose, his face as angelic as any five-year-old's, offers the ball for Dustin Doubleday's inspection.

"Forget it," grumbles Nathanael with a disgusted expression on his face. Doubleday shrugs and motions for Peres to return the ball.

Nathanael Isbister has a full count, three balls and two strikes. He lifts the bat expectantly, realizing that Tekel is virtually forced to send one through his strike zone. Unless. . .

Tekel throws a lazy ball well outside.

Nathanael drops the bat and takes a few steps closer to Tekel, his hands crumpled into fisted hams on his hips. "Ain't you a dandy, Ambrose? Ain't you the cat's pyjamas? First off you try to bust my jaw, then you throw me a spitball, now you walk me. Shit. . ."

Isbister turns away and starts off for first. He has not gone ten feet when he feels a hand tap him on the shoulder. He spins around to find Tekel's dark face inches away.

Something about Ambrose is screaming, bellowing away with unbridled fury, but it is not his voice; he voice is menacingly calm. "It ill becomes a man of your reputation to make such accusations. Especially as your team is losing by five points."

"Yeah?" blurts Nathanael. "And you know damn well that if you'd thrown me a good ball it would have just been four!"

"You had your chance to hit," returns Tekel. "I seem to remember you fell down."

"I want to know what the Bible's got to say about spitballs."

"There is nothing in the Bible about spitballs," states Tekel Ambrose.

"Gentlemen."

Both men turn to find Dustin Doubleday below them. "May we continue the game?"

Isbister nods. "Why not? Lemme see, I just got a base. *On balls.*" There he heads.

Tekel, on the other hand, tries to explain his position to Dustin Doubleday. "I am a very moral man," he says, laying a long hand over his heart. "Yet he keeps making accusations disparaging not only my character but that of the Brethren."

"Well, Mr. Ambrose, Mr. Isbister is a very passionate man. I can only advise you to ignore him."

"I do not throw spitballs," says Tekel Ambrose.

"I'm sure not," agrees Doubleday.

Tekel climbs up on his mound, turning his eyes upward to the sky.

Grotesque Robert Merrill enters the box; Nathanael notices that the Hippopotamus Boy and Zapper have been in conversation, the Wild Man from Brooklyn pointing at various locations in the field, whispering urgently. Zap sees Nathanael looking and slaps a forearm to his chest, pulling it away sharply. Zap jumps up and down, wiggles his fanny provocatively, and returns to the dugout.

What the hell was that all about? Nathanael wonders. There was something calculated about it, especially the arm motion. Then Isbister smiles. Zap was giving him a bunt sign—Bobby's going to bunt.

Tekel raises his arm to pitch, and from the corner of his eye detects Nathanael standing nonchalantly some fifteen feet off the base. He whirls around in a blinding flash, burning the ball at the first baseman. Isbister leaps for the bag, touching it before the baseball is in the player's glove.

The crowd cheers.

Tekel throws his first pitch, and Robert Merrill steps across the plate, lowering the bat. By some miracle he makes contact, the ball dribbling out in front of him. Tekel Ambrose is off his perch in a split-second, gulping up the ball. He spins around to second base, hoping to catch Isbister—he sees it is too late. Reluctantly and disdainfully he tosses the ball to his first baseman. Bobby's waddle has taken him only some thirty feet towards the bag, even though he's been running as fast as his body would allow. He returns to the dugout sadly.

Zapper comes up beside the Hippopotamus Boy, slamming a hand on the lad's bottom. "Dat's good," says Zap. "Ya did good."

Dr. Sinister picks up a bat and starts toward the box. Tekel eyes him closely, darkly—and if any thought is running through his bearded head, it is probably an idle wondering over which he detests more, Isbister or Sinister. At that moment, Nathanael would probably have won hands down, seeing as he was standing on second base—and Goldenlegs Isbister on second base was a pitcher's nightmare.

Accordingly, Tekel throws a couple of balls to the base, hoping to rivet Isbister more closely there. But Nate always gets back in time, and takes just as cocky a lead-off the next time.

Tekel throws, and the instant he does he hears a loud gasp from the crowd, a gasp that could mean only one thing—Nathanael is going. Dr. Sinister swipes at the ball, missing, and it lands in Peres's glove. Peres springs up and throws all in one motion, a picture-perfect throw (even though Lambert doesn't take a picture of it). Nathanael dives, reaching for the bag—no contest.

The crowd cheers; their Goldenlegs has made it to third.

Well, at least Tekel can relax a bit—it's highly unlikely Nate will steal home. He therefore drives a pitch at Dr. Sinister, a fast ball that rips through unmolested for the second strike. Then he hurls an inside curve for a ball. Next Tekel heaves one that the little Doctor goes for—there is the "pop" of connection.

The ball is going high out to shallow centre field. Mene Ambrose has claimed it, and is now circling restlessly on the ground beneath the ball, his glove in ready position. The crowd has silenced, each with a single thought: with a fly ball so shallow in centre, will Goldenlegs tag up?

Mene's glove swallows the ball, and Isbister bounces away for home plate.

Peres swings around to the baseline, straddling it, his glove stretched out as far as possible. Nathanael dives at him. Isbister makes contact an instant before the ball would have, flattening Peres Ambrose. The ball flies by. Nathanael's dive continues until his fingers touch the plate—then he is up in a flash, dancing on home like a drunken cripple.

"That'll learn you to put me on base, Ambrose!" he bellows. "That'll learn you!" Nathanael stops his words in order to regain his breath, and when he does so he becomes conscious of a strange sound—a low moaning. It is coming from Peres Ambrose, who is still on the ground, one leg folded awkwardly beneath the other.

"Jesus," says Nathanael, dropping to his knees. "You okay?"

Peres's face is as composed as ever, but he cannot prevent a moan from escaping his lips.

"I'll help you up," offers Crybaby.

Peres waves the offer away.

"You gets on the base line, you takes your chances," says Nate softly.

"Get away from him." A shadow falls across Nathanael's face, and he looks up to see Tekel Ambrose looming over them.

"He was on the base line. I'm sorry, but it wasn't my fault." Isbister rises to his feet and goes back to his dugout.

Tekel assists his brother Peres in getting to his feet, and they take a few steps together. Peres is obviously reluctant to put the full weight of his body on the left leg. Tekel points down to it, speaking urgently to his brother.

In the freak dugout Nathanael turns to Stella; "I hope it ain't broken," he says quietly.

If it is broken, Tekel seems to be trying to talk the limb out of it, speaking directly to his brother's leg. With a shadowed glance up at the clouds, Tekel falls to his knees. He brings his bony hands together and clenches them until they turn a ghostly white.

Anywhere else in America, the sight of a bearded ballplayer engaging in fervent prayer in the middle of a game would elicit huge and raucous laughter. But not in Burton's Harbor, not on that cold autumn day. The people stare in silence, unwilling even to breathe. Ernie Lambert does not take the picture, fearing that the click of the mechanism would be as loud and vulgar as a real ripper fart. All of us watch Tekel, and listen to him speak. We can hear none of the words, but the sound of his voice is mesmerizing, a wind with a will. Then, slowly, words become audible, until soon the stadium is ringing. "I refute thee in the name of Jesus our Lord! *Begone*!!" Then Tekel releases a hand, balls it into a first, and with every ounce of power he hits his brother's leg. "Hit" is a poor verb—in fact, Tekel smites it. He smites it once, twice, and then digs up an extra measure of force in order to smite the offending appendage thrice.

Throughout all this, Peres's face has begun to glow—by the third smite it has a visible sheen. Coincidentally with the third smite, Peres and all the Brethren scream, "Hallelujah!" at the top of their lungs.

Then Peres happily prances off to his position behind home plate.

Tekel rises from his knees, exhausted. He turns wearily to face Nathanael, and slowly he begins to smile. He speaks, and the stadium, still hushed, listens.

"Mr. Isbister, you said you would win this game in the name of the Devil. As you can see, there are more powerful forces at work here."

Mr. Isbister spits. "Well, I'll tell ya there, Tekel, I'm real glad that your brother's leg wasn't broken."

"On the contrary. I think I can say with reasonable assurance that you broke it very cleanly. What you just witnessed was a miracle."

Isbister nods. "Uh-ya."

"If you had faith, your legs wouldn't be so badly twisted."

Isbister nods again.

Tekel turns to the stands, spreading his arms. "A miracle!" he shouts. Then, once again to Isbister, "A miracle."

Nathanael barks, sounding more like a dog than Janus ever did. "The only miracle around here is gonna be if you end up the game with your hooter stuck in the same place it is now!"

Tekel advances on the timid Dustin Doubleday. "You heard him threaten me! What have you to say?"

Dustin Doubleday waits until Tekel is well with easy earshot, and then he mutters, "Fuck off."

Somewhat rattled by this response, Tekel lumbers back to his pitcher's mound. Dustin Doubleday calls out meekly, "Player to the box!", and the Alligator Man takes a deep breath and picks up a bat.

Tekel stares at him hard and hurls the ball. Ally ticks it and it fouls high, arcing backwards toward the stands. Peres Ambrose leaps up and charges after it, and it's hard to believe that just moments ago he was writhing about in pain. As the ball falls into his glove for the third out, Peres shouts, "Praise the Lord!" This is picked up by the other members of the congregation and is sung out often and cheerfully as they trot off the field. "Praise the Lord! Praise the Lord!"

And as he walks out to centre field, Nathanael takes a canny look skyward. "Let's hope You got something better to do than hang around and watch a baseball game."

2 0 4   3 0 −   − − − (House of Jonah)
0 4 0   0 1 −   − − − (Exhibition of Eccentricities)

Doc Sinister, who has been relatively quiet for a while, manages to whistle two baseballs very cleanly through Mene Ambrose's strike zone. The third one is driven out to right field, where the Hisslop sisters stand. They nab it after a bounce—Daisy catches it, flips it to Violet, who sends it to Zapper, the new second baseman. Mene is held to a single.

"Hey, dat's swell!!" exclaims the Wild Man from Brooklyn.

Peres drives the second pitch for a grounder down to the right of second base; Zap takes an athletic leap into the air, somersaulting and trapping the ball. He charges back to his base, but is not quite quick enough to stop Mene from arriving safely.

Nathanael calls out, "Nice play, Zap!" and the Wild Man spits in tacit acknowledgment.

The next batter, unfortunately for us, is awarded a base on balls. The Doc had got him up to a full count, but the last pitch broke to the outside.

The bases are loaded, and Tekel is coming to bat.

This time Tekel's approach to the mound is accompanied by boos. These are high-pitched, coming mostly from the young boys in the crowd. Tekel accepts them stoically, remembering that Christ had predicted such treatment for those who would follow him.

He hikes up the bat, and Dr. Sinister throws him a mean dipper.

". . .bisterIsbisterIsbisterIsbister. . ." goes the crowd, for once again that is the baseball's direction. This time it is not going as far, for Nate was standing well back by the fences. Crybaby has to charge forward this time, and he thrusts his hand ahead, bending over while still travelling full-tilt. The instant before the ball touches the turf, Isbister's glove appears underneath it. He snaps backward and holds up the ball, his eyes daring anyone stupid enough to tag up and try for a base.

No one does so.

Tekel walks calmly back to his dugout.

Everyone on the freak team is so delighted by this course of events that they don't really pay as much attention as they could to the next batter, who calmly and without fanfare drives one to the right of third base. Angus manages to get a hold of it, but not before Mene Ambrose has had plenty of time to score.

Dr. Sinister vows not to make any more mistakes, and he's the sort of man who's good at that kind of thing. Accordingly and matter-of-factly, Dr. Sinister strikes out the next batter. This he does with a complicated combination of dippers and change-ups.

The next batter pops up shallowly, just managing to clip the ball a bit. Zapper, on second base, waves away Ally and Angus, muttering, "I'll get dis one, I'll get dis one. . ." The ball lands with a soft sound into the Wild Man from Brooklyn's glove. He grins proudly. "Dat's it," he says as his team jogs in from the field.

```
2 0 4   3 0 1   — — — (House of Jonah)
0 4 0   0 1 —   — — — (Exhibition of Eccentricities)
```

Although the House of Jonah now have exactly double what we have managed to accumulate, there is a strong and victorious excitement buzzing around the freaks' dugout. As Nathanael puts it, if not poetically then at least succinctly, "We ain't doin' too bad." He holds out a bat to the Hisslop sisters. "Here you go, ladies." Daisy accepts the bat, looking at Nathanael questioningly, awaiting further instructions. Isbister shrugs. "Just try and blast it."

So the two girls enter the box, approaching from the right so that Daisy can swing. She gets into position, drawing the bat through the air—below her, the crouching Violet begins to sing.

This time Violet does not intone Stephen Foster's classic. Instead she sings a ditty called "Cats on the Rooftops", author unknown. Without taking the time to include all of the text, let me simply inform the reader that this song, also a classic in its way, is almost unbelievably filthy.

Daisy is instantaneously a mass of blushing pink giggles.

As Tekel's first pitch comes sailing at her she lashes out at it without thinking, bops it squarely with the bat and exclaims, "Hey!" as she sees it sailing away.

"Let's go!" shouts Violet, and she races away.

Daisy, naturally, goes with her.

"We're going to make it to first," whispers Daisy excitedly, watching the charging centre fielder head for the ball.

Violet shouts back, "We're going for second!" and although Daisy thinks this ill advised, she chooses not to argue with her twin.

They round first base and run fiercely for the next, all of their movements precisely coordinated, their feet touching around and pushing away at the exact same instant. Meanwhile the centre fielder has got hold of the ball and is rearing back to hurl it.

"*Dive*!!" shouts Violet, and with beautiful synchronization the girls lift off into the air, reaching forward with their long and graceful fingers. These fingers reach the second base bag a long moment before the baseball does, and the Hisslop Sisters have safely doubled.

The crowd response is automatic; they are up on their feet in a twinkling, cheering and clapping their hands. Hands that have known only years of futile farm labour are now joyfully applauding the Siamese twins.

Back near the on-deck circle, Nathanael Isbister is giving it one more try. "Hey, Major?"

"Yeah?" scowls the midget, practising swinging his pint-sized bat.

"Did I ever tell you how a few years back I played for a minor league team that had a little guy for a pinch-hitter?"

"Yeah." Major Mite pelts an imaginary ball.

"Yeah, 'cause he was so small no one could throw a strike against him."

"Imagine that," mutters the tiny man, but it's obvious that this information does not interest him.

"Anyway, the manager, he even said to this guy, he said, 'Look, you're gonna get a base on balls, 'cause you're so small.' He even said, 'If you swing the bat, you're fired.' "

"Yeah?" Major Mite tugs his miniscule hat down snugly and spits on his hands. "Is that what you're gonna do, Nate? Fire me?"

"Oh, hell, Major—"

"I'm up," announces the midget, and he turns away and enters the batter's box. "Hey, Tickle!" he shouts. "How about giving me something I can get a hold of?"

Tekel Ambrose fires one that is a foot above Major Mite's shoulders.

Whoosh.

That "whoosh" is the sound of the Major's bat swinging.

Strike one.

Whoosh.

Strike two.

Whoosh.

You're out.

Major Mite walks back into the dugout and meets Isbister's eyes calmly. He jerks a thumb toward Tekel on the pitcher's mound. "Luckiest son of a toad I ever seen in my life," he says; then he nods at Angus, who is waiting to go up to bat. "Good luck, buddy."

"Aye, thankee, Donny." Then the giant thinks of something. "C'mere, Donny."

Major Mite walks over to his friend. "Yeah?"

"Ye see this joker, this Tekel laddy here?"

"What about him?"

"D'ye ken that he reckons as I'm old?"

"No. . ." The Major feigns incredulity.

"Aye, an' sure he does."

"What are you gonna do about it, Angus?"

"Well. . ." McCallister pulls on his beard. "I can't say as theer's any logic to it, Donny me bosom, but I think I'll have to hit me a baseball."

"There you go."

The giant from Cape Breton moves into the batter's box slowly and lifts his bat. He directs his grey eyes at Tekel, and then, in an instant, both shakes his head with wonder and nods that he is ready. Tekel releases one toward McCallister.

"Theer ye go," whispers Angus, and he throws out his bat.

He hears a rich "thwock".

"Theer ye go!" he shouts, and he bounds away toward first.

The hit is a line drive that skins over top of the first baseman and lands gently between that player and the right fielder. Angus has ample time to reach second; more importantly, the Hisslop sisters have ample time to come in and score.

Off to one side of the makeshift stadium stands an aging Brother of the House of Jonah. His hair and beard have turned to snow. It is his job to keep track of the runs, tallying them up with little pieces of chipboard that he hangs on nails. When he sees the girls score safely, he takes down a piece marked "5" and puts up one reading "6". After a moment's reflection he replaces this one with another that says "7". He thinks again, and puts up the "6" once more. Which he changes to "7".

Tekel storms off his mound. "What are you doing, Brother Emmanuel?" he demands of the old man.   .

"They are two," answers Brother Emmanuel uncertainly. "Aren't they?"

"They are *one* player," states Tekel. "Put the "6" up again."

The old man does this hesitantly.

Inside the freak dugout there is much laughter. The two Brethren of the House of Jonah turn toward it; Tekel glares at his opposites, frightened by, but defiant of, their humour. The aging Brother Emmanuel has a humble look, and there is more than a trace of asking forgiveness somewhere in his wrinkled face. Nathanael Isbister nods at him. "Just score the one run," he says. "It don't matter." Brother Emmanuel smiles at Crybaby and shyly nods in return.

Infuriated, Brother Tekel Ambrose returns to his pitcher's mound.

Next up is Zap. Now that he no longer has to pretend to be the Wild Man from Borneo, Zapper is very businesslike in the batter's box. He marches in, raises his bat, and then, on an impulse, howls in horrible orangutan style. "Beg yer pardon," he mutters, and makes ready to receive his first pitch.

Zapper watches it, and it is called outside by Dustin Doubleday. He goes for the next one, and chips it. It shoots straight up and arcs backward. Peres Ambrose tears off his mask and charges for the ball. It is heading straight for his glove when Peres falls down for no good reason. That is, anyone focusing on his glove would think he fell down for no good reason. Anyone watching with a broader perspective would see that he falls for the very good reason that Zap, the erstwhile Wild Man from Borneo, has tackled him.

This particular stunt causes about a ten-minute delay in the game. Peres, of course, is awarded the out, and Zap is admonished sternly. "One more such display," announces Dustin Doubleday, "and I shall be forced to throw you out of the game." Tekel cannot understand why, quote, "The hideous little creature is not banished forthwith." The reason being, explains Doubleday, that emotional outbursts are not at all uncommon in sporting events. Isbister gets into the picture, telling Tekel that at least it was a fair tackle, not underhanded like all the junk the Brethren have been pulling. This fails to calm Tekel. And so they argue, as I say, for a full ten minutes before the game continues. Zap is out, but still a player, and on his very best behaviour.

Next up is Madame Tanya. We have two outs, and Angus McCallister is on second.

Nate says to the bearded lady, "Nothin' to tell you, darling—except he's gonna be merciless."

Tanya chuckles lightly. "I'll see what I can do."

Tanya swings for a strike and watches the next one curve outside for a ball. The third one she wallops, knocking it foul along the third base line. Then she braces herself, takes a deep breath, and waits for the fourth pitch.

She bops it squarely, and the ball finds a hole in the infield. Tanya gets safely to first, Angus to third, and up comes Golden-legs, er, Nathanael Isbister.

The stands start buzzing, "IsbisterIsbisterIsbisterIsbister..." and no one is wondering whatever happened to him, because nothing did—here he is.

Tekel Ambrose stares with his midnight black eyes. Crybaby meets the glare with his own, his deepest eyes like a couple of stones pushed into his tanned face. "Gonna walk me, Ambrose?" asks Nathanael quietly—and by way of response, Tekel rears back and hurls an incredibly fast pitch toward the plate.

Isbister lashes out at it and it soars away.

The crowd's "ooooo..." dies away as the ball sails foul.

"Lucky for you," mutters Nathanael, going into his stance again.

Tekel fires off another ball immediately, taking no time between pitches. His throws are powered by a monumental rage, and he wants to make sure he takes full advantage of it.

Isbister watches the ball approach, his mind working so fast as to make the ball's advent actually appear to slow down. He sees the ball begin to cut to the outside, so he relaxes his grip, lets out a small breath, and lets the pitch go by. Unbelievably, the baseball breaks back again, and screams straight through the zone.

"Strike two," announces Doubleday, and Isbister can only nod resignedly.

As soon as he receives the throw back from his brother Peres, Tekel launches his third pitch. Nathanael Isbister throws the bat back and swings with all his might.

And the only sound to be heard is the "oooff..." that Nathanael makes as he spins around. He continues spinning in a full circle, like a corkscrew or a demented ballerina, his twisted legs twisting even more. Then there is a small scream of intense pain, and as my grandfather sadly announces, "Strike three," Crybaby Isbister collapses on top of homeplate.

Angus trots in to help Nathanael to his feet. "Ye went fer quite a spin, laddy," he says quietly.

Isbister tries to answer, but his words are strangled by a gasp as more pain shoots through him.

Tekel Ambrose watches this scene for a moment before leaving for his dugout. Although there seems to be a kind of half-smile on his face (probably elicited by the sight of Isbister in considerable pain), mostly his expression is one of incredulity. There is something about Nathanael, about Angus, indeed about all the members of the freakish baseball team, that confuses and bewilders Mr. T. Ambrose.

2 0 4 3 0 1 — — — (House of Jonah)
0 4 0 0 1 1 — — — (Exhibition of Eccentricities)

As he limps toward his position in centre field, Nathanael Isbister is stopped by Dr. Sinister. That little man looks very sad. "I've just had words with the physician tendering to David." He speaks softly.

"And?"

And the hundreds of thousands of words in Dr. Sinister's fripperish vocabulary desert him, and he can only shake his head from side to side.

"Oh, Christ." Isbister kicks at a stone near his feet. "Well, what do you think? Call off the game?"

"Oh, my, certainly not!" The little Doctor seems genuinely shocked by the suggestion. "We should ask for an intromit and go speak with him."

"Now?"

"No." The Doctor looks at the men about to come to bat for the House of Jonah. "Let us wait a tad and see if we cannot go to David with a more favourable progress report."

"Okay, Doc."

The Doctor is obviously intent on improving matters for Davey's sake. He strikes out the first batter from the House of Jonah with three quick pitches—the first one is looked at and called, the next is popped foul, and the last is swung at and cleanly missed.

The Doctor does not fare so well with the next batter. It is, after all, the top of the seventh inning, and the little magician is far from young. One of his pitches to the next man slows down a little and is walloped toward second. Luckily, the Wild Man from Brooklyn is there. He reacts in a split-second, diving sideways, scooping the ball into his mitt, and throwing it to Ally before his body has crashed to the ground. The toss is a little off, and the Alligator Man has to lift his foot from the bag; the House of Jonahite takes that opportunity to place his own foot on safely.

Next up is Mene Ambrose who, like his brothers, has remained infuriatingly calm and collected throughout the proceedings. As he enters the batter's box, Nathanael Isbister can be seen backing up deep into the field, motioning with broad sweeps of his arm for the Hisslops in right and Janus in left to do likewise.

So now it's time for the catch that *still* has people in Burton's Harbor buzzing—the sons of sons of people who were actually there and claim to have witnessed it.

A very few know the truth; lucky for you guys, one of them is me.

This is how it looks: The Doctor's second pitch is belted by Mene Ambrose for all that man is worth, which baseball-wise is considerable. It sails into the air, deep into centre field. Nathanael Goldenlegs Isbister, his eyes trained on it, backs up slowly until his back is pressed against the boards there. The ball is obviously going over, but it is not going over by much. Nathanael reaches up and grabs hold of the top of the fence, pulling himself skyward, his eyes still trained on the approaching baseball. The baseball zooms over his head, a foot or two out of his reach. (Mene and the other Brother are meanwhile triumphantly running the bases.) Then Nathanael Isbister flips over the boards, so that his legs are suspended upright and that's all there is to be seen of him, and he stays that way for a full second. Then he flips over, dropping to the field—and he raises the baseball triumphantly.

This causes some confusion for the runners. If Isbister made that catch fairly, the man in front has neglected to tag up, and the ball is already in flight to Madame Tanya on third. Reluctantly the player heads back for second, and Mene holds up, bewildered, at first.

So that's the way it looks. Do you want to know what really happened? Nathanael watched with disgust as the baseball flew over the fence, just beyond his grasp. Then he noticed Gertrude—that is, he called her Gertrude, but we all know that it was Beatrice the Bovine Beauty, heartbroken ex-star of vaudeville. The cow stood calmly on the other side of the fence, as if knowing (remember, she was something of a clairvoyant) that she would be needed. The ball landed gently in her mouth, and without hesitation she flipped it into Nathanael's waiting glove.

(Afterwards, Nathanael demanded of the little Doctor Sinister, "Did we cheat on that play?" The tiny man shook his head vigorously. "Not at all. She's on our team.")

I stop typing and stand up. Very deliberately, and without trying to conceal an ironic tone, I read the previous four paragraphs to my grandfather.

"Nothing wrong with that," he says, a little defensively.

"There's nothing in that section that bothers you just a bit?" I ask. The old geezer shrugs, as if he can't imagine what's eating me.

"Look," I say to him, "if Isbister makes the catch, then Mene Ambrose is out, and the other Brother has to get back to first or he's out too. Am I right?"

All I get from my grandfather is another shrug, so I continue. "There's no getting around this one," I insist.

"You don't understand—"

"I understand the rules of baseball. What did Isbister say about this?"

"Didn't say nothing."

"Goldenlegs Isbister, the greatest competitor in baseball, stands back and doesn't say a word when he could have had a double play?"

The old man nods. "See, he knows that he didn't really catch the ball, that Mene should've had a home run. So it's a kind of compromise."

"There's no such thing as a compromise in baseball. You're safe or you're out. What did the umpire say?"

My grandfather squirms in his seat. "I *was* the umpire, remember?"

"And?"

"I don't remember if I said anything."

I stare at him in disbelief. "It was a long time ago," he says.

Peres Ambrose is up to bat next. The Doctor is obviously losing his arm at this point. He manages to throw one clean strike, and Peres blips another for a foul, but the Doctor also issues three balls. With a full count, and men on first and second, Dr. Sinister throws high and outside, walking Peres and loading the bases.

Dr. Sinister rounds his small hand into a fist and whaps himself sternly on the forehead.

The other troupe members call out encouragement. "Take it easy and slow, Doc!", "You can do it!", and stuff like that.

Major Mite does what a catcher should—he calls time and runs out to the mound.

"Hey, Doc!" he says, and the two men put their heads together conspiratorially.

"Yes, Major?"

"Well, um. . ." The Major looks around, trying to think of something to say. "Did I ever tell you my dick's the same size as anybody else's?"

"Is it? How very anomalous."

"Yep." The Major races back behind the batter's box, and play is resumed.

The Major's time-wasting tactics seem to have done some good because the next batter, the nameless third in the lineup for the House, swings wildly at the Doc's first pitch, wildly at the second, and, incredibly, wildly at the third. The freaks and the crowd are exuberant, cheering the Doctor's performance—only one person from that faction seems perturbed, and that is Nathanael Isbister. He mutters under his breath, "Fucking typical," as he watches Tekel Ambrose take his position in the batter's box. Crybaby can hardly believe it—Ambrose has told his own man to strike out, just so *he* could get the chance to hit the grand-slam homer. Isbister, out in centre field, becomes furious.

"You ain't gonna do it, you bastard, you!" he hollers, jumping up and down. It's his fury that is Isbister's undoing, for he continues to jump up and down in an attempt to release some of his pent-up anger. "You big show-off, Ambrose!" he shouts.

Dr. Sinister rears back and sends a ball hurtling toward Tekel. And something has changed in the bearded man, because instead of one of his smooth, almost relaxed swings, he pulls around with all of his force—the "cuurraacckk!" as he hits the ball echoes through the stands like a peal of thunder.

At this point in time, Isbister is suspended momentarily in midair, having jumped up to call out a spirited, "You *dawg* you, Tekel!" He sees the hit and tries to drop lightly to the ground—it does not happen. His legs buckle, and he crumples painfully.

Isbister is up on his pegs in a split-second, but he has already lost valuable time—the ball, naturally, is headed toward the fence. Nate wheels around and charges back for it, his little accident forcing him to run with a wobbling gait. In desperation he dives upward, toward both the ball and the fence. His gloved hand is about a foot short, but his forehead makes perfect contact with the wood. The crowd gasps as he bounces off some ten feet, ending up flat on his back and seemingly out for good.

The Brethren trot round the bases, and the score has to be changed to 14—6 in their favour. The stands are a beehive of unhappy murmurs and tongue-clucking; only a few are happy—those with bets with J.M.M. Brassiere.

Even Dustin Doubleday, who is supposed to be perfectly impartial, is scowling with a face full of disgust—and looking at this face from the stands, the young reporter makes the connection and chuckles. "Why, that little rascal," he whispers.

Out in centre field, Nathanael Isbister has pulled himself up to his feet. He looks like a drunkard, wandering around in lopsided, dizzy circles, taking vicious punches at thin air and shouting obscenities. No one dares go near him—his teammates wait patiently for him to regain his composure. When he has, Nathanael indicates it by raising his glove hand into the air and slamming a fist into its pocket. "Okay, let's go," he shouts from the field. "These suckers ain't beat us yet! And they ain't about to neither!"

His teammates look sadly at the scoreboard. The "14" there seems as massive and awesome as Everest.

Every team needs someone who, when things look blackest, gets their spirits up with a dazzling display of skill and courage. In our case, that somebody is a remarkably hideous two-headed puppy who is playing in left field. The next batter for the House of Jonah smacks the first pitch thrown to him in a high arc over that portion of the playing area, and everyone in the bleachers is certain that this hit, too, will be a home run.

Not the wonderdog. He races back toward the fence with a speed that is dizzying. One of the heads is craning backward and up, keeping its eyes fastened on the flight of the baseball; the other stares sternly forward, heading for the boards. The crowd gasps as the creature comes within two feet of the fence without showing a sign of slowing up.

The ball, sadly, is still some fifteen feet in the air.

Janus hits the wall—but instead of running smack into it, the dog begins to run *up* it, still showing no signs of slowing. When he reaches the top, Janus springs backward so that he is doing a graceful somersault in the air. Both of its mouths are open wide, and into one of them the baseball flies. Janus continues his backward flip and lands on the ground firmly.

And as the crowd jumps to its feet, the wonderdog disdainfully spits the ball out on to the ground and begins to trot back to the dugout, as if he is perfectly aware that his actions have ended the half-inning. And who are we to say that he isn't?

2 0 4   3 0 1   4 — — (House of Jonah)
0 4 0   0 1 1   — — — (Exhibition of Eccentricities)

Janus's heroics, though, do little to raise our team's spirits. What prevents this is the appearance of a small, oldish man at the dugout. He seems ill at ease, and asks quietly to speak to someone in charge. Dr. Sinister, Nathanael, and Angus crowd around him.

"I am Dr. Anderson," the man says quietly. He is at a loss for words after that, and merely waves a hand in a certain direction. "Your friend," is all he can say.

"Has the lad left us?" asks Angus sombrely.

"No," Dr. Anderson answers, shaking her head slowly. "But he's going. He asked to speak to all of you."

"Oh, shit!!" explodes Isbister, smacking his hands together. "And we gotta go now and tell him we're losing 14 to fucking 6!"

"Well," says Dr. Anderson, "he is sleeping right at the moment."

"Come on, then!" shouts Isbister. "Bobby, you're up to bat!"

"Nathanael!" says Dr. Sinister, obviously upset at what he considers a very insensitive reaction to Davey's condition. "You make a rodomontade of a game of baseball, reckoning it more cardinal than a man's life!"

"Doc," says Isbister, "do you know what it's like to have a guy like Dr. Hunter after you all the time? All I want is to be able to tell Davey that we got the bugger on the run. That's all."

"But he is passing away," whispers the Doctor, exasperated.

"Let's just play our half-inning, that's all. We'll go after our half-inning."

"Very well," agrees the little magician.

Bobby Merrill waddles to the plate—the tears in his eyes are unseen, trapped within the deep craters of his face.

He, like all the troupe members, has overheard the news.

The tears keep coming, filling the space before his eyes; soon he can see nothing.

While Bobby is in this condition, blinded by his own human pity, Tekel Ambrose whistles three fast balls cleanly through the strike zone.

The Hippopotamus Boy is called out by Dustin Doubleday.

Bobby Merrill lowers his huge, misshapen head toward the ground and the sadness spills out, forming a huge puddle. Isbister is the first to get to the boy, stopping him before the weight of his head topples him over. Nathanael walks him back to the dugout, while Bobby groans out miserably, "Whie Dah? I'n ni fah. . ."

Crybaby pats his shoulder comfortingly. "Yeah," he mutters, eyeing Tekel Ambrose on the pitcher's mound. "It's a son-of-a-bitch, ain't it?"

Nathanael jerks a thumb at the Doctor. "It's your turn," he snaps.

"Right-o!" chirps the Doctor, and he hops into the batter's box. "Come on, you hairy git!" he hollers at Tekel. All of the players, both on the House team and the freak team, stop for a moment and raise their eyebrows quizzically. Even Tekel Ambrose is a trifle nonplussed, but he raises only a single eyebrow.

Dr. Sinister covers his mouth as if he has just belched. "I *beg* your pardon," he says contritely—then he lifts the bat to his small shoulders.

Tekel is not only doing one-on-one battle with Nathanael; he is, of course, doing the same with little Sinister, whom he considers his archrival and enemy. Toward this end, Tekel feeds the magician a slow, low ball that the Doctor hits, sending it back in Ambrose's direction, except about ten feet to the left. Tekel leaps sideways and grabs the baseball before Dr. Sinister has taken more than a few steps. Ambrose appears to flip over a midair so that he lands standing, perfectly at ease.

Dr. Sinister acknowledges this feat with a barely perceptible bow from the waist, accompanied of course by his angelic smile. He walks back to the dugout. "That lad Ambrose," he informs his teammates, "demonstrates a most goetic adeptness."

Ally picks up one of the heavier bats. "I don't care what he demonstrates, Doc," he mutters, pulling the bat through the air. "Myself, I'm mad at the fucker."

The Alligator Man walks into the batter's box and assumes his stance.

Tekel issues forth his patented glare; he rears back and hurls. The ball shoots through the strike zone, and Dustin Doubleday calls out, "Strike one!" Ally remains motionless, staring at the bearded man on the pitching mound. Ambrose throws the second pitch, a ball that looks outside but curves sharply toward Ally, so that Dustin Doubleday is forced to pronounce it, "Strike two." Ally takes a couple of sweeps, wipes the sweat from his forehead, and waits. The third pitch is a fast ball, heading straight and true for the strike zone's lower right hand corner. Incredibly quickly, Ally takes a step back and pulls the bat up. He pulls it up with such force that his body continues with it, flipping him over and landing him on the ground.

It doesn't matter, however—the ball is headed out of the make-shift park. The left fielder is standing, hands on hips, watching it fly away.

Ally clambers to his feet and rounds the bases—when he reaches home plate, his friends and teammates are waiting to shake his hand in the traditional manner. At the end of the line are the His-lop girls, and the three of them embrace tightly. Then Ally lets them go, for it is their turn to face Tekel.

Violet takes the bat and they enter the box.

Daisy bends over double and begins the soft singing of "Camp-town Ladies".

Violet pops the first pitch high and back—Peres is instantly rushing for it, peeling off his mask en route, his dark eyes riveted to the flight of the ball. When he sees that it is headed into the front rows of the stands he takes a leap into the air, looking more like a Nijinsky than a ballplayer. He catches the ball and pirouettes on the way down. The moment he lands he is walking calmly toward his own dugout.

Our half-inning is over. We managed to score one run, bringing the tally to 14—7, which still looks mighty hopeless. Reluctantly, our freak team goes to have their last words with their dying friend, David Gray Goliath.

TIME OUT

Someone, probably one of the boys from the House of Jonah, had the foresight to set up a little first-aid tent just behind the stands. Our team knows immediately that this is where they'll find Davey, for there is a huge pair of shins and feet sticking well out from the opening. The team pulls apart the flap gingerly, and the sound of deep, irregular breathing can be heard. Inside the tent it is almost pitch dark. Dr. Anderson has lit only one small candle, not wishing to burn off more oxygen than necessary. The light is enough to show them Davey's face, twisted with internal agony but somehow peaceful.

Our friends initially think that the giant is asleep, but at their first movement they hear his soft voice.

"Come in, my friends," he whispers. "Come in, all of you, and sit around me."

The troupe moves in slowly, some to the right, some to the left of the giant. They kneel beside him. Madame Tanya, sitting at his head, strokes the thinning hair. Stella in her wheelbarrow blocks the tent's opening, making it even blacker inside. The candlelight dances on Davey's face as he struggles to smile.

"How goes the battle?" he asks.

There are many hums and haws, until Isbister finally says, "We're coming back, Davey."

"It's amazing," muses the giant. "Truly astounding. The man, although evil, does have his talents. Extraordinary ones."

The troupe members exchange quizzical glances.

"He has stalked me everywhere," Davey continues, "a relentless pursuer. But in my wildest dreams, I could not have anticipated that he would finally trap me here—at a baseball game."

"He hasn't trapped you, Davey," says Daisy Hisslop.

"Oh, he has," states David sombrely. "I am powerless to stop him now. I have no strength left in my limbs. I must lie here and wait for the darkness. Then I shall be a skeleton in his private collection. But I am not afraid."

"Well, you sure showed him, Davey!" Nathanael Isbister says. "You hit that ball farther than I've ever seen."

"Not far enough," whispers the giant. "Not as far as a man can dream, or as long as a man can hope."

The silence here is a long one.

"But anyway, Davey," says little Major Mite suddenly, "I don't know what you're worried about. He don't want you anymore."

"What do you mean?" asks the giant.

"What I said. Hunter don't want you anymore."

"You are lying to put my mind at ease. Why should he—" Here David stops to wince in pain; he continues after a few moments. "Why should he pursue me for all of these days only to decide that he no longer wants my skeleton?"

"I'll tell you," says the Major. "You should have seen his beady eyes light up when he got a look at Angus and me. So we told him, if you lay off Davey, you can have the *both* of us when we go."

Davey tries to raise himself to his elbows, groaning, "No. . ."

Tanya gently forces him to lie back.

Turning his head from side to side, Davey says, "I won't let you do that. Do you not realize what that means? Do you not realize that you will go to Hell if you allow him to have your remains?"

"Lad," asks Angus McCallister, "where is it ye figured we were off to anyway? Donny an' me have done a first-rate job of damnin' ourselves."

"I cannot let you do this. Let me talk to him."

"Talk to him?" repeats Stella.

"Bring Hunter to me. I want to speak with him."

"Son," Dr. Sinister whispers, "that might be a tad ugglesome right at the moment."

"This is my death bed—that is my dying request. Bring me Dr. Hunter."

"Well—" someone among them says uncertainly.

"Go and get him," insists Davey. "Tell him he owes me that much. He has made my life hell, and he owes me the courtesy of of speaking with me. It is funny that I never had the courage to do this before. Go and get him."

Slowly they get to their feet, exchanging glances and expressions of bewilderment. They hear David laughing lightly.

"I doubt very much that I shall survive the ordeal. If you should speak of me to anyone when I am gone, say simply that I was intelligent and could play a good game of bridge. Mention that I once hit a baseball a very long way. And if you must, tell them that I was tall. Thank you all for being my friends. Now, please go. I need to rest."

The troupe members file silently through the opening. The sunlight is almost blinding after the blackness of the tent.

They stand around in a circle and Major Mite wonders aloud, "What do we do now?"

"Well," says Isbister, "about all we can do is go and see if Ambrose will talk to him."

"That Tickle ain't about to do us no favours," snarls the Major.

"I'll go and talk to him," says Nathanael, and he walks toward the baseball diamond.

Tekel Ambrose, never idle for a moment, is throwing pitches to his brother Peres. His dark face is lined with concentration, and he doesn't notice that Isbister has come to stand beside him until Nathanael clears his throat quietly. Ambrose receives the thrown ball and turns to look at Crybaby.

"How is your friend?" Tekel asks.

"My friend is dying."

Tekel nods remotely. "The Lord giveth," he intones, "and the Lord taketh away. Do you wish to resign the game?"

"Nope."

"Very well. Let us resume."

"Listen, Ambrose, I know you don't like me very much—"

"I dislike no man among you."

"But you got nothing against Davey, right? The kid who's dying."

"I most assuredly have nothing against him." Tekel turns away and drills a curve ball at his brother.

"He wants to talk to you."

"Why does he wish to talk to me?"

Nathanael shuffles his feet. "That's kind of hard to explain."

"Surely, if he is passing away, he should want to see his friends."

"You see—" Crybaby tried to think of a simple way to explain about the menacing and relentless Dr. Hunter of the boiling cauldron, and comes up with nothing. In desperation he says, "You see, Davey is a very religious guy, and he thinks you're sort of like a priest."

"I am not a priest."

"But you're close, right? I mean, you could tell him things. Things from the Bible that might make his mind rest easier."

Tekel Ambrose throws another pitch to his brother, but this one is wild, and Peres is forced to trot after it. Tekel stares sternly ahead.

"I mean, offering comfort to a dying man," says Nathanael, "that's something Jesus would want you to do if you could."

"I am not a priest," repeats Tekel. "I can perform no last rites or final unction."

"We're not asking you to. All we want you to do is go and have a little talk with him. It'll make him feel better. Please. Not for me, for him."

Tekel throws his glove almost angrily to the ground. "Oh, very well. I shall go and see if I can comfort him."

"Thank you."

"Do not thank me," mutters Tekel. "Show me to him."

Nathanael leads Tekel to the tent. The other troupe members watch their arrival with interest.

"Does he know what gives?" asks Ally.

Isbister says quickly, "Yeah, he knows that Davey's dying," and then he silences any further questions with a flashing of his eyes.

Tekel looks at the tent for a long time, and asks, "Will one of you come in with me?"

"It'd be better if you went in alone," answers Isbister.

"Very well." Tekel moves to the tent and, after a moment's hesitation, disappears through the opening.

Ambrose is blinded by the darkness, then startled by Davey's ghost-like face.

The giant smiles slowly. "So you came."

"I came." Tekel crawls closer and kneels. "I will pray for you."

Davey laughs out loud. "You never cease to amaze me!" he says. "What gall you have!"

"You do not wish prayer?"

Davey, half-chuckling, does an imitation of Tekel, saying, "You do not wish prayer?" in a sombre, tight-lipped fashion. Then he laughs once more, saying, "Oh, give it up!"

Tekel asks, "Why have you sent for me?"

"All I really want is the answer to one simple question. The question is 'Why?' Why did you lead the life you did?"

Ambrose settles back on his haunches. "Why? It is not such a simple question."

"It's very simple."

Tekel breathes deeply and begins, "I love our Lord—" but David rudely interrupts with a sardonic chuckle.

"I might have known," says the giant. "You are simply going to repeat the dediction for me. Don't bother, I know it well. 'This for the glory of God.' "

Tekel Ambrose nods and states hesitantly, "Those words apply."

"And exactly how does it glorify God that you denigrate and belittle his creations?"

"I do no such thi—" begins Tekel, but Davey is on a roll.

"You dissect and dissect and dissect. You dissect until you come to the essence of life. Then you turn away, because you can't understand it. It frightens you, so you simply discard whatever it is you have in front of you and move on to something else. When you look at me, sir, you see a huge skeleton, because you are afraid to see what it is that makes me a man." Davey raises himself to his elbows and looks Tekel dead in the eyes. "You think you know so damn much. But what do you know of dreams or hopes or kindness or madness? What does it matter what an eagle's wingspan is? What does it matter that an eagle flies because of air currents? All that matters is that there is beauty in the flight. But you don't care!" David lies back again and speaks in a hoarse mutter. "You can learn nothing from my dead bones, nothing that is important. It does not matter that I am the tallest man that ever lived. What matters is that I am a man, with a capacity for love and hatred, for joy and sorrow. You can never know *me*. You can only know my bones." Davey Goliath's huge frame convulses suddenly.

"I will get your friends," offers Tekel.

"You will stay right there," whispers David. "What I want to tell you is, any deal you have with the Major and McCallister is null and void. They were willing to damn themselves for me. That is called friendship. There is nothing about friendship in your damn book. It is, finally, what you know the least about."

"I have my brothers," says Tekel meekly.

"Your brothers in the fraternity of knowledge, eh?" chuckles David. "I'll tell you a secret, sir. They do not like you. They are afraid of you."

Suddenly Tekel is angry. "You have no right to speak to me like this. What choice of life do you think I was given?"

"All you have to do is see that life is a miracle. Accept it as a miracle that you can never know. Then, perhaps, you will learn to love it a little bit. Because, sir, in your heart of hearts, you hate life very much."

"I hate nothing," snarls Tekel.

David shrugs, the last motion he will ever make. "More's the pity. I hadn't realized you were that dead."

And with those fitting words, Davey peacefully dies.

Tekel almost stumbles through the tent's opening and confronts the carnival troupe. "He. . ." begins Ambrose, searching their faces, "your friend passed away painlessly." The bearded man turns and starts back for the baseball diamond. Suddenly he spins around and addresses the freaks again. "I do not know why young men die. I do not know why children die. If life is such a miracle, why can it be snuffed out with more ease than a candle's flame?"

Tekel's eyes have been burning deeply into Nathanael's own. Isbister shrugs. "Well, you know, Ambrose. He," says Crybaby, lifting his eyebrows heavenward to indicate who "he" is, "must know what He's doing."

Tekel turns away once more. "At any rate, we know what *we* are doing. We are playing a game of baseball."

2 0 4   3 0 1   4 — — (House of Jonah)
0 4 0   0 1 1   1 — — (Exhibition of Eccentricities)

Before our team takes to the field they stand around awkwardly in the dugout. Several of the players are crying loudly, and others are comforting them. Amazingly, Nathanael Isbister is one of the comforters. He has his arm around Stella's fat shoulders and is talking softly into her ear.

Tiny Zap walks over to the Doctor and says, "He was a good guy." The little magician merely nods, muttering, "A fine man."

Bobby Merrill is the loudest of the mourners, seeming to weep in a general way for all of mankind, for the unjust and terrible burden of mortality.

Angus and the Major are silent, sitting beside each other and contemplating perhaps their own ends. Tanya strokes both of Janus's heads; the Hisslop sisters watch as Ally, the man they love, takes vicious swings through the air with his bat.

Tekel seems willing to wait for them, sitting in his own dugout. Several of his teammates approach him, to ask for instruction and guidance. He waves them away without saying a word.

Ernie Lambert takes a photograph of the freak dugout and feels very guilty for doing so. The little reporter takes out a hip-flask and drains about four ounces of liquor into his mouth. It burns, and he coughs for several moments, at the end of which he appears much calmer.

The Author watches the freak dugout with a detachment that he despises in himself; but it has been said that at the centre of any writer's heart is a sliver of ice.

Nathanael Isbister raises himself to his feet and says, "Okay, let's go."

His team begins to file out to their places on the pitch.

Crybaby calls over to the opposing dugout, "We're ready, Ambrose!" Tekel, again in silence, directs a bearded man into the batter's box.

This man hits the Doctor's first throw in a beeline between second and third. Angus McCallister, the shortstop, scoops it up into his massive glove and lobs it to Ally at first. The runner from the House of Jonah is out. The second batter is struck out by Dr. Sinister. The third hits a high pop fly into centre field, and Nate Isbister has little problem with it. The ball falls into his glove, and he continues his trot toward the diamond.

It takes a few moments before our team realizes that the House of Jonah have just gone three-up, three-down. When they do, the dugout erupts into a cacophony of cheers and hurrahs.

Crybaby Isbister calls over top of this, "Well, it's time to hit that comeback trail!"

2 0 4　3 0 1　4 0　— (House of Jonah)
0 4 0　0 1 1　1 — — (Exhibition of Eccentricities)

First up is our precious, tiny Major Mite. He walks to home plate dragging the bat behind him—this effort alone brings beads of sweat to his forehead. He pulls it up to his shoulder and casts a defiant look at Nathanael, challenging Crybaby to tell him to take a base on balls.

Isbister grins. "Take a good rip, Major."

Major Mite grins back and hollers, "Let's see some of your best stuff, Tickle! The faster they come, the faster they're gonna go out!"

Tekel Ambrose rears back and hurls one that is some inches above the Major's shoulders. The midget has to pull down on one end of the bat and use his back as a fulcrum to get anywhere close to the baseball. He misses and Dustin Doubleday calls out, "Strike one!"

"Just a little lower, Ambrose!" shouts Major Mite.

Tekel's next pitch is lower—in fact, it's too low, and by the time it reaches home plate it's skimming the earth. Major Mite goes for this one too, first dropping the bat to the ground and then pulling up with all his force. He manages to tick the ball off into the stands—right into the hands of the young reporter, who pockets it as a souvenir and even considers having it signed by the Major after the game.

Major Mite, meanwhile, is taunting Tekel. "Listen, Ambrose, I'm trying to tell you that I want that booger right about *here!*" The Major hauls his bat through thin air. "Got it?"

Tekel throws the ball—right where the Major wants it. Major Mite shoots the bat forward. Unfortunately, he misses it. The force of the bat continues to spin him around, and the Major ends up on his backside in the dust. He springs to his feet and spits on the plate. "Are you ever lucky, Ambrose!" he shrieks. "That one was *gone!*" He walks back to his dugout, holding himself as tall as he possibly can.

Next up is Angus McCallister. He is sent up to the batter's box with a chorus of encouragement, and those tall enough to slap him on the back do so. He raises up the bat and waits for Tekel's pitch.

Tekel doesn't feed him this time—the first pitch is an extraordinarily fast one, but its course is straight and it's headed for

Angus's enormous strike zone. The giant from Cape Breton is forced to go for it, but he gets bad wood. The ball dribbles off his bat and heads for the man at third base. That Tekel-clone picks it up and throws the ball leisurely to first. The player there almost has it in his glove when Angus is some ten feet from the base.

Angus doesn't slow down—he speeds up. He raises his huge hands into the air and fashions them into enormous claws. His grey eyes fire with red. And then, opening his gargantuan mouth, Angus McCallister bellows like a dying dinosaur. The scream fills the field like an air-raid siren. Angus takes a jump into the air then, landing on first base, his work boots producing a stomp of thunderclap proportions.

Many people in the stands are shaken by this performance. No one is more shaken than the poor boy on first base, who has a sort of glaze over his eyes. His glove is still raised to receive the throw from third, but the baseball is lying two feet behind him. It is some moments before he is able to collect himself and return the ball to Tekel.

Angus McCallister, safe on first, is a mountain of childish giggles. He hoots and hollers and beats his feet on the ground. "I may be old," he shouts to no one in particular, "but me God, I'm still *ugly*!" He lifts his arms in triumph, and the crowd cheers him.

Zap is contemplating Angus, a look of sincere appreciation in his eyes. He wags a finger at the giant and tells Nathanael, "Old Angus is almost as good at dat shtick as me!" Zapper selects a bat and enters the batter's box.

Tekel has a problem—that is, Angus at first. From the corner of his eye, Ambrose can see that McCallister is taking an enormous lead off the base—but whenever Tekel tries a throw to first, all Angus seems to do is take a single step sideways and he is safely back on the bag. This process is repeated four or five times before a single pitch is thrown to Zapper. And each time, McCallister's lead-off is just as gallingly enormous.

Zap misses the first pitch by half a foot, hauling off and taking a full-force swipe at the ball. (Isbister, in the dugout, nods appreciatively.) McCallister takes his cocky lead off first. Tekel throws the second pitch. The Wild Man from Brooklyn, in a twinkling, straddles home plate and raises the bat across his chest. The baseball hits with a tiny sound and dribbles slowly along the first baseline.

No one can stop Angus from safely reaching second base—the race is on between Tekel and Zapper. Both men charge with all of their speed, but Zap has the advantage in that Ambrose has to pick up the baseball en route. Tekel tosses the ball underhand as he falls on his face in the dirt. Zapper dives into the air, extending his arm as far as it will go. There is crashing and grunting and a great cloud of dust, but Dustin Doubleday is able to make the call without controversy—"Safe!"

The crowd goes crazy—some even get to their feet to applaud the Wild Man. Quietly and modestly Zapper explains to the first base player, "Ya can't spend half your life watchin' da Brooklyn Dodgers and not know nuthin'."

Madame Tanya is up next. Angus shouts to her, "Get me home, ·darlin'!" and the bearded lady smiles broadly at him.

Tekel's first pitch comes in a little outside. Tanya calmly watches it fly by. "Way to have an eye!" calls Stella from her wheelbarrow. Tanya goes for the next pitch, catching just a bit of horsehide and slicing it back into the stands. The ball lands where Yuccatan should have been—but the sucked-out sailor man is no longer here (much to the relief of the poor guy who was sitting next to him). Tekel's third pitch is a little low—Tanya checks her swing and Doubleday accurately assesses it as "Ball two." Tanya takes a deep breath, and when the next pitch comes she is ready for it. She belts it deep into right field, just far enough that the player there is forced to let it take a single bounce before he can get to it. Tanya, her skirts hiked up to her waist, makes it easily to first. The ball is played quickly to home, holding McCallister at third.

And now, with the bases loaded, comes the chant. . . "IsbisterIsbisterIsbisterIsbister. . .", along with a few, "Come on, Goldenlegs!" and even more, "Let's see you belt it, Crybaby!!"

Nathanael Isbister receives a kiss on the cheek from Stella the fat lady and slowly makes his way toward the batter's box.

The hobos, hidden underneath the stands, recognize something in Nate's eyes, and they get very excited. "Here it comes," one of them whispers; he takes a long draught of lord-knows-what to calm himself.

Tekel Ambrose watches the proceedings carefully, idly flipping the baseball in the air. Nathanael wonders why Tekel should be making such a show of not preparing the pitch and decides, on a hunch, to get ready for a knuckle ball.

Crybaby goes into his stance and the ball is thrown simultaneously. Sure enough, it's a knuckler, coming without the slightest spin. If Isbister hadn't been expecting it he surely would have missed the ball, its path as curvaceous as a snake's. As it is, Nate merely keeps his eyes trained on it every inch of the way, and at the last possible moment he lashes out.

There is a "pop!"

The crowd is up on its feet in a second. The hobos are up on their feet in a second, too—which is a shame, because several of them ram the tops of their heads on the boards above, knocking themselves senseless, and they are the only ones who don't witness the ball's flight out of the park.

Everyone else sees it, though. The ball travels through the air for a long, long time before disappearing over the fence at centre field. It falls gently to the ground beside Beatrice the Bovine Beauty. She picks the ball up with her mouth and begins to move away from the playing area. Her work is done.

Meanwhile, the freak team has tallied four runs, making the score a more competitive 14—11. The troupe members are a massive huddle of hugs, all of them grouping around Nathanael Isbister. Dustin Doubleday alarms Tekel Ambrose by joining their throng—the geezer shouts, "Horray! The great Nate does it again!" and looks anything but impartial.

Crybaby disengages himself, clapping his hands together. "Okay, okay!" he hollers. "We gotta keep this going!" He throws an arm around Bobby Merrill and walks him to the batter's box, talking quietly into the Hippopotamus Boy's ear, which is only a small flap of skin. "Just watch the ball," Nate says. "Don't think about hitting it or nothing. Just watch the ball, and if you hit it, run like the Devil was chasing you. You're gonna do okay."

Bobby nods his bloated head.

Tekel Ambrose has been merciless to Bobby all day, perhaps because the Hippopotamus Boy is so grotesque. His first pitch is extremely fast but its course is a bit off, and it comes inside for a called ball.

"Don't let him crowd you out, Bobby!" shouts Nate, and the Hippopotamus Boy takes a step closer to home plate.

Tekel's next pitch comes in below Bobby's knees and is called ball too. Then Ambrose hurls a screamer through the strike zone. Bobby takes a swing but misses by a good foot.

Just as Tekel gets ready for the fourth pitch, the Hippopotamus Boy leans in a bit closer in order to better see the ball's arrival. Bobby misjudges his balance though, and just as Tekel is winding up he begins to fall over. The crowd gasps as they realize that Tekel's pitch is going to hit the boy right in the side of the head.

Ambrose, however, never lets go of the ball. He manages to keep it in his hand, even though the effort of doing so causes him to fall face first off the mound with a sickening crunch. When he climbs to his feet his nose is bloodied.

Dustin Doubleday quietly says, "Balk," and waits for Tekel to explode at the call. Ambrose merely nods and resumes his place on the mound.

Bobby's teammates help him to his feet and walk him over to first base.

In the great tradition of baseball pitchers, Dr. Sinister is a real washout as a hitter. Coach Isbister spends a few minutes with him, discussing various fine points and strategies. The little magician nods and hurries out to the batter's box. He rolls up his shirt-sleeves and stirs up the dirt with his heels and toes. He spits into both palms, rubs his hands together, and dries them on the seat of his trousers. He takes a moment to make sure no stray hairs are falling into his eyes (not very likely). Then he hikes the bat, waits a moment, and smashes Tekel Ambrose's first pitch right back to Tekel Ambrose.

"Oh, piss!" the Doctor hisses, and many people watch him with wonder as he walks back to the players' bench.

The Alligator Man comes up next; like the Doctor, he rolls up his shirt-sleeves as far as they will go. Only the Hisslop girls, watching from the on-deck circle, realize that this is the first time he has ever done this. Ally has always kept his cuffs buttoned, covering as much of his scaly green skin as possible.

Next to the great Nate, Ally is the crowd's freak-team favorite. He goes into the batter's box accompanied by applause and whistles. A small group of young boys has even given him an affectionate nickname, and many people in the stands have picked it up. It is "The Green Machine."

Ally goes for Tekel's first pitch, missing it by less than an inch. He twists around and steadies himself. Immediately he takes his position again, taking full-force warm-up swings through the air. The Alligator Man lets the next one whistle by. Doubleday calls it low, and Ally has a one-one count. The Green Machine goes for Tekel's third pitch and connects with a resounding "Smack!"

It's not a particularly good hit in terms of power, but the ball is perfectly placed—it bounces halfway between first and second. Ally takes off with all his speed.

The right fielder from the House of Jonah has managed to trap the ball; he hesitates momentarily, and then elects to toss the ball over to second, because the slow-moving Hippopotamus Boy has yet to reach his base. But the second's hesitation proves costly, for Bobby Merrill manages to find some hidden reserve of strength. He shoots forward and then topples over, his huge head making contact with the bag before the player there can tag him.

There is a brief delay in the game as Angus and Nathanael have to hurry out to help Bobby back to his feet. When the Hippopotamus Boy is erect, Isbister studies his gruesome face for a moment.

"Hey, McCallister," Crybaby says, "it seems to me that this here boy is grinning. What do you think?"

Angus McCallister stoops over to look at the face that is hardly recognizable as human. "Aye," he concludes, nodding vigorously. "The lad is surely smilin' like the mouse that got the cheese."

A strange sound erupts through the bone-filled hole that is Bobby's mouth.

"Will ya listen to that?!" cries Nathanael. "Now the cocky son-of-a-bitch is *laughing!*"

Both men pat Bobby Merrill on the backside and hurry off to the dugout.

Daisy and Violet are very excited. It's Daisy's turn at bat, but she wants to decline in favor of her sister Violet. "You're doing so much better than me," she explains.

"Oh, don't be silly, Day," Violet snaps. "Come along now." Violet begins to march out to the box and, accordingly, Daisy goes with her.

Tekel Ambrose, gaunt and shadowed on the pitcher's mound, is absolutely impassive. He has his hands behind his back and is toying with the baseball inside the pocket of his glove.

While Daisy raises the bat to her shoulders, Violet bends over (which Peres Ambrose would have greatly appreciated if he'd been anybody else) and begins a soft singing: "Roll me over in the clover, roll me over, lay me down and do it again." Daisy struggles to control a giggle.

Tekel's first pitch whistles forward. Daisy starts her swing a little early, and only manages to tick it foul off the third base line.

"Take it easy, Daisy!" hollers Isbister from inside the dugout.

Daisy (still squelching a giggle) waits for the second pitch while her Siamese twin segues into, "Aboard the good ship Venus, you really should have seen us, with a figurehead like a whore in bed and a mast like an upright penis!" Daisy lets the second pitch go by, certain it is headed outside; but at the last moment it breaks in sharply and bisects the strike zone.

With an oh-two count, Daisy listens to her sister's voice—"And it's bow to your partner, backs against the wall! If you haven't been humped on a Saturday night, you've never been humped at all..."

Daisy giggles. Tekel's third pitch comes howling. Daisy lashes out with the bat. There is a "Thwock!"

The ball sails away into left field. It's not going anywhere near out, but it's going a long ways.

Nathanael knows that with two out the runners must be going. "Run, Bobby!" he screams. "Run, Al!" The players do as they are told. The girls take off for their base, perfectly synchronized, running with all their speed.

The left fielder dives for the ball. It is agonizingly close—some spectators are sure that the baseball was even inside his glove for a split-second. But as we all know, a split-second isn't long enough; and by the next split-second, the baseball lay about a foot away from him.

The midget Major Mite surveys the situation—the bases are loaded, there are two men out, and the freak team is a mere three runs away from tying the ball game. The Major looks with disgust down to the ground—selecting the most substantial-looking rock, he hauls off and boots it away. Then he storms over to Nathanael Isbister.

"I know, I know, I know!" he shouts, startling Crybaby.

"What is it, Major?"

"I know that every single time I been up to bat I struck out. And I know that if I just let Tickle hurl 'em at me, he'll rack up four balls, and I'll be on base and we'll score Bobby. So I'm just gonna stand there." The Major morosely turns away.

"Well, Major—" starts Nate, and the midget spins around.

"You are the most argumentative son of a mule-faced bastard that I have ever encountered!" he shrieks. "That's what you wanted me to do all game, and now I'm gonna do it! I'm old and I'm a little on the short side, no one has to tell me. I'll go for the walk."

Major Mite picks up the bat and drags it to the batter's box; he bounces it up to rest on his shoulders and waits for the pitch.

Sure enough, Tekel's first throw, although fast as a bullet, is about six inches over the line through the dwarf's armpits. Dustin Doubleday announces, "Ball one."

"Of course it's ball one, you bespectacled nimrod!" screams the Major. "Can't you see I'm a *midget*?!"

The second pitch is also high. "Ball two!" says Doubleday.

"Hey, you're pretty effing smart, ain't you?" shouts Major Mite, his miniscule features trembling with contained rage. "No one had to tell you that two comes right after one!"

Dustin Doubleday calls the Major out of the box. "What is your trouble?" he demands quietly.

"*Nothing*!!" With that bellowed response, the midget re-enters the box and waits for the third pitch. Which is also high.

"Ball three," says Doubleday, almost whispering.

"Hold on, hold on, hold on," says Major Mite and he steps backward, pushing the baseball cap off his head wearily. "Oh, my. . ." he sighs; he takes a moment to stare at the dark form of Tekel Ambrose.

"Fuck it," the Major says suddenly. He shouts back to his own dugout, "I'm sorry, Crybaby! I just can't do it."

Nate Isbister grins and nods.

The Major leaps back into his stance and for a few seconds he is a blurred fury as he takes a series of practice swings. Warmed up, the Major calls to Ambrose, "Now, listen, you! How's about puttin' one where I can get a crack at her?!"

Tekel Ambrose tugs the brim of his cap down until his eyes are hidden in darkness. He leans back and then bolts forward, releasing the baseball.

Major Mite, his grizzled face lined with concentration, watches the ball's progress until the last moment and then smacks at it for all he's worth.

The ball flies down the third base line—it's a good hit, a high fly, but everyone is sure it's going foul. Suddenly, a gust of wind, so strong that the whistle echoes through the stands, comes from out of nowhere and pushes the ball safely fair. The left fielder for the House hurries to make the play, but to no avail. The wind carries the baseball triumphantly over the boards.

The Major, halfway to first base when all this takes place, leaps into the air, thrashes while suspended there, and hollers, "Yahooooo!!!"—and that is Ernie Lambert's most famous photograph. It's interesting for many reasons—the look for defiant victory on the aging human face, the contortions of the deformed dwarf's body. But perhaps that photograph is most interesting because the midget appears to be a good eight feet in the air.

Bobby Merrill, the Hisslops, Ally, and the Major all come in to score, and the freak team tallies 15 to the House of Jonah's 14 in the bottom of the eighth.

Naturally, our team takes a long time in congratulating the Major—he brushes away the hugs and kisses irritably, saying, "I don't know what all the bother's about. I knew Tickle's good luck was bound to run out sooner or later."

Nathanael Isbister tells him, "I'm awarding you the MVP for that particular stunt, Major."

The midget grins up at him. "What's that, Crybaby? 'Most Vexatious Pisshead'?"

Angus McCallister says, "Ye did reet good, Donald," in a terse, serious manner.

"Thanks, Angus. But I'll tell you, I think maybe I got a little help." The Major raises a single eye toward Heaven.

"Aye, Him again," nods the giant from Cape Breton. "He's a good boyo." Angus walks away toward the batter's box.

It is natural enough, I suppose, that Tekel Ambrose is angry. At least, this is what we have to assume; his face tells us nothing. We can judge only from the mysterious intensity in his black eyes. At any rate, he takes full advantage of Angus McCallister's gigantic strike zone. The first pitch whistles through for a called strike. The giant ticks the next one foul for number two. And then Ambrose forces Angus to go fishing—he sends a low ball right through the outside corner. McCallister has to go for it, but there is no way he can get much wood on it. The baseball dribbles slowly to Mene at shortstop, who relays it over to first. Angus is out before he has a chance to terrify the player there.

> 2 0 4 3 0 1 4 0 — (House of Jonah)
> 0 4 0 0 1 1 1 8 — (Exhibition of Eccentricities)

The freak team is ecstatic, jumping, hooting and hollering in their dugout. Nathanael Isbister hurries to calm them. "Hey, now," he says, "we're nowhere near won yet. They only need a couple of runs and we're losing again."

The statement sobers everyone; they stare down to their feet, contrite.

Isbister laughs lightly. "But what I say is, there's no way in hell we're gonna let them get no couple of runs! So let's get out there."

The freak team takes to the field. There is great applause from the stands, cheers and whistles. Major Mite, donning his catcher's mask, accepts this tribute on everyone's behalf, bowing deeply from the wait.

Dr. Sinister, on the pitcher's mound, toys idly with the baseball and can be seen mumbling to himself. Then he appears to mumble directly to the ball. He tugs down his baseball cap and waits.

The first batter from the House of Jonah enters the box. Our team readies itself; the stands fall silent. The little Dr. Sinister pulls back, twists around, and hurls forward a baseball. The batter goes for it but misjudges the curve—the ball pops off the end of the bat for strike one.

"Attaboy, Doc!" shouts Major Mite as he returns the baseball.

"Thanks so much," mutters the magician, eyeing the man at the plate. He releases another pitch, which goes high for a ball.

The batter from the House of Jonah watches the next pitch; it cruises in low but appears to break upward (the dipper). Dustin Doubleday calls, "Strike two."

Dr. Sinister then pitches a change-up—in this case, the fastest ball he's thrown all day. The batter is completely baffled; he swings wildly and is pronounced out on strikes.

The crowd applauds the little pitcher, though Poindexter Sinister doesn't hear. He is concentrating solely on the task at hand. And with the appearance of Mene Ambrose, the task becomes a grave one.

On his first pitch, the little Doctor tries to fool Mene with the dipper, but the Ambrose boys are quick learners. Mene shuffles back and in the same instant slices upward with the bat, making perfect contact. The baseball sails away, dropping gently in mid-right field.

Nathanael Isbister, amazingly, is there to catch the ball as it takes its first bounce. He jumps into the air and traps it with his bare hand, then does a half-gainer so that he is facing first base. Reluctantly, Mene scurries back to stand beside the Alligator Man, who informs him, "The great Nate Isbister."

"Apparently," murmurs Mene.

Next up for the House of Jonah is Peres Ambrose. As he waits for the first pitch he hears a voice coming from behind him—you know the voice; it's like a nine-year-old with bronchitis holding his nose. "Did you see my hit, Perry? Did you see how far I whopped the bugger?"

Peres lets the first two pitches go by—the first is called a ball by Doubleday, while the second is judged to be a strike. Then he swings at the third—it screams out with a single bounce, headed for the hole about fifteen feet to the right of second base.

But Zapper makes a play worthy of the Dodgers he so dearly loves. He throws himself sideways, his body extended to its full length. The ball lands in his glove, and he collapses to the ground. In a twinkling he is up again, brandishing the baseball menacingly at Mene on second and Peres at first. "Come on, you joiks," he snarls, "let's see youse go for extra bases."

The Ambrose brothers stare incredulously at the hairy little pinhead.

The next batter from the House of Jonah can be seen conferring with Tekel Ambrose before entering the box. The player nods once and turns away—Tekel pats him lightly on the back.

After looking at two balls from Dr. Sinister, the batter from the House of Jonah connects with a pitch and sends one out to deep left field. Janus the Wonderdog is there, catching the ball and making the out. The Ambrose brothers, however, have tagged and are racing for second and third.

"Gimme the ball, Fido!" shouts Crybaby; the right head of the dog jerks back and lobs the baseball into Isbister's hand as that man circles around the face the infield.

Tekel Ambrose waves at his siblings, telling them to hold up.

"Good doggy!" shouts Nathanael, and he pats Fido's head lovingly. He notices the hurt look in Rover's eye so he rubs that head too. "He couldn't have done it without you," he says before he trots back to centre field.

Now, I know you probably won't believe it, but the old geezer insists that at this moment the skies were blackened with thunderclouds. He climbs up on the sofa to paint the scene with his scrawny outstretched arms. "From one end of the sky to the other they went, as black as the ace of spades." He pauses dramatically, under the impression that I am typing his words verbatim. "And lightning is forking up there, and the thunder is rumbling like the world hadn't eaten breakfast. And then, with two men in scoring position, he goes into the batter's box. You know who. . ."

Tekel Ambrose.

Well, I don't know if the thunder is rumbling or not, but I know that there is total silence in those stands. I know that no one in the stands dares to make a noise. The reporter scribbles no reports, Ernie Lambert takes no pictures. The hobos are afraid to guzzle their lord-knows-what. The truck driver's wife wakes him up, because his snores are too loud and vulgar for the quiet.

And I half believe my grandfather about the heavenly tempest, for if it isn't there in fact, it is certainly there in Tekel's eyes, in the cruel shadows he casts upon the earth.

Tekel Ambrose pulls up the bat and swings it loosely through his strike zone; he holds it back behind his shoulder. The tip of the bat spins tiny circles like the tail of a rattlesnake.

Dr. Sinister rears back and throws himself forward, releasing the baseball.

It is a good, fast pitch, but not good or fast enough. With a minute movement of his feet, Tekel draws himself closer to it and bashes the ball with all of his strength. It flies away down the third base line.

Nathanael Crybaby Isbister hurries into left field, but he knows he doesn't stand a chance. He, like everyone else, is watching with dismay what is surely a home run.

The baseball appears to be clearing the fence at a height of about forty feet, the best hit of the day (except for Davey Goliath's mighty drive).

Then the wind whistles and rises and pushes the ball sideways.

Dustin Doubleday grins. "Foul fucking ball!" he bellows, raising his arms in triumph. There are cheers from the stands, cheers from the freak dugout.

Tekel Ambrose, who has just passed second, turns away from the base line and trots back to the batter's box, apparently unperturbed.

He picks up his bat and waits for the second pitch.

The pitch is a long time coming—Dr. Sinister is obviously throwing some kind of knuckler. The little magician spends many moments preparing the pitch, working with the ball in the pocket of his glove. He turns his back to Tekel momentarily and then spins around, his arm shooting out almost underhand.

Ambrose chooses just to watch the pitch—it is, after all, high, outside, and wobbly as all hell to boot. But just in front of the plate the ball drops and comes inside, shooting through the zone as true as an arrow.

"Strike two!" screams Doubleday.

Tekel Ambrose nods.

Dr. Sinister giggles.

"One more pitch, Doc!" hollers Isbister from centre field as the prestidigitator receives the throw-back from the Major.

"One more pitch," whispers Dr. Sinister, and without hesitation he throws the baseball toward Tekel Ambrose.

The crowd groans.

The pitch is agonizingly slow, and placed perfectly for Tekel Ambrose. The tall, bearded man from the House of Jonah has more than enough time to line up the ball. He brings the bat back and swings it forward.

The crowd gasps.

Major Mite stares with disbelief at what he has in his glove: the baseball.

Dustin Doubleday's call is barely audible. "You're out," he whispers.

Out on the pitcher's mound, Dr. Sinister is chirping, "Capital! Capital! Capital!"

Dustin Doubleday regains his composure and repeats the call in big-league umpire style, jerking his thumb toward the skies. "Yoouuu'rreeee *OOUUTT!!!*"

And with that, all hell breaks loose.

The spectators are up on their feet in a flash, bellowing, cheering, clapping their hands together. People are embracing each other, kissing and hugging, even people they've never seen before.

Crybaby Isbister throws himself heavenward with a resounding, "Yaaahhhoooo!!" He is bowled over in midair by the two-headed, five-legged wonderdog, and they drop to the ground in tandem.

Dr. Sinister is still chirping, "Capital! Capital!" between massive fits of giggles.

Major Mite pats Tekel on the lower back. "Too bad, Tickle," he says. He races toward Angus McCallister, who is already jumping up and down with Madame Tanya in his arms. The midget disappears somewhere between them.

Ally and the Hisslops are a triangle of love and kisses.

Isbister throws the wonderdog off from on top of him. "Come on, Fido! Come on, Rover! We gotta go see Stella!" They streak from the outfield toward the fat lady's wheelbarrow.

Zapper has forgone human speech again, and is communicating only with howls, hoots, and bellows. Bobby Merrill answers with groans, grunts, and grabbling.

No one from the House of Jonah has moved. Mene and Peres stand still on the bases, and their teammates are lined up in the dugout staring ahead without expression.

Tekel Ambrose finally drops the bat and walks toward Dr. Sinister.

The two men stare at each other for a long moment—and then Tekel extends his hand. "Congratulations, Doctor."

"You can call me Pointy, Tekel," says the little magician, and they shake hands heartily.

With that, many of the House of Jonah players go off in search of a freak to shake hands with.

Dr. Sinister walks into the dugout, still piping out a merry little "Capital! Capital!" There he finds Nathanael Isbister buried deep in the fleshy folds of Stella.

"Hey, Doc!" shouts Crybaby. "How did you do that, anyway?"

"Didn't you see, Natty?" asks the little magician.

"I couldn't see too good from out there," says Isbister. "What happened?"

"Well. . ." Dr. Sinister leans on close and speaks in a secretive tone. "The baseball passed right through the bat."

Crybaby laughs. "Oh, come on, Doc!"

"It did, it did, and I don't know how! A capital! Magic with a capital!" Dr. Sinister giggles again.

Isbister turns to the fat lady. "Stel, did you see what happened?"

Stella considers her words carefully. "It was magic," she says, and she hugs Nathanael Goldenlegs Crybaby Isbister.

BOOK FOUR

AS THINGS TURNED out, the House of Jonah stayed in Burton's Harbor, Upper Peninsula, Michigan. Tekel Ambrose was more than willing to leave—such, after all, was the wager and immediately the game was lost, he ordered his Brethren to vacate the town. Dr. Sinister assured him that this wasn't necessary. The two men conferred for some minutes and the following was decided: the Brethren would stay where they were, but would give a horse to any member of the Exhibition of Eccentricities who desired one.

Dr. Sinister's troupe was disbanding.

"Why?" I ask the geezer.

He speaks more quietly than I have ever heard him. "The winter was coming. The war was coming. The way of the world had changed, just like that."

"I don't get it."

"Look at it this way, boy. It's a beautiful thing when a caterpillar changes into a butterfly. But once the change has taken place, the butterfly begins to die. . ."

The first person who wanted a horse was Bobby Merrill, the grotesque Hippopotamus Boy. He simply hitched up his caravan and left. For the next seven years he travelled the United States of America; he wore the monk's cowl for disguise and spent his time watching and writing.

His caravan was found one day outside Norfolk, Virginia, his body surrounded by reams and reams of verse written in his neat, precise hand. The official autopsy reports the cause of death as asphyxia—to be precise, Bobby choked on a chicken bone.

I shall always wonder why the Hippopotamus Boy tried to eat a piece of chicken. It would be simply that he was sick and tired of sucking gruel through a straw. Perhaps he felt ready to enter the world of human beings. . . perhaps he knew the attempt would kill him.

Robert Merrill was twenty-five years old when he died.

Angus McCallister wanted a horse too. "I kin always do with a good hard-workin' nag up on the Isle," he said. It was the giant's wish to live out the rest of his days on the farm, peaceful and serene. Then he noticed Madame Tanya's sad eyes. "Aye," he nodded. "Ye kin come with me if ye please."

Tanya said she wanted to.

"*But,*" said Angus loudly, "let's unnerstand one thing, lass. I'm old. Aye. Old an' reet set in me ways. An' that means thet if I've a mind t' have a pint I don't want no wooman tellin' me any other. I smoke me pipe when I wish an' scratch at me gobbles when they itch. I—"

He was cut short by Madame Tanya's laughter.

So the couple moved to Cape Breton Island, where they did indeed live peacefully.

Four years later, Angus got rip-roaring drunk and attempted to raise a massive and long-buried boulder. He managed to lift the stone a few inches, but the effort caused a blood vessel in his brain to burst. He lay in a coma for three weeks and then slipped away.

Angus McCallister never knew that he left behind a son. Tanya was but two months pregnant when the giant died. As the baby grew within her, Tanya's body began to undergo changes. Her breasts swelled, of course, and she was often dizzy and nauseous. But more importantly, her facial hair fell out. By the time the child was born, Madame Tanya's face was as smooth as the baby's bottom.

She named the boy Donald.

Madame Tanya is still an astoundingly powerful woman, and has been quite successful at working the farm by herself. She is known and loved throughout Cape Breton. (I've heard a rumour that, with the change of life, the whiskers have made a reappearance, this time white and scraggily. I've also heard a rumour that Tanya doesn't care.)

Donald McCallister is a very tall man, six foot six and a half; he is a Professor of English Literature at Concordia University. His main area of interest is medieval poetry.

Donald Pfaff, a.k.a. Major Mite, also never knew about his namesake's existence.

The Major, back at the baseball game, did not want a horse.

"I'm gonna take a train to where I'm going," he said.

"An' whither might thet be, Donny?" asked his friend Angus.

"I'm going to Hollywood!" announced the Major. "I heard that Singer wants every last one of us."

Singer was a man who ran a troupe of performing midgets, the largest in the country, numbering nearly a hundred. The Major had heard that for some purpose Singer needed more. Singer had let it be known that he wanted every professional performing midget assembled in the motion picture capital.

"I don't know what for," said Major Mite, "but it sure sounds like a lot of fun."

Singer needed the midgets to play the Munchkins in *The Wizard of Oz*. I'm not sure if you're aware of this, but there are no children among the Munchkins, even when there is a huge crowd of them—every last one is a midget.

And it certainly was fun.

The little people had never been brought together in such a huge number, and they had a party to end all parties. The midgets were constantly drunk. They delighted in tormenting Judy Garland, reducing her to tears on several occasions. They cost the studio no end of money in retakes—as when, for example, a tiny, angelic man would chirp, "Follow the yellow brick road!" and pull out of the shot to reveal a pair of pint-sized lovers happily copulating on the ground behind him.

Major Mite reigned over all this madness as a kind of king. He was, after all, the most famous performing midget of all time, and the others revered and worshipped him. He drank incredible amounts of liquor, and had his choice of any woman there. The poor Major couldn't choose, so elected to work through them one by one. On the last day of shooting, the Major's ticker gave up on him. He was thoroughly pissed at the time and cavorting with three naked little ladies.

Incidentally, the Major has a fairly big part for a Munchkin. He is the one who emerges from the crowd to proclaim:

As coroner I must confer,
I thoroughly examined her!
And she is not just merely dead,
She's really quite sincerely dead!

And with that the joyous news is spread: the wicked old witch at last is dead.

Daisy and Violet Hisslop returned with Ally to Florida, where they set up housekeeping. The Alligator Man got a job as a construction worker and laboured hard enough to support the girls well. In time it became clear that the relationship between Daisy and Ally was stronger than between Violet and Ally. This might have strained the whole arrangement were it not for the timely arrival of Benjamin Bell. Ben was a painter of extremely erotic sensibilities—Violet fell deeply in love with him. The two couples were married in a joint ceremony (naturally) on August 1, 1947.

Some time later, Daisy developed cancer in her left breast. She battled it unsuccessfully for over a year and died quietly. The doctors then tried to separate the girls' bodies. It was a simple operation, as I've said—Daisy and Violet had no common organs, they systems were wholly individual and self-contained. But for some reason, Violet passed away on the operating table.

The Hisslop sisters were buried, side by side, in Gainesville, Florida.

Violet's husband Ben was a moody, temperamental sort, and after her death he shot himself. This left Ally altogether alone in the world. He went back into the business, then, with a small show that still tours the country. Sometime, at a carnival or fair, you might stumble upon a freak show. There might be a picture of a smiling human head attached to an alligator's body. He is a very old man now. You should go talk to him—I've heard that Ally is friendly and affable. He especially likes to tell people about a baseball game.

Stella's marriage to Edmund was not an overwhelmingly happy one. The young man certainly had no drastic personality faults of the sort Nathanael had warned of—he was a kind and gentle man. But Stella had always attributed his taciturnity to a deep-rooted and painful shyness; after a few months of marriage she realized that, more than anything else, Edmund was stupid. Still, Stella was fairly content. Her husband made a good living as a garage mechanic, and he was almost always horny. All this ended when a car Edmund was working on rolled off its blocks and crushed him to death.

After that Stella married a diminutive fellow who'd made a fortune in real estate. She lived with him in a huge mansion in Beverly Hills, where her greatest pleasure was floating in the kidney-shaped swimming pool. In the water, Stella felt at ease and graceful for the first time in her life.

Stella caused something of a scandal in Beverly Hills. It is rumoured that one day a hobo had the audacity to walk up and knock on her front door. This fellow was patently a rounder—a tall, ugly-looking cuss with a face that had been beaten in bar-rooms from coast to coast. The bum was dressed in filthy rags and had a very peculiar way of walking. At any rate, rather than turn this guy away, Stella gave him the warmest welcome imaginable! The hobo lived in the mansion for three months before leaving silently in the early light of dawn.

Stella Stinton Raleigh Pauling (her married names) died on July 22, 1953. Her heart had worked overtime for many years and on that day decided to strike. She was found floating gently in the swimming pool.

"Oi'll 'ave an 'orse!" announced a voice to Tekel Ambrose. The troupe members all laughed loudly and heartily.

"Hey," shouted Nathanael, "will ya listen to the Doctor!"

"Oi ain't no doctor," said little Poindexter Frip with a wink.

Stella asked, "What are you going to do, Pointy?"

"Me, oi'm a-goin' to 'ave a look at these 'ere Americas. And wiv luck, at some point, oi shall find me a little bit of—" The Doctor gestured lecherously in the air.

"Come on, Doc," said Isbister, "you don't really talk like that, do you?"

"Well," admitted the little man, "I suppose I have acquired a modicum of eloquence that should not be so capriciously eschewed."

Herman Shepps, the Wild Man from Brooklyn, approached our little magician shyly. "Doc," he asked, "ya want any company?"

Poindexter Frip smiled. "I should be delighted."

And so the pair of them chose a horse (Tekel Ambrose thought they went out of their way to pick the most sway-backed rickety-legged creature he owned) and named him Floyd, the Equine Extraordinaire, Junior. They hitched up the Doctor's caravan, dragged it from the ground, and rattled, clattered, and bumped away happily.

Those two spent some very good years. Floyd pulled them over every mile of road he could find. If they ran short of funds they put on a little show. Poindexter Frip would perform his magic, and Herman Shepps would howl like an orangutan, the fearsome Wild Man from pestilential Borneo.

They met a woman named Bailey. Bailey was all she ever called herself. She was extremely beautiful and just as eccentric. So eccentric, in fact, that she developed an incredible fondness for both Herman and Poindexter and began to travel with them.

Bailey added to their little show a touch of class. Her act consisted of simply shedding her clothes with Dr. Sinister played his wheezy concertina. When Bailey was fully naked there was never a sound, even among the most drunken and loutish crowds.

That Zapper should lose his forty-year-old virginity to such a creation was to him empirical proof of an all-knowing and benevolent deity. The Doctor was as happy as he'd ever been, and I'll tell you why—Bailey was the spitting image of Marie, the model he'd loved so passionately when he was a painter in Paris.

Poindexter Frip's last works were these: a painting named *Bailey* (it shows her from the back, nude and glistening from a dip in some river); a novel named *Bailey* (which is an account of their many adventures); and a symphony, also called *Bailey*.

Poindexter Frip died as a result of beestings. He was merrily pursuing a butterfly through the woods when his net knocked a hive from a branch. It fell squarely upon him and that was that.

Bailey and Zapper continued to travel together until the late forties. Then, one dark night, a carful of drunken teenagers broadsided the caravan. Herman, who was perched up top driving, was thrown about fifty feet; he died instantly. Floyd bit the big one too. Bailey got away lightly, although her perfect beauty was marred by a scar that ran the length of her face. She is still alive today, in Chicago, Illinois, and if I ever get the money together, I mean to pay her a visit.

That left, of the troupe members, Janus, the two-headed, five-legged wonderdog. He left with Nathanael Crybaby Isbister.

I ask the geezer, "And what happened to you?"

He scowls—this, of all his memories, is the most painful. "Well, there I was hooting and hollering and thinking that I was thousands better off, when I hear this voice saying, 'Excuse me.' I turn around and who do I see? That pesky little reporter guy. And he says, 'Doubleday... Brassiere... whatever... the jig, as they put it, is up.' I knew he had me dead to rights. I ask him what he means to do with me, and he dwells on it for a bit and says, 'Well, I don't want to see you in jail, I guess.' I tell him them's my sentiments, too. So the reporter scratches at his head and finally decides, 'Let's go get the money. We'll get drunk and then tomorrow give back the rest.'

"I'd sure heard worse deals than that. So back we go to the Fulton Arms Hotel. On the way he tells me, 'You know, I'm going to have to write an exposé about shysters like you. I'm afraid it's my job.' I tell him I don't mind and he says thanks."

My grandfather pauses for a moment's reflection. "I don't know that he ever did write that exposé—leastwise, not so it affected business any. What happened to him is, he finally made it down to Gilbertsville. And what he saw down there twisted even harder at his heart. He wrote a book about tenant farmers—I forget what it's called. He died of a heart attack in the back seat of a taxi cab in New York City. They say it was the drink. I dunno.

"Anyway, me and that guy go back to the hotel. I'm practically in tears. It was the best thing I'd ever done, I'd finally made the big scam, and I was gonna have to give it all back. I might have tried to talk the reporter out of it, offer him a split, but you could tell he was one of those guys who have a thing about justice and fair play and similar doodley-squat. I never understood those guys, but they're around."

I grin to myself. The geezer, for all his advanced years and flim-flams, has never discovered that he *is* one of those guys.

"We go up to the room," he continues, "and I go over to the safe and open her up. And..." My grandfather thinks for a bit. "And..." He giggles. "And..." The geezer erupts into the laugh that sounds like a rusty water pump. "The fucking thing was *empty*!"

"What?"

"Bless his little heart, Yuccatan pulled a scam on *me*! He'd slipped out during the ball game and made off with all the goddam money!" My grandfather continues laughing, breathing in wheezily, slapping at his scrawny legs and shining a bright red. "Good old Yuccatan!" he hollers.

"Weren't you mad at him?"

"I might have been if I had got to keep the money. As it was, I just laughed and laughed. I told the reporter what had happened, and he started laughing, too. So, the pair of us had about three dollars between us, and we went out and got as drunk as we could on that.

"Turns out we got pretty goddam drunk. So drunk in fact, that the dumb kid loses all his notes, and in the morning he can't hardly remember the baseball game at all!"

"Aha! I was wondering why he didn't write about it."

"Yeah. Lambert's photographs got printed, sure, but nobody knew what the hell they were supposed to be of."

"Did you ever see Yuccatan again?"

"I ran into him a few years after that, in some bar somewhere. The first thing he says to me is, 'I owe you a drink!' " The geezer laughs loudly for some moments and then sobers. "He died not long after that. Drownded in a bath tub."

"So ever since that baseball game you've just been bumming around? Hustling old ladies and cheating at cards?"

"Well, sure. But all the time, at the back of my mind, I've been thinking that *someone* has got to write down the story of that baseball game. I always figured the Author would do it. He was there, after all, sitting right in the dugout and cheering for the freaks. And every time he'd have a new book out I'd buy it, or steal it. They were always real good books too, but they were never about the ball game. He died a few years back, and I figured that was that. But then, one day, I'm in a store—I confess, I was having a gander at the girlie mags and I see this book that was written by a guy named Quarrington. 'What's this?' I think. 'That's my name too.' So I check it out, and sure enough, you're my little grandson. That's why I came. Now we've done it."

"We've *almost* done it," I remind him. "You still haven't told me what happened to Nathanael."

The geezer grins. "You writers just can't stand loose ends, can you? That's what Isbister was, a loose end. He left with Janus, and that's all I know."

I suspect that my grandfather is not being candid with me. He knows what happened to every other person associated with the game—he could probably tell me what happened to our old friend the truck driver. I ask him, even though I've a good hunch what he'll say.

The answer is, "The truck driver fell asleep at the wheel and drove into a mountain."

I was right. "Now come off it, granddad," I scold him, "you know damn well what happened to Isbister."

"Nope. He was a loose end."

"He never said anything when the game was over?"

"He said goodbye."

"That's all?"

"Come to think of it, he did say something else. He said that he didn't think Tekel's third strike was Magic with a big one. He thought Tekel missed it on purpose."

"Hmmm. What do you think?"

My grandfather dwells on the question momentarily. "I don't know. It was a nice, soft pitch. Tekel should have clobbered it." He shrugs. "What do you think?"

If there is an answer, it probably lies somewhere in the history of Tekel Ambrose. I ask the geezer what happened to him.

"Nothing happened to him," replies my grandfather. "He stayed in Burton's Harbor with the House of Jonah. He played baseball and prayed, same as he always did."

"He didn't change?"

"What do you want to hear, boy? That he married a stripper and ran guns to Cuba?" The geezer scurries over to his pile of belongings, and rummages through it with a pirate's wink, as though it contained untold treasure. He pulls out a scrapbook, filthy and dog-eared. "I keep a lookout," he tells me. "Tekel was in the news a couple of times."

My grandfather spins the book around so that I can have a look. Taped to the page is a newspaper clipping, accompanied by a photograph. The picture stops me cold and I let out a small gasp.

"Yeah," nods the geezer. "It's his eyes, ain't it? Have you ever seen eyes like that before in your life?"

I don't know what to say. As I stare at the photograph of Tekel Ambrose it occurs to me that I have seen eyes like that before. In the middle of every face I've ever looked at. In fact what shocks me about the picture is how ordinary Tekel looks. His beard is perhaps extraordinarily long, but other than that he is almost non-descript. Where are the hellish shadows, the shades of midnight black?

My grandfather seems to see them. "It gives me the heebie-jeebies just to look at the photograph," he mutters. "It's those eyes."

I look away and then take a quick peek, hoping that I might catch a flashing of brimstone damnation. Tekel's eyes meet mine, calm and dull. I decide it has to do with the grainy texture of the newspaper, and I turn away to the clipping itself. The headline reads, "HOUSE OF JONAH TRIAL CONTINUES". I scan it briefly for the gist. Tekel and the House had declared themselves conscientious objectors as soon as the United States entered World War Two. The government did not like to see so many physically fit young men just sitting around, so they stated that the House of Jonah could in no way be considered officially a church. Tekel held fast, and although I'm sure he was far more eloquent, in effect he told the government to cram it up its hawk-like nose. Thus, the trial.

The clipping my grandfather had cut out concerned the testimony given by Tekel Ambrose himself. The prosecuting attorney had been particularly skillful. He'd browbeaten old Tekel mercilessly, and his coup de grace was in getting Ambrose to admit that participation in a war did not of necessity make a man morally bad. Tekel's response is underlined with pencil:

> Mr. Ambrose replied, "But it is not enough that a man simply not be bad. A man must do everything in his power to be good."

My grandfather tells me, "They let him off the hook. I like to think it was because he said that. But it might have been because he said, 'Gentlemen, I simply do not see why we are going through all this bother. The Brethren are not going to fight, and that is that.' " The geezer giggles. He flips to another page in the scrapbook, telling me, "After that I didn't hear nothing about him for years and years. Then, just a little while ago, I saw this." He shows me another clipping, this one from the *Burton's Harbor Bugle*. Tekel's face stares at me once more from a photograph, his beard now snowy white—and once more my grandfather suppresses a shudder. "His eyes never changed," he whispers.

For the life of me, I can see nothing unusual in them. Very quickly I turn away to the accompanying clipping.

Tekel was in trouble again, this time for refusing to send the House children to public schools. I should explain that the House of Jonah had traditionally taken care of their young ones' education. During the reforms of the sixties, various authorities decided that this was not good enough, and ordered Tekel to send the children to public schools. Although I'm sure he was far more eloquent, Tekel told them to shove it up their rosey-reds. Thus, the trial.

From what I gather, more than anything else Tekel was insulting. It was not simply the lack of religious tutelage that he resented, it was the whole public education system. This paragraph is underlined in pencil:

> Mr. Ambrose was particularly disdainful of the Natural Sciences and throughout his testimony made disparaging remarks about botany and zoology. When asked why he considered these studies so worthless, Mr. Ambrose replied, "The children can learn nothing of importance from them." Mr. Zurelli (the prosecuting attorney) then added a touch of levity to the proceedings by asking Mr. Ambrose if he felt that baseball was more important than botany. The humour was lost on Ambrose, who merely stated, "Of course."

"Hmmm," I hmmmed. "Did he get off this time?"

The geezer shakes his head. " 'Fraid not. The kiddies got bussed off to normal school, and old Tekel had to cool his buns in a jail-cell for six months."

"Is he still alive?"

"Yep. And he probably will be for a time to come. I reckon Tekel's a pretty hard man to kill."

This is not true of Peres and Mene, I next learn. The former died in 1972, the latter a year later, both victims of the plague-like and virulent "natural causes".

"There you have it," announces the geezer. He begins to gather up his belongings.

"All except for what happened to Nathanael."

"Loose end. You gotta learn to live with them if you want to get along."

"Okay, okay. . . but take a guess."

"I guess that Nate and Janus bummed around until one day Isbister got hit by a bolt of lightning. And I don't know if God did it or if the Devil did it. Seems to me they both had reason aplenty." My grandfather ties up his bag with binder twine and sighs heavily. "Now look, son," he says, "I know you're gonna ask me to live with you, but I been on the move too long. I'll write, let you know where I am." He heads for the door.

"Hey, geezer!" I shout, stopping him. "I wasn't going to ask you to live with me. But there is no way that you and I are not going to get royally pissed tonight down at the Sticky Wicket. You can leave tomorrow."

My grandfather grins. "That's my little grandson talking!" he cackles.

"All I have to do is finish this book. Any final words?"

"My final words are 'Play ball!' Now you write whatever you got to say, and let's get at that beer!"

Well, all right. It's very true, as the geezer said, that we writers don't like loose ends. It's simply not in our nature. Nathanael Crybaby Goldenlegs Isbister is a loose end, and there's nothing I can do about it. If I could, I most certainly would. The odd thing is, there's another loose end, and I don't care. I refer, of course, to this question: did Dr. Sinister perform Magic (note that capital), or did Tekel Ambrose miss that pitch on purpose? That loose end doesn't bother me one little bit. You people can tie it together if you want. Myself, I now see no distinction between Magic and human purpose. And for that, I am truly thankful.

The End